PROMISE
OF
VIPERS

PROMISE OF VIPERS

Riftborn * Book 4

STEVE McHUGH

Podium

For Barb.

My best mother-in-law.

Cover design by Pius Bak

ISBN: 978-1-0394-5453-8

Published in 2024 by Podium Publishing
www.podiumaudio.com

Podium

GLOSSARY

SPECIES

Ancients: The oldest, but not necessarily the most powerful, members of the rift-fused. They ensure that there are checks and balances between rift-fused and humans.

eidolons: Living embodiments of rift power that reside as caretakers of a riftborn's embers. Can change shape to most animals as needed. Are always two for every riftborn's embers.

fiends: Animals that die on Earth close to a tear and are brought back to life from the power of the rift. Comes in three kinds: lesser, greater, and elder.

practitioners: Those born inside the rift. Can create constructs along with using the rift to imbue writing and potions with its power.

Primes: The rulers of Inaxia, the capital city of the rift.

primordials: Creatures that live inside the Tempest in the rift.

revenants: Those who died on Earth as human, close to a tear, and were brought back to life by the power of the rift. There are ten different species of revenant.

rift-fused: Anyone or anything given power by the rift.

rift-walkers: Can create tears between the rift and Earth at will.

riftborn: Those who were mortally wounded on Earth as human but were taken into the rift and gifted incredible power. Can move between earth and the rift using their embers.

GROUPS

Guilds: Seven groups of powerful rift-fused who ensure that humans and rift-fused live in harmony.

Investigators: Police force of Inaxia.

RCU (Rift-Crime Unit): Multi-nation agency who investigate crimes committed by and against the rift-fused.

Talon: Guild member trained in secret to remove threats to their Guild.

PLACES

Agency: Largest Lawless City in the rift. On the boarder of the Vastness.

Crow's Perch: Prison city in the rift, run by the Queen of Crows.

embers: The pocket dimension used by riftborn to travel between Earth and the rift, as well as to heal any physical wounds the riftborn has sustained.

Harmony: The area surrounding the Tempest.

Inaxia: Capital city of the rift.

Lawless City: City in the rift that lives free from Inaxia rule.

Mercy: A place no one wants to admit exists.

Nightvale: Settlement in the rift.

Plainhaven: Largest settlement inside the Vastness.

rift: Dimension attached to our own that allows incredible power to flow out from it through tears between dimensions.

Tempest: The maelstrom of power at the north of the rift.

Vast Death: Otherwise known as the Vastness. Large area of the rift which is considered the most dangerous.

PROMISE
OF
VIPERS

CHAPTER ONE

The mountain crumbled after Callie died. Both she and it were consumed by the energy of the rift. The sky tore asunder as a power that had been contained for millennia flooded out of the mountain. And then, as quickly as it started, it stopped. And everything was okay.

Okay lasted three weeks.

To be as close as possible to exact, it lasted three weeks, four days, seventeen hours, and eleven minutes.

After that, it all went to shit real fast.

CHAPTER TWO

NOW

I sat under an oak tree atop a hill just outside of the town of Whitby, Yorkshire. During the day, it gave a good view of the local harbour, which led out into the North Sea. There were lights on the boats that were moored there. The pleasant scent of sea water was a constant, and the sounds of the ocean lapping against the nearby cliffs soothed me.

I looked up at the indigo-and-magenta tear as it ripped across the night sky. It resembled a wound that wasn't quite healing properly. Despite being three in the morning, the light of the tear illuminated everything. Not as powerful as sunlight but enough to see by without the need for streetlights, even if you were human. It flashed twice and disappeared.

"At least they're not becoming more frequent," Nadia said from beside me, the chains that were a part of her wrapped around her torso.

Nadia was a chained revenant, a being who could see all of their possible futures and, if they were unlucky, tear their mind apart in the process. Nadia had been lucky so far, and I hoped that would last. She was a good person and someone I considered a friend.

At five-five tall with olive skin and short dark hair, Nadia had several earrings in both ears and wore a pair of shorts, a baby blue vest top, and white trainers. She didn't much look like someone who had once murdered an entire Mexican cartel for killing her family, but to be fair, I'd long since stopped expecting people to look a certain way when it came to the revenants and riftborn of the world.

Up until Callie had swan-dived into a core of pure rift energy, tears were usually small and quick things, randomly appearing across the globe. They opened, flooded out power, and vanished. Sometimes, that power created a revenant or a fiend—an animal imbued with rift power and twisted into something monstrous—or a riftborn, although in the latter case, we were taken into the rift itself.

Now these tears had become more powerful, occasionally ripping the sky open for miles, pouring out rift energy before snapping shut. The small tears still happened too, but no one worried too much about a pin-sized tear in the middle of nowhere. This was on a different scale, and while humans and those of us born from rift energy had coexisted peacefully side by side for a long time, there were increasing calls for someone to figure out what the fuck was actually going on.

A scientific research team had gone into the rift, right up to where the mountain had exploded, to try and figure out what had happened. The resident primordials of the Tempest hadn't been pleased at first, but they also hadn't been thrilled that their sky looked like a Lovecraftian nightmare, so they sucked it up and dealt with their new reality. So far, no one had been eaten.

As someone with a degree in rift science, I'd also been asked my opinion on what was going on. Apparently, shrugging was not the best answer. Unfortunately, that was all I had. No one knew how to stop the tears from happening or close them once they started. The only thing we knew for sure was that they opened in the sky in the same places every time. That, at least, gave us a way to track the influx of fiends and revenants that were created, although the timing of the tears appeared to be completely random.

"It's peaceful here," Nadia said in a relaxed tone.

I nodded, staying quiet, enjoying what was almost certain to be a short-lived piece of tranquillity.

"You think that tear created a new fiend?" Nadia asked, making it sound that it was no big deal.

"I hope not," I said. "I could do without having to kill a twelve-foot-tall snail or something."

"You ever had to fight a twelve-foot-tall fiend snail?" Nadia asked curiously.

"No," I told her. "But there's always a first time."

Before the tears had started, the vast majority of fiends were created from larger animals; occasionally, three or four smaller animals had merged to form some kind of weird fleshy version of Voltron, but they were thankfully in the minority. Since the tears, however, fiends born from a mix of smaller animals had become a more regular occurrence.

"You're thinking of that *Voltron* line again, aren't you?" Nadia asked; she sounded like she was almost asleep.

"Have I said that before?" I asked, knowing full well I had.

Nadia gently patted my hand. "You're old; you forget these things."

I laughed. I was old enough that I'd fought alongside Hannibal against the Roman Empire. I'd died doing it, too.

"I have a question," Nadia asked. "Have you ever met another Carthaginian?"

"I lived there for most of my human life," I pointed out. "I grew up there, so yes, I've seen a few."

Nadia let out a low sigh. "No, I mean since then."

"A few, but not many," I told her. "Why?"

"Trying not to fall asleep," she said, lying down on the thick, insulated picnic blanket that we'd placed there so we didn't get drenched from the wet ground. "It's very relaxing here."

It was the middle of August, and the close, stifling heat of the last week had been broken with thunderstorms that had spent the entire day lighting up the sky while Nadia and I stayed in our hotel room. It was cooler now. Fresher. Certainly more comfortable.

Whitby consisted of two worlds that should really oppose one another but somehow managed to intermingle and work. On one hand, it was a seaside town, with all that entailed. There were amusement arcades and a beach that was usually packed to bursting. It was a place where many people went to spend their summer, bringing noise, buckets, and spades for building sandcastles, and brightly coloured inflatables.

The second world the town was renowned for was darker. One of vampires. Not literal vampires but figurative ones. Dracula, to be exact. Everywhere you went, there was something telling you how Dracula had visited the place in the book. The people of Whitby were proud of their association with vampires, and in turn, you had a host of tourists who came to the town to look at the gothic ruins, the old abbey, and museums, to walk where Dracula might have walked, had he been real.

It had long since been one of my favourite places to visit, although I wished I was currently there for more pleasurable reasons.

The headlights of the approaching vehicle illuminated us, and Nadia sat up, stretched, and yawned. Her chains flicked out in front of her like a snake's tongue tasting the air.

I got up, and after Nadia followed suit, picked up the blanket and folded it away. The silver Volvo XC60 pulled over to the side of the road nearby, and Hiroyuki stepped out.

Hiroyuki was, at a push, five foot six, with long hair on top his head that was in a ponytail. The sides and back of his head were shaved closely to the skin. He wore his usual dark grey suit and black shoes, and a silver pendant hung around his neck. It was in the shape of an Ancient Greek helmet and signified that he was a member of the Silver Phalanx, the bodyguards of the Ancients.

"Sorry it took so long," he said.

Hiroyuki had offered to question someone connected with our target. Apparently, Nadia and I make people we interview feel *uncomfortable*. Well, technically, only I make people uncomfortable. Nadia scares the shit out of them.

"So, what did you get?" Nadia asked as I popped the boot of the Volvo and dropped our bags inside.

"He's on the moors," Hiroyuki said, using his phone to show a map of the place to Nadia before coming over to let me take a look.

"How'd you find out?" I asked.

"Turns out Americans get noticed," Hiroyuki said. "He uses a local convenience shop."

We knew he had to be getting food and supplies, so we'd spent the day asking around the local shops and showing our target's photo.

"Apparently, creepy Americans who stare at the young lady behind the counter *really* get noticed," Hiroyuki continued. "He came into the store a few times in the last week. Each time, he buys some bits and pieces, creeps everyone out, and leaves. He's staying in a small holiday home on the moors. Driving a forest green Kia Sportage."

"So, Lucas, you been to the moors?"

I nodded. "It's a good job you got a location; otherwise, it would be like searching for a needle in a giant haystack made of needles. It's the kind of place you can get lost in if you don't know what you're doing. It's also the kind of place someone might go to get away from the rest of the world."

"Or hide from it," Nadia said.

"Or that," I agreed, and got into the rear seat of the Volvo, sitting behind Hiroyuki, who took up the driving position, with Nadia in the passenger seat. "That map said it's an hour or so away."

"Yeah, the satnav only goes so far," Hiroyuki said. "Apparently, this place is off the beaten path a bit."

"Anyone wondered why an American serial killer would flee to the Yorkshire moors?" Nadia asked as Hiroyuki started the car and we set off into the night.

"We'll ask him when we find him," I said.

I looked out the window as we left Whitby behind, and soon after, the streetlights started to become less frequent as we entered the moors, passing through the occasional tiny village on the way to the middle of nowhere.

The moors themselves are a mixture of heather moorland, woods, rivers, cliffs, and villages, interspersed with old ruins. It's the kind of place that if you run into trouble and need help, you're already in much deeper shit than you ever want to be.

"So, are we still classing him as a serial killer?" Nadia asked, breaking the silence.

"He's killed nine people!" Hiroyuki said fiercely.

"Well, yes, but seven of them came back as revenants," Nadia said. "And one went to the rift as a riftborn. So, is he still considered a serial killer when most of his victims didn't actually die?"

"I think that might be a case of semantics," Hiroyuki said. "This monster has hunted, kidnapped, and murdered nine people in six months. He kills them, seemingly deliberately, when the skies tear open. The fact that only one remained dead is neither here nor there. He must be stopped."

"No argument from me," Nadia said. "Just curious about whether or not we call him a serial killer. Also, curious about why he ran from Boston to here."

"You said," I mentioned.

Nadia looked back at me. "It *bothers* me. Something is . . . *off* about this whole thing. We spoke to his revenant victims; each one said that the killer only spoke about how he was helping them. He believes that he's making them better, yet he's human. If he believes he's making these people better by turning them into revenants, why hasn't he tried to do it to himself?"

I'd read the files on each victim and what they recalled about their interaction with Jacob. He'd been focused to a scary degree on making sure that *every* little detail was right before he hurt them. He mentioned a "Great King" more than once, about how he was going to bring us all into a new age. It sounded like the ravings of someone who had lost their mind, but whatever it was he believed, no matter how crazy it sounded, the important part was that *he believed*. He believed in something enough to hurt people, to kill people. That made him dangerous.

"Maybe he's a coward," Hiroyuki said, his eyes never leaving the road before us, illuminated only by the car's high-beam headlights.

Nadia faced forward again and shrugged. "I do not like this. I know that Ji-hyun couldn't spare people and asked us to come fetch this odious little man, but we found him awfully easily."

"Almost like someone wants us to find him," I finished.

"You feel it too," Nadia said.

I nodded. It *had* been weird that when we'd finally tracked down Jordan Chapman from his apartment in Boston, we found information on his email about flights booked to Heathrow, along with maps of the Yorkshire moors. The whole thing felt a little *too* easy, but it was also all we had to go on. Besides, this idea that serial killers are all super intelligent is nonsense, so maybe we just got one of the stupid ones.

The car came to a stop and Hiroyuki tapped the screen on the console, zooming in on our whereabouts. "The directions end here," he said. "The house is a quarter mile down that dirt road. We'll have to drive without lights in case he spots us."

"Okay, time to tell us," Nadia said. "How'd you know he's here?"

Hiroyuki grinned. "You remember the shop assistant he creeped out? He left her his address. Told her to come by and see him sometime."

"He *gave* someone his hideout address?" Nadia asked incredulously.

Okay, this was definitely one of the stupid ones.

"He did," Hiroyuki said, clearly trying to stifle a chuckle. "He thought he was being charming. Not at all creepy and weird."

"God bless stupid criminals," Nadia said, shaking her head in disbelief.

Hiroyuki took the Volvo along the dirt road, moving slowly in the darkness. After a few minutes, he stopped and switched off the engine. "We're blocking the road, so he won't have an easy time of running if he has a car or bike. I wouldn't want to try any off-road driving around here."

Everyone got out of the Volvo, and I opened the boot, removed three stab vests, and passed one to Nadia and one to Hiroyuki. I wasn't concerned about getting shot. It wouldn't kill any of us unless the bullets or rifle were rift-tempered, and if the bullets were, they'd be more likely to blow up in the face of the shooter.

Rift-tempered blades however, were dangerous to anyone who had rift energy inside of them. A riftborn could heal from an awful lot of damage, but a rift-tempered blade could kill us pretty easily. And while a revenant might pass through to the rift after they die, a rift-tempered blade made sure their death was permanent.

I tucked my Raven Guild pendant beneath my stab vest, feeling the cold metal against my skin. I had two daggers in sheaths against my back, their blades made from steel-infused primordial bone. I would have liked to have taken my short spear with me, too, but I was only hunting a human and didn't think it necessary, so had left it with Gabriel in New York.

Nadia wore a belt of a dozen throwing knives, and Hiroyuki removed a wakizashi and a tanto from the illuminated boot, and secured them against his hip. He'd left the katana at home in North America.

"We ready?" I asked as Hiroyuki closed the boot.

The moors were illuminated by the full moon, the sounds of various animals going about their nocturnal lives. Somewhere in the distance was the unmistakable sound of an owl.

Hiroyuki passed Nadia and me a small torch each and, using their light, we moved along the dirt road, keeping as quiet as possible, looking out for anything that might signal our arrival to Jordan.

The holiday home he was staying in was an old, converted barn. It was large enough to probably keep a family of five comfortable and had a large parking area outside the front. A forest green Kia Sportage was the only vehicle parked up.

I motioned for Nadia to go around to the rear of the property and for Hiroyuki to take the opposite route around while I walked up the path to the front door.

There were lights on inside the building but no open windows, and all of the curtains were closed. The lack of an easy ingress meant no turning to smoke to get inside. Not unless I wanted to move around the door-frame, and honestly, moving around the frame of a closed door sucks.

Both Nadia and Hiroyuki returned a few seconds later. "Nothing," Nadia whispered.

Hiroyuki shook his head, signalling that he had found nothing in his journey around the building.

Placing my hand tentatively against the door handle, I was surprised to find that it wasn't locked. It opened without resistance, and I stepped through the doorway into a large open room. To my right there was a brown leather sofa, which sat in front of a thick green rug, on top of which was an oak coffee table. A large flatscreen TV had been hung on the wall.

On the opposite side of the sofa and TV was a large table, which looked identical in colour to the coffee table, although it was several times bigger. There was a wooden bench on either side of the length of the table.

Next to the only door in the room was a staircase leading up to the bedrooms above. They would be searched last.

The three of us moved to the door and I pushed it open, stepping through into the short, dark hallway beyond. There were three doors, with the one on the far right open, revealing a bathroom. Nadia opened the one in the middle, which turned out to be a closet full of cleaning equipment.

We moved to the door on the left. As Hiroyuki reached it first, he pushed it open, barely making a sound as the kitchen was revealed before us.

Beside the large kitchen, with a centre console where high stools sat beside it, there was a dining table. The curtains on the kitchen window and door leading to the rear of the property were both closed. An open door beside the fridge and freezer, close to where we'd entered the room, showed steps leading down to a dingy basement, but none of that really mattered at that point.

"Oh, damn," Nadia said as we all stepped into the kitchen.

"Fuck," I said, staring at the dead body of Jordan Chapman.

CHAPTER THREE

J ordan Chapman had died hard.

No one was particularly upset about that fact, although I was pretty sure that Jordan hadn't been too thrilled.

"They beat the shit out of him," Hiroyuki said grimly, pointing at the swollen mass that had once been Jordan's face. Blood had poured down Jordan's face, saturating his T-shirt and the once-silver tape that bound his arms to those of the wooden dining chair he was in.

"Broke his nose, broke his fingers," Nadia said. "Lots of injuries but nothing that would kill him. Apart from the killing blow."

The cause of death was obvious, considering the dagger had been stabbed up under his throat, into his brain. The dagger had been slammed in with force, right up to the hilt. The death itself might have been fast, but the buildup to it had been slow.

"Lots of small cuts on his legs," Nadia said. "Bare feet had been hit with something too."

"They tortured him," I said. "You think maybe he held back and wouldn't talk?"

"Everyone talks eventually," Nadia said in a flat, unemotional tone, proving once again that she was terrifying.

"So, what were they asking?" Hiroyuki said. "And how long ago was he killed?"

"An hour, maybe," Nadia said, looking at Jordan's body. "Ninety minutes at the most. We just missed them."

Apart from the multitude of cuts on his arms, he had a tattoo that said *Ahiram* in a black Gothic font.

"Who's Ahiram?" I asked, pointing to the tattoo.

"Never heard of it," Hiroyuki said.

"Person, place, or something else?" Nadia asked.

"Person," I said. "It's an old name I've heard before, but not since I've been Riftborn. A few people in Carthage were called it."

"Maybe he really likes history?" Hiroyuki suggested.

"We search the building," I said, mentally reminding myself to check out the name when I had the chance. "If you find anything, note it down. I'll check the outside in case there's something the killer left there."

"I'll take the basement first," Nadia said.

No one wanted to argue with that, and we all set off to search the large house.

We hadn't even gotten out of the kitchen when an exhale of air left Jordan's lips. I turned back to him as his eyes opened.

"He's alive?" I shouted.

"How the fuck is he alive?" Nadia asked.

The tear opened beside Jordan, which quickly enveloped him and snapped shut before any of us could reach him.

"How was he not dead?" I asked.

"He had a dagger in his brain," Nadia almost shouted, her chains gesticulating wildly as they copied her hands.

"Well, I didn't bother to take his pulse," Hiroyuki said.

"Because he had a *dagger* in his brain," Nadia repeated.

Humans becoming riftborn are usually taken when they're mortally wounded. The fact that Jordan had been alive this whole time was, to say the least, unexpected.

"Okay, so, these tears are becoming more of a pain in the ass," Nadia said.

"On the plus side, Jordan is going to be in the rift very much alive and well," I said. "He'll end up in the caves near Inaxia. It'll be several hours before he arrives, but we can find him and, hopefully, get some answers."

"He might not be keen to see us," Hiroyuki said.

"Yeah, I'm okay with that," I said. "He'll be even less keen when we tell the Inaxian guard what he did as a human."

"So, we still have time to search the place," Nadia said, and returned to the basement, glancing over her shoulder at the empty chair before leaving the room.

I exited through the back door of the building into a small area with chairs that were turned to look out over the view. There was a small deck with a barbecue built on top of it.

I took a few steps across the garden, turned to smoke, and moved over the sizeable ditch at the end of what I assumed was the property line. I re-formed on the other side and used my torch to search the area. After a few minutes of walking around, and apparently disturbing every nocturnal critter in the vicinity, I decided that whoever had killed Jordan hadn't fled across the moors.

Turning back to smoke and moving across the landscape, I re-formed at the side of the building and moved around to the front, making my way to the Kia. The door was locked, and there was no obvious damage to the vehicle. I had no idea where the keys were, and I didn't want to break the window and set off an unrelenting alarm, so I left the car and resumed my search.

The second set of car tracks weren't difficult to spot. They were fresh, maybe an hour at most, our own tracks having partially driven over them. I followed them out onto the dirt road and all the way down to the main road. It was impossible to follow further, as the road beyond was tarmac.

I jogged back to the building and met Hiroyuki and Nadia, both of whom were stood outside. "You find anything?" I asked them.

"Jordan was going to kill again," Hiroyuki said, motioning to a black plastic folder in his hand. "Scattered all over the floor of the bedroom. There are photos and information on several people who live in the Whitby area. Including the shop assistant who was creeped out by him."

"Found these, too," Nadia said, passing me a flip phone and a USB drive.

"Where'd you find them?" I asked, flipping the phone open and switching it on.

"The phone was hidden inside a Velcro pocket that was under a sofa cushion in the basement," Nadia said. "The USB drive was inside a book. The psychopath had carved out part of a book and put this drive inside."

"Seriously?" I asked.

Nadia nodded. "Whoever killed Jordan didn't do a particularly through search of the place. It's a *really old* burner phone, already switched it on and off, doesn't even have fingerprint security. It had a total of two numbers in it."

Having booted up, the phone's small screen showed no apps. I scrolled through the saved contacts, and there were none, but there were two numbers called. One repeatedly over the last several days.

"Someone was keen," I said, flicking through the number. "Neither of them are British numbers."

"American, I'm pretty sure," Nadia said.

We returned to the kitchen, where we all spent a moment staring at the empty seat, Jordan's blood still covering the chair and floor.

I got out my own phone and took a photo of the numbers that Jordan had dialled. I sent the photo to Ji-hyun in Boston with a quick description of what was going on and a request for her to check the numbers.

Hiroyuki opened the folder and removed the photos that Jordan had taken of his supposed next victim. Among them was a Polaroid photo of a neon-yellow-and-black snake emblem. "What's that?" I asked, pointing to the emblem.

"Never seen it before," Hiroyuki said.

"Nadia?" I asked.

She shook her head as her chains moved across the table and wrapped themselves gently around the phone. I looked over at her as her eyes rolled into the back of her head.

"I don't think I'll ever get used to seeing her do that," Hiroyuki said.

I looked back over to him. "I'm not sure she's ever got used to doing it either."

"Use the phone," Nadia said, her chains flicking away as if the presence of being close to the phone hurt them.

I stared at the phone and looked over at Nadia. "You sure?"

She moved her hand from side to side. "Chains are a funny thing. But I think no matter what we do, that phone is going to start a path we're supposed to follow."

Chained revenants can't see the future in the way people expect. They see snippets of their *possible* futures. They see the people or objects who will be important to that future. A lot of chained revenants go insane as they delve deeper and deeper into the futures the chains show them, finding the one that they believe is the *right* one. I knew that Nadia's biggest fear was losing herself to her chains.

I picked up the phone, the screen coming back to life as I pressed a random button. The reception showed at one bar, which was good enough for a call. I guessed we were close enough to a mast somewhere that we should be thankful. "So, who do I call first?"

"The most-used number," Nadia said.

"And if that person expects Jordan?" I asked.

Nadia shrugged.

I scrolled though the numbers called on the phone. "This last call was six hours ago. This phone was hidden, so that call was before the attack occurred."

"This was a professional job," Nadia said. "They subdued Jordan with what looks like no struggle. It's possible that whoever is on the end of the phone knows more about this than we do. Maybe a loved one."

"We searched into Jordan's life," I said. "These probably aren't phone numbers of family members; he had nothing to do with any of them."

Jordan had been born and raised in Boston, where he worked in sales for a bank. Three years earlier, he'd moved to Wyoming and began work for a congressman. He'd stayed there for two years as an intern until a judge turned up dead. Fingers were pointed by the local police, and Jordan ran back to Boston, which was where he started committing more murders and trying to turn people into rift-fused. Once the RCU had become involved and Jordan had run again, we discovered diaries where he wanted everyone to know that he *hated* his family.

"Maybe he knew his time was up and wanted to make amends," Hiroyuki said, scrolling through the phone. "He called this number fourteen times in the last day alone. That's a lot of tries to get hold of someone. Whoever it was, they were important to Jordan."

"No time like the present," I said, and pushed the little green phone button. I put the phone on speaker and placed it back on the table as it rang.

After eight rings, the call automatically disconnected.

"Burner phone on the other end?" I questioned. "Maybe they don't expect another call from Jordan."

"You think that number belongs to the killer?" Hiroyuki asked.

I considered it and settled for a shrug. "There's no sign of the house being broken into. Jordan either let his attacker in or they gained entry quietly."

"Considering he was still alive, they weren't great at their job," Hiroyuki said, motioning to the empty chair where Jordan had sat.

"We didn't know he was alive either," Nadia pointed out.

"When I tell everyone about what happened here, I'm going to leave that bit out," Hiroyuki said.

I picked up the phone. The previous number was last called only a few times in the last few days. "Okay, so, next call?" I dialled the other number.

It rang once before being answered. "Congressman Mills' office; how can I help?" a woman with a high-pitched tone asked.

I immediately recognised the name. "It's the congressman from Wyoming," I whispered.

Hiroyuki was on his phone in a flash, showing me and Nadia the search results for Congressman Mills. He was a white man of fortyish years, with a tan, dark brown hair that was suspiciously perfect, and a smile that could have lit fireworks. He looked like someone for whom the phrase *snake oil salesman* was created.

Nadia gave me a thumbs-up, and I passed the phone to her.

"Hello?" the receptionist repeated.

"Hi, this is Linda," Nadia said in a Bronx accent. "I'm looking for Congressman Mills."

"Can I ask why you're looking to speak to the congressman?" the woman asked, her tone neutral but bordering on irritated.

Hiroyuki showed a picture of the congressman alongside a group of gathered children with the words *Together We Will Pass Proposition 816.* And under that: *Putting Children First.*

"I work for the *Boston Globe*," Nadia said. "I'd like to talk to the congressman about Proposition 816."

"I'm sorry, you'll need to make an appointment," the woman said, sounding a little confused as to why someone in Boston would care about what happened hundreds of miles away. There was a pause before she continued. "And the congressman is *very* busy."

"Is there anyone I can talk to in his organisation about this matter?" Nadia asked.

"Please wait," she said, and hold music filled the air.

We sat in silence for close to a minute before the woman returned. "I've spoken to his chief of staff, who is willing to talk to you on Friday morning at ten a.m. Call this number and I'll put you through."

"Their name?" Nadia continued.

"Elliot Webb," the woman told her.

The phone went dead.

"If this wasn't a phone call, it would seem like a trap," Hiroyuki said.

"Which we would walk into anyway," Nadia said.

"Of course," I agreed. "Nice accent, by the way."

"Thank you," Nadia said with a curtsey, her Bronx accent back.

"There isn't a lot on the congressman's website about Elliot Webb," Hiroyuki said. "There's a *Mister E. Webb*, labelled as his chief of staff, who I assume is Elliot, but there's no photo or details beyond a bunch of stuff about growing up in Boston and believing in the vision of the congressman."

"Elliot Webb and Jordan Chapman are both Bostonians," I said. "Maybe not a coincidence."

"Boston is a big place," Hiroyuki said. "But it could be that they're old friends."

"Something else to ask Jordan when we find him," I replied.

"Jordan is going to be in those caves outside of Inaxia soon," Hiroyuki said. "Few hours at most. I think someone should be there to greet him. Preferably before the Inaxian guards get to him first and whisk him off to the capital for his new life."

Technically, whoever you were on Earth doesn't matter in the rift. It's a clean slate, a fresh chance. It doesn't exactly work like that in practise, but if Jordan keeps his mouth shut and nose clean, it could be a long time before his crimes on Earth are uncovered.

"Is getting to him once that happens harder?" Nadia asked.

I nodded. "The guard will take him into the city, where he'll be put through a sort of orientation and then sent out to start his training on his new life. It'll take a while to find him, considering the increased traffic of new riftborn over the last few years. Then we have to prove he did these things to the rulers of Inaxia."

Technically, you got a new life, all previous crimes forgotten, when you went to Inaxia. But the people there also weren't stupid, and they have people working on Earth to do checks on new arrivals. Some criminals were a threat to the wider public and were monitored to ensure they didn't start a new phase of crimes. Killing people to bring them back as rift-fused might not go down well in Inaxia, especially considering the large influx of new people and the disarray it's caused throughout the city.

"And after all of that, we have to hope he hasn't done a runner or gotten close enough to those he's been placed with that going for him could trigger a fight."

"So, we need to get him in the caves?" Nadia said. "Will he be alone?"

"At some point, probably would have been," Hiroyuki said. "But there are so many riftborn created at the moment that chances are he will have others with him."

"He killed people to make them into rift-fused," Nadia said. "It's possible that as he can't do that to people in the rift, he wouldn't try to kill anyone?"

"Do you believe that?" I asked her.

"No, just trying to make it sound less likely that whoever goes is going to find Jordan next to fresh victims," Nadia said.

Hiroyuki took off his Silver Phalanx pendant and threw it over to me before removing the car keys and doing the same with them. "Take it to Boston; I'll come back through the rift there."

"What are you going to do with Jordan?" I asked, pocketing the badge and keys.

"I'm going to make sure that he gives me the information we need," Hiroyuki said. "I want to know *exactly* who killed him and why. Jordan ran here, but his killer knew exactly where he was. Now, maybe that means Jordan wasn't working alone and someone wants to cover their tracks. Jordan was a psychopath, but if he was set up, maybe he's not too thrilled about that. After that, I'm going to contact the law enforcement in Inaxia and make sure they give him *special* attention."

"Be careful," I told him.

A tear opened up beside Hiroyuki. "I always am," he said, and the tear washed over him before snapping shut.

"We should go," Nadia said. "We need to get back to Boston. And we've got a phone call with the chief of staff of Congressman Spencer Mills."

I took the phone and got to my feet, removing the USB drive from my pocket and moving it between my fingers. "I want to know what's on this, too. We can use the laptop back at the hotel before we leave. Whatever is on here was important enough to hide. Hiroyuki once told me that a member of Congress was one of the Blessed. And Zeke said that a member of Congress worked with Jacob Smythe."

The blessed were a group who initially wanted greater parity between practitioners and other rift-fused who used to be humans. Unfortunately, they'd turned into a terrorist organisation who tried to overthrow Inaxia. Long story short, it didn't go well, and the leaders were mostly exiled from the rift, where they became criminals of a different kind. There were only two surviving members we were aware of: Jacob Smythe, who used to be a Member of Parliament and was now in prison in London, and an unknown member of the Blessed who was apparently in the US Congress.

"You think it's this guy?" Nadia asked, holding the door open for me as I walked through, nodding a thank you on the way.

"I don't like coincidences," I told her.

"So, do we go to see Jacob?" Nadia asked as we started our walk back to the car.

I shook my head. "Last time I saw him was a few years ago, and it wasn't a great meeting. I don't think he'd be receptive to answering questions."

"Would Zeke?" Nadia said.

Zeke was . . . complicated. He was a riftborn who'd been extorted into working with Jacob Smythe, who threatened his family if he didn't comply.

They made him try to kill me. It didn't end well for him, and he'd come clean about everything, including how his family was being held hostage. That didn't end well for the hostage-takers.

We stopped by the Volvo and I unlocked the car, both of us getting in, with me in the driver's seat. "Ji-hyun will know where he is."

"You think he'll help?" Nadia asked.

"I think he *wants* to help," I said, starting the car's engine. "Been a few years since I've spoken to him, too. Maybe his help would be in exchange for some time served."

We set off back toward Whitby. We had time to get to the hotel, get some rest, and get everything ready before we flew home. Also, we had to arrange to fly home. The RCU had a private jet, but it wasn't exactly used for transatlantic trips.

I called Ji-hyun on the way back to the hotel and told her everything that had happened. I kept nothing back; there was no point. She was going to find out everything sooner or later, and telling her now had the added benefit of giving her time to be annoyed without me anywhere near her.

"You want me to get Zeke out of prison?" she asked after having waited for me to finish before speaking.

"I just want to talk to him," I told her. "Before Friday."

"Friday is two days away," Ji-hyun said. "Has anyone ever told you that you're a pain in the ass?"

"It's been mentioned," I said.

"I'll see what I can do," she said. "You want me to get flights booked for you?"

"That would be very nice," I said.

"First class," Nadia interjected. "The less people who see me on board, the less people who ask stupid questions. If I could sit in the baggage hold, I would."

"I'll call you both in a few hours," Ji-hyun said. "Get some sleep and head down to Heathrow in the morning. Do I need to send anyone into the rift to help Hiroyuki? He's only here as a favour from Noah Kaya. If something happens to him, I would hate to have to explain to an Ancient why one of his people got hurt."

"He'll be fine," I said. "But I doubt Hiroyuki would say no."

"Okay, I've got some calls to make," Ji-hyun said. "Thank you both for doing this. I'll see you when you're back in Boston."

The car was quiet for a few minutes until Nadia said, "I don't think this is going to be a fun few days."

I was about to speak when a tear opened across the skies above the moors. Whatever it was Nadia thought was going to happen over the coming days, nothing good was going to come of a closer link between Earth and the rift; I was pretty sure of that.

CHAPTER FOUR

The flight from Heathrow to Boston was actually in first class. The relief on Nadia's face as she walked onto the plane all wrapped up, her chains beneath her long coat, was palpable.

Chained revenants were a species who had become a sort of good-luck charm for travellers. The idea went that as they could see portions of their own futures, they would never step foot onto something that was going to crash. If they were safe, so was everyone else.

It ignored a few key facts. Firstly, that chained revenants knew that *they* were going to be safe. One could be on a ship that sank, but they would survive, while everyone else died. But secondly, it could also be that they were *meant* to die. That they boarded their vehicle of choice, knowing that they weren't getting off at the other end.

Despite most chained revenants not wanting to be seen as anything close to a lucky charm, they were still portrayed that way by a large number of humans. So, while most humans saw a chained revenant and inwardly sighed at their being there, a few were more . . . verbose.

Nadia going into coach had the unpleasant side effect of a number of humans wanting to talk to her, to ask about their future, like she was a walking, talking magic eight ball. No amount of explaining that she couldn't do that was enough. And there was always one person, every single time, who decided that Nadia was just being unpleasant and demanded information she didn't have.

It happened in first class too, often because the more money they have, the bigger the arsehole, but the fewer number of people clamouring for her attention made it a little easier to manage. And having good flight staff who made sure she was left alone was all the better.

I sat on the other side of the aisle to Nadia, who spent a large portion of the flight staring out of the window or sleeping. Oddly enough, the tears in the sky didn't appear to have any effect on travelling by aircraft. Flight paths had been changed to avoid the places we knew the largest tears occurred, just in case, but no planes had been struck out of the sky by them opening, or by the rift energy that flooded out. After a few tentative flights, I'd found the same sense of ease coming back when getting on a plane.

Once we'd gotten back to the hotel, I'd tried the USB drive, only to discover it was encrypted with a level I had no hope of breaking on a machine ill suited to such a task. Ji-hyun assured me that she had people, and equipment, that could do such a thing.

After several hours of researching any connection between Jordan Chapman and Elliot Webb, or the Wyoming congressman, and finding nothing beyond what we already knew, I decided to get some rest. There were no photos of Elliot on *any* websites, and he apparently had no social media presence, which was weird in this day and age of politics but not unheard of. As I lay back in my seat, I found myself being pelted with tiny pieces of bread until I removed my headphones and looked over at Nadia. "Can I help you?" I asked.

"The bread was too much, wasn't it?" she asked.

"Well, I'm not a duck, so yes," I said.

Nadia slowly put down the rest of the slice of bread she'd been tearing apart to use as a ballistic, and looked up and down the aisle of the aircraft. "I should pick that up."

I glanced down at the multitude of small balls of bread as she got up and began to pick up her ammunition, taking it back to her seat and placing it in her empty food bowl.

"Feel better?" I asked.

"I don't know why I threw bread at you," Nadia said. "I thought it was playful. But honestly, now I just feel a bit weird."

"Did you want something apart from to pelt me with pieces of sourdough?" I asked her.

"The phone we took from Whitby," Nadia said. "When I touched it . . . I got flashes of something. I don't know what it was, but since the tears have been opening more frequently, my powers have been fluctuating."

I sat upright and turned toward her. "In what way?"

"Nothing bad," she said. "It's just that when I touch something that has been in contact with the rift, I can see . . . things. Like looking through a stop-motion camera they used to have at old seaside resorts. That might not make sense."

I think I got what she was saying. "You see flickers of where that object has been?"

Nadia nodded. "That phone was with Jordan when he . . . hurt people. He's not just psychotic; he's a *believer*."

"In what?" I asked.

"In the idea that revenants and riftborn are who humans are *meant* to be," she said. "That we're the next step of human evolution. I know that's not how evolution works; it's just what he thinks. I saw images of him at a church. Like Gabriel's."

The Church of Tempered Souls was a religion that could be found both on Earth and in the rift and was mostly conducted by people like Gabriel who just wanted to support and help their local communities. They wanted to bring humans and the rift-fused together to work in harmony. The vast majority of human church members were peaceful people who felt like they needed to find a place to belong.

Unfortunately, not all were that way. There had aways been a small contingent of mostly humans who believed that the rift-fused were their rightful place, and were increasingly angry that they hadn't been brought into what they considered an exclusive club.

Since the tears began to appear across the sky and the number of rift-fused had exploded across the globe, these small groups had gotten larger. They believed that now was the coming of a new age of life for humanity, and that those who were transformed into the rift-fused were going to be taken into this new utopia.

"You think a church is behind Jordan's killings?" I asked Nadia.

"I think he was a religious fanatic, and religious fanatics are usually the product of someone else's twisting of the truth," Nadia said.

"Maybe Gabriel will have some ideas," I thought aloud. "Or Hiroyuki will be able to get something out of Jordan so we don't have to go hunting in Wyoming when we go to see the congressman's aide."

"You ever been there?" Nadia asked.

"A few times," I said. "Not recently. You?"

She nodded. "Few years ago. It's a peaceful place. Lots of open land, not many people. I'd have thought I'd have liked it, but there's almost too much quiet. That make sense?"

"There's a place in the rift about two days' ride from Inaxia which is just open tundra," I said. "It's called Vast Death, for good reason, although most call it the Vastness. I have no idea how many miles it is, but you could take a week to ride across it. There's a smattering of small villages here and there, but mostly it's just open land, plants, and animals that want to eat you."

"Vast Death?" Nadia asked. "Seriously?"

"There used to be a rule in the rift that if you find it first, you can name it," I said. "We don't have that rule anymore."

"Because someone came up with *Vast Death*," Nadia said with a laugh.

"No, someone found a forest to the south of the rift, wanted to call it *Big Tree Land*," I said. "His naming privileges were revoked at that point."

"The rift doesn't have a Big Tree Land?" Nadia asked, sadly. "It sounds like a terrible amusement park. I for one would like to go there. Are the trees even big?"

I nodded, remembering that they would dwarf even giant redwoods. "They are."

"What did they call it in the end?" Nadia asked. "Treetopia?"

"It's called Whistling," I said. "The trees make a noise when the wind whips across them. It sounds exactly like its name would suggest. It's so loud, though, that if you're in the middle of the forest when a storm hits, the sound could kill you."

Nadia stared at me for several seconds. "You know, considering how much these people like Jordan want to go live in the rift, it's not the most hospitable place."

I couldn't really argue with that. We both settled back as the plane landed at Logan International Airport just as the sun began to set. We left the aircraft, thanking the flight crew for their help, and made our way through the airport, where we grabbed our bags, including Hiroyuki's.

There was a car waiting for us outside. The half-hour ride to Moon Island was done in the setting sun. Moon Island was where the RCU had once built their Boston headquarters and was now where the vast amount of training was conducted for new recruits. We were let through the security checkpoint and taken around to the rear of the island before we boarded a small ferry for the short remainder of our journey to Fort Andrews on Peddocks Island.

What had once been derelict island off the coast of Boston, had been transformed into the RCU's new headquarters for the eastern states of America. Ji-hyun had taken charge of an organisation that was falling apart, and turned it into one of the most highly regarded law enforcement agencies in the country.

The main building was five stories tall, with a further ten stories—including a prison—underground. There were about two dozen buildings littering the island, one of which was inhabited by the resident blacksmith, Drusilla August.

We pulled up to the small harbour to be greeted by two RCU agents, both young men who I didn't recognise. Both of the agents stood to attention and saluted.

"You don't need to do that," I said, stepping off the ferry onto the pier.

"You need to salute me, though," Nadia said from behind me. "Actually, can you bow? I'd like that a lot."

The worried shared glances between the two agents made me look back at Nadia, whose smile was broad and beaming.

One of the agents started to bow, and I stopped him before Nadia could burst out laughing. "She's messing with you, lad," I said.

"I also want rose petals dropped at my feet as I walk," Nadia told the two agents.

"Where's Ji-hyun?" I asked the agents, as Nadia huffed behind me for stopping her fun.

"Main building," the agent who hadn't tried to bow said. "She's waiting for you. We can drive you."

I followed his gesture to the small vehicle nearby. "Let's go."

We followed the two agents, keeping our bags with us as we sat in the rear of what was essentially a golf cart painted red and set off. It was a short drive to the main building, and it would have only taken a few minutes of walking, but it gave me a short time to look around at the number of agents who walked the island.

Since the tears opened in the sky, the number of revenants had increased exponentially, and so, the number of people who decided they wanted to work for the RCU had also increased. Ji-hyun was choosy about who she allowed the honour of being an agent, and anyone who was shown to be overly aggressive, or corrupt, was out. Every new agent was paired with someone she trusted and was on probation for a decade, which seems like a long time, but revenants could live for hundreds of years, so in the scheme of things, it was a blip of their life.

She'd made a few enemies in the last few years by kicking out four police officers who had been turned into revenants after a shootout in LA. All four had shown to be the exact type of people Ji-hyun despised, and none had taken their dismissals well. One had thrown a punch her way. I couldn't remember if they'd been able to reattach his hand.

Ji-hyun was five foot seven, with long brown hair that was always in a high ponytail. As usual, she wore black boots and blue jeans, although this time, she also had on a green T-shirt with a picture of Donatello from the *Teenage Mutant Ninja Turtles* on it.

She pointed to her T-shirt and smiled. "Best. One."

I raised my hands in mock defeat.

"I like Michelangelo best," Nadia said, walking by Ji-hyun into the headquarters.

"What a fucking shock," Ji-hyun said, giving me a hug. "Hiroyuki not back yet, I assume."

I passed her his Silver Phalanx pendant. "You'd probably best keep this here."

"Come on; you can tell me everything that happened," Ji-hyun said.

We walked through the glass-encircled foyer and used a lift to go up to the top floor, where Ji-hyun's office was.

The entire top floor was designated offices for the highest-ranked people within the RCU, although, as it was getting late, the two dozen rooms were mostly empty. Ji-hyun stopped at the few offices still occupied, checking in with those within. Despite her own near-endless need to work all hours of the day, she was mindful that others did not do the same.

We reached her office at the far corner of the floor, walking by the empty reception area opposite a large window that overlooked Massachusetts Bay. It was now dark outside, but the nearby city of Boston was alive with light.

"So," Ji-hyun said, pushing open her office door and beckoning us both inside. "You've created a set of all-new problems for us."

The interior of Ji-hyun's office could be considered lived-in. There were windows, which gave a good panoramic view of the island and water surrounding it. There were bookshelves, which groaned under the weight of so many manga and books that it looked like a library. There was a wooden table in the middle of the office, which had a slight crack in it where Ji-hyun had punched it a few years ago. She had a desk with computer, a small fridge beside it, and a water cooler beside that. I glanced over at the pullout sofa next to the entrance, which I knew she slept on more often than just going home.

"I don't sleep here *every* night," Ji-hyun said, having noticed my gaze settling on the sofa.

"You shouldn't sleep here at all," Nadia said. "People need to be away from work."

Ji-hyun looked between Nadia and me. "You both go home all the time?"

"No," Nadia said. "But everyone says I'm crazy."

"And you?" she asked me.

"I agree; I think she's crazy," I said, pointing at Nadia, who laughed so much, she started to cough.

We sat and discussed our findings for a few hours, eventually ordering food from a Korean takeaway that had seen itself making record profits when you're close to a place where all-nighters are pulled on a regular basis.

"So, the problem is that if this congressman is involved," Ji-hyun said, tucking into a bowl of kimchi-jjigae, "then we're heading into human politics. We don't want to be messing with human politics."

"Because they all suck?" Nadia asked, taking a bite of fried chicken so spicy, it made my nose tingle even from several feet away.

"There's that," Ji-hyun said. "But mostly because we don't want to be accused of meddling. Should the phone call move toward a meeting, it might be an idea to get this chief of staff to come to us here. Or meet in neutral territory. We definitely can't accuse anyone of anything without proof."

"Zeke," I said, finally bringing up what I'd been tentative to mention. "I'd like to see him."

"Already in the arranging stages," she said. "He's in New York, so it should be sorted out within twenty-four hours. You think he'll be helpful?"

"Can't hurt," I said. "You didn't send him to the rift."

"He helped us," Ji-hyun said. "So, he didn't have to go to the prisons in the rift. I don't much wish that on anyone."

"He wanted to help when I last saw him," I said. "He agreed to be jailed for his crimes when he could have run."

"We asked about the congressman at the time," Ji-hyun said. "He told us he didn't know who it was."

"Maybe that's true," I said taking a bite of pork from my own bowl of kimchi-jjigae. "But if he met one of the aides of a congressman or even recognises the name, he might be able to confirm things. Jordan called the office of a congressman. Not saying he's a member of the Blessed, but someone in that office was important to a serial killer. I'd rather figure out who and why."

"Besides, someone had Jordan executed," Nadia said. "Probably a good idea to find out if that person is going to become a bigger problem."

"Any chance your chains are telling you anything useful?" Ji-hyun asked.

"Since the sky started tearing open, my chains are . . ." She paused for a moment to finish a piece of chicken. "Temperamental. Things tend to come to me much sooner than they used to. Right now, making those calls in England was something I knew we should do. After that, they're not showing much of anything."

I got up from the table and stretched. "I'm going to go see Drusilla. Unless we have other matters to discuss?"

"Go enjoy your time," Ji-hyun said. "I'll see you in a few hours."

"Oh, Ahiram," I said before I made it to the door. "You recognise the name?"

Ji-hyun considered it for a moment before shaking her head. "Should I?"

"It was tattooed on Jordan's arm," I said. "His victims said that Jordan kept talking about a Great King, wondered if Ahiram was that person."

"Maybe it's some old rift history," Ji-hyun said. "I can ask around, but I'd call Gabriel and ask him. The man knows rift history better than most."

"Good idea," I said. "I'll give him a call in the morning. Enjoy your food."

Nadia waved me away as she tucked into more of her chicken, and I left the office. I opted to walk across the island to Drusilla's blacksmith shop. The air whipped across the island more often than not, and even on hot days, it got noticeably cooler at night than it did on the mainland.

Drusilla was the granddaughter of Roman Emperor Augustus and his wife Drusilla, who the blacksmith had been named after. When we'd first met, she'd made a deal with me to take her out for a meal—definitely not a date—in return for working on my spear and daggers that had been fused with primordial bones. That promise had taken me a year to bring to fruition after the problems that Callie's death had caused.

In the past year, we'd quickly gone from friends to something more. I'd considered asking her exactly what we were, but the time never felt quite right. We were both busy, her with her forge and me with helping the RCU or trying to figure out how to stop the sky from tearing apart on a regular basis.

I reached the forge and knocked on the door. I tried the handle, but it was locked.

"That you, Lucas?" Drusilla asked.

"It is," I called back.

The door unlocked, and I pushed it open, stepping into the main forge.

Drusilla stood in the middle of her forge, next to her anvil, and smiled as I entered. She had long dark brown hair that fell over her pale shoulders. She had piercings in her lip, nose, and ears, and was otherwise completely naked.

"Had to make sure it was you," she said.

"I appreciate it," I told her, locking the door behind me. "This is quite the welcome home."

Drusilla crossed the floor and kissed me passionately. "Oh, this is just the preliminaries." She took my hand in hers and led me upstairs.

CHAPTER FIVE

I woke up to moonlight streaming through the window beside me. The curtains were still open, which was probably not the best way to ensure privacy, although if anyone had decided to watch earlier, I hoped they enjoyed the show.

Drusilla was already up; I couldn't remember an occasion where she wasn't awake before me once sunrise had started. She liked to rise early to get the forge going; she was a riftborn, and her power allowed her to manipulate metal. Usually nothing too fancy, but when it was heated, she could forge pretty much anything she could think of, using nothing but her own hands. I'd once seen her beat a red-hot axe head with the palm of her hand. It might have been the sexiest thing I'd ever seen in my very long life.

I got up and was about to put on some clothes when the door to the room opened and Drusilla came back in, wearing an oversized white T-shirt and a concerned expression.

"RCU are downstairs," she said as I pulled on a T-shirt and grabbed my jeans from the floor.

I picked up my T-shirt and continued getting dressed. "Did they say why?"

"Tear in Boston Common," she said. "Big one."

Tears above Boston Common were a fairly regular occurrence, but they were small and usually closed with minimal problems.

"How big?" I asked, putting on my socks and shoes.

"*Really* big. It's bad. Four greater fiends. That's all I got from them."

I paused for a second. "Four?" I half-whispered. Four was three more than had ever been created because of a tear over the common.

Four greater fiends in a heavily populated area was the definition of the word *bad*.

Now fully dressed, I stood and paused by Drusilla. "I'll see you soon," I said, giving her a kiss before reaching for the nightstand to retrieve my Raven Guild medallion.

It was in the shape of a buckler shield with a sword and hammer crossing over each other in front. A steel raven sat on top of the shield, as if holding it. I had once thought it was made from hardened stone; it turned out to be made of primordial bone, covered in copper.

There was usually a space between the shield and hammer, but it was filled with an oval forest-green gem. A promise crystal. Or heart crystal, depending on who you spoke to. At some point, it would break—either because I broke it or, much more likely, because Neb did—and it meant that I would have to fulfil my oath to return to Neb for whatever help she required from me. The crystal also gave Neb the ability to communicate with me while I slept, although thankfully, it was an ability she hadn't found a use for yet.

I slipped the cool chain over my neck, feeling the weight of the medallion in more than just its physical form.

"We need to talk soon," Drusilla said. "Nothing bad, I promise, but it's important."

I was a little surprised to find that I felt a pit of concern in my gut upon hearing *we need to talk*. I cared for Drusilla and enjoyed her company, but despite the fact that we hadn't discussed anything further, the possibility of her being unhappy unnerved me. "We will," I promised, kissing her again. "Soon as I'm back."

"Go do your thing," she said with a warm smile.

I left the bedroom and took the stairs two at a time down to the three waiting RCU agents—two women and a man—who all wore black tactical gear with a sidearm on their hip and two daggers that I could see. While I'd had the idea of making everyone in the RCU a primordial-bone weapon, there simply hadn't been enough to go around. They were kept under lock and key at the HQ and given out only when needed. Thankfully, taking down a few fiends didn't require specialist weaponry.

"Sir," one of the women said. She was short and pale and had her hair in a mohawk, the sides of her head shaved. "You're requested at the helipad."

I followed them out of the forge and climbed into the back seat of one of the carts, driven by the mohawk woman, as we sped as fast as the cart could go.

"Why me?" I asked. "I mean, you guys can all deal with this without my help."

"Lots of sky tears tonight," the male RCU agent said, turning around. "We're stretched a bit thin."

"How many tears?" I asked.

"Nine," the female agent beside me said. "Spread from here to New Jersey."

"They all in usual places?" I asked.

"No, we've got three new locations," she told me.

Nine sky tears in one night located in such a relatively close area was a lot. But three tears in new locations was bad news. If the tears were spreading and becoming both larger and more regular, we could have serious problems on our hands. The most in one night that I was aware of was fourteen, and that particular cluster of awfulness started in Toronto and ended in Mexico. The tears don't care about borders. The RCU in Canada, America, and Mexico had worked together to make sure that everything was dealt with. Another feather in the cap of an organisation that was undergoing a renaissance of a sort. No one would be getting much sleep tonight.

"Any chance they can figure out why these tears keep happening and stop them?" the male agent asked.

"If I knew the answer to that, I wouldn't be sat here with you," I told him.

The Boeing CH-47 Chinook helicopter sat on the helipad, the rotors already moving, the sound deafening. We all climbed aboard the helicopter, where I found a dozen more RCU agents already strapped in, along with Nadia, who waved enthusiastically from halfway down the fuselage and patted the chair beside her. I walked over and sat down, putting on the headset she gave me.

"This is exciting," she said with a large smile, and passed me my short spear, which she'd had under the bench we were all sat on. "Thought you might need this."

I nodded. "Thanks. Happy to have it back."

Unlike the other agents, Nadia didn't wear any tactical gear, as it messed with her chains. She continued to wave at several other agents, who waved back. She'd become a popular member of the team in the last few years, although she had refused to join the RCU on the several occasions she'd been asked and so was considered an *external contractor,* a bit like me.

"You have a nice evening?" Nadia asked.

The door to the Chinook was closed and locked, and a red light at the end of the fuselage near the cockpit glowed green, followed a few seconds later by the helicopter taking off.

I watched out of the circular window opposite me as the helicopter gained altitude and turned slightly, facing Boston and giving me an excellent view of the tear above the city. "It was until the sky opened up," I told her. "That's a really big tear."

In fact, it was a *fucking huge* tear and must have been several miles long. A large part of the city of Boston was bathed in an unearthly purple glow.

"The largest tears only happen at night," Nadia said. "You noticed that?"

I nodded. It was one of the first pieces of information we'd managed to glean from the sky tears. Also, despite the fact that the tears were huge, they never created more than a few dozen rift-fused at a time. However, nine tears in a few hundred miles meant a lot of fiends to stop and revenants to take care of.

"How's Drusilla?" Nadia asked me.

"Good," I said.

"You told her you love her?" she asked.

I noticed several people looking my way.

"Nadia, are you on comms to everyone in this helicopter?" I replied.

Several others nodded to me with a smirk as Nadia looked down at the comm switch on the lead that left the helmet. "Oops," she said with a shrug. "You want me to change it?"

"Bit late now," I said, stretching across the fuselage to tap the RCU agent opposite me on the knee. "What are we dealing with here, agent?"

The agent, a young man who looked no older than thirty but was probably three times that, looked back at me. "Becker," he said with a German accent. He was an RCU team leader, as was denoted by the three golden pips under his name on his lapel.

"Okay, so what are we looking at, Agent Becker?" I asked.

"Four greater fiends," he said. "All we know is that one of them is a bat and one a rat."

"Please let one be a cat," Nadia whispered, presumably forgetting that everyone could hear her.

"Any casualties?" I asked, noticing several RCU agents look away with grins on their face.

"Property damage, but it's late at night, and they appear to be confined to Boston Common," he said. "The Boston PD have put up a cordon around the park and are helping evacuate everyone inside."

"You got any more riftborn here?" I asked.

"Just you and me," he said. "One chained revenant, too. The rest are spined, horned, and a few bone revenants."

"Sounds like you've got it all sorted," I said. "Why am I here?"

"You can track these things, yes?" he asked.

"Yeah," I said tentatively. I'd been trained to track and hunt from young—trained to kill, too, although the addition of being able to track their trail of rift energy made it all much easier.

"And you've killed them before?" He continued.

"A lot of them," I said.

"Well, most of these agents are newbies," Becker told me. "They have power and training but very little experience facing down more than one greater fiend at a time."

"And me?" Nadia asked.

"You're here because you were the first person on the helicopter," Becker said. "Honestly, no one wanted to ask you to leave."

"Aww," Nadia said with a playful grin.

Becker pressed the button on his comms to make his channel private and motioned for me to do the same, which I did a moment later, sitting back in my seat and expecting something unpleasant.

"She going to be okay?" he asked.

"Yes," I said. "She's a highly trained and exceptionally dangerous revenant."

"And she's currently waving at people and smiling," he said. "Don't get a lot of waving and smiling on the way to fight monsters."

"Becker, I promise you if shit goes down, I would rather have Nadia at my back than every single other person on this helicopter," I said. "Not because you're not good enough but because she's *better*."

The team leader stared at me, looked over at Nadia, and nodded curtly. "Just wanted to check," he said. "These people are my responsibility."

"No, I get it," I told him, not wanting any resentment or hurt feelings about what I'd said. "But she'll make sure people come home tonight; I can promise you that."

I disconnected from the comms of the whole helicopter and closed my eyes, happy for the sound of the helicopter engine drowning out any conversations. I had managed about thirty seconds when there was a tap on my hand. I opened my eyes and found Nadia staring at me; she raised the wire on her headset to show me she'd flicked over to her private channel. I followed suit.

"Tears that big aren't normal," she said.

I made sure to keep my face emotionless and nodded. "Agreed."

"I know Callie is dead and everything, but is there any way someone else could have used her knowledge to *force* open tears from the rift?" she asked me. "Theoretically?"

I considered it for a moment. "I have no idea," I admitted. "If someone is forcing them open, we've found no evidence of it. The primordials believed that the tears are just a byproduct of the rift energy being warped by having someone die inside it. They believed that the tears would calm down over time, but they had no way of knowing what *over time* actually meant. Years, decades, no one knows."

"So, *theoretically*, it's possible," Nadia said.

I nodded, although I *really* didn't want to. "Yeah. *Theoretically*, someone could control the tears; that's what Callie was trying to do. But I don't know who, and I don't know where they'd be. The RCU raided her lab in Texas, took everything of value, and burned everything else. The tears have been opening at specific locations since Callie died, and with similar levels of power and size, but the times have been all over the place. The idea that they've now opened in new places and are considerably larger than they've been before is something we should all be concerned about. I've spoken to other experts in rift science, and no one has figured out anything close to a rhyme or reason as to when the tears open or close. The fabric between the two worlds is thinner than it's ever been. That's all we know for sure."

Nadia pondered my words for a moment. "Does that mean parts of the rift could go to here or vice versa?"

"I don't know," I said, wishing I had better information. "Callie's long-term plan was to control the tears, but she never wrote anything about opening the skies or merging the rift and Earth. She believed that she could control the tears as they used to be. Small, small, fast tears that were gone as quickly as they arrived. The only good thing is that while the sky is what stays open, we're unlikely to get any elder fiends."

Elder fiends were created differently to the lesser or greater variety. When a tear happened and an animal on Earth walked through just as an animal in the rift walked through, they merged and an elder fiend was created. The tears being high up in the sky meant that elder fiends were extremely unlikely. If they ever did, it would be bad for everyone concerned. No one wants to deal with a hyper intelligent and aggressive monster at the best of times, but one that could fly would be a cruel and unusual punishment.

Out of the window, it was easy to spot the gigantic flying bat. For the most part, greater fiends looked like the animal that the rift energy had come in contact with, transforming a living creature on Earth into something monstrous. I hoped that whatever fun extras the bat-fiend had been given by the rift power, it wasn't anything too problematic. Thankfully, greater fiends are only about as clever as the animal they're created from.

"People look scared," Nadia said.

I tore my gaze away from the ten-foot-high bat with a wingspan the size of a bus. I looked around the fuselage of the Chinook and saw the fear etched on the faces of many agents. There was no training that truly prepared you for going up against a greater fiend, let alone four of them.

I flicked my communication device over to talk to everyone at once. "This will not be fun," I said, feeling the eyes of everyone in the helicopter turn to me. "That big bastard out there is still made of flesh. It's big, it's probably angry, and it's definitely dangerous. But so are you. Watch each other's backs, trust in your training, and you'll all come back fine. You might have a few bruises to compare over drinks later, but bruises fade. You are better as a team; trust in that team. Ji-hyun would not have let you become RCU agents if she'd thought you weren't good enough."

The helicopter jerked suddenly and rose steeply as several of the windows exploded, raining glass down on those unlucky enough to be sat beneath them.

"What the fuck was that?" Becker shouted.

"Echolocation, maybe, or sonic boom," I suggested. Greater fiends can get some interesting amplification of their own natural abilities.

I caught a glimpse of the bat-fiend as it tracked our movement, having obviously seen us, or heard us, or whatever it was rift-powered bats did.

"Get us up high," I said, opening the comm channel to the pilot.

"How high?" the pilot asked.

"How high are we now?"

"Two thousand feet," the pilot said.

"Seven thousand feet," I told them, unconcerned about altitude sickness.

The helicopter banked sharply before moving vertically at speed, the shape of the bat-fiend and the surrounding trees disappearing below us. I was heartened to discover the bat staying where he was, its attention back to something under the canopy of trees.

"You got a plan?" Becker asked as the chinook stopped climbing.

"Yeah," I said. "I want all of you to enter the park from the south. Hopefully, you'll be able to find somewhere to land. I'm going to go keep those fiends busy."

"How do you plan on doing that?" Becker asked.

"I'm going to jump out," I said. "And piss them off."

"You're going to jump out?" Becker asked, speaking slowly as if he'd misheard.

I nodded. "I need that door released."

"We've been friends for far too long," Nadia said, although she was smiling as she said it. "You need a parachute?"

I shook my head. "I've been practising."

"Jumping out of helicopters?" she asked.

"Something like that," I said. "I'll see you on the ground. Be careful."

"You too," Nadia said.

The door to the helicopter opened, the freezing wind whipping in as I walked to the edge, looking down on the ground far below me.

"Do you know what you're doing?" Becker asked.

I nodded. During my year spent in the rift, I'd researched the constant tears, but I'd also worked with my primordial friend, Valmore, who trained me in uses of my power that I hadn't considered before. Or, more accurately, shouted instructions while I did something stupid. Over a year, I got fitter, stronger, faster, more so than I'd been for many years. But I also spent a lot of time finding out how far I *could* push my power.

Valmore's method for getting me to turn to smoke and back to human form had consisted of putting me in dangerous situations to see what I could do. Making me go underwater was one such pleasant task, but the other was climbing the mountains around the Tempest—the area of land where the rift power is strongest—and jumping off at various heights, some thousands of feet above the ground.

It turned out that I hadn't previously hit the limits of what I was capable of, and with a lot of practice—mostly trial and many, many errors—I improved myself.

"See you shortly, then," Becker said.

A quick glance over at the tear in the sky told me it was closing. Thankfully, that meant no reinforcements for the greater fiends. Hopefully, anyway.

I stepped out of the helicopter, and gravity did what gravity does best.

You'd think that seven thousand feet was a long way up, and technically it was. However, once I hit terminal velocity—an average of about twelve seconds—I had about another twelve seconds before I hit the ground.

It doesn't make much difference whether or not I turned to smoke before or after I hit terminal velocity; it sucked either way. Turning to smoke at ground level was something that had taken me a long time to master. When you add in wind speed, falling speed, temperature variables, and how quickly all of those particles of me get spread around when in smoke form, and you either get good fast or you get dead.

Thankfully, I was *very* good. Even if I do say so myself.

I counted to fifteen and turned to smoke, pushing it out far enough so that I could still keep my mind in contact with every piece of me while also making sure that nothing started to drift away. I transferred the speed I was going while whole to my smoke form and poured straight down toward the ground. It was a taxing and draining exercise, and the first time I'd done it after jumping out of a helicopter. The highest I'd done it in the rift was five thousand feet, and the first time I'd done it had been deeply unpleasant.

The cold tore through my smoke form, and I could feel it all. I felt the tug of the wind, the pull of the smoke as it tried to move further apart. And through it all, I felt my own nervous energy bouncing between the parts of me. Turning to smoke is a weird experience but not one I would trade for anything.

The bat-fiend looked up at me, having sensed something moving toward it at speed, but didn't react in time for me to re-form my body inches before its head.

The resulting feet-first impact was . . . *unpleasant*. More for the fiend than me.

CHAPTER SIX

The bat-fiend's head vanished in a plume of blood and gore. I immediately turned back to smoke and re-formed inches above the grass inside the park. The energy that I'd gathered from the fall dissipated in the most spectacular way possible, creating a twenty-foot-diameter crater in the ground, throwing up grass and dirt all around me and dumping me on my arse with a painful jolt up my spine.

I had a trick where I could fly at someone in smoke form, re-form into my human form, and punch someone hard enough to send them flying. The only problem was it usually did damage to my hand. Thankfully, falling and doing a similar thing with my feet only made my legs really sore the next day.

I didn't feel bad for the bat-fiend. Whatever animals they'd once been were dead long before I ever came along. Their amalgamated and twisted bodies only thought of causing pain and suffering to anything living nearby.

The bat-fiend had collapsed to the ground, its twitching corpse already beginning to decompose. The bodies of lesser and greater fiends didn't last long once dead.

It took me a few wobbly moments before I was able to stand up, and a few more before I walked out of the crater, still holding the short spear in my hand, using it as a makeshift walking stick. I looked down at myself and discovered that only my legs were bloody, an unpleasant side effect of travelling at speed feet-first to impact with something's head.

I placed my index finger inside the small ridge on the side of the shaft, turning it to smoke, and used my ring finger to push the small button beside it, activating the shutter on the end of the ridge, trapping the smoke that had once been my finger inside. Wherever my spear was thrown, I could immediately snap to it in smoke form. Another weapon I'd been practising with.

The usual streetlamps that sit inside the park were all off, and the only light came from the combination of the tear high above and the moon.

I crouched low, took a deep breath, and let it out in a long, slow moment as I scanned the area for any of the remaining three fiends, hoping to catch movement within the park.

It took a few seconds, but I eventually saw something between me and the flashing light of the police and ambulance vehicles on the edges of the park. Whatever I'd seen had been only for a moment, but it was quick and big.

Before I moved, I heard the crack of wood behind me. I froze, my grip on my spear tightening, as I slowly turned to face the noise. In the distance, I saw the George Washington statue bathed in the glow of the rift but nothing between me and it.

A helicopter flew overhead, the noise of the machine all-consuming as it moved to land, using searchlights on the underside of the aircraft to illuminate the park. Unfortunately for it, the light attracted the attention of a fiend, which bounded out of the darkness the trees gave it and jumped high into the air, revealing itself to be some kind of squirrel creature. Although squirrels don't usually have dark beetle-like armour across their back and side, and a stinger on the end of their tail.

The squirrel missed the helicopter, landing somewhere deeper in the park, which soon erupted with gunfire. I ran toward the noise, hoping to help the humans before they were turned to paste, and almost missed the rattling noise, throwing myself to the leaf-covered ground and barely avoiding the snake's open mouth as it darted up from under a bridge, crashing through a bronze statue as if it were made of paper.

The creature had once been a rattlesnake, which I didn't even know were native to Boston. And although it still looked pretty much snakelike, it was twenty feet long, with fangs that weren't far off the same length as one of my legs.

The rattler struck, and I turned to smoke, moving to the side of the creature, re-forming, and driving my spear into its belly. I tore down the side of the greater fiend, expecting it to be a short-lived encounter, but instead of blood and organs, a toxic slurry left the animal's body, the noxious fumes making me feel dizzy and light-headed.

The spear with primordial bone killed the creatures that Callie had created with no problems, but it turned out that it didn't always immediately end the lives of fiends and other rift-fused. Give with one hand and take with the other.

I turned back to smoke and moved twenty feet away before re-forming, taking in a deep lungful of beautiful, non-toxic air. The snake coiled around itself, the wound in the side of the creature still secreting a blood that wouldn't be out of place found inside a xenomorph. It bubbled and oozed as it touched a nearby elm tree, which began to die almost instantly, pieces of trunk falling away.

"That's not pleasant," I said as the snake hissed, its rattle shaking furiously.

The snake kept its eyes on me as I moved between the trees, using them as a screen between us. Occasionally, the snake hissed or moved slightly, but it didn't try to strike. I relaxed the grip on my spear, wondering what might happen should the blade—made from mixing the bones of a primordial with the very best in hardened steel—touch the sludge that had all but eaten through the tree.

Besides, I didn't know if the toxic mess was due to an evolution of the creature when it became a greater fiend, or if it was just the venom of the snake turned up to eleven. I didn't much want to find out.

Two more steps and the large elm tree gave way, snapping in half where the slurry had touched it and causing it to crash down where the snake was coiled.

The snake darted away, and I threw my spear, catching it under the jaw and pinning its jaws together. I turned to smoke and snapped toward my spear, re-forming, taking hold of the spear for a moment as the snake thrashed around. It slammed its huge body on the ground, and I only narrowly managed to turn back to smoke, moving back over to the trees as the snake stopped moving. The impact had driven the spear further up through the roof of its mouth, into its brain.

Its head flopped to the side, its eyes closed.

I walked slowly toward the dead fiend, took ahold of the end of my spear, stepped to the side, and tore it out of the snake's head, narrowly avoiding more toxic blood as it jetted from the wound I'd inflicted. The snake almost immediately began to disintegrate, and I was grateful to see the spear remained intact and the blade wasn't bubbling or damaged, although it definitely needed a good clean. Maybe with some bleach. I wasn't going to be able to hold it any further up the shaft, considering the venom there would eat through my skin in seconds.

I left the spear on the ground. It was unfortunate, but I couldn't risk infecting more of the park—or any of the people—with the greater fiend's venom.

The gunfire had stopped, but I ran toward the edge of the park anyway, hoping to get an update about what had happened with the other fiend I'd seen running their way. I found the RCU, several of whom looked a little worse for wear, and the decomposing bodies of two greater fiends.

The buildings close to the edge of the park had taken a battering, with several store fronts being smashed to pieces, their contents strewn across the sidewalk. A few buildings had claw marks on the edges of them where the greater fiends had tried to escape or get a better angle for attack, and one police car had been overturned, while another was . . . flattened.

"How many hurt?" I asked Nadia, who sat on the edge of the park, eating a chocolate ice cream in a cone. "And where did you get that?"

"The fiend smashed the front windows of an ice cream shop," Nadia said, pointing to the end of the block, where several more RCU agents congregated. She licked the ice cream. "Waste not, want not."

"And the injuries?" I asked.

"Four humans hurt," Nadia said. "None seriously, although one of them might not have all of his limbs anymore."

"That sounds pretty serious," I said.

"I mean, it depends on how deeply attached you are to both your hands," she said. "We told him to back off, he didn't, he aimed a gun at a greater fiend. It bit his hand off. Could have been his head."

She had a point. "And the RCU?"

"Two RCU agents, one with a broken leg, one possibly broken ribs, serious cut to her face, too," Nadia said. "She'll need stitches, fast healing or not. All are being seen to. Where's your spear?"

"In the park," I said. "Fought a giant rattlesnake that bled venom."

"Oooh," Nadia said, suddenly interested. "That's new. Let me see."

I pointed into the park. "It's probably decomposed by now, but I assure you it wasn't as much fun as you seem to think it was."

I looked around the mass of RCU agents, the Boston PD officers, and a smattering of federal officers from a variety of organisations with three-letter acronyms. Everyone had come together—human and rift-fused—to stop people getting hurt or worse. While there were politics to be played, and I was pretty sure Ji-hyun was fed up of it, the people on the ground still did their jobs. Lives had almost certainly been saved tonight.

There was a commotion from several uniformed officers inside the park, and Nadia caught me staring their way. She turned to take a look. "Problem?" she asked.

"Always," I said as one of the officers broke away and ran over toward where Nadia and I were.

The officer was a short lady, at barely over five feet tall. She had light brown skin and shoulder-length dark hair, her police uniform was covered in dirt and debris, and she had a cut on one cheek that had been taped shut, although there was still dried blood on her collar.

"Sir, ma'am," she said, her accent all Boston.

"*Lucas* is fine," I replied.

"I prefer *High Evolutionary*," Nadia said, and smiled warmly.

The officer stared at her for a second, presumably deciding whether or not Nadia was being serious.

"She's Nadia," I said.

"It's been a long night," Nadia said, finishing her ice cream and getting to her feet. "Let me have my moments of fun."

"Okay," the officer said, clearly no longer sure what the hell was going on. "I think you're going to want to see this."

"Lead the way," I told her.

The officer almost looked relieved as she turned and headed back into the park.

"High Evolutionary?" I whispered. "Seriously?"

"I thought it was funny," she said with a shrug.

We followed the police officer back to the group of five—three other Boston officers and two RCU agents—all of whom looked more than a little unhappy. They were stood on a bridge that went over part of the lake, the lights adorning the bridge itself were switched off, and the whole place felt still and eerie.

"There," the female officer said as we stood in the middle of the bridge, looking down at the bank. She pointed to what looked like a small box just under the shadow of the bridge.

"You been to look at it?" I asked.

"We did," one of the RCU agents—a tall man with pale skin and large bushy black beard—said. "Decided to get someone who might know what it is."

I walked to the edge of the bridge and swung down onto the bank of the lake. I removed my phone and used the torch to get a better view of the package. From first look, it just seemed to be a small metal box. Twelve inches long, six inches wide, and about as many high. There was a handle on top of it and a latch on one side of its length.

"What is it?" Nadia called down from the bridge.

"It's a box," I said, trying to get a good look at all sides of it just in case it was something that would explode when picked up. "Any of you touch it?"

"No, sir," the RCU agent said.

"Is it dangerous?" one of the Boston PD officers asked.

"I don't know what *it* is," I said. "Maybe you don't want to be standing directly above me."

Everyone decided that was an exceptional idea and quickly left the bridge, with only Nadia staying behind.

"You too," I said.

"Nice try," Nadia replied. "I'm not going anywhere. Pick it up; let's get this done."

"You're not the one picking it up," I told her.

"Is it ticking?" she asked.

"You are not helping," I shouted back.

"The bomb squad are here," someone called from the opposite side of the bridge.

"They've got a robot," Nadia said, sounding a lot more excited about it than I felt.

I climbed back up the bank, spoke to the bomb squad, wished them luck, and decided to go retrieve my spear rather than watch the little robot get exploded.

I'd just about finished cleaning the spear in a water fountain—the venom having turned to a thick goop, which thankfully seemed non-toxic to the touch—when Nadia found me again.

"It's not a bomb," she said, sounding disappointed.

I sheathed the spear in the scabbard on my back and followed her through the park to the bridge once more, where a large crowd of RCU agents now stood.

"I've never seen anything like it," Becker said as I pushed through the crowd to see a bomb disposal guy sat by a now-open metal box.

I crouched down and looked inside at the plexiglass container within. Inside the transparent container was a piece of what I instantly knew was primordial bone floating in cobalt-blue liquid that appeared to be almost frozen. I'd seen its kind before, although not for a long time. The back of the lid had a painted emblem of a snake in neon yellow and black. An exact copy of the image in the photo we'd found at Jordan's hideaway in Whitby.

"The snake," Nadia said.

"Yeah, I see it too." I nodded. "Is the snake because it had a snake in it?"

No one had an answer to that.

"What about the box?" Becker asked.

"The box is a new one on me," I said honestly. "The liquid is rift energy mixed with water. It comes from the east of the rift. There's a huge amount of rift energy in the mountains there, and it feeds into the water, making it look frozen and giving it the colour of this blue. It's . . . it's not something you want to touch."

Becker's hand was halfway to the box when I said not to touch, and it immediately shot back. "Why?"

"It nullifies the power of those who touch it," I told him. "You can't swim in it, because it doesn't behave like water, you can't drink it, you can't do anything with it except avoid it."

"You sound confused," Nadia said.

"I am," I admitted. "For several reasons. All of which Ji-hyun is going to want to know about."

Becker took the hint. "I'll make the call."

"Anyone who's human wants to be nowhere near this stuff," I said, loud enough to overcome the mass of whispering. "And anyone rift-fused *really* doesn't want to touch it."

Everyone moved away several steps, leaving only me, Nadia, and the bomb-disposal robot with the small metal box.

"You got any idea what it does?" Nadia asked.

I shook my head. "Not even a little bit. Never seen anything like this. No idea why anyone would take primordial bone and submerge it in that crap. And what's with the snake?"

Nadia's chains crept around the external sides of the metal box, and she jolted back like she'd been touched with a cattle prod, landing on her behind on the grass.

"You okay?" I asked her.

She stared at the box. "It's so cold," she said softly. "I saw nothing. Quite literally nothing. No chains, no me, no you, just a cold, empty, void."

"You sound like that's not all," I said.

"I don't know what that is, but it's the single most *terrifying* thing I've ever been in contact with."

CHAPTER SEVEN

The night only got longer from there.

Ji-hyun was contacted, and a complete search of the park was undertaken by everyone, no matter their employer. Hundreds of officers and agents searched every inch of the park in case more of the small boxes were hidden away.

Nadia and I joined in, although Nadia had become quiet since her chains had touched the box. Whatever she'd felt had given her an unpleasant jolt, and her usual careless vibrancy had dissipated.

By the time the park was completely searched, we found three more boxes. All of them had the same snake emblem on the inside lid, which meant that my initial idea of it being done because it had contained a snake was wrong. It also linked the photo of the snake image that Jordan had in his possession with the boxes in Boston. Had he created them before he'd escaped to the UK? It seemed . . . unlikely that these boxes were just sat in Boston Common without anyone having stumbled across them. Something didn't add up, and I *really* hated it when things didn't add up.

Ji-hyun, never one to do a half-arsed job, ordered a search of all streets, alleyways, and rooftops for every building in a two-mile radius. No one complained, although both the feds and the local PD called in reinforcements to get it done.

The search revealed another three devices, all on rooftops in the surrounding neighbourhood. All six devices were brought to the makeshift command centre that was set up in the middle of the park, which was closed to anyone who didn't wear a badge.

I stood by the table with the six devices, staring at them, trying to figure out what the hell they were.

"So," Ji-hyun said as she stood opposite me. "This isn't great."

"You touched one?" I asked.

She nodded. "Not the plexiglass, though. I know it's sealed tight, but . . . I just can't bring myself to do it."

I felt the same way, and looked up at the sky as the sound of a helicopter caught my attention.

"Noah," Ji-hyun said as the aircraft hovered above the park before landing some distance from us.

"You called an Ancient?" I asked. Despite my long and documented distrust of Ancients, I didn't judge her for it. Noah was about as close to trustworthy as Ancients ever became. Still, even then, I would never be sure if he was working with us or for himself.

"Where's Nadia?"

I looked around after Ji-hyun spoke, expecting to see the chained revenant, but there was no trace. "Her chains touched one of these things," I explained. "Don't think she liked the experience."

I told Ji-hyun what Nadia had told me, and the director of the RCU remained quiet until I'd finished. "Shit" was all she said, although that one word conveyed a lot.

"You ever seen anything like this?" I asked.

Ji-hyun scanned the table before shaking her head. "Are these things causing the tears? Because that sounds like a lot of rift-fused water, and a whole bunch of primordial bones. And how does sticking these two things in a box make tears in the sky?"

When I didn't say anything for a few seconds, Ji-hyun said, "I'm asking an actual question."

"Oh, no idea."

"What about the snake emblem?" she asked.

"No idea there, too," I admitted.

"But you said that image was in Jordan's possession?"

I nodded. "A photo of it."

"So, somehow, he's more than likely linked to this. Did you contact Gabriel about the name you found tattooed on him? Ahiram, wasn't it?"

"Shit," I whispered. "I was going to, and then all of this happened. I'll make sure to do it in the morning."

One of the RCU agents came over and spoke to Ji-hyun before hurrying away.

"Noah is here," Ji-hyun told me.

I turned to follow her gaze and spotted the Ancient walking towards us.

Noah Kaya was tall and broad, with bald head, dark skin, and black beard that was, as always, perfectly manicured. He wore a powder-blue suit—the jacket dropped casually over one of his huge arms—black shoes, and a black shirt. He had the aura of someone who was both powerful and happy to use that power to do what needed to be done.

As much as I didn't trust Ancients, I did actually like Noah. And Hiroyuki trusted him, which went a long way toward telling me the kind of man his boss was.

Noah was followed by three members of the Silver Phalanx but no Hiroyuki. I wondered if my old friend had returned from the rift yet, or if he was still chasing down Jordan. I hadn't heard from him since he'd entered the rift, and he hadn't returned via the pendant I'd given to Ji-hyun, so maybe something had happened while he was there.

"Lucas," Noah said, his voice warm and friendly.

"Noah," I said, getting a glare from his Phalanx for not bowing my head respectfully. The number of people I bowed to ran into the low single digits, and none of them were Noah. To his credit, the Ancient had never seemed to mind.

I noted that Ji-hyun didn't bow either, although as the director of the RCU, she wasn't expected to. The RCU were meant to be completely neutral, and bowing to Ancients might show an alliance to someone.

"Ji-hyun," Noah said, shaking her hand. "You have found some curios."

"You seen these before?" she asked him.

Noah picked up one of the boxes, lifting it to look at the bottom while turning it in his hands. "What happens if I touch this plexiglass?" he asked no one in particular.

"No one has wanted to do that yet," I said. "Nadia touched the box with her chains, and I think that was enough to swear people off."

"Nadia was injured?" Noah asked, a genuine concern in his voice. He had grown fond of the chained revenant over the last few years.

"I think it just freaked her out a bit," I said.

"This is primordial bone and rift-fused water," Noah said, passing the box to a young man beside him. "Find out what this is meant to do."

The young man gingerly took the box, and along with the other two Silver Phalanx, they walked back the way they'd arrived.

"So, this is new to you, too?" I asked.

"I believe this will be new to everyone," Noah said. "Never seen anything like it."

"I have a theory I've been considering," I said.

"Be my guest," Ji-hyun said, taking a step back from the table.

I opened my tear to the embers—an individualised pocket dimension that could only be accessed by the riftborn. My embers would be very different to Ji-hyun's, or any other riftborn, for that matter. I could step into the embers and move through into the rift itself with ease, but that wasn't why I wanted it open.

The embers was still full of rift energy, some of which showed itself as a dark shadowy smoke that billowed just off the ground. I looked into the tear that was only a few feet wide and saw the old buildings in my embers. They'd been torn from my memories of growing up in ancient Britain, and then in Carthage, but there were parts of the architecture that came from several periods in my long life.

"Is there something that is meant to . . ." Noah began.

The smoke inside the embers shot forward, slamming into the tear inside the embers, thankfully not spilling out into our world. It smashed against the tear again and again, like it was trying to break free of its confinement. Each time, a crack of power echoed around us, until I shut the embers. An awful tingling feeling moved up my hands and arms, as though I'd been asleep on them and they were just coming back from being numb.

I did not want to do that again.

"That was *new*," Noah said slowly, as though he was unsure where he was going with that sentence.

Before anyone else could say anything, several RCU agents arrived, carrying the remains of four metal boxes. Each of the boxes was three feet high by a foot long and a foot wide. The boxes were placed on the table in front of us. One of them had a large hole in the warped but still sealed lid of the box, while the two others looked like they'd been torn apart from the inside out.

I removed my phone and used the torch to look inside the box, and discovered it was thankfully empty of anything, although it stank of decay and animal.

"There's snake's skin in this box," Noah said, picking up a piece of skin between his fingers to show everyone. "Quite a lot of it."

"It *had* been a really big snake," I pointed out.

"They were up in the trees," one of the agents said by way of explanation.

"The animals were put in here dead," I said. "The boxes were sealed and placed to wait for a tear."

"Any idea how long they've been up in those trees?" Ji-hyun asked no one in particular as she inspected the third box.

"No clue," I said. "But there's at least one more box out there."

"No one goes home until every tree, bush, and shrubbery has been searched," Ji-hyun said. "If we have more of these boxes and the animals inside haven't become fiends, we've got the equivalent of ticking bombs in the middle of the city."

"This explains how the snake got here," I said, as Noah had one of his guards deposit hand sanitiser in his open palm before offering it to everyone else like it was a fine wine.

When we were all suitably sanitised, I looked around and found Nadia sat on the ground under a nearby tree, her chains flicking out in front of her like a serpent's tongue.

Nadia looked over to me and smiled. "This was done on purpose," she said.

"I know," I told her, taking a seat beside her.

"Those boxes with the bone and water, I think I know what they are," Nadia said. "I think they're designed to attract rift energy."

I nodded in agreement. "That makes sense, considering I opened my embers and the rift energy inside tried to smash its way out to get to one of the boxes."

"So, these boxes are creating the tears," she said. "Or at the very least, they're attracting the tears to where the boxes are."

"That would explain why we never had a tear this big over Boston Common until tonight. There's a cumulative effect of the boxes. The more boxes in one place, the stronger the tear. Someone is using these boxes to create tears in places they want them."

"Just like Jordan Chapman knew where to take his victims."

"You think Jordan had some of those boxes on him?" I asked her. "He hardly seems to have the brains to orchestrate something like this?"

"Jordan knew *exactly* where and when the tears would happen," she said. "I agree, though; nothing about him said he'd have this level of sophistication."

"Maybe Jordan ran from Wyoming because he found something he shouldn't have?" I suggested.

"He takes some of that water, creates a few boxes, starts fulfilling his crazy need to make people rift-fused."

"We didn't find anything like these where he lived," I said. "And none in Whitby, either. So, either someone else was using them to create these rifts, or someone was supplying him with the boxes."

Ji-hyun strolled through the park toward us. "Glad to see you're both comfortable," she said, with two bodyguards keeping a strategic distance.

"I killed two greater fiends," I pointed out. "Now I wish to sleep."

"I helped," Nadia said. "I'm just being lazy."

Ji-hyun glared.

I told her what Nadia and I had been discussing. I didn't want to be yelled at.

"Hiroyuki isn't back yet," Ji-hyun said. "That concerns me."

"It's been over twenty-four hours," I said, quickly doing the mental maths to see if that was right. "I'd have expected him back. He's not exactly a pushover. If he's found something, he may well be looking into it."

"Noah says the same, although he's also clearly worried," Ji-hyun said, taking a seat beside us. "I got you Zeke, by the way. Tomorrow at 1400 hours at Moon Island. He's being shipped to us."

Despite being where the training for RCU agents was conducted, Moon island was also where all visitors were met. It was safer for everyone if Peddocks Island was only used for trained personal.

I checked my watch; it was a little after five in the morning, so less than twelve hours to go.

"I hope they pack him properly," Nadia said absentmindedly.

Ji-hyun rolled her eyes, although I still caught the tug of a smile around her mouth.

"You really think Zeke can help?" Ji-hyun asked.

"I hope so," I told her. "If there's a congressman involved in the death of Jordan Chapman, or at least if his office is involved, maybe Zeke can recognise something. How many murderous politicians can there be in one country?"

"Seriously?" Ji-hyun asked, her eyebrows raised.

"Fair point," I conceded. "Even so, if Congressman Mills is involved and Zeke can corroborate that, we've got our man. And if not, then we've still got a possible link to a serial killer and someone who may be involved in the creation of greater fiends in a major city."

"And Hiroyuki?" Ji-hyun asked.

"I'll talk to his boss," I said.

"Excellent," Ji-hyun replied with a broad smile.

"You don't want to talk to the Ancient," I said. "Why not just say that?"

Ji-hyun's smile never wavered. "Because if you take up that decision on your own, it makes me feel better."

I found Noah directing the search teams, while his Silver Phalanx all remained close by. I understood their concern at their boss being in the middle of what had, until recently, been a battle zone, but I knew Noah well enough to understand that he'd probably rather they all left him be.

"Noah," I called out.

The large man turned to face me and waved me over, his bodyguard moving aside to ensure we had space to talk, although judging from the number of hands that fell close to the hilts of their blades, they didn't like it.

"Hiroyuki isn't back," I said.

"He is not," Noah agreed, his voice betraying his concern just a little. "I've sent two of my Silver Phalanx into the rift to find him. I didn't think he would be gone longer than a day."

"Yeah, it shouldn't have been particularly hard work," I agreed. "We both know Hiroyuki is thorough in his investigations, but he would have notified someone if he'd needed to stay longer."

"He would have gotten word to me," Noah said, giving no doubt about it. "The Silver Phalanx members do *not* vanish without trace for over a day."

"You want my help?" I asked.

"No," Noah snapped, wincing as the word left his lips. "Right now, my people and I will search for him. If that comes to nothing, I'll be glad of your help. Thank you, Lucas."

I nodded, turned, and walked away. I really wasn't concerned about Hiroyuki being away. I'd known him a long time—centuries—and he was more than capable of taking care of himself. But the more I saw the look of concern in Noah's eyes, the more I wondered if I too should be worried. At some point, no matter how capable you are, you're going to come across someone who is better than you. It happens to us all at some point, and when it does happen, you just have to do all you can to win, escape, or survive.

I looked around the park, seeing RCU agents working alongside police and federal agents, and wondered if this was only the beginning of something. There was a fear in my gut, something I couldn't shake, that whoever had perpetrated the act of creating four greater fiends, of getting all of these agencies to the same place at the same time, was doing it for a reason none of us could yet see.

The sun would be up soon, and I had yet another long day ahead of me. I'd hoped that after the mess with Callie, I'd have been able to take some time for myself to figure out what I was going to do. I didn't want to join the RCU, despite being happy to help Ji-hyun and her people. There were still Raven medallions out in the wild, after all, those of my Guild family who'd been slaughtered. I still hadn't figured out on whose orders those killings had taken place. I'd found some of the medallions purchased by people after the fact—including one owned by Callie Mitchell—but never found out who'd given the order to massacre my Guild. Instead, I'd spent several years running, trying to put out fire after fire, in a desperate need to make sure nothing else blew up.

What I'd done was important, it saved lives, and I was happy to help, but it felt like there were things I put on the backburner from investigating, because of the need to keep everything else from going to hell.

I removed my phone to text Drusilla, hoping she might have some information about these boxes with the water and primordial bone, and hit Send, then the light of the nearby park lamp caught my medallion.

I moved my medallion and stared down at the promise crystal. And then there was this fucker. Who knew when it was going to break; who knew what Neb would need my help with. Whatever it was, I could *technically* refuse to do it. But it would be walking away from Neb and her friendship, and quite possibly making an enemy of anyone she considered an ally.

I finished the text to Drusilla, sending her a picture of the box and snake image to see if she recognised anything, and put my phone back in my pocket. I'd hoped that once we'd found and removed Jordan as a problem, things were going to get easier, not considerably more complicated. I doubted the next few days were going to reverse that pattern.

Despite it still being dark, I scrolled to Gabriel's number and dialled it. He answered it on the second ring. "Lucas, you okay?"

"I'm sorry, Gabriel," I said. "I need to know if you've ever heard of the name Ahiram."

Gabriel paused for a moment. "Where did you hear that name, Lucas?"

"It was tattooed on the arm of a serial killer who was almost killed by what looks like a professional hit, and then he went into the rift as a riftborn."

"That's . . . a lot," Gabriel said. "Ahiram is a Phoenician mythological king of the rift. Or murderous despot, depending on which version of the story you read."

"You got anything you can send me on him?"

"I'm almost certain I do," he said, with a yawn. "Let me wake up properly and I'll send you what I have. And Lucas, you should know that this guy isn't a mythological king like Arthur is for the British. He's more like a despot who tried to conquer . . . well, everything."

I let out a sigh. "But he's not real, right?"

"Oh, no, totally made up," Gabriel said.

There was an uncomfortably long pause before I said, "Gabriel."

"Almost certainly made up," Gabriel amended. "Probably."

CHAPTER EIGHT

Despite a need for sleep, the next twelve hours were a tornado of activity. I stayed in Boston until nearly midday, helping search for more boxes, just in case a second attack happened, and was happy to be told to go back to the RCU headquarters in time to grab a quick shower and change of clothes.

Gabriel helpfully sent me a vast amount of information on the stories of Ahiram, which were several volumes in length, along with a thoughtfully brief synopsis written by Gabriel. Ahiram started off a hero. A visionary. A bastion of truth and integrity. Over the years, he turned from hero to villain and was killed by his own people when they refused to help him murder his own siblings or allies . . . that bit wasn't clear.

I put aside the homework for now and concentrated on getting the search finished, and at nearly two in the afternoon, I stood on the helipad with Ji-hyun and Nadia as the helicopter flew in from Boston, exactly on time.

The Bell 429 helicopter landed nearby, and we waited as armed guards moved up to the helicopter as it powered down. I watched the rotor slow to a crawl before stopping altogether, and two guards opened the side door while two more kept submachine guns trained on the opening. I thought it was probably overkill. We were the ones who wanted Zeke's help, we'd arranged to get him out of prison to do so, but I reminded myself they were only doing their job.

Ji-hyun marched across the helipad to meet Zeke halfway between the helicopter and where I stood. She spoke to him out of earshot of Nadia and me, and Zeke nodded a few times in response.

Zeke was flanked by two large and menacing RCU agents, neither of whom looked happy with the appointment. Zeke, or Ezekiel, also liked to be called Gunslinger, but I was never going to call him that under any circumstances.

Despite his having betrayed me by working with Callie's allies, it had been under the duress of his family being threatened. He'd accepted his punishment of being imprisoned for his crimes, but in spite of it all, I liked him.

He looked like he'd aged a decade in the few years since he'd been sent to an RCU prison. His shoulder-length hair was now longer and looked like it was in need of a good conditioning. It fell over his shoulders, meeting the light brown shaggy beard he'd grown. He had always been tall—taller than me, anyway—and slim, but he'd lost some weight during his incarceration.

The shock on my face at the gaunt man stood before me must have been easy to see as Zeke was brought over toward me, "Prison doesn't really agree with me. I am in need of a shave and haircut, but unfortunately, the few hours I've been out haven't really lent themselves to such frivolities. Apparently, I'm not allowed to handle a razor or scissors myself."

"He's a riftborn whose power allows him to pour the energy of the rift into inanimate objects," Ji-hyun said. "He could take a pair of scissors and turn them into a weapon that could kill a rift-fused."

"The boss makes a point," I said to Zeke, and shrugged.

"We'll get him groomed when we have time," Ji-hyun said as we started to walk toward the headquarters.

A short time later, we were in Ji-hyun's office, with everyone sat around the large table. Several large pitchers of cold water were on the table, along with half a dozen glasses. The moment Ji-hyun removed Zeke's cuffs, he immediately poured himself a glass and took a long drink before refilling it.

"Wasn't allowed anything on the flight," Zeke said. "I was deemed a possible risk."

"So, can you tell us about the congressman who worked with the Blessed?" I asked.

"I didn't know his name," Zeke said. "Never met him, never spoke to him."

"You recognise the names Spencer Mills or Elliot Webb?" I asked.

Zeke shook his head as Ji-hyun picked up a remote and pressed a button, the blinds in the room closing and a projector coming to life, beaming an image of Spencer Mills on the far wall, next to the door.

"What about now?" she asked.

Zeke stared at the image. "Never seen them before; who are they?"

"Congressmen Mills of Wyoming," Ji-hyun said.

"Sorry," Zeke said. "You know you could have just shown me the pictures in prison. Would have made life easier for you."

"Actually, I want your help, in person, on this," I said. "You know the Blessed; you worked for them, whether by choice or not. If the last member alive and free is causing hell with these tears and fiends, you might recognize patterns of behaviour that we could miss."

"We're offering you a chance at freedom," Ji-hyun said. "You help us, you get out. You do anything outside of that remit, you go back and serve the rest of your sentence."

"I don't know who that is," Zeke said helplessly. "I can't help find someone I don't know."

The picture on the screen turned into one of Jordan Chapman.

Zeke's eyes bulged. "Jordan," he said. "Now, *him* I recognize. He's a low-level employee of the Blessed. Used to run information from his higher-ups to me. He was strictly a *do as you're told* kind of employee. The man was, frankly, an idiot. Kept talking about how the rift-fused should inherit the world, how it would be better if everyone was rift-fused."

"He murdered a lot of people," I said.

"He's a murderer?" Zeke asked, shocked. "No way."

"He wanted to turn people into rift-fused," Ji-hyun said. "Mortally wounded them, and some got turned and some died."

"I don't think he intended to kill anyone," Nadia said. "I think he intended to make them all rift-fused."

Zeke nodded. "That I could see. He said something about wanting it for himself one day, that he'd considered ending his life to try and become rift-fused, but that there were no guarantees he wouldn't just die. There was always a fringe element of the Blessed who thought that the best way forward for humanity was to erase it, make everyone live in the rift. No idea how they thought that might work, but that's why they were considered idiots."

"You don't know who he worked for?" Ji-hyun asked.

"Not directly; it's not like we all shared names," Zeke said. "He was just a general gofer."

"What about Elliot Webb?" I asked.

"Never heard of him," Zeke said. "What's he look like?"

"We don't know," Ji-hyun said. "I've had people researching him for a day now, and we've gotten no photos, no information of any kind."

"Fake name?" Nadia asked.

"Fake existence," Zeke said. "I'm here because I might be able to visibly ID him, yes?"

I nodded.

"And when will I be going to do that?" Zeke asked.

"We have a phone call with him tomorrow," Ji-hyun said. "I'd like you to listen in just in case you recognise his voice. We're going to get a face-to-face visit arranged."

"Sounds like a plan," Zeke said, and turned to me.

I opened my mouth to speak and felt a jolt of electricity that ran from where the medallion touched my skin on my chest, up toward my neck, along my shoulders, and down my arms, ending in my fingertips. It wasn't painful as such, but it wasn't exactly fun, either, and it had made me drop my phone on the floor beside me.

"What the . . ." I began, but was stopped by the sound of stone cracking.

"Lucas?" Nadia shouted.

I moved my medallion and the once-whole promise crystal fell from its mounting into my hand.

"Lucas," Nadia repeated.

I looked up at her, "Nightvale; be a few hours." I stared at the two pieces of crystal as I was engulfed in rift energy and immediately found myself inside the rift. "Bollocks," I said out loud.

CHAPTER NINE

U nfortunately, because I hadn't used my embers to enter the rift, I had two large problems. One, I had no idea where I was and could only assume that the breaking of a promise crystal meant I was immediately whisked away to wherever it had been activated.

There were old ruins a few hundred meters' walk north from where I'd landed, but otherwise, it was open plains to the east and a river to the west.

The second problem bubbled up and left my body shortly after.

Being dragged to the rift without the use of my embers makes riftborn sick. It's neither pleasant nor dignified, but Valmore had assured me that if I kept doing it, eventually I would just feel a bit unwell for a few seconds. So far, that theory hadn't borne much fruit.

The sky above was its usual mixture of bright blue and purple, but in the distance I noticed dark clouds. I did not want to be out in the open during a storm. I hurried up to the ruins, seeking shelter, and hoped nothing else from the local wildlife already called them home.

The ruins themselves looked like part of what had once been a fortification of some kind. They jutted out of the soft burgundy soil at strange angles, as though the ground had tried to swallow them whole.

I'd expected when the promise crystal was activated to be taken to Neb's settlement; Nightvale. However, it was pretty clear from the surroundings that I was not in a settlement of any kind.

As I got closer and found myself stood atop a hill, it was easy to see that the ruins stretched much farther than I'd first assumed, as they moved with the undulating landscape. This hadn't just been a fortification but potentially a village or something even larger. There were dozens of buildings, all in the same state of dilapidation, with partially destroyed white stone walls, or red tiled roofs that had long since stopped being able to keep the elements out.

Since my encounter with Callie in the Tempest and being so close to the rift energy that consumed her, I'd started to feel changes in myself whenever I was in the rift. I was tired less; I appeared to *feel* more of my surroundings. I could also see a violet shimmer over things with a large connection to the power of the rift.

They were little things, and Valmore had suggested they were because I'd been training so hard in the Tempest, and put it out of my mind. But seeing the ruins before me, I was struck by the violet shimmer that covered them. Whatever they'd used to be, they still had a powerful connection to the rift.

The violet colour dissipated as I reached the ruins, leaving me wondering if it had been something connected with how I'd been brought there. Something to investigate when I had the chance.

Vines the colour of burned orange snaked around several of the buildings, and I wondered just how long this had all been there. I'd lived in the rift for hundreds of years on and off but was still constantly surprised by what I found there.

Two figures left one of the dozen scattered buildings farther in the ruins; both wore black hooded cloaks and stood motionless, looking up at me. As they were the only people I'd seen since arriving, they'd get the lucky job of answering all of my questions.

I set off toward the two newcomers, who were a good hundred meters from me, and when I was halfway there, a third figure left the building. Neb.

She wore black leather armour with various buckles at the top of both legs, where throwing daggers nestled. Steel vambraces sat on each forearm, looking dulled, as though someone had rubbed dirt on them to remove the shine. Midnight blue boots adorned her feet, and a jade Greek cloak sat around her shoulders, the hood remained down, showing her nearly black hair, which was plaited and coiled atop her head.

Nearly every time I'd seen Neb in the last thousand years, she'd been adorned with jewellery: bracelets, rings, earrings, and necklaces. But here she looked ready for war, with a short sword against her hip and a longbow across her back, next to a full quiver of arrows.

Neb was nearly six feet tall, with brown skin and the aura of someone who commanded respect no matter whose company they were in. Her slate-grey eyes looked my way, and she gave the barest hint of a smile.

So, I knew who had brought me there and how, but the why was still a little iffy.

The two guards remained where they were as Neb walked toward me. "Lucas," she said warmly.

"This is a little weird," I said to her.

Neb removed a forest-green promise crystal from a dark brown leather pouch on her hip and dropped it into my hand. The crystal was a larger version of the one I was given, but otherwise, they appeared to be identical.

"So, I guess I'm here because you need something," I said. "Because you could have just called or sent someone to get me."

"Let's get out of the open," Neb said, turning and walking back toward her guard, and I followed.

When we were all inside the building they'd originated from, it turned out to be a bit more than a run-down shack. A spiral staircase started in the corner of the floor and went down twenty feet to a large, open room. There was a table in the centre made of dark grey stone with white stone chairs around it and several more chairs against the edges of the room.

"What is this place?" I asked no one in particular.

Neb took a seat at the end of the table and motioned for me to sit opposite her. "You may leave us," she said to the two guards, who nodded and did as they were told.

I took a seat opposite Neb and waited to find out what the hell was going on.

"You might have noticed that I'm prepared for battle," Neb said. "Commander Pike is missing. Along with six of his people and six of mine, including Kuri."

"I think you might want to start from the beginning," I pointed out, while wondering just how bad everything was about to get. Commander Pike had worked for one of the rulers of Inaxia—a Prime—but had been undercover the entire time. He'd pledged his allegiance to the Queen of Crows, and while he wasn't exactly what I'd call a friend, he was loyal to the Queen. Also, I enjoyed the fact that he was an open book. Too many people try to hide who they really are; Commander Pike proudly wore who he was as a person like a giant neon sign around his neck.

Neb nodded. "Over the last few months, there were several attacks on small Lawless villages to the east of Nightvale, along the border of the Vast Death," she began. "At first, it was nothing major. A few people got hurt, some seriously, but it was like they were being tested. Over time, the attacks increased in both frequency and aggression. I sent people to protect the villages. But it wasn't enough.

"Three weeks ago, a village was slaughtered not far from here. The attack happened at night, and it left two hundred people, almost all of them revenants, dead. These were farmers, Lucas. Not warriors. They had lived their lives on Earth as revenants and, after death, had come here, looking for peace. And they were murdered for it. The village is one of a number that have been attacked, all of them without large numbers of guards or soldiers to defend them. Whoever did this knew which ones to hit."

Neb remained silent for a moment before continuing, a slight catch in her voice. "The Queen of Crows sent several of her people to check out the site of the attack. We both agreed that should these attackers start to move west, toward either Nightvale or the Crow's Perch, we could have serious problems. We needed to know who, or what, we were up against. We both sent a small contingent of people to investigate. The group was led by Commander Pike and Kuri. That was a week ago."

I'd met Kuri for the first time a few years earlier; he'd been a stern but passionate supporter of Neb and her ideals. Much like Pike, I didn't get the impression that Kuri would be a pushover when it came to a fight.

"That's why you're heading out?" I asked.

Neb nodded. "My people are missing, as are those who work for the Queen of Crows. And the Queen of Crows is an ally. I practically had to force her to stay in the Crow's Perch and not go out alone."

The Queen of Crows was *officially* meant to be a prisoner, along with everyone else in the Crow's Perch. Unofficially, she was pretty much given free rein to do whatever she wanted. Despite having enemies in Inaxia, some of whom were quite happy to try and kill her, no one was stupid enough to try and take the prison city of Crow's Perch by force.

"How far were your people going from here?" I asked.

"Three days' ride east," Neb said. "To a town at the start of the Vast Death: Agency."

I let out a long sigh, because that's my usual response to hearing the words *Vast Death* said with actual reverence. I mean, technically, it lived up to its name, but how I wish they just changed it to something less . . . dramatic.

"I've been before," I said. "Has Agency been hit?"

The city of Agency had been founded by clerics from the same religion that Gabriel was a member of. In the centre of the city sat the Glass Cathedral, which loomed hundreds of feet above everything around it. They'd built the Glass Cathedral as a symbol of . . . hope; at least, that's what the official line was. Unofficially, I was also pretty sure that if it was ever a partially bright day, it would turn the cathedral into a Death Star.

Besides, I'd always assumed it had been built so that those who lived and worked in there could look down on everyone else in the city, but I had to admit that it was a truly impressive piece of architecture.

"Not to our knowledge," she said. "But it's the largest settlement along the border of the Vast Death, and several villages north and south of it have been attacked. We need to know where those attacks were coming from. The prevailing idea is from within the Vast Death itself."

Not a single bit of information that Neb had told me sounded good. "So, am I here because you want me to come with you? Because we're dealing with some serious shit back on Earth, too."

Neb got up from the table, walked over to a small wooden cupboard, and opened the top, removing a metal box, which looked suspiciously similar to the ones we'd found in Boston. She carried it over to me, placing it on the table and removing the lid, revealing the same snake emblem.

I stared at the cobalt-blue water and wasn't really sure what to say that didn't include a steady stream of increasingly offensive swear words.

"We found this one outside of Nightvale," Neb said, retaking her seat at the opposite end of the table. "We've also found them in the Crow's Perch and a few dotted around Inaxia, although obviously, that's just between you and me."

"You know who made them?" I asked.

Neb shook her head. "Not this particular version, no. I'm guessing our friend Callie Mitchell had a hand in it, though."

"Even in death, she's still a pain in the arse," I said.

"Do you know what they do?" Neb asked.

I pushed the box away. "We've found them on Earth as well. I've been thinking about that. I think they attract a tear—like lightning to a metal pole. I opened my embers when we found one, and the smoke inside of them tried to get out at one of these boxes."

"That's my summation, too," Neb agreed. "Except I also know for a fact that these things weaken the membrane between Earth and the rift. They cause tears to be more powerful and thus create more fiends, but they also attract things to them on the rift side."

"Fiends?" I asked.

"Elder fiends," Neb said grimly. "I think these are designed to give both Earth and the rift a new set of problems to deal with. One of these was found at the destroyed village."

That couldn't possibly be good. "So, you're thinking that someone is sending the various monsters that dwell in the rift to wipe out villages?"

Neb nodded.

"Have they attacked any of the villages or settlements affiliated with Inaxia?" I asked.

Neb shook her head. "Inaxia has its own issues, considering the number of newcomers. Attacks from the rift version of elder fiends might overwhelm them; we need to find out what's happening and put a stop to it before then."

I considered what Neb had told me. "It all feels a little like too much of a coincidence, but then, I also don't know what the link is. We have a serial killer who might have been using these to make sure the tears happened when he killed his victims. Potentially, it's linked to a sitting US congressman. That snake emblem, any idea what it means?"

Neb stared at it for several seconds. "A gang, maybe?"

"A gang?" I asked, getting the feeling there was something she wasn't telling me. "We've got these things on both sides of the tears. Someone is tagging their own signature so everyone knows who's doing it. If it's a gang and you don't know about them, I think we should be worried."

"I am worried," she said. "I don't actually know what's going on. That in itself worries me."

"We're going to talk to one of the people possibly involved," I said. "I say *possibility* because while we have a link between our serial killer and the congressman, right now, it's nothing concrete."

"So, we have potentially two people making these things." Neb waved disdainfully at the box. "One here, and one on Earth end."

"Unless they're making them here and shipping them through to Earth," I said. "Although it means someone is still taking primordial bone and rift-fused water through to Earth by unknown means."

"Embers, or maybe a rift-walker?" Neb asked. "Either way, we're walking into a problem we can't ignore."

"It's not embers," I said. "Those shadows went mad when I opened mine. So, unless they can stop that from happening, it'll be a rift-walker."

Neb rubbed her eyes with her hands. "It's not a great choice either way."

"Okay, we both have a lot of shit to deal with," I said. "But why am I here? Why use the promise crystal to bring me here?"

"Because I need your help," Neb said. "I don't know how long I'm going to be away or what I'm going to find at Agency, but if anything happens,

I need to know that things will be looked after. Do you swear to do whatever I ask in fulfilment of your promise to me?"

"No," I said. "I won't do *whatever* you ask. I think we both know that."

Neb nodded in agreement. "Yes, okay. I've promised your assistance to the Queen of Crows. You will promise to help her however she needs aid. Except for outright murder and the like."

I sat dumbstruck for an unknown amount of time. When I finally felt like I could talk again, I said, "You what?"

"I have given your promise to the Queen of Crows," Neb repeated.

"You've outsourced a promise crystal?" I asked, feeling slightly betrayed.

"What's wrong?"

"I'm just wondering if this is a prank of some kind," I said, looking back at Neb. "You *gave* my promise to the Queen of Crows. To use as she sees fit. I don't think I've ever heard of such a thing. Why would you do that?"

"She wanted to go after Commander Pike," Neb said. "The only way I could stop her was to say that I will go and I will give her your promise. If I don't come back within a suitable amount of time, she's going to call on you."

"To find you," I finished for her.

Neb nodded.

I had no idea what the Queen looked like behind the mask she always wore; I didn't know her real name or anything about her beyond what I'd learned since discovering she even existed a few years earlier. And while I wasn't entirely sure I could trust her, I did trust that she did everything possible for the betterment of her people.

Unfortunately, the fact that she'd turned the Crow's Perch from what was meant to be a prison into a working town away from anything Inaxia could touch angered people with vested interests in making sure that such things didn't happen. The Queen was to stay in the city at all times, and if she left, her life was considered forfeit. Her riding around the rift to find out what had happened to her people would end up with the wrong people knowing she was outside of her city, which could potentially cause her a lot of problems.

While the Queen was alive and healthy, no one wanted to attack the city she called home. The cost to take it would be astronomical, and the potential for people to be drawn to her cause was too high of a risk for anyone considering it. No one really knew what would happen to the Crow's Perch should the Queen no longer be in charge. I was pretty sure it would involve a lot of bloodshed.

"How is she going to contact me?" I asked.

"I'm going to give her the crystal," Neb said. "If there are any problems that have occurred, she's going to use it to make you aware that she needs you. You can't be dragged back here, because there's no crystal on your end, but you're going to get a hell of a headache until you actually return here. Your task is that you will return here if she calls, and you will aid her in any way she needs. After that, your promise will be fulfilled."

I found that I had more questions that needed answers. "You want me to come find you or avenge you?"

"I'm not planning on getting killed out there, Lucas, but we need to know what's going on," Neb said with a slight smile. "We need to find out why these places are being attacked and maybe their link to these boxes. I need to know that you will do whatever is needed to help the Queen and her people."

"I agree," I said, not really seeing as if I had much choice.

Neb got up from her seat, removed a dagger from her belt, and made a shallow cut across her palm. She passed me the still-bloody dagger, and I did the same on my own hand. Neb removed the smooth crystal from her pouch again and pressed it into her palm, and I placed my own hand over hers.

"Do you swear to keep your promise to help the Queen of Crows?" Neb asked.

"I do," I said, my eyes never leaving Neb's.

There was a jolt like an electric shock that went up into my hand, up my arm to my shoulder and neck, which made me wince.

"It's done," Neb said, retrieving her dagger and wiping it down before sheathing it on her belt. She placed the crystal on the table as it pulsated green, the blood completely gone.

I pushed it across the table to Neb with a little more force than necessary, and she had to catch it before it flung off the edge.

"Really?" she asked, placing the crystal in a second pouch.

I got to my feet. "I want you to know that I'm not *thrilled* about this. I get you're giving my aid to the Queen of Crows so she doesn't leave her home and ride around the rift, almost getting herself killed in the process. I just don't understand why she's so important to whatever plans you have going on. And I'm *deeply* unhappy about you promising my aid to someone else, and am only doing this because it's you."

"I understand," Neb said. "Once either I or the Queen utters the phrase *Your promise is fulfilled*, the crystal will break, and you will be completely free from any future obligation."

I looked up at the ceiling and counted to ten, calming myself, before looking back at Neb. "Don't *ever* force a promise crystal on me again. I don't care what our relationship is; you ever do it again, and we're done. Where's the nearest tear stone?"

For the first time I could remember, Neb looked genuinely upset. "Outside of the ruins."

I turned to walk away and stopped, looking back at Neb. "Be careful, Neb. I'd rather this whole thing was just sorted without me having come find you. Or avenge you."

"I truly hope that you will not need to be held to your promise, Lucas," Neb said.

"If you find nothing in Agency, are you crossing the Vast Death?" I asked. "That's several days' ride to the nearest village."

"The villages that were attacked were all along the border of the area," Neb said. "The attacks came from out of the Vast Death. My guess is there's a staging post somewhere inside it. Maybe one of the scattered villages within its borders knows more. They'll be my next destination after Agency. The town I plan on checking first once inside the Vast Death is called Plainhaven; it's a few days' ride from the border, but you can trust the people who live there. Go there if you need to, find Timo."

"Be careful," I told her, and paused. "You ever heard of someone by the name of Ahiram? Gabriel says he's some kind of mythological king, but our suspect had his name tattooed on his arm."

There was something in Neb's face that I couldn't read before it vanished and was replaced with a weary smile. "It's an old story about the folly of thinking you can solve everything yourself. Man goes from hero to villain. It's not my favourite piece of rift mythology."

I left the ruins, asked one of the guards where the tear stone was, and followed his directions for the five-minute walk until I found it.

I looked down at the six-metre-diameter black stone. There was purple-and-blue writing all over it, which glowed when activated. I glanced back at the ruins and wondered just how bad things were going to get. I'd been angry when the promise stone had been forced upon me, but the idea of my promise being passed from person to person had set off a deep-seated dislike. I was not a commodity. My word was not a commodity. No matter what happened, my relationship with Neb would need to have new boundaries set.

Stepping onto the tear stone, I opened my embers and walked through.

CHAPTER TEN

If I was going to the Tempest to the north, I wouldn't have needed the tear stone to enter my embers from the rift side, but unfortunately, things weren't always as easy as I'd like them to be.

The tear snapped shut behind me and I stood in my embers, looking around at the mixture of architecture.

A strange grey facsimile of Gabriel's church in New York sat between two Carthaginian villas, and a short ways later was the forge where Drusilla worked and mostly lived. Oddly, my own New York apartment wasn't among the buildings, although that might have been because I considered it more a necessity than something I felt was a part of me. It was a place to store stuff and sleep, and I hadn't been back there in a year.

I stopped outside of the forge, the dark swirling smoke moving around my ankles as shadows of people I'd once known walked around. All of them journeyed a pre-scripted routine or carried out the jobs they'd done when I'd known them, but none of them were people I could talk to, just a strange shadowy version of them.

When night fell, they would hunt me down to try and consume the power inside of me. Thankfully, they couldn't enter any of the buildings, so once I was inside, I was safe until morning.

Time in my embers was a weird thing. I could come there, sleep for a night, and leave, but how long I stayed depended on how injured I was. A serious injury might mean the difference between being in my embers for hours or days. And there was no way to know which it was until you left again.

Thankfully, I wasn't hurt, so I could leave my embers to return to Earth having only been away for the few hours I was in the rift. Which, in and of itself, was probably enough time for people to have started freaking out but hopefully not freaking out *too much*.

A large black bear padded along the street toward me, sat down, and let out a world-weary sigh normally reserved for parents who've had their children for an entire summer off school.

"Casimir," I said. "Still liking the bear form, I see."

"I can't decide on what *kind* of bear," Casimir replied.

Casimir was one of my two eidolons, creatures of pure rift energy that stayed inside my embers and protected it from external threats. On occasion, I'd taken one of them through to Earth or the rift, but it was dangerous to keep them out of the embers for any real length of time.

A few years earlier, Casimir had saved my life by turning from bird to bear while several hundred feet in the air. The resulting encounter had almost pancaked an exceptionally awful riftborn by the name of Matthew Pierce. Since then, Casimir had been in a constant state of indecision as to what form they preferred.

"They're doing my head in," a tawny owl said after landing on the post of a fence nearby.

"Maria," I said with a nod hello. "As much as I love staying to chat with you both, I need to get back to Earth as soon as possible," I explained. "Neb has asked me to return to the rift and find her if she goes missing."

"If she goes missing?" Maria asked.

"She's Neb," Casimir said. "I'm pretty sure she's capable of killing anyone who crossed her."

"I would have said the same thing," I replied. "But something feels wrong about all of this."

As we walked through the embers toward the exit that both Maria and Casimir instinctively knew the location of, I explained everything I'd discovered in the last few hours.

"You need one of us to come with you?" Casimir asked.

"No," I said. "If that changes, I'll contact you. If something happens to a riftborn as powerful as Neb, I don't want to risk either of you being in the firing line."

While I could take one of my eidolons into the rift without any problems, if they were injured in any way, it meant me being forced to stay in my embers for an extended period of time. On top of that, it made the embers unstable and the shadows that were usually passive during the day somewhat more dangerous.

We stopped walking outside of a small building that appeared to be in the middle of merging a lot of different styles of architecture into one. A mishmash of Carthaginian villa, ancient rift ruins from the time I'd spent in the Tempest, and several other parts I couldn't quite identify. "What happened to it?" I asked.

"You care about places," Casimir said. "I mean, you always cared about places, but you actually consider yourself to have a home for the first time in centuries. Every time you considered yourself a home before, there's always be a little something holding you back."

"Are you suggesting I'm at peace?" I asked with a chuckle.

"You've found places you can be at peace," Maria said. "The Tempest is one I wasn't expecting, though."

I walked over to the door and opened it, revealing the tear back to Earth inside. "I'll be back soon," I said and stepped through into . . . Ji-hyun's empty office room.

My spear lay on the table.

I picked it up and examined it, making sure it was still in good condition. I hadn't really wanted to plant it tip-first in the soil, but I also hadn't wanted to toss it aside, so I was glad to see it was still in a pristine state. I only hoped that Drusilla hadn't been informed of its treatment.

Pulling back one of the blinds revealed that it was nighttime, though there were still plenty of people on the island working, the floodlights from the dock illuminating several people nearby. More floodlights were situated around a two-storey building that I could have sworn had been unused the last time I'd been there but now appeared to have several guards out front.

I couldn't make out details about anything, but it looked like I'd missed something in the last few hours of being in the rift. Needing to know exactly how long I'd been, I walked over to Ji-hyun's desk. The red numbers on the digital clock said it was four-forty-seven a.m. I hadn't been hurt when taken into the rift, so I figured I'd been gone a little over an hour.

I decided to go discover what was going on or at least try and find my phone, which I remembered I'd dropped in the Boston Common. It had, all in, been a rubbish night and one I'd quite like to end by getting a shower, some food, and some sleep. Not necessarily in that order.

I used Ji-hyun's desk phone to call her mobile.

"Who are you?" Ji-hyun asked, her tone sharp and irritated.

"It's me," I said.

There was a pause that lasted a few heartbeats. "Lucas?" she asked, a slight quiver to the word.

"Yeah," I said. "I'm in the office on your floor of the RCU building. The island looks like it's busy, so didn't want to just—"

"Shut up a second, Lucas," Ji-hyun said. "You *vanished* in front of me."

"I know," I said. "I wanted to explain in person, but I guess now is as good a time as any: Neb activated my promise crystal. It's a whole thing. I need food and sleep. I know I've only been gone a few hours, but I'm ravenous."

"It's been a week, Lucas," Ji-hyun said softly.

"It's been a what?" I asked, wondering if I'd misheard. It wasn't unusual for a riftborn to enter the embers and exit it days or weeks later, sometimes even longer, but it was only when the riftborn was injured. Otherwise, very little time should have passed.

"You stay right there," Ji-hyun said. "I'll be there in ten minutes. People have been worried about you. Do *not* leave my office, Lucas." Ji-hyun hung up.

A week. I was not thrilled about that. I wondered what I'd missed. I called Drusilla's home number but got only an answerphone, and I did not want to leave the *hi, I've been in my embers for a week, sorry about that* message on a machine.

I decided that if I was going to have to stay put, I'd have something to drink, and opened Ji-hyun's small fridge that was behind the desk. I removed a bottle of water and a packet of chocolate shortbreads, removing two of the round snacks and putting the rest back in the fridge.

The water was cold and the shortbread was delicious, and seeing how I had no phone of my own and no idea what Ji-hyun's computer password was, I settled for lying back in her chair relaxing.

I'd just started to drift off to sleep when the door to Ji-hyun's office opened, and I sat bolt-upright as Ji-hyun and Gabriel walked into the room.

Gabriel Santiago was a spined revenant, capable of growing huge spines all over his body and using them for both defensive and offensive purposes. He was also a cleric for the Church of Tempered Souls, the only religion to involve the rift-fused.

He wore the same long black coat I often saw him wear and had the same blue-and-gold clerical band around his bicep he always wore. His being there was more than a bit of a shock, considering his church was in Hamble, New York.

"Gabriel what are you doing here?" I asked, getting to my feet and walking over to my old friend.

A guard stepped between Gabriel and Ji-hyun, a gun pointed in my direction.

"Okay," I said slowly, holding my hands up. "What's going on?"

"We just need to make sure that you are *you*," Ji-hyun said.

"What the fuck does that mean?" I snapped.

"You remember that spirit revenant who could make himself look like other people?" Ji-hyun said.

"That doesn't work on riftborn," I reminded her. "But if you need conformation of who I am, then by all means, how can I confirm it?"

"Who are you dating?" Gabriel asked.

"What are we, fourteen?" I replied. "Fine, Drusilla. Is she okay?"

"She's fine," Ji-hyun said. "Just worried about you, like everyone else."

"If I've been gone for so long, what about Hiroyuki?" I asked.

"We're meant to be asking you the questions," Ji-hyun reminded me. "We'll explain shortly. He's fine too."

"Did you make him answer a bunch of questions, too?" I asked.

"Yes," Ji-hyun said.

"Fine," I said. "What else do you want to know?"

"Who gave you the promise stone?" Gabriel asked.

"Neb," I said, moving my medallion from behind my chest to show the crystal was still there and would remain so until I'd fulfilled my promise "You *really* think I'm pretending to be me?"

No one spoke.

"I will concede that there could be riftborn or revenants who could mimic another of their kind," I said, "But we know even that best revenants can't just take all of the memories of a person without getting them all jumbled up; they can't take my personality, just the memories. And they won't remember all of the details in the right order in such a quick time as I've been away.

"So, how about this. At the end of the year 2000, you, Ji-hyun, practically forced me to play three video games from a certain series, in order. They were roleplaying games. We had both taken some time out to heal up and step away from all of this nonsense. You believe that number seven is the best of those three games. You are wrong. We have had far too many discussions about it, but after all of these years, you're still wrong. Nine is the best one; deal with it."

Ji-hyun stared at me before tapping the guard on the shoulder, who immediately lowered his gun.

"Lucas," Ji-hyun said. "We had to be sure."

"Yeah, okay," I said, not really understanding why they had to be sure. "I get that it's been a week, but this all feels a little overkill."

"After the last week, it's definitely not overkill," Ji-hyun said.

"What the fuck happened?" I asked.

"Someone tried to kill Ji-hyun," Gabriel said.

CHAPTER ELEVEN

For the briefest of moments, I figured Gabriel thought he was being funny, or that it was some weird gotcha prank that only idiots appear to enjoy. But I'd known him long enough to know that pranks and Gabriel did not exactly go together.

"Who tried to kill her?" I asked. "When did it happen? Are you okay? Is everyone okay? And how the *hell* has it been a week?" I found myself sitting at the table in the office, although I didn't remember actually sitting down. The last few seconds had been a bit of a blur.

"Everyone is fine," Ji-hyun said softly. "The bomb failed, we took the human prisoner, and . . . asked him nicely about who sent him."

I took a deep breath and let it out slowly. "Okay. What happened?"

"You vanished a week ago," Ji-hyun said from opposite me. "You mentioned Nightvale, so we presumed that you'd gone through to Neb. When you didn't come back after two days, I sent Dani through to talk to Neb, and when Dani returned, she said that Neb hadn't been in Nightvale for days. That she'd gone off to investigate something. She spoke to one of Neb's people in her stead."

"Dani returned okay?" I asked, looking between Gabriel and Ji-hyun, who both nodded. Dani was a rift-walker, able to move between the rift and Earth with ease. She'd also been through a lot in her short life. She'd turned into a rift-walker just after a car accident that also turned her brother into a revenant. Unfortunately for Dani, she'd been stuck in the rift for years. When she'd finally built up the power to create her own tear and leave, Callie and her merry band of psychopaths had wanted to capture her to use in their experiments.

After Callie's death and the disbanding of her followers, Dani had decided to join the RCU.

"Although it took her five days before she could reopen a tear," Ji-hyun said. "She didn't go through, just in case she couldn't open another, but she seems to be able to open them from this end fine now. She just hasn't gone through to see if it screws around with her ability."

That wasn't good news. "So, I went through to the rift and got stuck there for a week, despite thinking it was only a few hours, and Dani just came and went as normal?" I asked, wanting clarification.

"That's about the size of it," Ji-hyun said.

I wondered whether it was the embers—as a go-between—that were causing the issue or something else.

"And Hiroyuki?"

"He arrived back four days ago," Ji-hyun said. "He told us he left the rift only a few hours after arriving. So, the same issue."

I looked between Ji-hyun and Gabriel. "He okay?"

"He had a similar expression to the one on your face right now," Gabriel said. "Took him a while to come to terms with how much time he'd missed."

There was a noise from the hallway beyond the office; a few seconds later, Nadia practically sprinted into the office. I'd only just gotten to my feet when she launched herself in my direction, hugging me tightly.

"You're okay, you're okay, you're okay," she said, the words spilling out without breath.

"I'm fine," I said. "Are you?"

"You weren't in my chains," she said. "And I know there are times when you're not in my chains, and that's fine, because it's not like there's a void where you were. This time, it was like a void. Like someone had cut up part of the chains and stitched them back together without you in them."

"I think I was stuck in my embers," I said, looking around the room. "I was dragged to the rift by Neb, and she seemed to be expecting me at that exact time. So, I don't think it took long, but then I didn't use my embers to get to the rift. Those boxes with the rift-fused water have been placed in villages in the rift that have been attacked by the creatures living there. There's that snake emblem on them, too. Neb thought that there was an effort to make the membrane between Earth and the rift thinner. Maybe it screws with the embers at the same time. It would explain me and Hiroyuki taking so long to get back and why it didn't affect Dani in the same way."

"You've got a lot to catch up on," Ji-hyun said. She turned to the guard. "Can you get Dani, Drusilla, and anyone else down in the lobby? I imagine they're all waiting to find out what's going on."

"They're in the lobby?" I asked, watching the guard head off.

"I was with Dani when you called," Ji-hyun said. "She went to get Drusilla."

"What about the congressman and his aide?" I asked. "Did Zeke recognise him?"

"The chief of staff?" Nadia asked. "That's where it gets complicated."

"We spoke to the Elliot Webb on the phone as arranged," Ji-hyun said. "Zeke didn't recognise the voice, but he couldn't be certain. Elliot said he was in Rochester on a meeting, and asked if I would be able to come and meet him. He wanted somewhere out of the way, somewhere the media wouldn't be paying attention. I chose Gabriel's church. Twenty-four hours later, after confirming with Gabriel that it was okay, I went to meet him. Zeke was going with me to hide in the church and wait to get a good look at him. We arrived early and set up. But when Elliot Webb's car arrived, a car I was told would be coming, I was instead met by a young man with a bomb in his bag. He had been ordered to detonate it beside me as we entered the church. The aide, Elliot Webb, was nowhere to be found. "

A deep anger settled Inside of me. "Where is the bomber?"

"In holding," Ji-hyun said. "You will not be talking to him, as that's probably unwise. He's been treated well. No bumps or bruises. Nadia spent some time with him, and he told us what we needed to know."

I looked over at Nadia.

"The chains told me a lot about him," Nadia said. "He's a fanatic. Like Jordan. Went to the same church in Wyoming. He said he believes in the coming of a warrior who will join the rift and Earth together as one."

"Ahiram's name was mentioned a lot," Gabriel said.

"Same as with Jordan's tattoo," I said. "I asked Neb about him and she said he was a mythological king. Same as you did. But there was something not right in what she said; she was . . . worried. Maybe. It's hard to tell with Neb. What about the USB drive?"

"We hacked it," Ji-hyun said. "Lots of encrypted files, which, annoyingly, we only managed to get access to after the little bombing incident."

"It pointed the finger at Elliot Webb, I assume," I said.

"Webb and Congressman Mills. They're both heavily involved in the same church as Jordan. He kept recorded conversations with Webb about creating more tears, making them more powerful. We confirmed that Mills is a practitioner, as he mentions it several times during the recordings. We think he bugged someone's office, as there's stuff with Mills on there where he's talking to Webb as if no one else is there. We checked it all to make sure it was legit. It is."

"Anything else?"

"Lots of stuff about bringing back the king."

"Ahiram?" I asked.

"He's not mentioned by name," Gabriel said. "And there's nothing in the mythology that says he's going to return. It's a cautionary tale of how power corrupts."

"They also mention a *she* several times," Ji-hyun said. "She is helping them, giving them information about how to proceed. It's all quite vague. Any idea who it might be?"

I shrugged. "Not a clue. Have you spoken to Webb or Mills?"

"Webb has vanished," Ji-hyun said. "Mills is holed up in his own private cabin in the middle of nowhere, surrounded by armed guards."

"You haven't taken him in for questioning yet?" I asked, a little surprised.

"We know where he is," Ji-hyun said.

I looked around the room. "How do you know he won't run?"

"We have someone monitoring the situation," Ji-hyun said. "Becker."

I remembered the RCU agent from my time in Boston Common; I got the impression he was good at his job. "How long has he been there?"

"Few days," Ji-hyun said. "I don't want him to stay out there any longer than he has to; I just need to make sure that us and the humans are all working off the same page. This needs to be done on the quiet."

"And how's that going?" I asked.

"Not as fast as I'd like," Ji-hyun said. "I've met with the heads of several government law enforcement organisations, all of whom have vested interests in members of Congress not being outed as murderous psychopaths to the general public. If he's not human, we definitely don't want that. Not after what happened in London with Smythe. In principle, we've got the go-ahead to do what we need to do, but they've asked we wait until they're ready."

"The church that Mills and Elliot are a member of are called the Promise Bearers," Gabriel said. "They're little more than a cult. If we get

Spencer in any way that isn't quiet, we risk them scattering. We've been looking into members of the congregation based on the intel in that USB drive, most are human. Jordan kept meticulous records on everyone who wasn't him. Almost like he was paranoid."

"Never heard of them," I said.

"Neither has anyone else," Nadia said. "We've looked into the church, which is actually a run-down old factory in the middle of nowhere. The humans want to go in, grab everyone they can during a meeting, and remove the problem all at once."

"So, that's what you're waiting for?" I asked. "The humans to get themselves ready?"

I nodded as I mentally went through everything I'd been told. "Where's Jordan now? Can he help?"

"He's dead," Gabriel said.

"Dead, dead?" I asked.

Ji-hyun nodded. "His head was removed from his shoulders and nailed to a wall, dead."

That was pretty dead.

"Hiroyuki know who did it?" I asked.

There was a lot of shaking of heads.

"Where's Hiroyuki now?" I asked.

"With Noah," Ji-hyun said. "After you called, I called him; he should be here within the hour."

"Well, don't I just feel special," I said.

Dani entered the room with Drusilla, the latter of whom walked over to me and hugged me. "You had us all worried," she said, pulling away. "When I say *all*, I mean *everyone else*. Clearly, I was fine with it."

I smiled. "Clearly."

"So, you found out the divide between the rift and Earth is fucked," Dani said, patting me on the shoulder. "That's not going to make things easier to deal with." She had olive skin, and had cut her dark hair short in the few years I'd known her. Since the death of Callie Mitchell, Dani had thrown herself into training and was now a capable RCU agent.

I glanced over to Ji-hyun. "If I need to get back to the rift and have to use my embers to do it, then I'm going to be gone a while. There's a possibility that Neb is involved in something shady. She gave my promise crystal over to the Queen of Crows. She can't drag me back there like Neb could, but I'm going to feel pretty unwell until I return should she decide to use it."

"I'll take you," Dani said.

The memory of having gone through a tear opened by a rift-walker was not one that goes away quickly. But there were precious few options opened to me.

"Okay, that's a plan, then," I said. "If the worst happens, I'll go with Dani, and she can bring me back if all is fine."

"And if it's not fine?" Gabriel asked.

"Then she can come back here and grab a few people," I said.

"That's going to take several days," Dani said. "You'll be alone in the rift with no backup."

"Can you take more than one person through?" Drusilla asked.

"Probably three at a time," Dani said. "The more I take, the longer it'll be before I can go back and get more though. Or, potentially, it could mean I won't be able to open a tear here for longer than a week. Something weird is happening with the tears, and I'm not sure what effect it'll have."

"Okay, that's one potential problem solved," I said.

"Now we just have to deal with the next problem," Drusilla said.

"Any chance you already have a way for me to get to the congressman?" I asked. "And, more importantly, a way to get out in one piece?"

"You can't kill a sitting Congress member," Gabriel said. "Sorry, you just can't."

"*Can't* is doing a lot of heavy lifting in that sentence," I said. "Maybe . . . *shouldn't* is a better word."

"Lucas," Gabriel chastised.

"I have no intention of killing him," I said. "Which is why I wanted a way to get out. I should have said for *both of us* to get out. We need answers, not dead politicians. I assume not killing him is a part of the deal you made with whichever agencies you're talking to."

Ji-hyun nodded.

"Then we need to get him somewhere secure and safe but do it so he remains in one piece."

"Okay, everyone go home, get rest; tomorrow is going to be a busy day," Ji-hyun said. "Not you, Lucas; stay a second."

Everyone filed out of the meeting room until it was just Ji-hyun and me.

"I've had other RCU branches look out for those boxes where large, powerful tears keep happening," she said.

"And?" I asked.

"We've found a dozen boxes all around the USA," she said. "Another three in Canada, and two in Mexico. I asked the RCU branches in South

America to be on the lookout, and after two days of almost-permanent rifts above Buenos Aires, they found three more there. They've also found several cages of animals in the region of those boxes."

"If the congressman is the same one who was once a member of the Blessed, it's possible this was their and, by extension, Callie's plan?" I asked. "Like a Blessed-light?"

There was the barest of smiles on Ji-hyun's lips that I was certain she was trying to fight. "I think someone wants us busy. Lots of big, powerful rifts all over the world, lots of fiends, lots of RCU doing firefighting instead of looking into crimes."

"How are the other RCU branches doing across the world?" I asked.

"Not as bad as here," Ji-hyun said. "There are large tears all over the world, but they haven't found the boxes there, and the number of fiends hasn't exploded because some asshole is putting dead animals out for the rift energy to feed."

"They want the North and South American RCU branches busy," I said.

Ji-hyun nodded. "More the USA than anywhere else. We've had something like eighty percent of all boxes found."

"The others are to help throw off the scent," I suggested.

"That's the prevailing idea. Although quite why they want us to be running around, no one is certain of. We have a lot of questions for Congressman Mills." Ji-hyun sat on the table and rubbed her eyes with the heels of her palms. "To change the subject, while you were gone, Drusilla told a lot more people to piss off than usual, *a lot more*. I think you and her are closer than you might think."

I sat beside her. "I agree. I was going to talk to her about it before the night in Boston. She wanted to talk to me too . . . Not sure what about."

"She's not exactly the most personable person I've ever met," Ji-hyun. "Maybe that's why I like her. But I do know that she would have torn this city apart to find you. Hell, she would have torn apart the rift if I hadn't stopped her from going after you. It's just a good thing I was the one to break the news; I'm not sure she wouldn't have just left if it had been anyone else. I put a block on anyone leaving to go to the rift to find you. After Dani came back, we figured something was going on, and didn't want to start losing people. Then Hiroyuki returned and we concluded that something was wrong with the connection between the two worlds."

"I've been thinking about the strengthening of the connection between the rift and Earth," I said. "It might be worth getting some people on your end who know about such things to investigate it further. We don't want part of these worlds merging."

"You think they can?" Ji-hyun asked, with more than a little concern.

"We're into theoretical rift science here," I said. "And I have no idea. I'm pretty sure no one wants to find out first-hand, though. Technically, if you weaken the barrier between the rift and Earth, you strengthen the link between the two, and nothing good happens."

"I'll have my people look into it," Ji-hyun said. "Go, sleep, eat, whatever you need to do."

I tapped my hand against the table and pushed myself away. "I'm glad you're in charge, Ji-hyun," I told her.

"Oh, why's that?" she asked.

"Because I'm pretty sure that I don't want any part of the job you have to do," I said.

Ji-hyun laughed. "Most of the time, I'm not sure *I* want any part of the job I do. Unfortunately, I sort of tripped and fell into it."

I left Ji-hyun in her office and made my way through the building until I found myself outside in the cool fresh air. There was no tear in the sky, just the usual twinkling of stars that were trillions of miles away, the lucky bastards.

Drusilla sat on a bench nearby and called me over.

She patted the bench as I reached her.

"We need to talk before you vanish *again*," she said, without looking back at me.

"Yes," I agreed. "You wanted to say something to me just before I went to Boston, which for me was only a few hours ago."

Drusilla glanced back at me. "I'm not great with people," she said. "I mean, you might have noticed that. I'm not what you might call a *people person*."

"Yes, we've met," I said.

"Well, despite my hundreds upon hundreds of years in age, and all the apparent wisdom that comes with it, I've never been great at divulging how I feel," she said, keeping her gaze firmly ahead. "I enjoyed spending time with you, and then you vanished, and . . . I am not used to feeling what I felt when you weren't here. Not just that you weren't here but that no one knew *where* you were. I wanted to search for you; I wanted to turn the rift upside-down. Ji-hyun talked me out of it, she sent Dani, and we figured something had gone wrong. But we still didn't *know* what had happened to you. I have not felt that way about a person in a long time.

I was worried, and it left a tightness in here." She stabbed her chest with one finger.

I reached out and placed my hand on her back.

"I don't want to lose you, Lucas," she said. "And, honestly, I'm not sure I've been able to say that about a lot of people in my life. The idea that someone had hurt you, or worse, it made me want to hurt people. Before you left, I wanted to talk to you about where we were going. I wanted to know how you felt before I said anything. I'm fine with telling people I love them, but I'm not so great with putting real meaning into those words. And goddamn it all, you make me feel the real meaning, but if you turned around and said you were just enjoying yourself, I would have put some distance between us. I can't do that now, Lucas."

Drusilla turned back to me, and I kissed her softly on the lips before pulling away. "I love you too," I said softly. "And I'm sorry if you were hurt while I wasn't here."

Drusilla stared at me for a moment before smiling and kissing me again.

CHAPTER TWELVE

I woke up with Drusilla beside me in bed, as sunlight tried its best to break through the thick bedroom curtains. I checked my phone and found that I'd actually gotten a few hours of sleep.

Drusilla and I got up, showered—taking somewhat longer than we would have if we'd done so separately—and, after getting dressed, went downstairs for some coffee and a bite to eat. By the time we were both dressed and ready to go, it was the afternoon, and Drusilla had work to do.

"I assume you'll be heading out to Wyoming," she said, her arms around my waist after kissing me.

I nodded. "Not much I can do about it. Can't just ignore the congressman."

"You're going to take him into the rift, aren't you?" she asked.

I nodded again. "Can't question him here; need to take him somewhere the human authorities can't look. Rift is the best bet; also, it means I can check in on the Queen and make sure that Neb isn't involved in something I need to worry about."

"You told Dani she's going to have to go with you to Wyoming?"

I shook my head. "Figured that was going to be the conversation today."

"If you're not back in a week, or if there's any problem that Dani says happened, I'm coming after you, Ji-hyun's order or not," Drusilla told me.

I kissed her again. "You'd better."

Drusilla sat beside me, a cup of hot coffee in her hands, as we looked at the satellite images Ji-hyun had given me. I didn't even want to know how she'd acquired them, and I wasn't sure she'd have told me if I'd asked.

"You could go via the lake," Drusilla said. "Maybe a HALO jump. The lake there is deep enough for you to hit. Although would Nadia and Dani jump with you?"

I remained silent.

"Okay, Nadia would *definitely* do the jump. She'd be the first out."

"They're not entering the estate," I said. "I'm going to need them to cause a distraction while I get inside."

"Nadia is going to *love* that bit," Drusilla said. "Have you told her?"

"Not yet," I said. "I'm pretty sure she's going to be giddy about it, though."

"Oh, before you go," Drusilla said, and retrieved a set of tactical black leather armour from inside a window seat. "It's made from steel, leather, and primordial bone. It's thin and lightweight but should be strong enough to resist a blade or even a bullet, although I wouldn't try the latter out too much. It should also lessen the impact of rift-fused power. Hopefully. I hadn't fully tested it. It's a prototype."

"Did you make this for me?" I asked, getting changed while Drusilla checked that the primordial bone and steel lining inside the armour didn't restrict movement.

"Yes," she said, looking up at me. "It was going to be a gift, but then you vanished. Seems like it might come in handy, knowing the trouble you get yourself into."

The black-and-grey armour was comfortable and resembled a bulletproof vest although with pouches on the chest and sides. There were matching trousers, too, which also had more pouches on the side and padding around the knees and shins.

When she was done, Drusilla returned to her window seat and removed a navy-blue-and-light-grey jacket, passing it over to me. "Same material is inside the lining of the jacket," she explained. "This is waterproof, though, so should keep you warm and dry. Same technique used as with the vest and trousers but even more lightweight, so it might not be as durable."

"Thank you," I said. The armour was light and comfortable. I walked over to a full-length mirror to get a look at it. "Honestly, this looks *amazing*."

Drusilla kissed me on the lips. "Now don't break it," she said with a smile.

I left Drusilla to start forging and made the short walk back up to the main RCU building, where Gabriel was waiting outside on the same bench I'd been sat on with Drusilla not long previously. He held a cup of coffee in his hands and had the appearance of a man who knew every-thing was about to go to shit and was enjoying the calm before the storm.

"Please, join me," Gabriel said.

"So, how'd they get you to come here?" I asked taking a seat. "Or did you volunteer after the attempt on Ji-hyun?"

"Partially the bomb," Gabriel said. "Partially because you called and put that idea in my head about someone who's meant to be a story. And partly because I figured something bigger was going on that Ji-hyun would need non-RCU help with. Also because Ji-hyun didn't want any-one going into the rift after you until they knew what was happening. I was asked to come and be a voice of reason. I think she figured if one of your friends who knew you best was calm about it, others might be."

"Were you calm?" I asked.

"Not really," Gabriel said. "But I also knew you'd be fine. I think every-one knew that, even Drusilla, who did *not* like being told to stand down."

I looked down the hill toward the port. "What's going on down there?"

"There were a lot of fiends over the last week," Gabriel said. "Most were just lesser, easily dealt with, but some of the greater fiends were hard work. And then there was an elder fiend."

"Wait, *seriously*?" I said.

"Ji-hyun killed it with help from her RCU agents but not before it hurt a lot of people," Gabriel said. "First one in North America in a century, so they tell me. Or at least the first one we know of. We got it just as it came through, thankfully."

"No wonder everyone was on edge when I arrived," I said. "An assas-sination attempt on the head of the RCU and an elder fiend in a week."

Gabriel took a long drink of coffee. "Ji-hyun leads her people like a general. It's like she was made for this job, even if she tells everyone how much she never wanted it."

"Wait, does that tent over there contain the remains of an elder fiend?" I asked, guessing they'd want to keep the thing close to investigate it further.

"Turns out if you can freeze one quickly enough, you can keep bits," Gabriel said. "But it was too big to transport by helicopter, so boat had to do. I think a lot of it has disintegrated by now, but it's not often you get to examine the remains of an elder fiend, so Ji-hyun had people who are interested in that stuff."

"Rather them than me," I replied. I watched the workers go in and out of the building where the remains of the elder fiend were. I hadn't met an elder fiend in a long time, and I wasn't entirely sure how I felt about part of it being kept on the island where people I cared about lived and worked. Yes, it was dead, and elder fiends, even the most powerful of them, couldn't regenerate themselves from death. And yes, there was no way that Ji-hyun would allow it on the island unless she'd spoken to several experts on the matter. Even so, it creeped me out, knowing it was there.

"The smell on the docks when they brought it in was quite pungent," Gabriel said.

"Something on your mind, Gabriel?" I asked. "You're not normally one to discuss the smell of deceased fiends."

"I do not like where this is all going, Lucas. Since everything with Callie, it feels like the connection between Earth and the rift has gotten more and more temperamental. People are afraid. They come to me for guidance, they come to me for reassurance, and while I do the best I can, I'm not sure I'm reassuring myself when I tell them all will be fine."

I patted him on the shoulder. "I wish I could tell you differently."

"I know. Maybe these idiots with their boxes and snake emblems will be able to illuminate our situation." Gabriel looked behind us. "I think Ji-hyun got tired of waiting."

I turned back to see Ji-hyun striding toward us with Nadia, Dani, and Hiroyuki. While Nadia wore her usual attire, Dani wore jeans and a T-shirt, with no indication that she was heading anywhere close to a battle. Hiroyuki wore red-and-black leather-and-steel armour that looked like something he might have actually worn during his time as a samurai.

"It's good to see you back in one piece," Hiroyuki told me, placing his helmet and mask on the bench where I'd been sitting. He carried a katana in his hand, while a wakizashi and tanto sat against his hip. He was most definitely ready for battle.

"You too," I said. "You dressed for war."

"As did you," Hiroyuki said, glancing at the armour Drusilla had gifted me.

While he could see the spear in the sheath on my back, he didn't know about the rift-fused knuckledusters, nor the daggers and knives hidden about my person. All courtesy of Drusilla.

"We have a private jet taking you from Boston to Wyoming," Ji-hyun said, looking around to check we were completely alone. "You won't be coming back that way, I assume."

I told them my plan.

"It could work," Hiroyuki said.

"You know," Dani told me, "If there's a problem, it could be a while before I can get the cavalry to you," she said.

I nodded. "I'm going to do my best to not need the cavalry."

"I've met you," she said.

Gabriel snickered behind his hand, which turned into a cough, which in turn made me laugh. Gabriel flipped me off, because while he might have been a cleric for the church, he also lived in New York.

"We might be gone a while," I said, adjusting up the spear against my back. "Hopefully, everything goes to plan."

"Something is bothering me," Dani said. "Why hasn't the congressman run into the rift to hide? The evidence on that USB drive is pretty damning, so what's he waiting for?"

"If he's the member of the Blessed that we believe, he's a practitioner," I said. "The Blessed were exiled from the rift. They can't go back without a rift-walker, and if they do go back, there's a good chance someone will recognise them at some point, and then they'll be executed on the spot. It's not a concrete theory, but it's all I've got at the moment."

"I'd take the risk," Dani said.

"Me too," I told her.

"Maybe he's staying here to wait for orders," Ji-hyun said. "We'll add it to things he needs to tell us. Is your plan going to work, Lucas?"

"I hope so," I told her. "Dani, Hiroyuki, and Nadia are going to cause merry havoc, and I'm going to get into the property, find the congressman, have a little chat. Once done, I'm going to bring him to everyone, Dani will open a tear, and we all slip away. That way, we don't need to worry about getting out of the property."

"What happens if there's a problem?" Dani asked. "Besides, I can't take Nadia into the rift."

Revenants couldn't normally enter the rift until they died on Earth and were reborn there. Why that happened, and why it wasn't *all* revenants, no one was ever sure. Another quirk of the rift.

"You can if she's masked up," I said. "Remember those revenants who worked for Callie. They were going into and out of the rift, but they had to wear masks and suits. So, Nadia will need to be wearing a mask."

Everyone turned to look at Nadia.

"Okay," she said after a few seconds. "But I'd rather not have to get dragged into the rift for longer than necessary."

"I can get us in and out in no time at all," Dani said. "But I'm going to need a destination for both the rift itself and where we get out."

"The tear stone near the Crow's Perch," I said. "You remember where it is?"

Dani nodded. "I've got it. And back here?"

It was my turn to nod. "We take the congressman to the ruins where I met Neb, and I go talk to the Queen while Hiroyuki questions him."

"You land via private airplane at Jackson Hole Airport," Ji-hyun said. "Take the twenty-minute drive to the congressman's property. You've given all of this actual thought."

"You sound surprised," I said.

"I am," Ji-hyun told me. "I've met you."

"The other agencies know what's about to happen?" I asked.

"In a roundabout sort of way," she said. "Turns out most of them don't want to know stuff they wouldn't be able to deny if it went to shit. So, let's make sure it doesn't go to shit."

Before I could reply, she said, "Let's go question one of the most powerful people in the country without causing a massive incident."

CHAPTER THIRTEEN

The flight was all perfectly normal, which after the last few months was practically a godsend. We landed in Wyoming, which was freezing cold, and exited the airport, picking up our prearranged rental BMW SUV, which had all of the gear we'd need in the back.

The drive to where the congressman was hiding was a short one, but it was early in the morning and the roads were deserted, so Dani took her time. We were in no hurry. She pulled over to the side of the road, letting me off at the halfway point. I ran into the dense forest, which covered the whole area, and was soon out of sight of the road.

Nadia, Dani, and I had earpieces that allowed us to remain in contact with one another, but otherwise, we were going to be on our own until we met up again, hopefully with the congressman in tow.

To that aim, I carried a small black rucksack, which contained a map of the area, a small but powerful satellite phone, just in case, and a chemical compound that I didn't even know the name of, but was designed to knock someone out once injected into them. We might have been given the go-ahead by whoever Ji-hyun had been in contact with, but I doubted any of them would be happy if there was a . . . commotion.

Spencer Mills was a practitioner, which meant he could create potions, charms, and a host of other things, and fuse the power of the rift with them. Callie Mitchell had been a practitioner too and had used her power to help make things that limited the powers of the rift-fused. They were a dangerous species and, like all rift-fused, were not allowed to take any office of public power on Earth. If the world knew about Spencer, there would be more outrage, more concern, and a lot more people wanting us tagged. That couldn't be allowed to happen.

I ran through the forest until I reached a sign on a tree that declared this to be private land. There were no fences this far into the forest, but I did spot several sensors attached to trees. Turning to smoke might help me avoid the sensors; doing so, I moved up the tree and re-formed on the thick branches high above.

Turning back to smoke and moving through the trees was easy enough, although it's a lot easier to billow along in smoke form at six feet off the ground rather than forty-six feet above it.

The house came into view on the opposite side of the lake I was on. I remained where I was and looked around at the open land on either side of the house. I remembered the photos of the area: the mountains in the distance, the stillness of the lake, the multitude of flowers around the lush garden. It was a tranquil place to live, and even in the darkness, with the cloudless night sky showing the multitude of stars above me, it was beautiful. I settled in to watch the activity across from my position.

Despite the lateness, there were still guards, or agents, or whatever they were, patrolling the perimeter of the property. Ji-hyun had told me that I wasn't to hurt them unless strictly necessary, and certainly no deaths. She hadn't said if they were FBI, CIA, NSA, or whatever other jumble of letters agency they belonged to, but they *weren't* the enemy there.

A sizeable contingent of the agents stood in the large parking area at the front of the house, but there were a few walking along the bank of the lake, flashing torches around. I had no problems taking out law enforcement if necessary . . . and avoiding them made my job harder, but hurting people for no reason is the way of arseholes and psychopaths, so I knew I would do what needed to be done.

The guards would carry guns of some kind or another, and while there was a larger degree of probability they wouldn't be rift-tempered, Congressman Mills wasn't human, so maybe he ensured that at least a few were equipped with a more-dangerous-to-rift-fused weapon.

The house itself was made of wood and glass, with huge windows in the three-storey building. There was a porch over the front door and an outdoor seating area at the rear, next to floor-to-roof glass windows. According to the estate agent floor plans, that room was a large living area connected to the foyer. The photos of the house from when it had been up for sale showed me everything I'd needed to see. The basement area below the front room, the large spacious kitchen, the large study just off the side of the main foyer, the five bedrooms and three bathrooms split between the two floors. The whole place was a warren of hallways and rooms, and there was no telling exactly what room was the congressman's.

I considered getting a set of night-vision goggles, but with the amount of lights still on in the house and surrounding area, it would have made the whole operation even more difficult. And cutting the lights was out of the question. I needed to get in and out without causing suspicion; plunging the whole area into darkness was the exact opposite of that.

I turned to smoke once more, moving low across the surface of the water, trying to scatter myself as much as possible in case someone saw a dark cloud shifting toward them.

It's harder than it sounds to make myself more dispersed, and even more difficult when I'm so close to the water that I can almost feel its coolness, but I got across to the opposite bank, moved up the side of the building, and re-formed on the tiled roof. There were no guards up there, although there was a balcony on the third floor that did have a guard on it, but that was pointing at the rear of the property, and I had no intention of heading into the building that way.

Fireworks went off in the distance, lighting up the sky in a variety of colours. Nadia and Dani were almost certainly enjoying themselves. I lay down on the cold roof and listened to the guards talk amongst themselves about what was going on. More fireworks, this time seemingly closer, inside the forest. I really hoped they didn't set anything on fire.

While everyone on duty was more interested in the night sky, I returned to my smoke form and moved up one of the exterior chimneys. I was grateful for the architect of the house, who had decided they still had to have an old-fashioned fireplace. I headed down the dirty chimney, also grateful the fire wasn't actually on as I came out in the empty living room and re-formed.

There were no lights on in this part of the house, so close to the congressman's office. I moved down the hallway, stopped outside of the office door, and pushed the ajar door open fully. The office was completely dark. It was also empty, which meant having to look through the house to figure out where the congressman might be.

First stop, the master bedroom.

I turned to smoke and moved through the house, not daring to make a sound as I reached the illuminated foyer and the dual staircases that went up to the floor above. I moved quickly, hoping that the guards outside wouldn't turn and see me. Thankfully, I reached the next floor without incident and continued right, along the dark hallway, toward the master bedroom at the far end.

The door to the bedroom was closed, so I moved around the frame into the room itself, only to be met with the sounds of gentle snoring.

The bedroom was in complete darkness, and I re-formed myself beside the door to the en-suite bathroom, which had a light emanating from it.

I was reaching out for the door handle when it turned, the door opening, leaving Congressman Webb in the doorway. He wore jeans, boots, and a large fluffy, white jumper. He looked like he was about to go drink cocoa on the veranda.

I pointed the dagger at Spencer. "You are coming with me. You have answers I need."

"I knew someone would come for me after Elliot vanished," Spencer said, sounding almost sad. "I'll tell you whatever you want; just please don't kill any of my people."

"I'm not going to be killing anyone," I told him. "We have evidence that you aided a criminal organisation and helped Elliot Webb make the tears worse. Right now, we've got you on a host of charges, and I'm not even including aiding Jordan, who was running around, murdering people."

"Jordan ran off and did his own thing," Spencer said. "I found out that he'd killed someone, I . . . I freaked out. No one was supposed to be butchered by a maniac because he wanted to create a world of only rift-fused. Elliot told me he'd deal with it. But they were all . . . I don't even know. Fanatical. Insane."

"You're going to tell all of that to the people who sent me here, once we're gone," I told him. "Which is what we're doing right now. Move."

"I need to go to my office downstairs," he said. "I have files there you'll need. Actual files, not on a drive."

"About what?" I asked him.

"Just please, let me get those files," Spencer told me.

This wasn't going as I'd intended. I expected fire and brimstone; I expected screaming about how the Blessed had been unfairly treated. I expected a lot of things, but capitulation was not one of them.

"Please just don't hurt any more guards," Spencer said. "None of the others were involved; they're just humans doing their jobs. They don't know anything about me, or the rift, or any of that."

"You got a way to get out of this house and to the forest without being seen?" I asked him.

"Basement has a tunnel that goes out to the forest," Spencer said.

"Lead the way," I said. "If we get caught, someone gets hurt. So, make sure we don't get caught."

Spencer nodded and walked out of the room into the hallway beyond. I followed at a distance, keeping the dagger in my hand as we went down the hallway, and took the stairs while more and more fireworks continued to be let off.

"That your doing?" he asked as we reached the foyer below.

"Something like that," I said, giving him a gentle nudge in the right direction. "Go."

Spencer didn't argue, and we were soon in his office, the door closed behind us, the blinds still pulled down, as he removed an abstract painting of . . . blotches of colour, I guessed, from the wall and revealed the safe. A four-digit passcode later, and the safe was open. He removed a black holdall and passed it over to me.

"Take one step to the side of that safe," I said.

Spencer sighed and did as he was told, revealing the gun inside it. "Seriously," I said.

"I wasn't going to use it," he said.

I pointed to the chair behind the desk. "Sit."

He did as he was told, which gave me time to open the holdall, removing the large file inside along with a USB drive. I pocketed the drive, as that would wait for later, and opened the file. It was . . . extensive. Photos of Spencer with various other high-ranking members of governments, not just American. There were photos taken in the rift, too, although I'd never known anyone to be able to get a camera in there and back out in one piece.

I flicked through more and stopped when I saw the photos of my old Raven Guild members, me included. I forced myself to carry on and found more lists of names, numbers beside them. There was a whole extra file inside the larger one that had *Vipers* written on the front in big green letters. I opened it and all of the names were redacted.

"Who or what are the Vipers?" I asked.

"You fulfil your end of the bargain, and I'll tell you."

I looked up at Spencer. I really wanted to hit him.

"They're on the USB drive," he said. "Only I have the password. I don't want to be killed the second I give it to you. I want assurances."

"Let's go." I put the file back into the holdall and motioned for Spencer to leave the office. I'd expected a ruthless fanatic, someone who *believed* in the cause of the church, but Spencer didn't believe in a damn thing. He didn't seem to care about the cause at all. It made me wonder exactly what Spencer's role in all of this really was.

He stepped out first and I winced as a voice said, "You okay, Congressman?"

"Yes, sorry," Spencer said. "The fireworks woke me up. Thought I'd go check on something for the meeting tomorrow. Everything okay?"

"Kids in the forest being stupid," the guard said. "Just thought I'd come in and do a quick sweep, make sure no one has decided to misbehave."

From my vantage point to the side of the door, I saw Spencer Mills shake his head. If he did something stupid, we'd be leaving there a lot louder than I wanted.

"I'm going back to bed now," Spencer said with a yawn. "Thank you for being so vigilant."

"Good night, sir," the guard said.

I waited as the guard's footsteps receded and the front door opened and closed, before coming out of the room. "Good job."

"I don't want anyone to get hurt," Spencer said. "You're that Raven Guild member who survived; I can see the medallion around your neck."

I nodded. "And we need to go, now."

We hurried through the house until we reached the door to the basement on the far side of where we were. Spencer opened it and I motioned for him to go first, closing the door behind me and descending the wooden steps into what some would call a man cave, although it was a term I loathed. There was a bar in the corner, a pool table, a darts board, various old arcade video games, a TV that almost fit the entire far wall, and honestly, the whole thing looked like a good place to spend your time off.

There was a bookcase on the wall next to the bar, and as Spencer walked behind the bar, I had a horrible thought of him coming up with a shotgun, but instead, there was a click and the bookcase slid to the side, revealing a metal door with a number pad beside it.

"You don't have a panic room," I said as Spencer input the numbers and the door hissed as the airlocks were released.

Spencer pushed the door open. "I never saw the need. I knew eventually what I'd done would come out; I knew it when the Blessed started to die or get arrested. I knew it when Jacob decided to be an idiot and go into business for himself. I never wanted any of this. Well, that's not true. I wanted the wealth and power, but by the time I had both, they had me. I knew the only way out was to do what they wanted until they did something so big that someone like you would come along. And here you are."

The tunnel beyond had steps leading down several dozen feet and lighting all the way that I could see. Spencer went down the steps first, and we followed the tunnel in silence for ten minutes until we reached an identical door, and he opened that with another numbered code. The door opened, and we stepped out of what was revealed as a small hut at the edge of the forest, close to a lay-by on the highway just a short distance away.

The hut was surrounded by a chain-link fence with DANGER OF DEATH written on an orange warning sign. I pressed my earpiece. "Got him," I said, and looked at my phone, which gave me the exact location.

"Be there in ten," Dani said. "Nadia is still setting off fireworks."

On cue, the night sky lit up again.

"I didn't really want to do any of this," Spencer said again. "I wanted to help people; it's why I became a Blessed. It's why I became a member of Congress, but over time, what starts off as good intentions becomes a need to gain more power, more money. I'm not sure when I finally gave in to corruption, but it's all I know now."

"You need a priest or something?" I asked.

"You hate me," Spencer said.

I shook my head. "No, I don't feel anything for you. I just want this done so I can stop whatever nonsense you've started. We're going to take you to the rift and we're going to question you."

Spencer chuckled, although there was no humour in it. "Back home, finally."

We went back to blissful silence until Nadia, Hiroyuki, and Dani arrived, with Nadia now sporting a full-on hazmat suit.

"You ready?" Dani asked.

I nodded. "Let's get this done."

CHAPTER FOURTEEN

I wasn't actually sick. I mean, I felt like warmed piss, but that was it. Hiroyuki looked like death warmed up and ran behind the nearest boulder outside of the ruins where I'd met Neb. Dani, Nadia, and I waited as Hiroyuki had some alone time. Congressman Mills sat on the ground, his knees up to his chest, his breathing shallow.

"So, maybe your primordial friend was right about you getting used to travelling between the two worlds," Dani said conversationally.

"I have to admit that being able to do this without feeling dreadful for five minutes after is a benefit," I replied as Hiroyuki reemerged from behind the boulder.

"You good?" I called over to him, and he gave me a thumbs-up in reply.

When Hiroyuki reached us, the five of us walked into the ruins, only to be met by half a dozen armed guards in red-and-silver armour, all with feather-like capes, all carrying a bow in one hand and a sheathed long-sword against their hip.

A woman walked out of the same building that Neb had exited the last time I'd been there. She wore almost identical clothing to when I'd last seen her: a long black cloak that was cut to resemble feathers, and a hooded mask that completely covered her head. The mask was designed to look like a beak and put me in mind of the old plague masks. She wore a silver-and-dark-grey dress that stopped mid-thigh, long black gloves that ended at her elbows, and black boots.

"You brought friends," the Queen said as she walked toward me, her guards all remaining motionless but watching Dani, Nadia, and Hiroyuki with barely veiled distrust.

"This is Hiroyuki, Nadia, and Dani," I said. "Dani and Nadia aren't staying."

"Oh?" the Queen asked, and turned to Nadia, who was busy looking around at everything in sight. "You're a revenant."

Nadia glanced back at the Queen. "Chained. My first time here. It's . . . it's not what I imagined."

"What did you imagine?" the Queen asked.

Nadia shrugged. "Not sure, just not something so . . . pretty. I'm only here as backup in case the dipshit on his knees did something stupid."

I turned to look at Spencer Mills, who was staring at the Queen with open hostility. The first time I'd seen anything on his face that wasn't abject pity for himself.

"Is there an issue here?" Hiroyuki asked Spencer.

"I'll deal with him in a moment," the Queen said, and turned to Dani. "And you?"

"Rift-walker," she said. "Just here to drop and run."

"The embers are fucked," I said. "It took me a week to return to Earth."

The Queen nodded as if she'd been expecting the information. "So I've been told. I've been a little preoccupied with the tear storms that keep happening. You spoke to Neb before you left?"

I nodded. "She okay?"

Queen removed the forest-green promise crystal from a dark brown leather pouch on her hip, and dropped it into my hand. "She has not returned."

"That's not great," Hiroyuki said.

I went to pass the crystal back and the Queen held up her hands to stop me. "You can keep the crystal; as far as I'm concerned, your promise if fulfilled. I doubt I'll need it to force you to find her."

"You want me to find her?" I asked.

The Queen nodded.

"You need to say the exact words," I said.

"Lucas Rurik, *your promise is fulfilled*," the Queen said with an overly exaggerated flourish.

The crystal in my hand cracked in half, the sound loud enough to make me wince.

"Damn it," Dani said, rubbing her ears. "A little warning next time."

"There's never going to be a next time," I said, my tone cold and hard.

"Neb is missing," the Queen said, getting back to more important matters. "Kuri, my people, her people, and Commander Pike. All missing."

"Have you been to where they were last seen?" I asked.

The Queen shook her head. "That is why I need you to deal with this. No matter what we find, I need to return to the Crow's Perch. But if I were to find evidence of wrongdoing against Neb, against my people, I might do something that would not benefit those who remain at home."

"You mean chase after those responsible?" I asked.

The Queen nodded.

"And if we don't find them?" I asked. "Or . . . well, worse?"

"We will decide what happens next after that," the Queen said, her tone hard as stone. "I regret that I will be unable to join you. My guards were annoyed that I insisted I leave the Crow's Perch to see you here. There is a concern that people within Inaxia will use it to try and assassinate me."

"They have a point," I said, looking around at the guards in the ruins.

We remained silent for a few seconds before the Queen said, "Neb is not immortal or impervious to harm."

"I know," I agreed.

"If someone has harmed her, they will not be someone to underestimate."

We went back to silence for a few more seconds.

"Neb thinks highly of you and your abilities as a warrior," the Queen said. "And from what I've seen, she has reason to."

"Are you asking me if I can beat whoever hurt her? If someone hurt her," I added quickly. "Because I have no idea. Even with Hiroyuki's help. We have no clue what we're up against."

"I'm asking if you will do what needs to be done," the Queen said, looking between me, Dani, and Hiroyuki. "Callie's death was not your doing, but would you have killed her if you'd needed to, despite Neb asking for her to be brought in alive?"

"We both know I would have," I said. "Are you suggesting I might need to kill Neb?"

"No," the Queen said with a wave of her hand. "I'm suggesting that someone who can take Neb out would need to be an Ancient themselves. Or at least have their level of power. Can you kill an Ancient?"

Considering my close proximity to a member of the Silver Phalanx, the question made me uncomfortable. Besides, if I was honest, it was a question I'd asked myself over the years. Could I? Almost certainly.

With enough time to plan, anyone can be killed, no matter the wealth, power, or ability of the target. Would I? "Yes," I said after a moment's hesitation.

To Hiroyuki's credit, he didn't turn my way and glare at me.

The Queen turned and spoke to one of the guards, who hurried over to Congressman Mills and dragged him to his feet.

"You betrayed us all," Congressman Mills seethed in the Queen's direction.

"Do you have anything you'd like to know?" the Queen asked me, pointedly ignoring Spencer Mills.

"The boxes," I said. "You're going to confirm who made them."

"Elliot," Mills said, still staring at the Queen.

I snapped my fingers next to his head, and he finally turned toward me. "Explain better."

"I wasn't privy to know," Congressman Mills said. "He would come here and return with whatever he needed."

"Why'd you make them?" Hiroyuki asked.

"I was not privy to know," Congressman Mills repeated.

"That pretty much sums Spencer up," the Queen said. "He never was one to be told what was going on."

"Fuck you, traitor," Mills snapped.

"I'll go check on things elsewhere," the Queen said. "Maybe he'll be more receptive without the cause of his hate being right in front of him."

"So, you're just a dumb patsy," Nadia said to Spencer. "What about Jordan?"

"He was supposed to place the boxes where they needed to go," Mills said with a sigh. "But he decided he could make the world better by actually turning people into rift-fused. He was always a little unhinged. Like I told you, I found out he'd killed someone. He was never supposed to kill anyone."

"Who removed his head?" Hiroyuki asked.

"Elliot had him dealt with," Mills said. "When the RCU investigated, we got Jordan to run abroad, keep him well away from anything linking him back to me. Elliot had someone find and kill him, but the lucky bastard got taken into the rift, so he had to come here and finish the job."

"Who did it?" I asked.

"I don't know," Congressman Mills said. "The less I knew, the less I could say to anyone should an eventuality like this happen."

"What about the snake emblem?" I asked.

"The Vipers are a gang," Mills said. "Elliot was part of them, said they worked in the rift. I left it at that. I don't know who they are, but they're rift-fused of some kind or another, and they're trained to a high standard. These aren't typical thugs. They're dangerous."

"What makes you say that?" I asked.

"I know the difference between dangerous people and those who pretend to be."

"Ahiram?" I asked. "Mean anything to you?"

"Who?" Mills asked.

"Ahiram. Someone tried to blow up Ji-hyun on your idiot orders."

"Elliot's," Mills said.

"The bomber said Ahiram was returning," I finished. "You know the name?"

"Some old warrior," Mills said. "When we were Blessed, before I was exiled because of that traitorous bitch, people mentioned him. He's a myth."

"That's what everyone keeps saying," Nadia said. "People sure are willing to do a lot of awful stuff for a myth."

"You do know that the Queen didn't betray you, right?" I asked. "Callie Mitchell and Prime Roberts did that. They set you up and then used your anger to get whatever Callie needed. You have been played your entire life on Earth. You stupid twat."

Congressman Mills stared at me. "You lie."

"He tells the truth," Hiroyuki said. "They arranged for Callie to get taken to Earth because she needed to conduct her experiments there. Needed a steady supply of unwilling subjects. The Blessed were never meant to succeed; you were just a means to an end."

The Queen returned, along with two guards.

"Is that true?" Mills asked. "Callie betrayed us?"

"Repeatedly," the Queen said dismissively. "You will come with us, and we will discuss it further. You will tell us everything we ask of you. Do you know who has Neb?"

Mills shook his head. "I don't know what happened to her. My job was to do as I was told in return for a comfortable life and vast wealth. Asking questions was a good way to end those in a painful way."

"They'd have killed you?" Dani asked.

"I want to kill him now, and I've only just met him," Nadia said.

The guards grabbed the congressman and marched him away.

"He was always someone who would take all of the credit and not do any of the work," the Queen said sadly. "Imagine he really doesn't know anything, but we'll find out everything he *does* know."

"Thank you," I said.

"I'm going to head back with Nadia," Dani said.

"Neb's missing, so I'm going to stay and have a look to see what's going on," I said. "Any chance you can pop back after your power returns."

"Five days last time," Dani said.

"Five days, then," I said. "Just come back here and check we're all in one piece."

"Can do; where?"

"We're going to the Vast Death," I said. "Neb was headed to Agency, so that's where we're going. If we don't find her or anything to say where she's gone, we'll go to Plainhaven, as that was her next destination. Between the two, we should hopefully be able to pick up a trail. Can you get into the Vast Death?"

"You really hate saying that, don't you?" Hiroyuki whispered.

"Yes," I seethed between clenched teeth.

"I can't get into the Vastness," Dani said. "But I can get to Agency. I'll take people there and we'll have to ride through. Can you leave word with someone you trust about what you need and, if you need our help further, make sure there are half a dozen horses there?"

"We can do that," Hiroyuki said.

"Be careful, you two," Dani said. "And you, my Queen." She opened a tear.

"Don't do anything stupid," Nadia said, although it wasn't entirely clear who she was talking to. "Keep safe. Lovely to meet you, Queenie."

The pair stepped through the tear, which shut behind them.

The guard returned, leading two large black stallions by their reins. Soon after, a half dozen more guards arrived, all on identically coloured horses, each of them leading one without a rider. The guards who had been watching us all moved over and mounted their horses, leaving the two in front of us without riders, along with one stood by the guards.

"Where's Mills?" I asked.

"Already heading back to the Crow's Perch," the Queen said. She strolled over to the one horse without a rider that was with the guards, scratched the large animal on the side of its face, and swung up onto the saddle with grace. She pointed to the two stallions in front of Hiroyuki and me.

I walked over to one of the horses. "Does he have a name?" I asked, my voice loud enough for all to hear.

"Roar," one of the guards told me, before pointing to the second horse. "That one is Pride."

"Roar like a yell?" I asked.

The guard nodded.

I looked back at the stallion, who stared at me with what I hoped was friendliness. Roar had a light grey patch on the side of his head that stretched from under his eye to below his mouth, like a bolt of grey lightning. "So, Roar, you okay with being ridden?"

"He's a warhorse," the Queen said. "All of these horses are bred for battle. They are from Nightvale."

"Pride," Hiroyuki said. He'd been oddly quiet during our time with the Queen. "He is a good horse."

"Why is Neb breeding warhorses?" I asked, and scratched the side of Roar's large neck, which got me an affectionate nuzzle from the animal. A small satchel hung from his saddle on one side, and a sword was sheathed on the other. I drew the broadsword; it was well made and would make an excellent weapon, but I was happy with my spear.

"You'll have to ask her," the Queen said. "Let's go; there's something I want to show you before I leave."

I sheathed the sword and swung up onto the horse, trotting after everyone else, the Queen of Crows beside me as we left the ruins. Hiroyuki rode behind us. Once out in the open, three of the guards moved back to our rear, while the others spaced out in front and to our flanks, effectively forming a shield around the Queen and me, although I was pretty sure it wasn't for my benefit.

"How far are we going?" I asked.

"To a settlement a few hours from here," the Queen said.

"Does it have a name?" I asked her.

"It's a Lawless village," she said as she rode beside me. "I'm not actually sure it had a name yet. It was attacked several weeks ago, before Neb contacted you. I believe she mentioned to you what happened. They were farmers. Two hundred dead. I think you need to understand what we're dealing with here."

We moved at a brisk pace across the plains, occasionally spotting one of the many local animals who might have been considered a problem if we'd been alone. Thankfully, even the hungriest predator in the rift would think twice about attacking a dozen heavily armed soldiers on horseback.

After two hours in the saddle, the village came into view ahead of us. A settlement in the middle of nowhere. We rode down a large sloping hill until we reached a fast-flowing river, and continued alongside it for another hour until we reached the village.

Or what had used to be a village.

There were few buildings still standing, and those that did were badly damaged with fire, the roofs caved in, the stone walls pulled down. Whatever had been used as a fortification around the village was all but gone, leaving jagged stone walls in its wake.

The guards remained behind as I climbed down off my horse and walked into the remains of the village, with the Queen of Crows standing at the perimeter. Hiroyuki followed me, and together we searched the remains of the settlement.

Revenants were a hardy group and were difficult to kill, but they weren't immortal. Even so, I would have expected some signs of them fighting back, even with their own powers. But it was as if something had descended upon the village and tore it asunder.

We spent an hour walking through the village alone, looking in the remains of any buildings we found. The farther we went, the more the constant bubbling rage inside of me grew. Several small scavengers ran when I came close. It wasn't until we left the settlement at the other end and entered what had once been farmland, and was now just a smouldering mass of destruction, that we found out the true horror that had been inflicted on the community.

It had been over a week since the attack, and I could still smell it in the air well before I saw them. Next to a burned-out shell of a barn, a few hundred meters from the village itself, were several dozen mounds of earth. The dead had been buried.

Hiroyuki cursed under his breath in Japanese.

I don't know how long I stood there, but I didn't move until someone cleared their throat behind me.

I turned to see the Queen of Crows and her guard. Despite the fact that she still wore her mask and therefore I couldn't see her expression, I knew she was angry. Her entire body radiated incandescent rage.

"None of these are the people I sent out to Vastness," the Queen said, each word wrapped in tightly controlled emotion. 'But they were just innocent settlers trying to make a living; they didn't deserve any of this. I had my people bury everyone."

"They burned the bodies," I said, and I found myself wanting to be as far from this settlement as possible.

"Whoever did this killed everyone and set the whole place alight," the Queen said. "We found this place a week ago, just after Neb set off to do whatever it is Neb is going to do. I just wanted to show you what these . . . *animals* are doing to people. We got here too late. Things are escalating, and I think Neb expected it to happen."

I glanced back at the bodies in the barn. "How far from the Crow's Perch are we?"

"An hour or two," the Queen said.

"How far from here is Agency?" I asked; I remembered Neb telling me, but I couldn't remember what she'd said. It had been a long few hours.

"Three days," the Queen told me. "You been before?"

I nodded and swung back up onto Roar.

"It might be my eternal optimism, but Neb's alive, you know," the Queen said as she turned her horse before looking back at Hiroyuki and me. "My people too. But if this is what these attackers are doing to people, I don't think they're going to stop unless they're someone puts an end to them."

"I know," I said. "We'll find Neb. Did you find a box here?"

The Queen nodded.

"Viper emblem inside it?" I asked.

The Queen nodded again. "There was a huge tear all across this place just before these bodies were found. The tears attract the creatures that live here, send them into a frenzy. I would not wish to have been in their way when it happened."

"We'll find out who did this," I said.

"Be careful, Lucas," the Queen told me. "I don't know what's happening, but none of it is good."

Hiroyuki and I watched the Queen of Crows and her entourage ride away.

"This was a test," Hiroyuki said. "Whoever did this hasn't gone further to the west toward the more populated areas like the Crow's Perch. Agency is closer to a bustling city than a town. If they've done this to anything close to that size, we have a real problem on our hands."

"The Queen said that one of those boxes was found here," I told him. "If the more-powerful creatures of the rift descended on this place and razed it to the ground like this, we're talking *a lot* of very powerful creatures."

"Elder-like power?" Hiroyuki asked.

I nodded. "But animals don't loot. They just kill. And that village was stripped bare of any valuables." During my time of searching the settlement, I'd seen no coins, no jewels, nothing that could fetch money.

"You think fiends are sent in to kill everyone, and someone cleans up after?" he asked me.

"I don't know what I think," I told him.

"This is going to get worse, isn't it?" Hiroyuki said, although it didn't sound like much of a question.

I looked back at him and nodded before the pair of us started the three days' ride to Agency and hopefully some answers.

CHAPTER FIFTEEN

Hiroyuki and I rode for several hours with the sun slowly lowering toward the horizon. We spoke rarely and paused for nothing, pushing the horses as much as we could. We needed to get to Agency as soon as possible, and what might have been a three-day ride normally was something we needed to make in two days. At most.

Unfortunately, if there was one thing you didn't do in the rift, it was travel by horse at night. You found shelter, you made a fire, and you hoped it would deter anything from seeing you or your horse as a snack.

The sun was a few hours from setting when Hiroyuki, who had been leading for almost the entire time we'd been riding, slowed down.

The scenery had been the same for almost the entirety of our time in the rift. Vast open plains populated by hills, a large forest to the far south, and pieces of ancient ruin protruding out of the ground.

"We should stop at that ruin over there," Hiroyuki said. "It's not too far from fresh water; we can fill our canteens at the lake and go hunker down."

"You want to check the ruins first?" I asked. "We can leave the horses there if it's safe." The horses had come with full saddlebags, each containing food and enough water to last us for the journey. They also contained an assortment of things we might need to start a fire or tend to a wound. The Queen's people had made sure we were as prepared as we could be.

"Sounds good," Hiroyuki said, bringing his horse to a trot, which I followed, and together we headed to explore what shelter there was available to us.

We left the horses just outside the entrance to an old white stone building that was still in one piece. Mostly. The building was one of a dozen, all in various states of disrepair, with the one we'd chosen looking a little better than the others. The entire door and its frame were missing, and the red-tiled roof had more than its fair share of moss growing out of it, but otherwise, it was at least a shelter with all four walls and a roof. Practically a luxury.

I stepped into the building first, my spear drawn, and found that it was just one large empty room, albeit one covered in dust, grime, and old leaves.

I looked around the house. "I think this was some kind of storeroom," I said. "There's a hole in the ceiling over there, but the horses will be safe in here. With a fire out front and one of us keeping watch, we should be able to make it through the night without being attacked by something. Or at least give something a pause before it attacks us."

"We should take the horses down to the lake," Hiroyuki said. "If there's something living in it, they're unlikely to be able to outpace a horse at full gallop. If we're lucky, the lake might be resident-free, and then they can drink awhile."

I didn't think we'd be that lucky and looked beyond Hiroyuki to the lake in the distance, unable to tell from here if there was a current resident that called it home. The odds were good it wasn't going to be free of local wildlife. Even so, Hiroyuki had a point, and we were both soon moving down the hill toward the body of water.

"Can I ask you something?" Hiroyuki said while we trotted down toward the lake.

"Sure," I told him.

He leaned down against his horse and patted his neck before looking up at me.

"You ever been to the Vast Death before?"

"A few times," I said. "I mostly just wish whoever named it that had been yelled at before it stuck."

"I think people like calling it something overly dramatic," Hiroyuki said with a chuckle. "It takes away from the seriousness of the actual place."

"Why did Noah send you?" I asked once we'd reached the shore of the lake. "You specifically."

Hiroyuki paused without looking over at me and climbed down from his horse. "Neb," he said. "He's worried she's building up forces to do something stupid in the rift."

I looked down at the stallion. "Like breeding warhorses."

Hiroyuki ducked under the horse's head and patted him on his neck. "Yeah. Aren't you worried?"

I got down from the horse and smoothed his neck. He'd been a good companion for the ride so far, and I hoped he still would be over the coming days. "Yes," I admitted. "She said that there have been a lot of attacks on Lawless villages. People killed. We both saw that village. Something out there is killing people, but . . ."

"She's hiding something," Hiroyuki said.

"She's always hiding something," I told him. "She's an Ancient. Or an ex-Ancient. Is there such a thing?"

Hiroyuki shook his head as he stood close to the bank of the lake and watched across the water. "Not that I've ever met."

I stood beside him and searched the bank for signs of something lurking beneath the surface. The water was clear enough that you could make out the sediment on the bottom several feet down, and it was easy to make out the fish that lived in what was probably one of the largest bodies of water for many miles. However enticing it appeared, predators in the rift had long since evolved to take advantage of their surroundings, and it wasn't unknown for creatures to use camouflage as they moved slowly across the bottom of rivers and lakes.

The lake was probably a hundred feet across and double that width; it was a source of drinking water for many of the animals that called the rift home. Three-quarters of the lake had large reeds moving from inside the water along the banks, making small forests of the five-foot-high vegetation. I did not want to go scrambling about in them.

A few hundred meters to the south was a large rocky area that rose up a hundred feet, where it was met by the beginnings of a woodland. I didn't want to go scrambling about in there, either.

Thankfully, there were plenty of reeds nearby, and I removed my spear and began to cut them down, scooping them up and dropping them on the bank as Hiroyuki watched the horses drink their fill.

I'd managed to get quite the bundle of reeds, and had made it a quarter of the way around the lake when I heard a loud whine accompanied by the sound of rustling in the reeds close by. I turned to look just as something ducked back out of view.

"You saw it," Hiroyuki called out, moving the horses back from the water's edge.

"I did," I told him as the reeds swayed ever so slightly. I kept my eyes on them as I picked up the reeds and moved slowly back toward Hiroyuki and the horses. "You know what it is?"

"When I was stationed here after I first arrived, we called it the three-tailed shadow," Hiroyuki said, helping me attach the reeds to the saddles. "They hunt all across the plains, but they're usually in the forest to the south."

"What do they look like?" I asked, wondering if I'd known them by a different name.

"Like a panther," Hiroyuki said. "Black, sleek, with three tails and armour plating around the top of their skull. Big teeth, foot long spines on the tips of one of their tails too. They're ambush predators, and we were warned never to enter the forest alone because of it. Hopefully, they'll see that we know it's here and go away. They usually attack in the dark. Odd that it's coming this way during the day. You ever seen one before?"

I nodded. "Sounds familiar."

"What did you call them?" Hiroyuki asked.

"*What the fuck was that spiny-tailed bastard?*" I said.

Hiroyuki laughed, but neither of us took our eyes away from where we'd seen the shadow last.

The tip of an indigo tail bobbed out among the top of the reeds.

"I think we need to get these horses out of here," I said, not taking my eyes off the creature in front of us. I drew a rift-tempered dagger and crouched low. The long, feline-shaped face of the animal poked through the grass.

The horses had smelled or seen something and were now much more interested in the new danger. They weren't panicking, but they weren't happy about being there.

The three-tailed shadow left the grass and started to pace up and down in front of it. The flank of the animal had four deep gashes on either side, as if something had grabbed it from the rear, but the three-tailed shadow had managed to flee before becoming a meal.

The creature was maybe nine or ten feet long including its tails, one of which—the spiny-tipped one—flicked around as if tasting the air. The creature had four muscular legs, and paws that were the size of my face, each one tipped with black claws that did not look like something I wanted to be near. The boned ridges on top of the creature's skull wrapped around to the side by its eyes and ears. It certainly looked the part of a dangerous hunter.

"It's wounded," Hiroyuki said.

"It looks angry," I said, standing. "It's hurt, hungry, and desperate."

"We have part of the lake between us," Hiroyuki said. "If we move further down, we could lead the horses around the hill and back to the hut."

We moved slowly around the side of the lake, the animal watching us the whole way, until the horses appeared to feel more comfortable with the distance between us.

"It's not stupid," Hiroyuki said.

The animal moved slowly toward the lake, crouched low, and started to drink.

"What could have hurt it?" I asked, looking around. The gouges in the flanks of the three-tailed shadow were deep, and now that I was able to see them clearer, it was obvious that they were fresh. "It wasn't long ago."

Like everything else in the rift, the creatures healed quickly; the wounds couldn't be more than a few hours old.

I kept watch on the creature as it drank, searching the reeds around us for any signs of what would attack a creature the size of a Siberian tiger.

There was an almighty roar in the distance.

"Any chance that's thunder?" I asked, fully aware of the answer.

"What do you think?" Hiroyuki said as the nine-tailed shadow in front of us stopped drinking and turned back to face the way it had come, ignoring us altogether, its hackles up.

Another roar. Closer.

"What hunts three-tailed shadows?" I asked.

"Something much bigger," Hiroyuki said grimly.

"Get the horses out of here," I said. "Fast. I'll catch you up after I've made sure it doesn't follow us."

Hiroyuki didn't argue, swinging up onto one of the horses, and, with the reins of the other in his hand, rode away.

I'd taken two steps after Hiroyuki when the three-tailed shadow roared in defiance as the earth shook so violently that both of the horses reared. Hiroyuki managed to keep on the saddle of one, but Roar's reins slipped through his fingers, and the black stallion galloped away.

Hiroyuki regained his composure and rode after Roar, while I picked myself up from the dirt, the shaking ground having thrown me unceremoniously to my knees. The earth in front of the feline erupted and a creature leapt out of the hole. The thing was twenty feet long, with four huge talons on each of its front legs. They were weapons designed to disembowel. It had a wide tail that was flat but ended in a large ball covered in bone and mud. Its scaled body was pale blue-grey with orange ridges down its back and around its underbelly and throat. Its face was catlike, with scales where there would otherwise be fur, and covered by bristling orange-and-black whiskers.

"What the *fuck* is that?" Hiroyuki shouted from up the slope, having managed to catch Roar.

"A mudrider," I said. "We need to leave right *now*."

The mudrider's jaw snapped open, elongating like a snake, as it launched itself at the much-smaller creature. It clamped onto the flank of the three-tailed shadow as the feline tried to bite and claw its way free.

The three-tailed shadow swiped at the mudrider, catching it on the snout, causing a roar of pain, but the smaller animal was too injured to run, and within moments, the mudrider had used its huge claws to tear into the panther-like creature, before its jaw snapped open again and it bit down on the feline's head, killing it.

I reached Hiroyuki and the horses and paused. "Fuck," I shouted.

"What?" he asked.

"These things can track over a long distance," I said. "If it decided that horse meat is a succulent delicacy, we're going to be in for a long night."

The mudrider looked up across the lake. It roared, showing all manner of gore in its mouth I'd rather not have seen. It stepped over the corpse of the three-tailed shadow, moving slowly, purposefully. Unsure if we were a threat or meal. Either way, running was not going to solve our problem."

"Okay, so what's the plan?" Hiroyuki asked. "Can we get to higher ground and outwait it?"

"We need to make sure it doesn't hang around here," I said. "They don't normally come this far north, as the ground isn't soft enough for them. We need to make sure it understands that it would be best to leave. Once it has our scent, it'll keep hunting us. They're not known for giving up easily."

"I'll get the horses put back and run down toward you," Hiroyuki said. "I'll be as quick as I can. You think you can make sure it's not happy about staying here?"

"Piss off a mudrider?" I asked. "Sure, why not? I've lived a long life."

I drew my spear, looked down at it and then over at the mudrider, who was thankfully decided on continue feasting on the three-tailed shadow. If it came down to a straight fight, the dagger would do some serious damage, so long as I was willing to get close enough to something that would rip me in half.

"You've fought fiends," Hiroyuki said.

"This isn't some lesser fiend," I told him. "This is an elder fiend in the waiting. If this thing ever got through a tear and bonded with an animal there, it would be catastrophic."

"Go now," I snapped as Hiroyuki rode off without looking back. It was a short distance from us to the hut and wouldn't take him long to get there and back. Time is relative when you're trying to keep something busy that looks at you like a snack.

I held my spear tightly as the mudrider walked through the lake, causing a large wash to cascade over one bank. It stopped before it reached the bank, looked up at Hiroyuki and the horses, and roared. It began to gallop toward them.

I turned to smoke and moved toward it as quickly as possible as it reached the bottom of the slope. I reached it, re-formed, and dragged the blade of the spear along the side of one massive leg. I turned the spear in my hand as the mudrider roared in agony and lifted its leg off the ground. I drove the tip of the spear up into the soft underside of the creature's foot, dragging it clear, turning back to smoke and re-forming by its back leg, where I cut through thick cartilage. Blood poured out of the wounds on both legs while I backpedalled toward the lake.

Mudriders were an intelligent and dangerous foe. There had been research done on them over the centuries, and it was deduced that they were capable of understanding, but more importantly, capable of holding a grudge. As the mudrider turned back toward me, it was evident that it *hated* me.

The creature leapt toward me, but I turned to smoke, harmlessly moving to the side as it crashed into the lake. I re-formed several feet away from the edge of the lake, right in the middle of a shower of rain as the lake water met gravity.

The mudrider lowered itself in the lake, then gave a low rumble as the creature leapt toward me, showing a lot more grace than you'd think possible from an animal the size of a bus.

I was already in smoke form when the mudrider landed with an almighty crash. I swirled around the creature's body, moving back toward the site of its kill before re-forming. I didn't really want to kill the mudrider, but it wasn't giving me many options.

The mudrider spun back toward me just as ice formed around its legs, freezing it in place. The creature struggled, tearing off huge slabs of ice, but they were quickly re-formed.

"I've got it," Hiroyuki said. "Kill it."

I ran up to the mudrider, avoiding its huge jaws, and drove my spear into a soft spot where its ear was, piercing the brain and killing it instantly.

"Fucking hell," I snapped, dragging my spear clear.

"You're not normally one to hesitate," Hiroyuki said when he caught up to me as I cleaned my spear in one of the large holes of water the fight with the mudrider had created.

"There's going to be enough killing," I said, looking up at him. "Just wanted to avoid it."

"Let's make some distance between us and it," I told him. I wondered how long before the body of the mudrider would bring something else along. "I think we're stood in the way of what is about to become an all-you-can-eat buffet."

CHAPTER SIXTEEN

Hiroyuki caught several fish, using his ice powers to freeze the water of the lake and grabbing the fish as he thawed the water around it. We returned to the hut as darkness settled in, and decided to move the horses back to a ruin that was farther away from the lake while still letting us watch it. Just in case.

It took us a few goes, but eventually we found a similarly sized hut that had nothing in it but dirt, and I set about building a fire that would hopefully deter anything from coming near. Hiroyuki used his riftborn powers to create a fence of ice spikes a dozen feet out from the hut, hopefully giving us more time to react should something from the local wildlife decide to investigate us.

Once everything was settled, Hiroyuki prepared and cooked the fish, while I divided up the bundle of reeds I'd collected and gave them to the horses, both of whom were seemingly very happy with their evening meal.

The smell of cooking fish, mixed with the smoke of the fire from whatever kind of wood Hiroyuki had found to make it, made my mouth water, and I was soon happily tucking in to a large, white-fleshed fish, the name of which I had no idea. I hadn't exactly been a keen fisherman in the rift, even when I'd lived there full-time.

Among the saddlebags prepared by the Queen of Crows people were small tubs of herbs and spices, which turned out to be essentially chili.

"We should come here more often to fish," Hiroyuki said as he tucked in to one of the large fish.

I was quiet for a moment, listening to the sounds of the rift around us. It was dark, and punctuating the sound of the wind whipping across the plains were chirps and squeaks from the various small nocturnal animals that lived in the vicinity.

By now, the dead mudrider would be awash with various species of carrion eaters, and it was quite likely that by sunrise, the carcass would be picked clean. It didn't make me feel better to know what *could* be only a few minutes' walk away, but I was sure we'd be fine while they had something bigger, and considerably easier, to feast on.

"You know, this is the longest I've stayed in the rift for centuries," Hiroyuki said. "Once I left and came back to Earth, I never wanted to come back here. It's too . . . chaotic."

"And Earth isn't?" I asked.

"Earth is more of a tamed chaos," Hiroyuki said. "Maybe it's just that I'm used to the craziness of Earth. I can anticipate and deal with whatever might be thrown my way on Earth. In the rift, anything thrown my way could range from a mudrider twenty miles out of its usual hunting ground to a primordial who goes insane and tries to destroy a town. There's no telling day to day exactly what ludicrous thing I'm going to have to deal with next. Combine that with the sheer amount of people who have a huge amount of power but are content to live as a farmer or blacksmith, and I never know quite what this place is going to drop on me next. I find the rift . . . exhausting."

I said nothing.

"I assume from your smile that you don't feel the same," Hiroyuki said after several seconds.

"I understand what you're saying," I told him. "I also find the rift to be a chaotic mess of a place, but so is Earth. Anywhere humans are—and no matter how much we all distance ourselves from being human, we all were one at some point—chaos reigns. It's basically their main creation."

"Chaos and death," Hiroyuki said. "Sometimes, it feels like that's all humanity, and by extension the rift-fused, are capable of doing."

I stared at my old friend for a few seconds. "You okay?" I asked eventually.

Hiroyuki waved away my concern but didn't say anything.

"Don't do that," I said. "Don't dismiss it. If there's something wrong, you can talk about it. It's not like there's anyone else around here who can listen in."

Hiroyuki stared at the fire for some time. Eventually, he said, "I find it difficult to discuss matters such as these."

"As what?" I asked.

"When we were young, when I was young, anyway, men were not to discuss such things," he told me. "I don't mean all of men in Japan were like that, but my family certainly were. We were not meant to talk about how we felt. My father was a samurai, I was a samurai. We were to hold ourselves to a higher regard, to hold our lord in the highest regard. Anything that seemed like weakness was to be pushed aside. I fought in wars, I fought against my own countrymen and with them, and I did things that, looking back, I know were wrong. I did those things because loyalty to my lord was placed above all. My own ethics and needs didn't come into it.

"When I died, or when I became riftborn, it was a happy day. I arrived here and was told I didn't need to follow anyone's orders. I could just do what I wanted. Get whatever job I wanted. I had skills, I had the drive, I could be soldier, an officer of the law, or a farmer. I knew how to read and write, I enjoyed art, there was so much I could do. The world felt open to me. It was terrifying. And now, after all these years, I am still in the service of someone else."

"You want to leave the Silver Phalanx?" I asked.

Hiroyuki looked over at me. "I do not know *what* I want to do. I have spent so long working for someone else that when I started to work with the RCU, I discovered that I *enjoyed* helping people. I *enjoyed* investigating crimes, helping you and Nadia. Working with you and Nadia. It was . . . *Fun* probably isn't the right word."

"Satisfying," I suggested.

Hiroyuki pointed at me. "Yes, that's it. I was satisfied. Like I had a purpose beyond that of keeping Noah safe. I love Noah. That is not hyperbolic. I love him. He is like a father to me. Probably more so than my actual father ever was. However, I am no longer sure being a member of the Silver Phalanx is enough. It hurts me to think that I will disappoint Noah, but it also hurts to think I will disappoint myself."

"Is that why you're here with me?" I asked. "You volunteered."

Hiroyuki nodded. "Noah did want someone to check on Neb. But, yes, I volunteered. Primarily because I hoped some time away from Earth and everyone on it might give me fresh perspective." He removed a pad of paper and a metal case of pencils from his saddlebag, neither of which I'd seen him bring with us. "I'm going to do some drawings. It . . . it calms me."

"I'll go for a walk," I said.

Hiroyuki gave me a concerned look.

"I'll be safe," I assured him before he could say anything. I got to my feet and stretched. "Thank you for telling me all of that."

"Thank you for listening," Hiroyuki said. "You were a warrior when you became a riftborn. You worked for Hannibal. How did you overcome that link? How did you decide to stop living your life in the service of one other?"

"I was never in service of Hannibal," I said. "I admired him, but I'd spoken to him maybe a dozen times in my entire life. He was . . . intense. Driven like no one I'd met at the time. I thought I wanted to be just like him, but I didn't. I just wanted to make him proud. I think a lot of us in that army did. A lot of us died because of it, too."

"So, you were never beholden to someone else's ideas?" Hiroyuki asked.

"Oh, I was," I said. "I was beholden to so many people, it's hard to pick one. Neb was a big one. She trained me, made me a better soldier, but, more importantly, made me a better man. At the same time, she turned me from being an ordinary, if talented, soldier, into . . . whatever I am now."

"You hold back," Hiroyuki said. "When I've seen you fight, you hold back. You only let yourself go when someone you care about is in danger, not when you're in danger. You could have killed that mudrider before I'd ever returned, and you know it. I heard what you did to those monsters Callie was making. You killed all of them in moments. I saw you fight to protect everyone in Boston when we first met one of her monsters. I saw you fight to protect me. You are a dangerous man."

"I don't want to be known as someone who is always dangerous," I said. "I don't want people to fear me."

Hiroyuki raised an eyebrow.

"Okay, fair," I agreed. "I don't want *everyone* to fear me. So, sometimes, I hold back. The talon mask made it easier to be feared. When you're just an anonymous entity, you can detach yourself from it all."

"You don't wear it anymore," Hiroyuki said.

I shook my head. "Seems pointless. I'm the only Raven Guild member left, so wearing a Talon mask does nothing but make everyone stare at me. I've worn them when making a point, but otherwise, I'm not really interested in keeping one on me. Besides, Talons are meant to keep their Guilds safe, so I didn't quite live up to that expectation."

"May I ask you a question?" Hiroyuki asked.

"Go nuts," I told him.

"Why haven't you restarted the Raven Guild?"

"You want the honest, no-bullshit reason?"

Hiroyuki nodded.

"I don't know how to," I said, and leaned up against the wall beside me. "Or, rather, I don't know how to start something I'm not convinced should be reborn. I don't know why we were killed, and I feel like that's something I should discover before I decide whether or not to recreate the Guild. There's just too many questions that haven't been answered, and every time I think there's time to look into it, a whacking great tear opens in the sky and I'm now on 'kill all the fiends' duty."

"Maybe we should all take time away," Hiroyuki said. "Spend a few centuries finding ourselves."

"I was a hunter for a century," I said. "Here in the rift. A settlement to the south of Inaxia. Five hundred rift-fused. I did farming there, too, and learned how to do pottery, although I'm terrible at it. I sometimes think about going back to it and living for a few hundred years in the forest again. Then something else happens, and I'm suddenly chasing criminals, or hunting a murderer, or trying to figure out why there's a bloody great fiend rampaging through a human town. But as for you, honestly, it sounds like you need a break."

Hiroyuki nodded. "I think you're right. I just don't know when I'd be able to have one."

"Maybe once we've got Neb and everyone else, we can figure out what had happened and then go off into the sunset as heroes," I said. "Heroes who are left alone for a while."

Hiroyuki laughed, and settled in to work on his art, which I took as an indication that the conversation was done.

I walked through the dark ruins until I could see over the lake. The sounds of animals squabbling over the mudrider floated across the tear-lit landscape. The mixtures of blues and purples hitting the still water of the lake created a strange, almost-psychedelic visual effect.

Just as I was about to head back, I spotted something odd in the distance, over by the rocky hill that led up into the forest. There had been movement; I was certain of it. It had been only a quick thing, and only for a fraction of a second, but there had been something moving fast.

I wasn't concerned about another animal coming up toward us, as they'd probably have to move a little too close to the party of scavengers below. I remained still, shrouded in the shadows, and watched the rocks. It didn't take long to see more movement. One . . . two . . . three.

Three humanoids running among the rocks, moving from cover to cover quickly.

They remained motionless in the nighttime, only the light of the tear high above us allowing me to see that they were even there. Something felt off about them. I couldn't put my finger on it, although certainly someone running through the rift during the night was weird in and of itself.

I concentrated on being able to spot them and noticed the mass of blue and violet that swirled around where they'd been, leaving a trail that led up to . . . only one person. It wasn't three people at all, but a single person moving in a way that I'd never seen before. While the actual physical person moved normally, it had two copies always looking like they were trying to catch up. I wondered if whoever it was had done it to ensure any threats didn't know which one was real. It was an odd thing to witness.

The now-singular person moved forward until they reached the reeds, and they disappeared from view. I stayed still, keeping an eye on the violet colour as it moved through the reeds. I hoped that they'd pop back up somewhere, as I had no idea what they were actually doing or if they were a threat. I couldn't even tell what they looked like, apart from wearing dark clothing, so I had no idea if they had on any markings that might identify them or who they worked for.

The figure emerged from the reeds and edged closer to the lake, where they removed something from a backpack. Canteens. Several of them, from the look of things. The singular spilt into two this time, with one filing the canteens while the other kept watch over the area. Once they got all the water they would need, they packed up and returned to the reeds. It was a well-drilled and organised way of moving through the area.

I remained where I was for several minutes, wondering what I'd just seen, before I risked moving back through the ruins to Hiroyuki.

"What is it?" he asked as I sat beside him.

I told him everything I saw, although I kept quiet about being able to spot rift power inside the rift. Primarily because I hadn't told anyone else about it apart from Valmore. I wasn't entirely sure it wasn't just a short-term by-product of my time in the Tempest. Or maybe I just hoped it was.

"We're being followed," he said, an edge of hostility to his voice.

"Honestly, I'm not sure," I told him. "I'm not saying it's just an exceptional coincidence, but it could just be a hunter from a village. They moved like they'd been trained to keep hidden. I'm feeling a little twitchy about everything that's happened the last few weeks."

"Let's hope it's something innocent," Hiroyuki said doubtfully. "Either way, I will take first watch."

"Wake me when you're ready to switch," I said, walking into the hut where the two horses were already lying down and sleeping.

Hiroyuki put his head through the doorway. "I'm going to move to a building over from here. I'll leave the fire." He left without waiting for a reply.

I removed my weapons and placed them beside me before lying down next to them and placing a hand on the pommel of my sword. Just in case.

CHAPTER SEVENTEEN

W e were packed up and ready to go just after dawn broke. Despite Hiroyuki saying he would wake me so he could rest, he didn't, but he assured me he was fine. He'd even brought some coffee with him, and we used a canteen of water to brew it up and pour it into the now-empty canteen. It was quite possibly the strongest coffee I'd ever drunk, but the caffeine hit alone made it worthwhile.

"I watched for that person you told me about," he said as we set off. "Didn't see them again, although that doesn't mean they weren't there in the shadows. Lots of places to hide out here."

I nodded, although I still had a feeling of anxiety about the whole situation.

While we rode the horses at a sedate pace through the ruins, we kept away from the open ground where we might be easier to spot, and the moment we were away from the ruins, we galloped as fast as we could. We needed to make Agency by nightfall. The quicker we found out what had happened to Neb, the faster we could get home and help with the investigation there.

After several hours of riding over open, occasionally hilly plains, we slowly began to be joined by pockets of woodland, until we found ourselves riding along a creek with forest on either side. We let the horses rest and drink for a while, and Hiroyuki and I took the opportunity to eat some of the food that had been packed for us and drink the still-warm coffee. The food was essentially jerky, although I didn't even want to think about what animal we were consuming. Not a lot of cows and pigs in the rift.

"You still thinking we're being followed?" Hiroyuki asked as we packed up.

"The one I saw last night?" I asked, forcing myself not to look behind me. "No. You?"

Hiroyuki shook his head. "Lot of open ground between there and here; it would be foolish of them to follow us over something where they could be spotted so easily."

"I thought you were sure they were just out hunting," I said.

"Yeah, well, I like to be sure we're not riding into trouble, too."

"Like an ambush ahead," I said, scanning the trees as I climbed back into the saddle.

Hiroyuki did the same and turned to look at me. "If you can turn into three people, that means you might not need help. It's what I'd do."

"Me too."

"Keep your eyes open, Lucas," Hiroyuki said, and set off at a trot along the riverbank.

I followed a short distance behind, wondering if the three I'd seen last night were there to stop us from reaching Agency or to stop us from going further. Presumably the latter. Maybe they were just there to keep an eye on us, see what we did. Too many variables. I was certain we'd be seeing them again, though.

If it wasn't for the increasing feeling that we were being watched, the ride would have been a nice one. The scenery was stunning, the vibrant colours of the various foliage looking like something out of a cartoon in places. The rift was a beautiful place when it wasn't trying to kill you.

We rode along a trail that moved up gradually, but over a long distance, and after a few hours, we were several hundred feet higher than we'd been when we'd stopped. The two halves of the forest, separated by the river, had merged into one, and while there was a well-used trail, the sense of unease at riding through it never went away.

A few hours later, and after nothing had tried to eat us, we exited the forest onto an open grassland as far as the eye could see. The pale green grass was six feet high in places, but thankfully, the trail we'd been using continued on through it. After hearing the sounds of creatures living in the taller grass, I doubted deviating from the trail was a good idea.

We made good time along the trail, occasionally passing a wagon pulled by oxforth—a massive animal that was a mixture of an oxen, camel, and horse. The wagon drivers usually ignored us and we them, but after we'd passed a half dozen, one slowed down and said hello.

The wagon looked like something that was used when the early Americans travelled west, although considerably tougher in construction, with armour around the wheels and spikes on the sides. A Mad Max version of the American West, then.

"You off to Agency?" the middle-aged man driving the wagon asked. Hiroyuki nodded.

"We're doing a run to some of the villages," the man said, and I glanced behind him through the opening in the thick covering of the way that there were half a dozen people in the back of the wagon. All of them were armed and looked like they could take care of themselves.

"My best for your journey," I said with a slight nod. "How is Agency these days?"

"Been better," he said after thinking about it. "Been worse, too. If you're going there, be sure to go to the committee office first and get yourself a pass. You don't want to be walking the streets without one."

Someone in the back banged with their hand on the side of the wagon.

"Thank you," I said.

"Go with God, my friends," the man said, and they set off.

"If God is real, they gave up on this place a long time ago," Hiroyuki said with a touch of bitterness to his tone as he began riding again.

"You ever heard of needing a pass?" I asked Hiroyuki after catching up with him.

He shook his head. "First time for me."

An hour later, we passed two women riding horses. "Good day," one called out to us. They both wore leather armour and carried swords on their backs. A pair of claw weapons, the metal showing they'd been imbued with rift energy, hung from the belt of one woman. She had dark skin, her hair short, cropped to her skull. She had a scar that ran from under her ear to just above her jawline. The second woman was white, with long light brown hair and a dozen earrings between both ears. Tattoos adorned her bare arms. They were either seasoned travellers or they'd purchased enough gear to make it look like they were.

"Good day," Hiroyuki said, slowing down.

"I've heard you need a pass for Agency," I said. "Is that a new thing?"

The women nodded. "You not been here for a while, then?" one of them asked.

"Not for a few centuries," I admitted. "Didn't need a pass back then."

"It's been in place maybe a year," she said. "You need a pass to be out after dark."

"Officially," the second woman told us. "Unofficially, you need a pass to walk the streets. Otherwise, the guards hassle you, rob you, sometimes

worse if you can't pay. A pass means you've paid your way and are protected by those in charge. Guards don't fuck around with those who pay
them."

"Can we get in without a pass?" I asked.

"Of course," the first woman said. "But good luck getting out again."

"Where would we get a pass?" Hiroyuki asked.

"Go to the committee office in the centre of town," the second woman
said. "It'll cost you either cash or favours. If you've got the cash, I'd advise
you to go that way."

I picked up on the fact that the women weren't telling us the whole
story.

"Is there another way?" Hiroyuki asked.

"Not for people we don't know," the first woman said.

"Have you seen a woman called Neb?" I asked as they started to trot
again.

They stopped and stared over at me. "You know Neb?" the second
woman asked.

"My name is Lucas," I told them, removing my Guild medallion.

"The Raven Guild is dead," the first woman said.

"Not all of us," I said.

"That's Neb's Guild," the second woman whispered.

"You both know of her?" I asked again.

"*Everyone* knows Neb," the first woman said with a shrug. "Look,
don't get into Agency through the front gate; you'll get grabbed, taken to
the committee, forced to pay a huge amount of coin. Or worse. There's
another way."

"Can you show us?" I asked.

The two women shared an expression of concern. "No, we have to
reach our village by nightfall. Keep this way, and an hour from here, there's
a crossroads. Take the left, go another hour, and there's a pond. Wait until
nightfall, and someone will come find you. Do *not* make them angry."

"Do we have a name of someone so we can prove we're not there to
cause trouble?" Hiroyuki asked.

"Ask for Tess," the first woman said.

"It's very trusting of you," Hiroyuki said.

"Not really," the second woman said, before nodding in my direction.
"He's a Raven's Guild. We trust those. We trust Neb. Besides, if you fuck
with them, they'll cut your heads off and leave them on pikes for people
to see."

"We're too far from anything close to Inaxia law," the first woman said. "Rules are different out here."

"Thank you for your help," I said, and the two women rode off as Hiroyuki and I continued on our way.

"I can't believe that the lawlessness around here has gotten worse over the decades," Hiroyuki said after a few minutes of riding in silence.

"Like they said, we're too far away from Inaxia for any of them to care," I said. "They care about their own lives and their own little kingdom, and anything outside of it can fend for itself. It's been heading that way for a long time."

"I remember when Inaxia would send people out to the Lawless towns and villages to ensure they were still safe," Hiroyuki said. "It wasn't official, but it was beneficial to everyone if people got food and were protected from bandits and animals."

"If Prime Roberts is any indication of what those are in charge are like—I wouldn't trust them either," I said, remembering the sack of crap in Inaxia who I'd rather never interact with again.

Just like the women had said, an hour's ride led to a crossroads. It was a simple, eight-foot-tall black metal pole with two pieces of arrow-shaped steel riveted into it. The steel arrow pointing right was marked AGENCY, and the arrow pointing left was . . . blank.

"That's not ominous or anything," I said as we turned to go left as we were instructed.

"Do you think we're being directed into a trap?" Hiroyuki asked.

"I think there's two outcomes to this," I said. "Either they were telling the truth and we'll be very grateful for it, or it's a trap and we get to put the heads of some people on spikes."

"That's a confident outlook," Hiroyuki said.

"I'm feeling positive," I assured him with a smile. "Also, I'm in no mood for people to play games. If someone comes for me today, they're not going to get a second chance later."

Hiroyuki gave a nod, and we returned to our peaceful ride along a path to what I hoped was going to be a helpful meeting rather than a bloodthirsty one.

After some time, we reached a large open area where the grass had all been cut back. If I'd been on Earth, it would have looked like it was due to be a park for the local kids to kick a ball around.

I left Roar with Hiroyuki and walked across the grass to the edge, looking over into the steep ravine of several hundred feet. Despite the jagged rocks, there did appear to be a trail along the side of the ravine, leading down to the river that ran along the bottom.

I glanced back to Hiroyuki and waved him over.

"That does not look like a fun time," he said, taking a quick step back from the vertical drop.

I walked along the cliff top for two hundred feet until I reached the start of the trail down the ravine. Next to it was more tall grass, meaning that someone had carved out this little patch, presumably for easier access.

There was painted graffiti on the large boulders close to the trail start. *Tesscaster* was written in green on the boulder, although it wasn't the most interesting feature of the area. At the start of the trail, like a macabre doorway, were a dozen heads on spikes, twenty feet in the air. Six had been placed on either side of the stone trail, and I had to admit they had the desired effect of making me not want to go down there.

"Not exactly welcoming, is it?" Hiroyuki said.

I looked between the horses and the trail. "Can they make it down there?"

"Yes," a voice said from the grass as they stepped out of it, a crossbow pointed at me, the top of the arrow shimmering blue from rift energy. If it hit me, it would do serious damage.

"You're the woman from earlier," I said.

The woman in question had been the first of the two we'd met. She smiled at me as the other woman we'd met earlier and a huge man with dark skin and a large mohawk hairstyle, who was well over seven feet tall and carrying what appeared to be a small tree in one hand, all stepped out of the grass,.

"Which one of you is Tess?" I asked.

"None of us," the first woman said. "I'm Naomi. This is Lara."

"And that is?" I asked, pointing to the large man.

"He is Kulan," Naomi told me. "He is deaf and does not talk. He would prefer it if you didn't try to have a conversation with him."

Kulan used sign language to say *I am not a people person.*

I signed back. *Considering the size of that hammer, you can be whatever you want.*

Kulan laughed, and I felt the gaze of everyone on me.

"You can sign?" Naomi asked.

I nodded. "We can learn any language we hear in the rift; it felt remiss of me not to be able to communicate with people who can't talk."

I can read lips, Kulan signed.

I nodded a thank you, and he looked visibly more relaxed.

"So, are you here to rob us or take us to see Tess?" I asked.

"We were here to watch what you did," Lara said. "We listened to you talk; we made sure you were who you said you were."

"And those people up there?" I asked, pointing to the head.

"They were not who they said they were," Lara said, and she moved her arms from behind her back, showing the set of claws on each one.

Hiroyuki stroked his horse as he tried to pull back. "Tesscaster," he said. "Is that her name?

"You'll see," Naomi told us. "You can bring your horses to the stables."

I looked around. "What stables?"

Naomi, Lara, and Kulan turned and walked back into the grass. Presuming that we were meant to follow, we did just that.

It was a five-minute walk, with one of our guides calling back to us every few feet to make sure we didn't get lost, but eventually the grass stopped, revealing a hill, at the bottom of which was a large patch of land, with a stable and home.

"It's like a bowl cut out of the land," Hiroyuki said.

We continued around to a set of steps that been carved out of stone and placed on the side of the bowl, which was easily two hundred feet across and completely hidden from anyone and anything until you stumbled on it.

"What is this place?" I asked as I led Roar down the gentle slope that sat beside the steps.

"It's a place of peace," Naomi told me. "No one knows this is here. The grass keeps it hidden. Most think that the trail around the ravine is the start of the path to the river below; most believe it to be treacherous. It is, and always has been, but in the last few years, we've made it more so. It's not a path you go down if you want to make it to the bottom unscathed."

We reached the bottom of the bowl and found that we were several dozen feet below the grass itself, which looked down on us like an army of protectors.

The stable was big enough to house six horses, and Hiroyuki and I placed our own mounts among those of our hosts.

"We're going to need them to continue on if Neb isn't here," I said.

We followed Naomi, Lara, and Kulan into the house. Which turned out not to be a house at all but a large, open building with a dividing wall about three-quarters of the way across. There was an archway in the wall, revealing a table, chairs, and several foldaway beds. Two men and two women sat in there, each of them raising a hand in hello to their companions and eyeing Hiroyuki and me distrustfully.

The rest of the room was taken up by a lift.

Rift energy bathed the whole area in a purple light, and when we stepped onto the platform, one of the people in the adjoining room came out and pressed a large red button on the wall. Four-foot-high metal barriers rose out of the floor, and we started to slowly descend into whatever awaited us below, hoping we weren't about to walk into something that would get us killed.

CHAPTER EIGHTEEN

We moved slowly, and I tried to judge how far down we'd come, but it was difficult after the first dozen or so feet, when the hole above us closed and we were left in only the pale purple light of whatever rift energy was being used.

We still had our weapons, presumably because we weren't considered to be enough of a threat to take them. Possibly not the smartest choice on their part, but I got the feeling that if they'd wanted us dead, or at least seriously hurt, they could have done that at any point from the moment we'd met them on the road to Agency.

The lift took what felt like an age to reach its destination, which it did with a bone-jarring bump. The cavern we found ourselves in was lit up with rift-energy torches, and the mixture of turquoise, cobalt blue, and purple made it look like I was standing in the middle of a lava lamp.

"This way," Naomi told us, descending the steps from the lift to the cavern floor.

While there were no guards inside the lift area, there were a dozen just beyond the archway you had to walk under to leave. They were all sat off to the side, several of them playing cards on a large wooden table, while a few of them watched us suspiciously, prepared for any trouble. These people had some real trust issues.

Beyond the guards lay ten minutes of walking through pale rock tunnels. We passed by several intersections, and it was soon evident that the whole place was a maze.

"This is quite the fortification," Hiroyuki said after we walked by the third set of tunnels branching away from the main thoroughfare.

"We don't want people coming down here and knowing where to go," Naomi said.

"It's not as echoey as I expected," I said, stepping over a piece of loose stone on the ground.

"How long have you all been down here?" Hiroyuki asked.

"A few years now," Lara told us.

"Why?" I asked.

"Tess will explain," Lara said.

The roof of the tunnel lowered, and Kulan had to duck to get under it without serious injury. It continued along like that for several minutes, until the roof of the tunnel rose and we stepped out into a large chamber that could have easily fit a full-sized football pitch.

There were over two dozen tunnel mouths leading into the darkness beyond; it was like walking through a human-sized ant's nest. In the centre of the chamber were chairs and tables arranged in front of a dais. Atop the dais was another table and what looked like one of the old black chalkboards used by Victorian human schools, partially covered by a navy-blue sheet.

The chamber was mostly empty except for four guards, all of whom wore armour that reminded me of the Crow's Perch guards, although these were black and grey. Their faces were covered by various helmets and masks, and all carried a broadsword against their hip.

Beside them was a woman who appeared to be of middle age, although judging age on sight was almost completely useless where the rift-fused were concerned. She had pale skin, long grey hair that fell freely over thin shoulders, and piercing green eyes. She wore burgundy robes with black and white accents, similar leather boots to those worn by the guards, and several bangles of various colours and shapes on each wrist.

"Tess, I assume," Hiroyuki whispered.

"Whoever she is, she's in charge," I replied.

"These are the men we came across above," Naomi said to the woman Hiroyuki had identified as Tess.

"You Tess?" I asked as the woman got to her feet.

She smiled and nodded. "Tess Macallister." She had a Yorkshire accent and a warm smile; she struck me as someone who people found disarming. That didn't mean she was safe.

"You named this place after yourself?" I asked looking around.

"I didn't get much of a choice in it," she told me. "I'm from Doncaster, and my name is Tess, so people called it Tesscaster. We were running for our lives at the time, so it didn't feel like the right time to argue it."

"You're from Donny?" I asked.

"You been recently?" she asked eagerly. "I haven't seen my birth home in hundreds of years at this point."

"Not recently," I said. "Although I doubt you'd recognise it after a few centuries away."

"Where are you from?" Tess asked, looking between Hiroyuki and myself.

"Kyoto," Hiroyuki said.

"That's a complicated question for me," I answered. "Britain. Ancient Britain, before even the Romans arrived. Then was raised in Carthage. Or near Carthage."

"Carthage?" Tess asked with a raised eyebrow. "Not many of you around in the rift these days."

"I'm looking for Neb," I said. "And several of her people. Along with several from the Crow's Perch."

"The Queen of Crows is involved?" Tess asked.

I nodded.

"That bodes ill for all of us if she feels a need for retribution," Tess said. "She is sitting on an army who would follow her to hell and back."

"Let's not give anyone the opportunity to act rashly," Hiroyuki said.

Our three guides who had brought us through the caverns all exited without a word, leaving Tess alone with Hiroyuki and me, although I noticed a few guards lingering in the tunnels.

"Neb was here," Tess said. "She came to see me a few weeks ago. Said she was looking for some people. I'm guessing the Queen of Crows' people. We spoke about the attacks on the Lawless villages on the borders of the Vastness—I'm not using that stupid name. She's concerned that these attacks are the start of something awful. Or more awful, anyway. Something about the creatures of the rift being used to massacre populated areas. If that's true, it's changed a lot. I've lived a long time and never heard anything about *anyone* controlling creatures of the rift."

"Not controlled so much as weaponised," Hiroyuki said.

"How?" Tess asked.

"Boxes with primordial bone and rift-fused water," I said. "Crystallised blue water. The boxes are being used to attract tears. They make new ones in places they haven't been before, and they make them larger and more powerful. We've had some problems on Earth with them. We just don't know *where exactly* the water is being taken from."

"From the rivers to the east of here," Tess said. "Or from the north by the mining operations in the mountains. A lot of rift energy flows into the water there."

"Yes," I said, fully aware of everything that Tess was saying. "My guess is that Neb knows and didn't tell anyone."

"That sounds like Neb," Tess said with tone of someone who had dealt with Neb on more than one occasion.

"Did she tell you where she was going?" I asked.

"She went to see our new Overlords of Agency," Tess said, her words dripping with venom.

"What happened to you in Agency?" Hiroyuki asked.

"I was part of the council for the city. I wasn't so much overthrown as banished for asking questions they didn't like," Tess said through gritted teeth. "Apparently, the traders in the city believed they should be getting a bigger cut of the profits for less work. They managed to convince a lot of the guards that they would be richer if they agreed with them. There were protests about it. I was arrested. *Arrested.* For trying to keep my people safe, and for wanting the mountains of coin that these people earn to go towards making the lives of everyone in the city better. Do you know how much trade comes through this city? We're probably the second-biggest after Inaxia, certainly the largest Lawless settlement. Close to a hundred and fifty thousand people call Agency home, and that's not including the thousands who come here to trade from the farms and Lawless settlements throughout the rift."

"So, you were exiled bloodlessly?" I asked, hoping to bring Tess back from what was very quickly turning into a rage-filled ramble. Although I understood her need to vent.

"Thankfully, yes," Tess said. "Several of the council's most trusted advisors were exiled. People who only wanted the best for the city. You met Naomi and Lara already, and Kulan, the head of my personal bodyguard. No one was killed, but I think that was only because who wants to go trade in a city where they execute their leaders for paying the people who live there? Even so, since they've taken full control, they've implemented the pass that essentially bleeds dry anyone who doesn't have one. You get in without one, then you have to pay to get the pass. You can't leave until you have a pass. And if you don't have a pass, you're racking up a debt every single day. Eventually, you're given the choice to work off your debt. And then the city has you."

"What do these people do?" I asked. "For work, I mean."

"They work for the traders, doing deliveries, doing whatever shitty work needs doing," Tess said angrily. "It's basically imprisonment without the prison. People are forced into more debt to live here, to eat, to do anything. You're working to pay off something you're never going to be able to pay off. They only pick revenants, too, no riftborn."

"Why?" I asked.

"Riftborn can leave the rift," Tess said. "That's the only reason I've come up with. Someone escapes, flees the rift, and is never seen again. A revenant can be hunted all across the rift."

"What happened after Neb went to see the new leaders of the city?" I asked.

"She wanted information about the attacks, about anything that has happened in Mercy," Tess said.

"The village to the east?" I asked.

"Garrison," Tess corrected. "Not a village. It's a garrison. A hundred soldiers. Most of whom are loyal to Inaxia. No one has had contact with them for several months."

"Months?" Hiroyuki looked alarmed. "How can a garrison go dark for months?"

"It's a week's ride from here," Tess said. "And it's there to guard . . . Well, that's the question, isn't it?"

"I don't understand," I said. "What are they guarding?"

Tess shrugged. "No one knows. Neb sure seems to, though. Maybe she told the Overlords what she knows, but it's Neb, so who can tell."

"We need to speak to the people in charge of this city," I said. "No offence."

"None taken," Tess said. "I'll take back control one day. For now, we live down here, help people where we can. We're getting those who have become indebted out of the city. A few dozen so far. Hundreds left to go."

"*Hundreds?*" I asked. "Seriously?"

Tess nodded sadly. "Agency has become a different place in recent months. There's a fear to go out at night. Before the coup, there were a lot of new guards brought in from . . . Well, no one seems to know. Lots of the old guards suddenly found themselves indebted. Most of whom didn't back the new laws. They've had their passes revoked and aren't allowed out at night. There's a curfew in force."

"Your city has fallen to totalitarianism," Hiroyuki said. "I am not a fan."

"Even so, we need to talk to those in charge," I said. "Which one person rules?"

"There are six of them," Tess said.

"Nah, there's always one more powerful than the others," I said. "The one no one else wants to cross, that one who says things like 'Whatever the group thinks' when they mean themselves. Who is it?"

"Pierre Lebelle," Tess said without any hesitation. "He runs most of the weapons trade in the city, exports a lot to the local villages, exports a lot more to those settlements in the Vastness. He was rich back when he was a human on Earth. He's a riftborn. About eight hundred years old. He lived in Inaxia for a long time, made a lot of connections. When the French Revolution happened, he returned to Earth and made even more money making sure he was on the winning side. Also, it's said, he took money from those being executed in return for a guarantee that they'd be resurrected as revenants or riftborn."

"No one can guarantee that," Hiroyuki said.

"He's a scam artist," I said.

"Was," Tess said. "Now he's rich, powerful, and has the backing of more rich and powerful people. Specially Inaxian people. They want my city to be closer aligned to them."

"Of course they do," I said. "Can't have a Lawless City get too far above their station. It would look bad for everyone who lives in Inaxia."

"How do we go about seeing this man?" Hiroyuki asked.

"You're a Silver Phalanx, and you're a Guild member," Tess said. "Just go knock on his door."

"And the pass?" I asked.

"They're not going to make people of your station pay to get one," Tess said. "The fear of having an Ancient arrive at your door, asking what the fuck they're playing at? They're going to be as nice as pie to you. Lara will take you out of here, back up toward the city. She'll ride with you to the gates, explain who you both are, and the guards will fall over themselves to let you in. My people have passes, so they don't need to worry. I have a request, though."

"What is it?" I asked.

"I assume my old study in the underground of the city is probably ransacked at this point, but there are things inside I need to know if they've been found. Important things. They could turn the tide of overthrowing the corrupt government. Naomi and Kulan will go up through the ravine into the city through the underground complex beneath it, where they will wait for Lara. They know the area and will be safe, and before you say anything, no, you can't go with them. You need to be seen by the guard at the gate; you need to have them call Pierre to come see you. Get Lara into the city, and she can meet up with the others. No one gets hurt; I don't want a bloody coup. I just want Agency to be a symbol of hope, not one where the rich get richer and everyone else suffers."

"We'll need supplies," I said. I didn't know Tess, I didn't trust her, and I was fully aware that Hiroyuki and I weren't overburdened with other ideas. Until I could get into the city and talk to those who ruled it, hopefully getting a clearer picture of who I could trust, I was going to take the help.

"I'm certain Pierre will be happy to provide you with them," Tess said. "Probably labelled with a picture of his own face just to make sure everyone knows who's supplying you both. A word of warning: don't believe a damn thing he says. He's a liar, always been a liar, and even when he's telling you the truth, it's only because it means he benefits somehow."

"Thank you for your help," I said to Tess as she walked over to one of the holes in the chamber, reached inside, and rang a bell.

Tess turned back to Hiroyuki and me. "No bother. Just be careful. My city has gone to the dogs, and if Neb went to see Pierre and she's missing, it's not out of the realm of possibility that he was involved."

Lara returned, and we said our goodbyes before retracing our footsteps back to the lift and up to the exit outside, where our horses were already waiting for us.

Hiroyuki and I greeted our mounts, who both looked like they'd been well taken care of for the few hours we were below. I checked my saddle and reins, because you always check your own saddle when in company of people you don't know, and, when satisfied, climbed on up.

"We've got a few hours of riding," Lara said. "You're going into a nest of vipers. I hope you're both prepared for that."

"I've worked with Ancients," Hiroyuki said with a chuckle. "Vipers don't bother me anymore."

"And you?" Lara asked, turning in her seat to look over at me.

"Been dealing with vipers my whole life," I said thinking about what the congressman had told us about the Vipers being a dangerous gang of well-trained people. I pushed the thought aside and started Roar off at a trot.

CHAPTER NINETEEN

The ride through the rift toward the front gates of Agency felt sedate. We were heading toward something that might not be outwardly dangerous but had that insidious menace that creeps up on you. People who smile and welcome you with one hand while holding a dagger behind their back with the other. It sounded like Pierre was one of those people.

The city of Agency hadn't changed much from the outside since I'd last been there some time previously. The walls loomed over everything around it. They were a hundred feet tall, made from the dark stone dug from quarries by people who probably wished they'd stayed on Earth. There were ramparts on the top of the walls, where it was easy to spot the guards patrolling.

The glass cathedral, which looked like it was twisting as it went farther and farther up, was nearly four hundred feet tall. At the very top was a viewing platform so that you could look out over the land all around the city. Legend had it you could see Inaxia from up there, although I doubted that very much.

As we reached the kilometre-long bridge that led up to the city, it was clear from the six flying banners that adorned the outer walls that this was a different Agency to the one I'd last visited. Neither Tess nor her predecessor had needed to display their own personal banners from atop the walls of the city.

There were two main entrances to the city, one on either side of the oval-shaped settlement, many miles apart. Each one served as the only way into and out of the city for the vast majority of people. They were forty-foot-high archways, with a dozen armed guards checking everyone coming and going. Half a dozen more stood away from the rest, each with a bow or crossbow.

The line to get into the city wasn't particularly long, as each person was asked their name, reason for entering the city, and whether or not they had a pass already. Hiroyuki and I had been told by Lara what to expect on the way in. The majority of what she'd told us was to keep our heads down and not get involved in whatever we saw, no matter how bad it was.

When we were next in line, I got a good view of the opposite line waiting to leave, and that one was much longer, and the conditions were much more thorough. People and wagons were searched; passes were asked for and inspected like the guards didn't believe these people could have gotten one.

I saw no trouble, just a lot of nervous people being forced to belittle themselves as the guards used their considerable power to humiliate as they felt necessary. I remembered Lara's words to keep my head down; it wasn't something I found easy.

The guards themselves all wore leather armour, with chainmail over the top, which shimmered with rift energy. They had a sword at one hip and a dagger at the other. They wore helmets that reminded me of something you might see on a SWAT officer on the TV. A mixture of new and ancient pretty much summed the rift up.

The three of us were motioned to dismount, which we did wordlessly.

"Name," the guard said as he stepped up to me, his hand on the pommel of his sword.

"Lucas Rurik," I said, glancing around to see that Lara and Hiroyuki were having similar interactions.

"Don't mind about them," the guard snapped. "It's me you need to be paying attention to."

The man was a little taller than me but thinner, his shoulders almost a vertical slope. What he made up for in an imposing presence, he put into his lack of personality.

"Why are you here?" he asked.

"I'm here to see Pierre Lebelle," I told him. Lara had said be honest.

The guard laughed in my face. Right in my face. He actually leaned in to me and laughed into my fucking face, little bits of spittle landing on my cheek.

I badly wanted to break his face for him.

"And I want to fuck the Queen of England," he said.

"She's dead," I pointed out. "I think that's probably frowned on."

The man's jaw dropped open, and I inwardly cursed myself for being unable to keep my gob shut. "When?" he asked, all pretence of power gone.

"What year were you last on Earth?" I asked him.

"Eighteen forty-nine," he told me.

"Well, add about a hundred and eighty years, and you're in the ball-park," I said. "We've gone through maybe half a dozen monarchs at this point."

"Shit," he said, removing his helmet and bowing his head slightly. "Too soon."

I had no idea what to say to that.

"So, why are you here?" he asked me, but before I could respond, he said, "Yeah, you want to see Pierre. But that's not going to happen."

Another guard, this one large and imposing, placed a hand on my guard's shoulder. "Let him through; it's good."

The guard was about to ask why, but he saw the Silver Phalanx pendant around Hiroyuki's neck and nodded. "My lords and lady," he said with a respectful bow of his head.

The smell of the markets was the first thing that hit you in Agency. In total, they made up about a third of the entire city, with each end of Agency being where the vast majority plied their trade. The living quarters made up the next third, with most of that being low-class homes for workers. The centre of the city, raised high above everything else, was the gleaming white stone pyramid, called the Stone Eye, where the rulers of Agency—and those who worked for them—lived and worked. It was modelled on Inaxia, although on a considerably smaller scale.

The houses were mostly two or three storeys in height, with cream brick extras. They appeared to be modelled on the Roman style, with grey slate roofs in place of red. We passed by a wall where a man in a black hooded robe was painting something on it.

The guard shouted, and the man ran off, giving us a look at the graffitied word left behind: *Ahiram.*

"You see that?" I asked Hiroyuki.

"Oh, yes," he said. "No matter how much everyone keeps saying that Ahiram is a myth, these Promise Bearer psychopaths believe in, and that makes it dangerous to everyone, apparently even this far into the rift. We need to tread carefully here."

"Agreed," I said as the guard returned and caught us staring at the graffiti.

"Old tale from this part," the guard said. "Apparently, he's some old hero of the Vast Death. He conquered it or something. Honestly, one tale says he's nineteen feet high, so I'm disinclined to listen to them."

"He was a great man," Lara said, and if I was being honest, I'd completely forgot she was with us, as she'd been silent since we'd arrived in the city.

The guard shrugged that he didn't much care, and we were hurried along to the pyramid without any more explanations. There were steps leading up to the Stone Eye on three of the four sides, with the final side being a smooth slope for merchants to take their wagons up.

A pass was hastily thrust into my hand, and I looked down at the parchment that was about the size of my palm. It had my first name on it, and the words *City Pass* written in gold.

"Do not lose these," the guard who brought us into the city said. He bent down toward us and whispered, "Seriously."

I placed it in the zip-up pocket on the inside of my jacket and nodded to him that I would keep it safe.

The smorgasbord of scents in the marketplace, combined with the general loudness and feeling of being crushed by the number of people, did little to make me want to be anywhere but as far from there as possible. I'd lived in New York, London, and a variety of other massive cities, but this felt overwhelming.

I followed the guard, with Hiroyuki beside me and Lara several steps behind us, as we pushed through the crowd, although the guard shouting at people to move helped.

Once we were by the trading area of the city, it quietened down considerably. There were still the occasional shops, but they were for those who lived and worked in the city, not for traders.

I dropped back to walk with Lara, who didn't appear to care much if I was there or not. "So," I said, trying to sound as nonchalant as possible. "This Ahiram guy. Everyone keeps saying he's a myth, but you think differently."

Lara looked over at me and nodded once.

"Why?"

"Why what?" she asked.

"Why do you think differently? I've been told about the mythology; I've read the stories about how he allowed his power to corrupt him. He let himself go from hero to villain in his quest for power."

"That is not what happened," Lara said, her tone stone-hard.

"Tell me what happened," I said. "I'm genuinely curious."

"He tried to unite the rift," she said with warmth. "He brought us all peace, and then he was betrayed by his own people. His own family. They decided that they wanted the rift for themselves, that he should forever be banished from this place. But one day he will return to unite us all, to bring about a new paradise. And he will turn those who stand against him to ruin."

"So, it would be best to get on board with his plan."

Lara turned to look at me and smiled. "Maybe all of this is mythology, Mr. Rurik, but it's nice to *believe* in something. Nice to think that out there somewhere is someone who might actually make this place better. Don't you think?"

I nodded, unsure what to think about Lara. "You ever heard of the Promise Bearers?"

She shook her head. "Should I?"

"No," I said. "They're . . . Actually, I'm not sure what they are apart from dangerous."

"If I hear about them, I'll make sure to let you know," she said, and walked away, letting me know the conversation was over. She would be one to keep an eye on.

I walked back up toward where the guard was and said, "You ever heard of Tess Macallister?"

The guard bristled but nodded once.

"Not a fan?" I asked.

"We're . . . We don't talk about her," he said, keeping his gaze straight ahead. "The city is better off without her. Without her influence. Those were dark days."

It was pretty clear that conversation was over too, so I fell back to walk beside Hiroyuki. "I don't think Tess was telling us the whole truth," I whispered.

"Yeah, I mentioned her to the guard, and he did not like it," Hiroyuki said.

It was nearly an hour's walk before we reached the centre of the city of Agency, the bottom of the Stone Eye.

I looked up at the monstrosity a hundred feet above us and wished I didn't have to climb that many steps. I assumed they were there for the same reason there are so many damn steps in Inaxia: to make sure that by the time you reach the summit, you're either too knackered to be any kind of threat, or you've had time to consider your place.

"I do not like this Pierre already," Hiroyuki whispered when we were halfway up the stairs.

By the time we'd made it to the top, I was ready to believe that Pierre was guilty of anything and everything he'd ever been accused of.

We were taken through an outer ring, which was made up of Roman-style columns—also in white stone—and through a courtyard, where there were a number of gardeners working on the multitude of colourful flowerbeds. In the centre of the courtyard was the Glass Cathedral.

I looked up at the magnificent structure of blacked-out glass. However awe-inspiring it looked from outside the city walls, it didn't do justice to the level of intricate detail that had been used in its creation.

The doors to the cathedral were open, and two guards, both wearing black fatigues and boots that made them look like modern-day soldiers, came to meet us.

Both wore black helmets with red stripes down the middle that were more akin to what motorcycle riders might wear. They removed their helmets and revealed that they were wearing balaclavas underneath. The level of weirdness about the whole thing made me want to shake my head in disbelief. One was well over six feet tall, while the other barely broke five feet, but other than that, it was impossible to know what either of them looked like.

"You are dismissed," one of the new guards said to our guide.

"Thank you for your time," the second guard said.

The guard nodded, turned to us, and nodded, then walked away without a word.

The two cathedral guards waited until we were alone before they removed their balaclavas. "Welcome to the Cathedral," the tall young man with brown skin said.

The second, shorter guard had their head shaved around the edges, with slightly longer hair on top. I couldn't have told you from looking at them whether they were male or female, although considering it was none of my business, I didn't suppose it mattered.

"Grand Master Lebelle will see you now," the shorter guard said, motioning for us to follow them.

"*Grand Master?*" I asked, and could have sworn I heard Hiroyuki chuckle, which was masked by a sudden coughing fit and a glare from the taller of the two guards. I looked back at Lara, who had an expression of disgust on her face. Hopefully, she'd be able to keep it together for long enough to not get us all into trouble.

Once Hiroyuki stopped sounding like he was going to cough up a lung, we followed the first guard through the rest of the courtyard and into the cathedral itself.

The interior foyer had what looked like a marble floor, with high ceilings and two receptionists who sat behind an almost-black wooden desk. They both stood as we walked by them, bowing their heads to us as if they thought we were the kind of people for whom that kind of thing was perfectly normal. We weren't, or at least I wasn't, and I found it weird.

We walked up a set of steps to a floor which looked down on the reception area.

"There are elevators here," the smaller guard said, taking us through a set of double doors, where one of three large elevators sat in an open chamber. I looked up at the vastness above me. It was high enough and had just enough light bouncing around carefully placed panels that it made me look away. Vertigo wasn't something I usually suffered from, but looking up the chamber of the cathedral certainly did me no favours in that regard.

We stepped onto one of the lifts, and the taller guard pressed a button. The floor of the lift lit up in a spider's web of blues and purples, which merged together as the rift energy moved beneath our feet, bathing all of us in an ethereal glow as the lift began to slowly trundle up the chamber.

The glass panels on one side of the chamber gave a spectacular view of the surrounding area of the Stone Eye and the city as a whole. The higher we went, the more of the city I could look out over. And as we reached our destination and the lift stopped, we were hundreds of feet above the ground level were people lived and worked. I saw the bridge outside of the city, the lands that Hiroyuki and I had ridden though. It was breathtaking.

"You coming?" Lara asked me.

I nodded and turned away from the view.

"Are you okay?" she asked as we followed the two guards and Hiroyuki, the latter of whom was busy looking around at everything, taking it all in. Presumably in case we needed to get out quickly.

I nodded again and stepped out of the lift chamber and into an open room that took up the entire floor. A large table sat in the centre, with a dozen chairs on each side but none at either end. There were more guards, a dozen in all, stood to attention around the circumference of the room, but there was no one else there. We walked along the dark tiled floor, our footsteps echoing until we reached the far end of the room, where the glass wall slid aside to reveal a large balcony.

The balcony floor itself was not, thankfully, made of glass but of black metal. The five-foot-high railings were made of glass, though, with gold etched along the top. The balcony stretched around the sides of the cathedral, the edges disappearing from view as it circled around the large building. The balcony had a little flower garden that divided the section we stood in from one farther along.

In our section was a large white sofa that had more throws and cushions on it than was probably necessary. A table sat in front of it, adorned with a variety of pastries, meats, breads, and fruits. There were pitchers of various liquids that were cold enough to leave trails of condensation. The combined aroma made my stomach grumble, reminding me that I hadn't eaten anything in several hours.

"I didn't see this from below," I said to no one in particular, while trying to ignore my complaining stomach.

"A trick of the building," a voice said in a French accent.

I turned as the doors opened and a tall, slender man with long white beard, tanned skin, and an air of power stepped onto the balcony. He wore grey robes with orange accents on the sleeves, and a red belt around his waist, along with a pair of sandals. He looked, for all the will in the world, like someone cosplaying Gandalf but not quite getting the outfit right.

"Please do take a seat," he said, motioning to the sofa. "And help yourself to any of the food and drink you'd like. When I heard that someone from the Silver Phalanx was here to see me, I thought it best to prepare something."

"Pierre Lebelle?" Hiroyuki asked.

Pierre nodded.

"The Grand Master himself," Lara said, her voice tight, her expression completely devoid of emotion.

"Yes," Pierre said, his eyes flickering from Hiroyuki to Lara and then over to me as I grabbed a croissant the size of my head and tried not to get covered in flaky pastry.

"And you two are?" Pierre asked Lara and me.

"I'm their guide," Lara said quickly. "I brought them here through the rift."

"Ah," Pierre said, almost visibly deciding Lara was no longer worth talking to.

"And you, sir?" he asked me.

I swallowed the mouth full of delicious pastry, removed my guild medallion from around my neck, and showed him.

His eyes bulged. "Raven Guild," he said, almost breathlessly. "You're the last Raven."

"Most people call me Lucas," I said, taking another bite of croissant. Hiroyuki could do the talking; I was hungry. And hungry Lucas tends to be short on playing nice with idiots in positions of power.

"We're here to find Neb," Hiroyuki said, regaining Pierre's attention as the *Grand Master* waved away the guard, including those who had brought us up to him.

"Neb?" Pierre said as thought testing the word for the first time. "She came here maybe a week ago. She spent the night and went on her way the next day."

"And what did she talk to you about?" Hiroyuki asked.

"She wanted to talk about the attacks on Lawless settlements throughout the rift," Pierre said. "I told her it was a dangerous time but that I had no idea who was responsible. I explained that we have increased the guard here and sent out more patrols into the area around this city, and so far, we've had no major issues."

"It's too big," I said, pouring myself a drink of what turned out to be almost ice-cold water. I took a swig and sat back on the sofa, feeling content.

"What is?" Pierre asked.

"This city is too big," I repeated. "Too many people, too many guards, only two main entrances and exits, easy visibility on the walls. It's too big, too well defended. The people attacking small villages and farms aren't about to send their troops here to get slaughtered."

Pierre practically puffed out his chest with pride.

"You ever heard of someone by the name of Ahiram?" I asked him.

"Old mythological tale; why?" Pierre asked.

"Saw someone writing the name on a wall; the guard weren't thrilled about it," I mentioned, almost as though it didn't matter. I didn't want to mention how often I'd heard that name recently, although the look in Pierre's eyes told me it mattered a great deal.

"I've been part of the council in charge of this city for several years now. Since then, we have brought the city of Agency to unheard-of wealth and importance within the rift," Pierre said. "The last . . . maybe year or so, we've heard mention of a group of people who did not like that their control over the city was removed to ensure the interests of the many were listened to. Since then, we've found several people writing that name on walls within the city. We don't know why."

Lara yawned. "My apologies, but is there somewhere I could freshen up? It's been a long ride."

"Of course, my dear," Pierre said. "Tell my guard just beyond this wall; they will take you to a bathroom. Take your time."

When we were alone again, I said, "We heard rumours that you force people into debt to pay back their passes to leave the city."

Pierre looked genuinely horrified, which meant either he should be awarded an Oscar at any moment or he actually had no idea what the hell I was talking about. That didn't bode well for whatever Tess had told us.

"It is true that it's free to enter the city to trade or work," Pierre said. "But that you require a pass to walk the streets at night."

"So, you don't force your people into indebted slavery?" Hiroyuki asked.

"Good grief, who told you that?" Pierre said, looking between the two of us like he was a rabbit caught between two exceptionally large wolves.

"You know of a Tess Macallister?" I asked.

Pierre's face clouded. "She was banished from this city. She's a criminal, and we discovered she was making and selling weapons to the highest bidder."

"Hiroyuki," I said softly. "I think he's telling the truth."

Hiroyuki nodded.

"Pierre Lebelle," I said. "I think you need to tell us what the hell is going on in your city and how it involves whatever Neb is doing."

"I genuinely don't . . ." he began before the wall opened and Lara returned. She had a smile on her face, and her hands were balled into fists, which she opened, and vines erupted out of her palms. One struck out toward Pierre, who was now on his feet, but Hiroyuki was up and pushing him aside in a moment. The thorn-covered vine slammed into Hiroyuki, punching through his armour as if it wasn't even there.

CHAPTER TWENTY

The vine that had come out of Lara's hands smashed through the glass barrier at the end of the balcony, Unfortunately, Hiroyuki was still attached to said vine, and as his feet dangled into the air, Lara retracted the vine, letting him fall hundreds of feet to the ground.

I turned to smoke and flew out of the balcony, down toward a barely conscious Hiroyuki. I reached him, wrapped my smoke around him, and managed to slow our descent to what was, in the end, an unpleasant but survivable landing.

"Get people up to the balcony," I screamed at the guard. "And get this man help."

The two guards from earlier rushed over to us. I looked down at my friend. His shoulder and side were covered in blood, and his face had an unhealthy shine to it. I turned to smoke and flew up toward the balcony, just as more glass tumbled down toward me.

I had almost reached it when a crossbow ploughed through my smoke form, the rift-energy-treated arrow forcing my smoke apart and causing agony to course through my disembodied form. The bolt had come from below me, but whoever fired it was going to have to wait.

I metaphorically gritted my teeth and continued on in my smoke form, managing to re-form myself on the balcony to find three dead guards, all of which had pieces of vine punctured through their chests and heads, but no Lara or Pierre. There was a shriek from inside the cathedral, and I drew my spear and took a step toward it before dropping to one knee as the world spun.

Goddamned rift-energy arrows. It wasn't permanent, I'd had plenty of rift-energy-enhanced blades go through my smoke form over the years, but occasionally, it can cause me a few moments of dizziness.

A second shriek was followed up with a cry for help.

I forced myself to my feet, tightened the grip on my spear, and vaulted over the partially damaged couch before making my way into the cathedral.

There were a lot of dead guards. At least six by my quick count as I ran through the large room to the lifts and caught Lara and Pierre in time as they travelled up one. Lara fired spines at me, which were easy to dodge but made a horrible decaying smell as they hit the wall behind me. Poison.

Another lift was just going down when I turned to smoke and moved up the chamber after the would-be assassin and her captive. I stayed below the lift itself, not wanting to try and dodge a bunch of spines.

"Just fucking move," Lara said, followed by a grunt of pain from Pierre.

There was a sound like someone being hit.

"Why are you doing this?" Pierre demanded, and I was quite impressed that he still maintained enough dignity to not sound like he was terrified. And I doubted anyone with a working brain would criticise him if he were scared.

"You took this city from its rightful ruler," Lara said as footsteps told me that the pair had left the lift.

"She's a fucking criminal!" Pierre shouted.

I moved up around the lift and re-formed on the platform beside it. Lara couldn't possibly think she was going to escape this city by going up, unless she suddenly evolved the ability to grow wings, or a bunch of giant eagles were up there, waiting for her.

Pierre had been taken to the very top floor of the cathedral, which was not only a small floor but, judging from the lack of fighting ahead, had no guards stationed there. I left the lift chamber and found myself in a long glass-surrounded corridor with one door at the far end a good fifty feet in front of me, and that was it.

Lara stood on the opposite side of the glass door, with Pierre wrapped in vines, on his knees beside her. She glared at me from beyond the glass, placed her hand against it, and fired a spine into the glass, but it was too thick to do anything but crack a little.

"You can't get to us," Lara said, almost manically.

"Tess wasn't overthrown, was she?" I shouted as I walked down the corridor, my voice echoing around me.

Lara continued to glare at me.

"Let me guess: the guard and merchants here got a little bit fed up of her lining her own pockets?" I asked. "Maybe a few people who disagreed with her started to go missing."

"She's practically a cult leader," Pierre shouted, only to receive the back of Lara's hand across his cheek, leaving a nasty-looking cut in its wake.

"A cult?" I asked. I was halfway along the corridor now; I just had to keep Lara's attention on me, and hopefully I could figure out a way to rescue Pierre. "Tess led a *cult?*"

"We were not a cult," Lara snapped. "We waited for *his* return."

"Funny thing about cults," I said. "Lots of them are waiting for someone's return."

"We're not a fucking cult," Lara practically screamed at me; spit covered the glass in front of her.

"You'd be amazed at how many cult members don't actually think they're in a cult," I said conversationally. "Have you had to get branded, or a tattoo, or something? Maybe you all chant together about the good times, or do you sacrifice goats?"

"Fuck you," Lara said, stabbing her finger against the glass. "This weasel and his . . . *cabal* took our city, and we're going to take it back."

"*Your* city?" I asked. "You mean Tess's city, I assume."

"No, Tess said it belongs to us all," Lara told me. "But this piece of shit only wants it for himself." Lara smashed her knee into the side of Pierre's head and the man went limp.

"Tess sent you with us to kill him?" I asked, reaching the door.

Lara turned back to me. "I broke the mechanism; you can't get in here."

"You never answered my question," I told her. "Tess sent you with us to kill him."

"Throw him from the heavens," Lara said. "Her exact words."

"You hurt my friend," I said, letting my anger out in my words.

Lara sneered. "He shouldn't have dived in front of this piece of shit. You're both just propping up a system that needs to be brought low. The Silver Phalanx turn a blind eye to whatever injustices their *masters* commit. And the old Guilds might as well be the secret police. I won't lose sleep over one less of either of you."

I placed a hand against the glass door, my smoke curling up from my fingers, probing the door, trying to find a crack.

Lara dragged a still semi-conscious, vine-wrapped Pierre across the terrace to the edge. "You think it'll kill him? You think you can get to me before I throw him over?"

I retracted the smoke. "You want to talk, right?" I asked. "You want people to know why you're doing this. Surely, you know you're not getting out of here alive."

"I'm not alone," she said.

I remembered the arrow that hit me as I flew up to the balcony. "How many of you are there?"

"Too many for you to stop," she said.

"You know they tried this in Inaxia a few years back," I said. "They nearly all got killed. The Blessed. You remember them? Ring a bell?"

Lara's eyes blazed with . . . something . . . determination, maybe.

"Is that what you call yourselves?" I asked.

"The Blessed were idiots," she snapped.

"Wait, *you're* the Promise Bearers," I said as the sound of fighting filtered its way up toward me from the lift chamber nearby. "Ah, you think that Ahiram is going to come back and save you all. He's a fucking story."

If in doubt, make the crazy person angry enough to focus on me and hopefully do something stupid.

"Ahiram is a hero," Lara said, almost beaming with pride. "He will return to us and save us all."

I took a few steps back from the door. "Save you all from what?"

Lara waved around her. "What do you think?"

I took a few further steps back. "And how is he going to return? Where is he?"

"Exiled," Lara said. "But when we need him most, he will return and take his seat as our leader once again. He will lead us into the light once again."

"He's a Phoenician," I said, remembering what Gabriel had told me what felt like months ago.

Lara nodded.

"You make him sound like the myth of King Arthur," I said. "But at the end of the day, he was just a story—how do you know your 'hero' is even real?"

"He is our—"

"Your man is slipping," I said, pointing to Pierre.

Lara's head moved, and I turned to smoke, billowed forward as fast as possible, re-formed, and hit the glass with my hand. The former exploded, and the latter didn't feel too good about it. I rushed into Lara, tackling her as her vines uncoiled from around Pierre, leaving him lying on the glass-bottomed terrace.

A large thorn shot up out of her palm, cutting across my cheek, which burned from the touch, but I turned partially to smoke and pushed it down her throat and nose into her lungs, until she panicked from being unable to breathe. I left the smoke there for a few seconds, until the oxygen finally cut out and she passed out.

I removed the smoke, re-formed myself, and dragged Pierre back inside the cathedral, resting him up against the corridor wall beyond. The sounds of fighting had become more intense, and I didn't want to have to carry him back down through a war zone if I didn't need to.

"You should have let us kill him," Lara said, now on all fours as she coughed and spluttered.

"You didn't stay out long," I said, frustrated, moving back toward her. "I really don't want to kill you. I will, you understand; I just don't want to. Is there a cure for whatever shit you pumped into my friend?"

"Bite me," she snarled, spitting in my direction.

I held the tip of my spear under her jaw, the blade touching her neck enough to draw a bead of blood, which fell onto the glass floor. "Antidote," I said. "You don't get asked again."

"He'll be fine," Lara said. "He's riftborn; he can just go into his embers and heal. The venom slows down my prey. You going to kill me or what?"

"You brought Pierre up here for a reason; why not just throw him over the edge?" I asked.

"He needed to confess to his crimes," she said, nodding to an amplifier that was at the edge of the terrace.

"He gives speeches to the whole city from up here," I said.

"He is a *parasite* on our fair city," Lara said. "Everyone will hear that Tess was overthrown. Everyone will hear that we are to be saved, that those who sided with Pierre should be brought low and destroyed."

"The city increased security because of your stupidity," I said. "You're not saving people who *want* saving; you're just trying to reclaim something that was never yours, and you don't seem to care that a lot of people would have died. You're either brainwashed or delusional. Maybe both."

Lara did something approximating a shrug. "They would have died on their feet instead of their knees."

"You appear to be on *your* knees," I explained.

"Remove the spear and let's see who ends up on the ground," Lara said with a lot of conviction for someone in her position.

"Tess left you here to die," I said, removing the spear from under her neck. "I don't plan on giving her what she wants. Don't make me fight you; it's not a fight you'll win."

"I will not be taken prisoner," Lara said, and threw herself to the side, jumping up and over the balcony.

"Well, that was unpleasant," I said, and watched as Lara hit the ground several hundred feet below us.

I turned back to Pierre, who was awake but still seated. "You saved me," he said.

"I did," I told him.

"And my assailant?"

"Squishy," I said. "She jumped over the edge. I'm pretty sure that even a riftborn is going to need years inside their embers for that one."

"What did she want?" Pierre asked, offering me his hand so I could help him up.

Once Pierre was on his feet, I slapped him on the shoulder. "You dead, I think. To have the people rise up and fight against their supposed oppressors."

"We're not oppressing *anyone*," Pierre said. "Tess was a criminal. She was exiled because she a criminal, using her gang to make herself rich at the expense of everyone else in the city. And then there were . . . other things."

"Other things?" I asked. "Actually, we'll get back to that. Stay here; let me check what's happening below."

"Tess was selling weapons to the highest bidder," Pierre said as I started to walk away, stopping me in my tracks. "We had a workshop in the dungeon, and we found multiple devices, most of which we destroyed, but a few we thought were too dangerous to meddle with."

"And also because they might have come in useful, yes?"

Pierre looked away, which more than likely meant yes.

"Did Neb go to see Tess?" I asked.

Pierre nodded. "I think so. I showed Tess's workshop to Neb. She wanted proof of the things Tess had done. She was furious. I think she felt betrayed because Tess had once been her friend. The morning after, Neb was gone. Just gone. I don't know where she went."

"You should have gone after Neb," I said.

"And give Tess's insane idiots a chance to get back in the city?" Pierre nodded and looked up at me. "They weren't a cult as such, but they treated her like she was some sort of god amongst them. She believes in nothing but coin and power, but they believe in whatever she tells them to do. You've seen how that works out.

"I would have gotten around to telling you, but . . . You want the truth? This place is under siege from Tess and her terrorists. That's why the security increase. They live in the ravine and we've sent people to try and get them, but they never come back. They attack our troops, our merchants. We asked for Inaxian help and were practically laughed at. Tess worked with another woman; a lot of the stuff in Tess' workshop was written by her."

"Who?" I asked, hoping I was wrong.

"Some of the work is signed by a Callie Mitchell," Pierre said. "I showed some to Neb; she said that if you ever arrived, we were to let you see. Which, obviously, we would have done sooner if people hadn't tried to kill me."

"Tess had Callie's research," I said. "Where is it?"

"Under lock and key," Pierre said. "It's all in the workshop still; Neb said it shouldn't be moved. Said it could be booby-trapped. I can take you there."

"Tess told me that she was sending people to the city to try and reclaim stuff from her underground study," I said. "It seems like Lara was never meant to let them in, just kill you. I'd send people to check that everything is where it should be."

Pierre nodded.

"I'm going to check on my friend, and then I want to see everything Tess had here," I told him.

"Not a problem."

"*Old Guilds,*" I said almost to myself.

"What?" Pierre asked.

"Lara said, '*The old Guilds.*'" It implies the existence of new Guilds."

Pierre thought about it. "I guess it does."

The lift reached our floor and two individuals got out, both wearing all-black leather armour and a black mask with charcoal-grey slashes across them. "They look like Talon masks," I said, taking a few steps forward to put myself between them and Pierre. "But that would mean you two are Talons. And I just don't see that being the case."

The two newcomers shared a glance before looking back at me and drawing their swords. Neither individual spoke.

"We could do this the easy way," I pointed out. "No one has to die."

Both newcomers put themselves in attack stances.

"Hard way it is," I said. "Hope you said goodbye to anyone who gives a shit about you."

Spines shot out of the hand of the hooded assassin closest to me, but I was already in my smoke form, moving around them, preparing to strike.

One of the assassins tossed a glass bauble onto the floor, which exploded, billowing blue gas all around, and causing me to instantly re-form as it touched me. I staggered forward, tripped, and crashed to the floor, rolling over and coming back onto my feet as the two assassins turned back to me.

That's new, I thought to myself, rolling my shoulders as I tightened the grip on my spear once again. "The *really* hard way."

I darted toward the nearest assassin, striking out with the tip of my spear, which was batted away by the sword of the assassin before they jumped back out of range. The second assassin took the initiative and sprang toward me, but I was expecting it and rolled under the swipe.

Unfortunately, I was now in between the two assassins.

With a hastily drawn dagger, I blocked and parried blade strikes from both sides, using my short spear to keep one attacker at bay while deflecting the other with the dagger as I tried to close the gap between us. It was an exhausting way to fight and not exactly what would be recommended when training, but then there's no training to teach you how to fight two people in an enclosed space, with no access to your powers. An oversight, to be sure.

The two assassins were good fighters, and I was tagged more than one across the arms and hands, and, on one occasion, a nasty cut along my ribs. Thankfully, I gave as good as I got, and it wasn't long before all three of us were bleeding from a variety of wounds.

Pierre was about as useful as a glass hammer at this point, and after a particularly nasty wound across my cheek, which made me taste blood, I began to wonder if it was too late to throw the useless bastard off the terrace myself.

The assassin on my left was more daring than the one on the right, the latter of whom tended to opt for more-defensive attacks and quick movements away. The one on the left wanted to get close, get physical, and overwhelm me. I could practically hear the satisfaction as it came off them in waves with every landed blow.

I took a step toward the assassin on my right, who darted back, as I knew they would. It left my left side open, and the assassin on my left took the bait. They darted in fast and low, trying to land a strike with their sword to my kidney. I'd planned for it, moving at the last second to show my back to the assassin on my right and drive my spear tip up into the chest and throat of the left assassin.

The assassin's eyes bulged in what I suspected was a mixture of surprise and horror, but a fraction of a second later, I'd removed the spear, spun around the mortally wounded assassin, and, when I was behind them, drove the blade into the back of their skull. The primordial bone in the blade made sure that nothing was surviving that.

I took a moment to move back, the spear making an unpleasant noise as it left the assassin's skull. The assassin fell to the ground. It wasn't like in the movies, where the dying person drops to their knees and pitches forward; this was standing to lying in one motion. No dramatics necessary.

The remaining assassin stepped over the corpse and flew at me with a fury I hadn't expected. I deflected blow after blow, moving around the confines of the long corridor we were in, until they let their anger overtake them and they got too close. I used my arms and chest to wrap and pin their sword arm up against their chest before head-butting them on the bridge of their nose, which crunched from the force. I kicked them back, leaving them open for a stab to their throat with my spear. I twisted the spear free as blood poured from the wound.

They grabbed their neck with increasingly blood-slick hands and collapsed to the ground, the hate in their eyes replaced with fear. They were dead a few seconds later.

I looked over at Pierre. "You good?" I asked.

Pierre looked down at the two dead assassins and back up to me. "Thank you," he said.

I dragged the mask off the closest body, hoping for something that might identify them, but didn't recognise the man beneath. The second face didn't jog any recognition either, but a medallion fell out from beneath their armour, and I picked it up, turning it over. It was sized like my own Raven Guild medallion. It depicted a snake, its fangs bared, coiled around a dagger.

The old Guild.

I checked the other body and found an identical medallion. "Shit. Looks like someone made a new Guild."

CHAPTER TWENTY-ONE

I took Pierre down in the lift, the man gaining some semblance of composure on the way. To be fair to him, I got the impression that people trying to murder him wasn't exactly an everyday occurrence.

I held the chains of the two snake medallions in one hand, the medallions themselves dangling free, occasionally clattering together when I walked. I wanted to throw them off the damn terrace, but that wasn't going to get the answers I needed.

I wondered why Lara hadn't been wearing a medallion. Maybe because she was a part of the Promise Bearers, a part of the church, and the Vipers were something else entirely. The idea of having two groups of psychopaths to deal with wasn't an endearing one.

Pierre had, not unexpectedly, known nothing about the new Guild. I was going to need to find Tess or her friends and ask them some very pointed questions. Not least about why they were such lying pieces of shit with an obvious death wish.

It turned out that the Vipers were a little bit more than some random gang. They were, at least they appeared to be, the Guild I'd just killed members of. What the hell was Neb involved in?

The lift stopped, and the thoughts of my injured friend came to my mind. Hiroyuki was my first port of call. I left the chamber before Pierre, who did not seem in any hurry to find out if anyone else with a sharp object was waiting for him.

I walked back into the large room, where several more dead guards lay, accompanied by people in normal daily clothes. There were no more masked assassins, which I was thankful for; despite wanting to punch a few more people, I wasn't sure I actually had the energy to do so.

Hiroyuki was still on the balcony, although he had two people knelt beside him, and two guards stood to attention close by.

"They dead?" he asked, looking clammy, his face awash with sweat.

I nodded.

"Saw Lara make her exit," he said. "Can't say I feel bad about it. Any chance you got an antidote for whatever this shit is?"

"She said you'll heal in the embers," I told him.

"If I go in there, I'm useless to everyone for weeks," Hiroyuki said bitterly.

"And if you stay out?" I asked, looking over at the bearded man who knelt beside my friend.

"We can make him comfortable," he said. "And I don't think he's dying. His riftborn physiology simply won't allow it, the same way those cuts on your arms and face look healed."

I touched where Lara's thorns had torn my face; it still stung. "So, what happens if he doesn't go back into the embers?"

"He'll eventually get better," a middle-aged female doctor said as she passed Hiroyuki something to drink. "We're talking a few weeks. At best."

"Great, so it's a few weeks here, with my insides feeling like they're on fire, or a few weeks getting back from the embers," Hiroyuki said, making neither option sound like one he wanted to be a part of.

"You saved my life," Pierre said, dropping to his knees by Hiroyuki. "If you choose to stay, we will put you in the finest rooms we have."

"We need to get a message back to Earth somehow," I said. "Ji-hyun and her people are coming through from Earth in under a week, and we have assassins and now a new Guild. They need to know what's going on."

"What?" Hiroyuki asked, a little more forcefully than he'd probably meant to, considering the immediate wince.

I dropped the medallions onto his lap. "Took these from two arseholes who tried to kill me. They had this bauble that, when shattered, put out blue smoke; I couldn't use my powers."

"We've seen those used," the female doctor said. "They toss them at patrols before attacking. We've had more than a few injuries since Tess was overthrown."

"Pierre, did you not think that was information that might have been *useful*?" I asked. "Oh, by the way, Tess is some kind of arms dealer and I'm about to be taken to her study to find out what she was involved in. Apparently, Callie Mitchell was involved."

Hiroyuki let out a soft moan. "Just great. Even in death, she's a monster."

"We need to strike back at Tess," Pierre said.

I didn't disagree. "They have a hidden maze, underground caverns, your typical evil villain–style lair. Although I doubt they'll be happy to see any of you, so you might be in for a fight if you try. Either that or they're waiting for you to take an army there, and they'll slip back in here."

"I hate that woman," Pierre said, his voice dripping with venom. "I knew that eventually they'd try to kill me or the others who worked together to banish her after we discovered her corruption, but it seemed like they were happy to attack our fringes. Whenever we caught one of them, they'd take their own lives. They really are little more than a god-damned cult."

"Yeah, I got that when Lara swan-dove over the side of the balcony hundreds of feet in the air," I said. "What happened to the body?"

"It's being dealt with," the male doctor said. "She didn't survive. Even if she'd been riftborn and dragged into her embers, she may not have survived. Besides, there wasn't much left of her head."

"And that was an image I didn't need," Hiroyuki said.

"Right, are you staying or going?" I asked him. "You can't come with me; don't argue. You're hurt, you look like death warmed up, and frankly, we both know you're going to do yourself more harm than good if you pretend you're fine."

"You have a terrible bedside manner," Hiroyuki said.

"You want me to wipe your brow for you and tell you you're a big, strong boy?" I asked him.

Hiroyuki laughed, winced, coughed, and eventually told me to fuck off.

"You're going after Tess, yes?" he asked.

"She was the last person to see Neb," I said. "So, yes, I'm going to go find her and ask her *nicely* about what happened. And then we're going to talk about a new Guild that shouldn't exist."

"I always wondered why new Guilds weren't created," the female doctor said.

"It was agreed upon," Hiroyuki said. "The Ancients created the Guilds thousands of years ago. No more. That was the promise they all made." He picked up the medallions. "Snake Guild, Viper Guild, Python Guild, I'm not really sure which one they're going for here. I don't know much about snakes."

I took the medallion off Hiroyuki. "Can I have a moment alone with my friend, please?" I asked.

Everyone left and I took a seat on the cold tiled floor beside Hiroyuki. "This is bad," he said. "All of this is bad."

I nodded. "New Guild, Neb missing, blue-water boxes that attract tears, and a group of people who *really* want Pierre dead. The man has all of the defensive capabilities of a chipmunk. You really going to be okay?"

"That's what they tell me," he said. "I can't stay here, though, can I? If they come for Pierre and his people, I'm going to be no use at all."

"You could be in the embers for an unknown amount of time," I said. "Two weeks to heal here, might be a few days in the embers normally, but with them being utterly knackered, it could be a month."

"There's no good option here," he said. "If they have a rift-walker, I could get back to Ji-hyun, tell her everything, then dump myself in my embers for two weeks. At least everyone would be informed."

"I'll check," I said, patting him on the shoulder. "Just as I was getting used to having you around."

I left Hiroyuki alone and went back into the cathedral, where the doctors and Pierre waited. "Do you have a rift-walker?" I asked. As a species, rift-walkers were rare, but I hoped that a city the size of Agency would have a few.

A woman I hadn't seen before nodded. "I am. They asked me to come see you. You need my help?"

"Excellent; can you take Hiroyuki back to Earth?" I asked. "He has information that the people who are coming here to help are going to want. The embers are, to put it mildly, fucked. That extends to rift-walkers creating tears."

"The constant tears in the sky is the cause, I assume," Pierre said.

I nodded. "One problem is that the rift-walker who goes through to Earth can come back, but you're going to be exhausted for a few days. No power for maybe a week. Like I said, fucked."

"He needs to go to his embers," the female doctor said.

"He will," I told her. "But Ji-hyun needs this information. The Promise Bearers, they're on Earth, too, and if they're all prepared like Lara was, there could be trouble. Also, they need to know there's a new Guild."

The two doctors shared a glance, and the rift-walker nodded. "I can do it, but he's not going to feel good."

"Yeah, we've been through a rift-walker's tear before," I said. "Can't say it's a fun time. Any more attacks reported?"

Pierre shook his head. "Apparently, they expected to get to me through you. I've sent guards to check on the other rulers of the city, though. They weren't all in the cathedral when the attack happened."

"You said earlier about how Tess was selling weapons," I said. "Any chance she was making boxes with rift-fused water in it? Or those damn baubles with the smoke in?"

Pierre nodded. "Very possible; the doctor here examined all the material we found, so she may have a better idea than me what Tess was trying to do".

The doctor looked at me seriously. "Tess had grabbed everything she could before she was forced to flee. We still don't know *how* she escaped. It's assumed a secret passage in the dungeon, but we haven't been able to find it."

I considered it. "Can someone show me?"

The male doctor nodded.

"I'll take your friend now," the rift-walker said.

I thanked them all and went back to Hiroyuki. "You're being taken back to Earth," I told him. "Sorry."

"I look forward to feeling even worse," he said with a wry smile. "You look angry."

"I am," I admitted. "They hurt you. They pulled some inexplicable power-draining smoke on me. And if they've done something to Neb . . ."

Hiroyuki smiled. "When you find whoever is behind all of this, and we both know it's probably not Tess, punch them in the face for me."

I offered Hiroyuki my hand, which he grasped. "Of course," I told him. "Be safe. I'll see you soon."

"Be safe, Lucas," Hiroyuki said. "Try not to get into more trouble than we're already in."

I laughed. "Yeah, that's not going to happen. No point in trying."

Hiroyuki laughed, coughed, sputtered, and called me a *goddamned bastard*, but it was done with warmth, so I was fine with it.

I left my friend alone with the rift-walker and found the male doctor waiting for me at the exit to the large chamber, along with the two guards who had taken us into the cathedral. Both of them looked like they'd gone several rounds with a large, angry rhino.

"How many attackers were there?" I asked.

"Half a dozen," the taller of the two guards said. "But they had these smoke bombs that stopped us using our powers. Made everything a lot more complicated."

"How can *they* use their powers still?" I asked.

"We don't know," the guard said, and his anger bubbled to the surface for a second before being sucked back down. "Many of the people who live in the rift aren't used to fighting without powers. Even guards don't get a lot of training in it. We lost some good people here today because of that oversight."

"You okay?" I asked the shorter of the two guards, who had a look of barely contained rage.

"No," they said, "but I might be once I find out who did all this and beat the shit out of them".

I smiled. These were my kind of people. "Let's go see these dungeons, then," I said.

I followed them back to the lift chamber, where the lift began its descent. I thought about Hiroyuki on the way down. I was alone now, no backup, no friends to count on. At least not until Ji-hyun and her people arrived . . . *if* they could arrive. Who knew the damage that had been done to the rift since I'd been gone from Earth. Maybe we were all stuck where we were. I pushed the thought aside. Nothing much I could do about it if that was the situation.

The lift bumped as we reached our dingy destination, and rift-energy torches flickered to life when we stepped off the lift.

"It's like a catacombs," I said. "Similar to Tess's little village in the ravine."

"You went there?" the short guard asked.

"Before we came here," I explained as we walked down a snaking tunnel. "She'd told us that you were the bad guys here. That her people were basically freedom fighters. After we're done, I'll take you there if you still need vengeance for what she's done."

"Don't you want vengeance?" they snapped.

I stopped walking and turned to them. They were illuminated by the nearby light, which only helped me see the anger on their faces. "What's your name?" I asked.

"Heleen," she said.

"I'm Dakini," the taller guard said.

I looked between the two guards. "Right, well, Heleen and Dakini, I would love some good old-fashioned blood-curdling vengeance. I'd like nothing more than to head back to Tess's home and kill everything that moved. Unfortunately, all that will achieve is to make more dead people. No answers, no idea what the hell is going on, and no information on whoever Tess and her people are working with. More importantly, it tells me nothing about Neb's location. My friend met with Tess and is now missing. So, yes, vengeance sounds great but not as great as actually getting information that will help."

Heleen nodded that she understood, and we continued our walk through the tunnels beneath the cathedral, stopping by a large wooden door.

"That's where . . ." the doctor said. "The dungeon. Do you need to go in there?"

"Is there anything useful in there?" I asked.

"No," Dakini said. "Just the perpetual smell of death."

We continued until we reached a set of dark stone circular stairs that we followed down to a large room below.

Books were everywhere. They sat on barely functional bookshelves or piled in corners. Some of the piles had fallen over and spilled across the floor.

"We came down here and went through everything," Heleen said. "We boxed everything up, put it in her study, and locked the door."

I looked around the room that was twenty feet by twenty feet. There was a wooden door in the middle of the wall adjacent to the entrance, and there was writing etched into the frame in what appeared to be a rushed carving: *fuck Agency*.

"She was not happy," I said.

"Tess left here in a hurry," Dakini said.

"She had enough time to leave a message," I told him. "I mean, it's more pleasant than leaving a giant shit in the middle of the floor, but even so. She was caught, fled, came down here, grabbed what she could, paused, and wrote that. You made her angry or stupid, or maybe both."

"I never thought she was stupid," the doctor said. "She was just . . . We always thought she cared about the city, but she didn't. She cared about money and power."

I placed a hand against the door and pushed slightly, ignoring the sharp inhale from someone behind me. "You all searched this place, yes?" I asked without turning around. There were a dozen wooden crates piled on top of one another all around the room.

"We did," Heleen said.

I pushed the door open, revealing a smaller and much tidier room. There was a desk that had a multitude of papers and scrolls covering it at the side of the room. A table with more scrolls sat in the centre of the room, and another door was to my immediate left as I stepped inside. That was it. No poison-dart traps or large monsters falling down from the ceiling. I was a little disappointed.

"What's in there?" I asked, pointing to the other door.

"It's her workshop," Heleen said.

I started to explore the room, moving the paper and scrolls around but finding that they were mostly just diagrams, doodles, and scribbles about whatever Tess had been thinking about that day. I found a few where she mentioned Callie Mitchell or, more specifically, her work. It looked like Tess had found Callie interesting, had met her at least once, and that everything she was doing was because of Callie's work. She had photos of Callie in a folder and had written notes about how important she was to the cause. Whatever the cause was. Some of the writings were bordering on the obsessive. She was an . . . obsessive fan. A *really* creepy fan.

"Because that's what we need, fangirling over a psychotic doctor," I said to myself.

"Callie Mitchell was a great mind," the doctor said.

I looked back to him. "She was a psychopath who tortured countless innocent people for her *advances.* And now she's dead."

"When I knew her, she was just a great mind," he said, almost absentmindedly.

I looked back at the doctor. "You knew her?"

"In Inaxia, centuries ago," the doctor said. "She was inquisitive, smart, driven. Before the Blessed stuff."

I dropped the paper back on the wooden desk and continued to the door, which was locked. There were dents in the wooden frame and a few in the metal hinges. More dents on the handle, the lock, and . . . Honestly, the door was more dents than not.

"You broke the door down?" I asked.

"We kept trying, but it was decided that we didn't know what Tess might have done to the door," the doctor said.

I looked between the door and the doctor. "You decided that *after* you beat the shit out of it."

"We . . . When Tess was found to be the person we now know she is, there was a lot of bad feeling," Heleen said. "Took a while for people to realise this wasn't the best way forward."

I turned to smoke and moved through the gaps in the door, re-forming in the room beyond. The door had been several inches thicker than I'd expected and was reinforced. This was not somewhere Tess had wanted people to go.

Blue lights blazed all around the thirty-foot-long by twenty-foot-wide room, revealing two large metal tables, a variety of substances that . . . Actually, I didn't want to know. There were three drains in the floor, hooks hung from the ceiling, and there were more attached to the black tiled walls. A hose was attached to the wall too; the constant dripping onto the tiles made me want to go over and turn the red handle one further rotation.

There were shelves with baubles with blue smoke in them, identical to the ones that I'd seen used earlier. A dozen of them in all. A long table sat on the far wall with six metal containers on them; two large, clear containers, each with a tap attached, held the blue crystallised water I'd seen several times at this point.

A notebook sat on the table, and I opened it, thumbing through the pages.

"All okay in there?" someone asked from beyond the door.

"Sorry, give me a second," I called out.

There was a lever next to the door, which I pulled, forcing the door open, although it practically fell off its hinges as it did.

"What is this?" Dakini asked, looking around.

"There's a notebook," I told them, going back to it and flicking through more pages. "It's instructions on how to make the baubles, and a bunch of other stuff."

I passed it over to the doctor, who started to look through it.

"Tess was making the baubles," I said, motioning to the mass of equipment that sat around the room.

"Oh, no," the doctor said, dropping the book on the floor.

I picked it up before he could and looked at the last page in the leather-bound book. I caught the fear in the doctor's eyes and read the note in the back of the book. All notes in this book are the sole property of *Callie Mitchell.*

The date written beside it, in the same handwriting, was a year earlier.

CHAPTER TWENTY-TWO

Tess was making all of these from Callie's instructions," I said, passing the book to Heleen. "That date is a year ago. Callie was dead a year ago. Doc, you want to explain the fear on your face?"

"She came to me a year ago," the doctor stammered.

"*She*?" I asked.

"Callie Mitchell."

I stared at the doctor in continued disbelief. "Like I said, she's dead. Very dead."

"No," he said with a shake of his head. "She's . . . something else. Tess was already exiled from the city. Callie needed a place to work. I told her to take Tess's study. This was the best of both worlds."

"She made the boxes that are wreaking havoc with this world and Earth," I almost shouted.

"I didn't know what she was working on," the doctor said. "She had been my pupil in Inaxia, so long ago. She turned up needing help, and I helped her. Told her to stay here. She came in here and found some of her notebooks and research here. She was . . . livid. Tess had stolen her work; she'd made copies of it, sold it on to the highest bidder.

"Most of the experiments that Tess tried to recreate were apparently not worth the time and effort, but she got the baubles to work. She told me that Tess would get what was coming to her, that no one was to come down here, that it was dangerous."

"And you didn't ask what she was doing?" Heleen asked, incredulous.

"Of course I did," the doctor almost snapped. "I asked. I wanted her to turn herself in. I wanted her to see the folly of her ways, but she just kept saying she had to fix it. Had to fix it all."

"You know anything about those boxes being made?" I asked. "Or someone named Elliot Webb?"

"Not a clue about either of them," he said.

"That's it?" I asked him.

"Callie said you would come eventually," the doctor continued. "That I wasn't to stop you. She left you something."

"Keep him here," I said to the guards, who both nodded and looked down at the doctor with disgust.

I followed his pointing hand to a large wooden box at the end of the room. I walked over, feeling more exhausted than ever, and saw that there was no keyhole. No way to open it.

"You can't force it," the doctor called out. "She said you'd know how to open it."

"I see she's gotten cryptic in her old death," I said without turning around.

I rapped my knuckles against the large box, but nothing happened. The top of the box had an inlay that was about the size of my guild medallion, so I removed it from around my neck and placed it in the inlay, the chain draped over the box.

I stepped back several paces as there was a loud click, and the box slowly opened on its own. Nothing exploded.

"I expected a little more . . . you know, stuff happening," I said to no one in particular.

"She did not hate you," the doctor said.

I turned toward him, unsure I'd heard him correctly. "What?"

"She was different to how I remember," the doctor told me. "Driven, certainly, but she had no anger in her apart from having her creations used to make Tess money. She told me that you had tried to save her from being taken into the core of the Tempest. She said she saw things clearly now. She knew what she had to do."

I walked back over to the box and peered inside. It contained a few things. The first was a small vial of dark blue liquid that had the word *Antidote* on the side. The second, a note explaining that the liquid was the antidote to the cloud of gas that removed powers, although I wasn't about to drink it to check.

The third thing was another, longer note. I read it, not really sure what I was expecting, but it wasn't this:

Lucas,

The vial will stop the gas from removing your powers. It won't last long, but it should be enough. When I say not long, I mean seconds, so make them count. I know you don't trust me, and you have little reason to, but I have no reason to hurt you. Okay, that's not true, is it? I have many reasons to hurt you. But I don't wish you harm. I will be seeing you soon, you can count on that; the other object in the box should be obvious to you. It can't be removed, so please don't try. Just take the box back to the city, give it to Pierre; he's not actually a bad man, just one who likes coin more than he should. It needs to be taken to the Crow's Perch. I trust the Queen, even if I don't always agree with her. Tell her to keep it safe.

You will have many questions, and I can't answer them all, but know that, yes, I did create those boxes that are causing havoc with the tears. I passed them to Elliot Webb, who took them where they needed to go. There's little point in denying it, because there's little anyone can do to stop what needs to be done. I assume the doctor has followed his instructions, and you should know that he only wanted to help me because he was a good man.

I know I should say that I've done many things I regret, but they all led to this, so it seems pointless to lie to you. Things have changed for me, and things will change for you, too. Everything is going to change, Lucas. And you'll see that I'm right. Follow Ahiram and you'll learn the truth.

When you're ready, open the door.

Callie Mitchell.

"Fucking hell," I whispered, and looked in the box, removing a sheet of black velvet to reveal . . . a tear stone. "Fucking hell again."

Dakini walked over to the box and looked inside. "That's a tear stone."

"Yes, it is," I agreed. "It's smaller than the ones out in the wild, but that is a tear stone. Why is there a tear stone built into a box?"

Tear stones let riftborn move from the rift back into their embers, so the idea of putting one in a box seemed . . . weird. I picked up the box, which felt lighter than it should, considering what it contained, and placed it on the table behind me.

"You knew about this?" I asked the doctor.

"No," the doctor said.

"And Ahiram?" I asked him.

The doctor shrugged. "No clue. I don't know who this Ahiram is. He's a story told to children."

"Tess and her friends certainly think he's real," I said.

The doctor shrugged. "I've known Tess for a decade, and she was always . . . secretive. Only really her assistants knew her, people like Lara and Naomi."

"I've met her," I said. "Kulan too."

"The mute?" the doctor asked. "I always thought he was a good man. Mocked as a child, and used as weapon when an adult. Lara was an elemental revenant, able to tap into the earth element. She used it to make plants, as you saw."

"And Naomi?" I asked.

"Blood revenant," the doctor said. "She's . . . dangerous. I saw her fight someone who came to challenge her in combat over some slight. It was meant to be until one could no longer answer a five count, but she made sure to inflict maximum damage on him before that happened. There were others."

"The Viper Guild?" I asked.

The doctor shrugged. "Never heard of them until those medallions showed up."

I rubbed my eyes with the heels of my hands. "*When you're ready, open the door,*" I repeated from Callie's letter.

"What?" Heleen asked.

I showed her Callie's letter and pocketed the vial. I wasn't about to drink it and check, but better with me than with someone else.

"I don't understand," she said, passing the letter back. "There's a door down here?"

I turned a full circle, looking at everything around us. "*Where* is the question."

I looked back into the room with the drains in the floor. Too small to get a person through. The walls were solid, no cracks, no holes, no nothing. I pushed out smoke from my hands, testing for anything in the room that might suggest a hidden door, but there was nothing.

I returned to the room where the doctor and two guards stood. "*Open the door.* What else is down here under the city?"

"The dungeon?" the doctor asked. "That's not a nice place."

"Worse than seeing an elemental revenant fall four hundred feet, headfirst into a stone floor? Because I'm pretty sure we're well beyond this being even close to a *good place.*"

I stepped back into the first room and stared at the wooden desk. I dropped to my knees and looked under the desk, finding what I was looking for. A button. It was about the size of my thumbnail and black, so it didn't stand out in the darkness of under the desk. I pushed the button, and part of the wall made a sound like two large pieces of stone rubbing together and being unhappy about it.

The wall in front of me slid to the side, and I got to my feet, thinking better of brushing myself down. I felt like I needed the world's hottest shower.

"A secret passageway," the doctor said.

After grabbing one of the torches from the wall just inside and taking a few steps into the escape tunnel it became pretty apparent that the newly revealed passage wasn't the boon I'd hoped for. "It's narrow and low," I told everyone when I emerged. "It'll be single file for anyone going in there, and you'll have to do it at a crawl, which means if they're waiting, you're a sitting duck.

"Damn it," Heleen said, taking another torch and going off to check for herself.

"Can we make it bigger?" Dakini asked.

"Do you have an industrial digger?" I asked. "Or one of those machines that dig out the tunnels for subways?"

Both men exchanged confused glances. Sometimes, I forget that not everyone in the rift has been to Earth in the last hundred years.

"I'll take that as a no," I said.

"We could use our powers to break it," Dakini said. "I'm a horned revenant; I could move stone, no problem."

"Moving it isn't the problem," Heleen said, leaving the tunnel. "There's no telling what moving part of the tunnel will do. Could cause a cave-in, which would be bad for anything directly on top of us. Or us if we're underneath it!"

"So, we're stuck here?" the doctor asked, sounding genuinely annoyed by the idea. "We come this far, and we can go no further. We go to where you say they took you outside of the city, and they're going to have an army waiting for us. How many more people need to die for this . . . evil woman?"

"You helped one evil woman have some time away here," I pointed out. "You don't really get to have ethics now."

"Callie isn't evil," the doctor said. "Not the one I knew in Inaxia, and not the one who came here."

"Clearly, you didn't know Callie." I took a deep breath. "You're all going back to the city. I'm going to turn to smoke and go through that tunnel.

Doesn't much matter if someone is waiting for me while I'm smoke. But if Tess knows that not only did her plan to kill Pierre not work but it got Lara and several of her new Guild members killed, she's going to think that either she needs to run as far and fast as possible or hunker down and wait for the inevitable retaliation. She didn't strike me as an idiot, so I expect that letting Hiroyuki and me into her lair was the last time she was planning on using it. Probably already preparing to run off somewhere. Killing Pierre was a shot in the dark, so to speak.

"Besides, I'll be sneaky. I'm not planning on charging headfirst into the fray with a bunch of people who would probably be just as willing to dive headfirst into pavement as Lara was."

"What can we do?" Heleen asked.

"You could get Pierre to take a large number of soldiers out to the crossroads and make a lot of noise," I suggested. "Make sure people know you're searching. Go to the ravine; kick some rocks down it. Don't actually find anything, don't go to the lift, just make a large commotion where Tess and her people can hear it."

"What if they attack?" Dakini asked.

"That's why you take a large number of people," I pointed out. "Take some horses, too. Turn into your revenant forms and throw a few things around. Don't leave the city unguarded, but go out there and make Tess think you're looking for her. Might help."

"We'll do that," Dakini said, drawing himself up to his full height.

Heleen shook my hand, and the doctor told me to be safe, passing me the key to the dungeon and Tess's workshop. I watched the three of them leave, taking the box with them. I heard the click of the door and stood in the light as I stared at the hole in the wall before me. This was going to suck. A lot.

I thought about Hiroyuki. I thought about Neb. I thought about what I'd seen happen in Boston, about my friends who were still there, waiting to come through and help. About Drusilla. I missed her.

Callie was alive. She'd created those damn boxes, although Tess and, I presume, Elliot, if he had access to their instructions, had been making them. I still didn't know why anyone would want to screw around with the tears, but Callie was always working ahead of everyone else, it seemed. The box was . . . weird.

Tess had lied, had taken weapons and sold them, had hurt people. She had been a criminal and she knew where Neb was. She was going to answer my questions. There was no second part to that sentence. And then she was going to feel justice, either at my hand or the hands of the people she'd betrayed so readily.

I walked toward the tunnel, and the entrance behind me slid shut. There was no obvious switch to reopen it, so I had little choice but to continue on with my plan. I made sure that everything I had on me was strapped down and turned to smoke.

CHAPTER TWENTY-THREE

Keeping myself together when I was in my smoke form wasn't the easiest thing in the world. A gust of wind or something moving through the smoke meant having to recalculate where all of me was. It was a weird sensation to still feel like you're one body, when in reality you were hundreds of millions of particles—probably; I'd never counted—all moving in unison.

Moving through the narrow, claustrophobic tunnel wasn't a lot of fun. Especially considering there were parts where it got even narrower, and I had to spread my smoke out further and further. I didn't know if there were traps, although I doubted it, but I still had to check. It was a slow, unpleasant process, and after what felt like an eternity, I began to hurt everywhere.

Several hundred meters—give or take—later, the tunnel opened up, and I re-formed, lying on the ground. I was bathed in sweat and needed a moment to gather my thoughts. Moving slowly and being in my smoke form for so long is a not-altogether-pleasant experience. It's weird, getting echoes of your own thoughts as parts of you that are farther back finally catch up.

I removed my canteen from my pack, which I'd thankfully taken with me, and had a long drink. I ate some jerky, no longer caring about whatever animal it had been, and hoped that no one was going to walk down this tunnel to find my dilapidated form. I was *exhausted*. In-my-bones tired. The one night in I didn't know how long I'd actually spent in my own bed with Drusilla, I'd been woken up early to go fight fiends in the middle of Boston Common.

After a few minutes of sitting in almost-complete darkness, wondering if I was seeing the edges of light bleeding in from an unknown distance away or if it was a weird optical illusion, I got back to my feet. I didn't know what I was going to face in the walk ahead. I didn't know how long that walk was going to be, so I turned back to smoke and moved quickly and silently down the dark tunnel.

It was a *long* tunnel. Several kilometres at least, and while I was thankful it was in a straight line, it was still a long tunnel. I could stay in my smoke form for a while if all I was doing was moving slowly, but after every few hundred meters, I re-formed and took a minute to myself before setting off again.

The bleeding light I'd seen when first starting at the collapsed part of the tunnel had turned out to be a weird surface of the tunnel wall, which must have had a large amount of rift energy inside it, as it glowed faintly.

Eventually, I reached a curve in the tunnel where light shone. I stopped, re-formed for what felt like the hundredth time, and walked around the curve in the tunnel, finding, at the end, a set of stairs that led down into more darkness.

Thankfully, torches came to life on the stairs, and I used the blue light to navigate the steep stairwell to the bottom, some hundred steps below.

At the bottom of the staircase was . . . another tunnel, this one lit with torches. I walked for twenty-five minutes and wondered just how far below the ground I actually was. I looked back up the tunnel and found that it had indeed been a gentle slope the whole way. I was maybe dozens of feet below where the steps had started, and judging from the tunnel in front of me, I had plenty still to go.

Another ten minutes later and the torches stopped, but instead of being plunged into darkness, there was a door before me, light bleeding in from around the edges of the wooden frame. I tried the handle, but the door was locked, and I quickly found what should have been the keyhole on my side was covered with a metal plate and smoothed over.

There was no way of knowing what was beyond the door, but there was no way I was heading back, so onward it was. I turned to smoke, moving around the doorframe and into what I hoped wasn't a shark tank or something equally annoying beyond.

It was . . . not a shark tank. But it wasn't good.

I re-formed in a large chamber that mirrored the one I'd just left behind in the city dungeons. There were tables in a circle around the outside, though thankfully no manacles on the wall. Blue light from the torches made the whole room look quite peaceful, when in reality it was anything but. In the centre of the chamber was the skeleton of a primordial.

It couldn't have been anything else, considering the size. Pieces of bone had been taken from the creature's remains and placed on the tables. Each one had a saw beside it and a bucket on the floor. Several of the buckets were empty, but some still had shards of primordial bone.

I looked back at the remains of a creature that had once roamed the Tempest, the lands in the far north of the rift.

The skeleton was about as large as a bull elephant back on Earth, and judging from the size of the claws that still remained on one paw, whoever it had belonged to hadn't been a pushover. I'd brought primordial bone back to Drusilla so she could make my weapons, but I'd been given those remains by another primordial. My Guild medallion was made of it too.

Some primordials worked with the rift-fused, some hated them, but some wanted power and influence. It was conceivable that those who wanted such power and influence might hunt one of their kind to give to people like Tess.

I dropped the bone back into the bucket and continued around the outside of the chamber until I reached the only door apart from the one I'd entered through. It was wooden and painted blue, and with a slight push, it fell open.

The room beyond was fifty feet long and looked like the playground of a serial killer, with the tables and hooks. I didn't bother to stop and examine the metal tables, or the books on the shelves; that wasn't my prime focus right now.

After the two rooms of death, I opened the door and found myself in the centre of a forty-foot-long hallway. There was a red door opposite me, and one on either side of the hall. I heard no sounds from farther in the compound that suggested anyone was close by, although that didn't mean I could just go charging around.

I decided that I'd check the door in front first, but that was just a place where scrolls and books were stored. The books were all over the floor, many of them missing covers, with dog-eared pages or water damage to the pages. The lack of care of the books alone should get someone arrested and imprisoned.

The door on the right of the hallway was my next stop, and it too was unlocked. It led to a large dining area with a dozen tables, several dozen chairs, and the aura of a place where food is more consumed for calories than because it was tasty. An archway on the right wall took me into a rudimentary kitchen, complete with still-burning fire in the corner and potatoes in several sacks that were larger than I was.

I headed back into the dining room, where I was greeted by a smug-looking Naomi, who wore her set of claws, which shimmered purple and blue.

"To be honest, I thought there would be more of you," I said conversationally.

"The second you were sent to the city with Lara, we started evacuating," Naomi told me. "I was to wait here for Lara, who was going to use that tunnel to escape after killing Pierre. I assume because you're here, you killed Lara?"

I shook my head. "She dove off the terrace of the cathedral rather than face being caught. Headfirst four hundred feet down."

"So, the answer is yes, you killed Lara," Naomi said through gritted teeth.

"No, gravity killed Lara," I said. "Actually, I think gravity just aided. If you want to be technical about it, the ground killed Lara."

"I'm going to kill you slowly," Naomi said, a cruel smile on her face.

"I assume the death rooms I've just walked through are yours?"

She smiled. "You're going to take pride of place in one."

"Actually, here's what's going to happen," I told her. There was fifteen feet between us, more than enough to deal with whatever she decided to do. "You're going to tell me where Tess is; you're going to do nothing else. I know that Tess is a weapons dealer. I know that she's the leader of some kind of cult."

Naomi laughed. "You still believe that? Oh, plenty of the Promise Bearers think that Tess is leading us all into a new enlightenment, that she's working with Callie to bring back a dead king. I don't care about any of that, and neither does Tess. She's making money and gaining power, and that's *all* she cares about."

"And you?"

"I get to enjoy myself."

"So, you're just playing at being a cult?" I asked. "Lara said something similar before her skull impacted with some concrete."

The second Naomi screamed in rage, I unsheathed my spear, deflecting her claw attack after she charged at me. She swiped at me with the claws for a second time, and I stepped back, tripping on one of the benches and almost finding myself disembowelled as I fought to keep my feet.

I deflected a swipe with the claws, knocking her arm aside and driving the spear into her elbow, twisting the blade and dragging it out in one smooth motion.

Naomi's screams were now of pain as she ran back from me, blood pouring out of the large wound in her arm. The limb hung loosely, the forearm barely attached to her elbow. I didn't wait, diving over the table to end the fight.

Blood erupted from Naomi's wound, smashing into me like a hammer and throwing me back across the room, the spear skittering out of my hand as I landed awkwardly on one of the tables, the back of my head cracking sharply on the wood.

Naomi was laughing now as I rolled back to my feet, spotting the spear ten feet from where I'd landed. Her arm was covered in thick black blood and, where the fingers had been, was now a huge hammer.

I hate fighting blood revenants.

I dove for the spear, landing awkwardly on the stone floor, but managed to grab my weapon before Naomi caught up to me, smashing her hammer inches from my head as I returned to my feet. I ducked under a second strike, drove the pommel of my spear into her face, took hold of her, and threw her over my shoulder into the wall behind me.

She collided headfirst, making a sickening noise as she fell to the ground, but the silence that followed was quickly broken with the kind of giggles you hear in a horror film when the hero or heroine is all alone in the darkness.

As she stood, the dark blood from her arm had covered her entire body. She jumped toward me, the claw she still wore slashing down as I turned to smoke and moved back across the room to put distance between us.

She collided with one of the tables, shattering it in the impact but barely stopping as she charged toward me again.

I spun the spear in my hand, the blade pointing down at the ground, and as Naomi reached me, slicing at my face with her claws, I turned to smoke and snapped to the side, ducking under what would have been a horrific blow from her hammer. She smashed into the wall behind where I'd stood only a second before. I re-formed beside her and stabbed her in the side of the head with the blade of the spear.

"Primordial bone blade," I hissed, not sure if she could even understand me.

Naomi convulsed as though she'd been shot with electricity, and I twisted the blade, punching it through her skull, before removing it and letting her fall to the ground.

I walked out through the kitchen doors where three more of Tess's people waited for me in a circular room with five doors leading out of it. The fight was short, sharp, and bloody. I was cut on the arm from one wielding two daggers, but all three were dead within minutes of the fight starting.

I picked the first door along from where I'd entered, and, after a brief walk down a dark tunnel, ended up in the hanger-sized room where we'd been taken to see Tess. There was no Tess, though, which was more than a little annoying. The tables and chairs had mostly been destroyed, their remains thrown around the room. There were four dead people on the floor, all of whom were wearing the uniform of Agency guards. All of whom were missing pieces of their bodies. I'd been in that tunnel for a few hours, and apparently in that time, the guards of Agency hadn't wanted to wait around to just cause a ruckus.

Kulan sat atop the dais at the far side of the room, the shaft of a double-headed battle-axe resting against his gargantuan knees. He'd turned into his horned revenant form; he was now over eight feet tall and had two foot-long black horns protruding from his temple. His skin was burgundy red, and hardened bone had jutted out from around his jaw and nose. He looked terrifying, and the fact that he needed an axe was almost comical. He wore no armour; there was none big enough that would fit him unless they happened to have African war elephant armour hanging around. His horned revenant form made him considerably harder to kill than he would have been usually. I got the feeling that no matter what form he chose, he was going to be hard to kill.

The floor was slick with the blood of Kulan's enemies, and while I was covered in my fair share of it, he looked like he'd bathed in it.

I wondered if you'd come, Kulan signed.

I placed my spear on top of one of the few undamaged tables and took a seat on the bench beside it, making sure to keep Kulan directly in front of me, despite the twenty or so feet between us. *Don't like to disappoint,* I signed.

Kulan smiled as people charged into the room, shouting and roaring, as though that would make the difference in the fight ahead. His hand immediately went to the axe.

"No," I shouted, looking back at them for an instant, noticing the two guards who had been with me in the dungeons, along with six others. "Take the doors there; make sure no one is about to do anything stupid out there."

All eight of them froze in place until Dakini barked an order at them to move.

"Do you need help?" Heleen asked.

"No," I said, never taking my gaze off Kulan.

I cannot let you hurt Tess, Kulan said. *I pledged my loyalty to her centuries ago.*

"You kill for her," I said, signing at the same time.

I do whatever I need to do, Kulan signed. *I'm sure you do the same for your Guild. Tess said you were a Talon.*

"Where is Neb?" I asked.

It's not going to be that easy.

"You want to die?" I asked.

Kulan laughed, the sound vibrating in my chest. *Maybe. Think you can do it?*

I looked down at the dead bodies littering the room and strolled toward Kulan, and he hefted himself upright and roared. Like all horned revenants, he moved quicker than his build suggested, covering the space between us in under a second.

Kulan brought the axe down where I'd been standing, but I was already in smoke form. The blade caused me pain as it cut through my smoke, but pain I could deal with a lot more than losing a limb in a fight for my life.

I re-formed behind Kulan, who spun on me with his axe, forcing me to move back. There was no point in deflecting or parrying. Kulan was considerably stronger than I was, and I didn't fancy being thrown across the room or injured because I tried to beat him in a straight-up fight.

I kept moving back toward the dais, turning to smoke and re-forming behind it, noticing the ajar door off to the side, in an alcove.

Kulan smiled, reminding me, as though I needed it, that I had more important matters to attend to. I turned to smoke, moved toward Kulan as quickly as I could. He swung the axe through my smoke, and the second it had gone past, I re-formed and kicked him in the chest.

The horned revenant flew back across the room, impacting with the wall on the far side of the cavernous room. Pieces of stone rained down over him, and Kulan used his axe to help him get back to his feet.

I wasn't about to let him get back to anything.

I threw a throwing knife at Kulan, and it caught him in his shoulder blade, causing him to roar in pain but giving me the time to close the distance between us and stab at him with my spear. But he was fast and used the axe blade to parry my strike, opening him up to my knuckleduster, which I'd put on after kicking him.

My fist met his jaw, and the primordial-bone-covered knuckleduster shattered the armour around his face like it was made of china. Pieces of his jawbone ricocheted off the wall behind him as I punched him in the face over and over again, each blow driving him farther down to his knees.

He pushed me away with one large hand, which sent me a dozen feet back, and by the time I'd returned to him to continue the assault, he caught me in the sternum with the pommel of his axe. The wind driven out of me, I staggered back. I didn't really want to kill him. I wanted answers, and everyone else had been far too keen to die rather than talk. I got the feeling that Kulan wanted both. Some people just live so long that they start to put themselves in positions where someone might take their life from them.

Kulan swung the mighty axe toward me as I rushed in with my spear, throwing it at the last second and hitting him in the chest. He roared again, unable to finish the axe-swing, as his arm was too damaged. He tried to headbutt me as I grabbed the shaft of the spear and drove it through his chest and out of his back.

I fell back against the table behind me as Kulan's axe finally fell from his hands with an echoing clatter as it hit the ground. He slumped down to his knees a moment later.

I pushed myself back to my feet, walked over, and pulled the spear out of him. Blood poured out of his chest, black and thick, and in seconds his torso was covered. A rift-fused blade would kill him with a wound this deep, this close to his heart.

You want to rethink telling me where Neb is? I signed.

She came here wanting answers. They argued. Tess used those baubles on her. Took her power and dragged her down to the river. Sent her away.

"How do I get to the river?"

You take the right tunnel.

"I don't see a tunnel," I said.

It's there. Now finish it, he signed, his hands barely able to move.

I picked up his axe. It was heavy, too heavy for me to use as an effective weapon, but as an executioner's tool, it was fine.

Mercy, he signed, and I paused, the axe resting on my shoulder, ready to strike.

He rocked himself forward, presenting his neck.

"Wait," Heleen said from behind me. "He signed *mercy.*"

I shook my head. "Not the word, the place," I told her without turning to look her way.

Kulan looked up at me and mouthed, *Thank you.*

I brought down the axe.

CHAPTER TWENTY-FOUR

I didn't enjoy executing people, and anyone who says they do is probably someone who needs executing. I let the axe fall to the ground and released a long breath. It had been a long few days.

I walked through the ajar doorway behind the dais and stood in what I was pretty sure was Tess's private chambers.

"She lived lavishly," Heleen said from the doorway.

"You all got here quickly," I said, glancing over at her.

"We were making noise near the ravine, and some of Tess's people came out to fight us," she said. "We beat them and followed the path down."

The floor of Tess's chamber was covered in thick animal furs from a variety of species that lived in the rift. There were tables along one wall that held a collection of jewels, pieces of jewellery that would probably fetch a small fortune back on Earth, and several lists of people and how much money they were going to spend, or had already spent, on the weapons she was supplying them. The baubles appeared to be a particularly good seller.

Heleen picked up one of the pages. "She's obsessed with Callie."

I took the page off her and started reading. "She wrote fanfiction about them becoming friends. I think Tess may have a few issues."

A turned-over bowl sat in one corner, several golden coins strewn about the floor beside it. A bed was covered in silk drapes and had enough bolstered pillows of a rainbow of colours that it was probably harder to sleep on the bed than was strictly necessary.

A set of bookshelves that didn't have any books on it was on runners and hadn't quite closed properly when a pillow had fallen off and stopped it from moving all the way shut. I pushed the bookcase to the side, revealing a hole in the wall.

Warm air rushed up the passageway behind the bookcase, greeting me with a mixture of scent of flowers, giving a pleasant floral aroma. Certainly the most pleasant thing about Tess's life in the rift.

"What was Tess's plan?" I asked. "She was caught being a criminal, exiled, lived out here, causing issues within the city. Then she sends someone to kill Pierre and rabbits. Leaves her people to die to aid her escape. Why? That makes no sense."

Heleen picked up another piece of paper. "Maybe something among all of this will tell us what her actual plan was. What happens when you find her?" Heleen asked, picking up more paper. "Now that you know Neb is in Mercy."

"Neb planned to go to Plainhaven," I said. "It's supposedly a large town at the far end of the Vastness. Mercy is a garrison nearby. I've never been there, but I've heard that the soldiers sent aren't there because they're well thought of by the Inaxian military. I wonder if maybe they're there to keep an eye on Plainhaven; maybe there's a link between them and Inaxia. I guess I'll find out when I get there. Not sure how delighted people who live there are going to be to see me, though."

"Us. They won't be delighted to see us," she told me firmly. "I'm coming with you."

"You're needed here," I said.

"Well, I suspect you're going to need me more," Heleen pointed out. "No one goes across the Vastness alone. Not unless you're insane. I assume you're *not* insane."

I moved my hand from side to side.

Heleen sighed. "I'm a hooded revenant, and I'm over two centuries old. I know my way around here. You don't."

"Good point."

"Let's go look down that tunnel and head back," Heleen said, shivering. "This place creeps me out."

"Okay," I said, holding my hands up, and glanced down the tunnel. I was getting really fed up of tunnels and secret passages all over the place. I wondered if this tunnel was going to actually lead anywhere useful.

The land of the Vastness is soaked with rift energy, so anything that grows is unpredictable, and anything that feeds on it is . . . problematic. That includes those people who live there. People who shun society for one reason or another, a population of the lost and discarded. There's lots of caverns in the mountainous rock faces that litter the area. Lots of places for ambushes. It's said that people who live there are either so awash with rift energy that it fries their brain, or they consider anyone who isn't from the Vastness as trespassers. And trespassers are either killed or, if legend is even close to accurate, eaten. It's a whole *The Hills Have Eyes* sort of situation.

I was never sure how much of that to believe, as I'd been within the Vastness a few times and had only ever had dealings with small Lawless villages who wanted nothing to do with Inaxia but didn't want to eat anyone's face, either.

The river that went through the Vastness wasn't much better, and no one in their right mind wanted to go swimming in that particular body of water. It might actually work out safer for me to travel along it. So long as I didn't have to make my own raft or something.

There was a scream from somewhere down the passage.

I ran down the tunnel as quickly as I dared, until I reached a large cave at the bottom. Blue and purple lights covered the area, but it couldn't quite make the enclosed feeling go away. The cave consisted of a small hut, a pier that sat above bright blue water, and an entrance and exit to the cave itself. I stepped onto the pier and glanced down the tunnel leading out of the cave, the water gently lapping against the stone cave. The water constantly glowed, making it look almost radioactive, and occasionally shimmered when it touched the stone wall. It looked like someone had made a gigantic, deadly, luminescent slushy.

Everything had that same violet shimmer that I'd been seeing on anything with a large amount of rift energy. When all of this was done, I was *really* going to have to figure out exactly what the rift power had done to me.

Tess knelt on the edge of the pier, holding her stomach as blood poured out of it. Beside her was Callie, holding a large dagger.

She kicked Tess in the face, sending the woman into the water.

"No," I shouted, but it was too late.

The second Tess hit the rift-fused water and was submerged beneath it, her body began to rapidly age; she broke the surface and screamed, the water going into her mouth, accelerating the process further. Her body began coming apart in the water, and she screamed in pain, allowing more water to enter her mouth. After a final scream of agony, she fell silent. Seconds later, the flesh and muscle on her body had dissolved into nothing, leaving only skeletal remains that would also dissolve over a longer time.

I gripped my spear and turned to Callie, who was now stood floating above the water, her bare feet almost kissing the surface. She wore a set of charcoal combat trousers, a dark green jumper, and matching cloak. Her eyes and long hair were both aqua blue. She looked a lot more alive than the last time I'd seen her.

"What the actual fuck?" I asked.

"Tess was becoming problematic," Callie said. "She sent people to kill Pierre because of her own need for vengeance. She sacrificed plans and people because of it. She had to go. Besides, she *stole* from me. Do you know that? She took my designs for the baubles, and she sold them to anyone with coin. She's little more than a thieving rat."

"How are you alive?" I asked.

"You get my box of goodies?" she asked, as if I hadn't spoken. "I had to create my own tear stone so I could come and go as needed. I told Elliot how to make those boxes, but I've seen his work, and honestly, it's absolute garbage."

"I have so many questions," I told her.

"How am I alive, where is Neb, what the hell is going on?" Callie asked. "Something like that, yes?"

"Ummm . . . yes," I replied slowly.

"That spear isn't going to hurt me," Callie explained. "Oh, hello, new person."

I turned to see Heleen stood beside me.

"You can see the floating, shimmering woman, yes?" Heleen asked.

I nodded as I looked back at Callie, and noticed that she was actually shimmering, even more so than anything else around her.

"So, you want to tell me what's going on?" I asked. "Why has Neb been taken away? Why not just kill her if she's a problem for Tess?"

"I told Tess to send her to Mercy," Callie said. "I'm alive because the rift wills it."

"You just murdered your friend," Heleen said.

"I already explained that bit," Callie said. "See, this is what happens when people arrive late."

"Tess was an idiot," I said without taking my eyes off Callie. "I get the feeling whatever you are doesn't like idiots."

"Whatever I am?" Callie repeated. "I am Callie Mitchell."

"No, you're not quite the Callie I met," I said. "She was arrogant and filled with a need to be right. She didn't much care about leaving me gifts. You seem more . . . contented."

"I am content," Callie said with a smile. "The rift has seen to that. It has seen to so much, Lucas. We shouldn't be fighting; we should be working together."

"To do what?" I asked.

"Remake the world," she said as if that was the most normal thing for a person to say.

"How?" I asked because I wasn't actually sure what else to say.

"Oh, you're not ready yet," she said. "You will be. You have a lot to learn; you have a lot to see. You must come to Mercy. There's a town nearby, Plainhaven. I'm sure Neb told you about it. Go there, rest, and then come to the garrison. Things will be explained. Do not bring the citizens of Plainhaven with you."

"Why do you need Neb?" I asked her.

"We needed her to unlock something," she said. "But now that I see you, I'm thinking that maybe we got the wrong person. Neb will be at Mercy. She will be unharmed because I do not wish her harm at this moment. You will come to Mercy, after Plainhaven, and you will do as you are asked. Do not dawdle. You have no idea what you did under that mountain, what you set in motion. But you'll learn."

That was a surprise. "What is she unlocking? What did I set in motion?"

Callie shook her head. "I can't tell you yet; that's not how this works. You'll have to ride the way. You'll get the answers you want. You'll find out what's happening."

"How can you know that?" I asked. "Are you in charge of the Vipers or whatever this Ahiram is?"

Callie smiled.

"I'm not a fan of being drip-fed information," I said.

"The Vipers are a Guild but not of my creation," she said. "I find them somewhat distasteful, if I'm honest. Ahiram is a much-longer conversation than we have time for. You've been back in the rift for a few days now; can you feel it?"

"Feel what?" I asked.

"You'll see," she said, and vanished.

"What just happened?" Heleen asked.

"I don't actually know," I said, and stared at my hands. "Can I feel what?" The way Callie had phrased it sounded like something had happened to me, yet I felt no different to how I had felt before I came to the rift. Did she mean the fact that I felt *better* in the rift? That I could see the accumulation of rift power?

There was no boat in the cavern, so going along the river was never going to happen, but as I turned to walk away, I saw something floating in the water. It bobbed gently just below the surface.

I looked around, found a metal boathook leaning up against the hut, and used it to fish out the black garment, which dropped onto the pier with a heavy thud. A skeletal hand dropped out of what was quickly discovered to be a tunic.

"She tossed the bodies of her victims in there, didn't she?" I said. "Anyone who crossed her. Whoever this was wasn't killed long ago. Few days, maybe."

"My god," Heleen said, transfixed by the hand, which was missing its index finger. "We're never going to know who it was."

I glanced between the remains and the water. "Whoever it was, they probably didn't deserve to die like that." I felt something warm on the back of my hand. I turned my hand over and realised that some of the water had gotten onto it. Touching the water wasn't really an issue; I could touch it and feel nothing but a cold discomfort. But staying submerged in it, or even wading through it for any length of time, would kill even the most powerful of rift-fused.

However, instead of the chill I should have felt, it was . . . pleasant. Soothing. It felt good. I wiped it off on my leather armour and stared at the water in wonder.

"You okay?" Heleen asked.

I nodded.

Having decided that there was nothing else to be done, Heleen and I returned to the city of Agency, telling the guard on the way about the remains. Hopefully, whoever it was could be identified and maybe bring some peace to their friends. It was unlikely, but sometimes, hope was all you had.

Pierre ensured we were fully stocked up on food, water, and any other supplies we might need. He'd suggested we take an oxforth instead of the horses, as they were much faster. I'd had to explain that they were faster in a straight line, over well-trodden terrain, but that I'd take a horse over an oxforth in any other set of circumstances.

The rift-walker returned with news that Hiroyuki had been delivered safety to Ji-hyun and had imparted the knowledge they had. She would be arriving with reinforcements within a few days, as Dani was still unable to access her abilities, and it would take as long to get someone in to help.

She explained that she'd been unable to bring anyone through the tear into the rift because of exhaustion, but that I should be assured that help would be on the way.

It was a shame that after what happened with Callie a few years earlier, so many rift-walkers had gone into hiding rather than help the RCU. I understood why they wanted nothing to do with any of it, but I wished more of them had stayed around.

Agency's rift-walker had collapsed after that and was taken to her home to rest. Pierre suggested we wait, but a few days waiting was a few days more that Neb was in the hands of Callie Mitchell. And I'd seen the kinds of things she did to the people she took prisoner. Her guarantee of leaving Neb unharmed wasn't something I was about to believe.

Despite not trusting old Callie as far as I could throw her, new Callie appeared to be . . . different. It bothered me that I couldn't quite put my finger on it. I asked Pierre to send the tear stone to the Queen of Crows, not because Callie wanted it there, but because my choice of people I trusted was limited, and I knew that the Queen was more than capable of handling whatever nonsense Callie might be up to.

After one final check, Heleen and I were on our way riding the road south to the entrance to the Vastness. Technically, you could enter the place from anywhere along the border, but there was only one road that was on any maps, so that was the one we decided to take.

The further into the Vastness we got, the stranger the landscape, with forty-foot bright green-and-blue trees, and soil that appeared to bleed as we rode over it. There was an almost-constant tingling in my back of my neck, as though something was watching us, and more than once, I looked around, expecting marauders to come running across the vast open space that gave the place its name.

Hills and mountains in the distance were no-go areas, the sky above them a dark purple and pink, as though someone had hit it hard, leaving an awful bruise. Lightning streaked down, and the sound of rock being torn apart from the destructive force occasionally rumbled across the plain as we rode further east.

"How far across this place have you been before?" I asked Heleen.

"Past the bridge," she said. "You?"

I recalled the kilometre-long bridge. It was made of old, twisted, burgundy wood and looked almost alive. Considering how high across the ravine below it crossed and how strong the winds had been, it had not been a pleasant experience.

"There used to be a settlement across the bridge," I said. "About twelve hundred years ago, everyone in it vanished."

"Everyone?" Heleen asked.

I nodded. "I was sent to figure out what happened. Turned out the people living there just didn't want to live there anymore. Too close to the ravine, too close to the only road in this place. They moved to the mountains."

Heleen shot me a look of horror. "They *willingly* moved to that place?" She pointed off to the distance.

"It was my job to track them down," I said. "I had to contend with a particularly unpleasant group of people whose brains had been completely turned to mush by the rift energy. Oddly enough, they had no problem with those who moved there, but they *hated* me. I think if you stay here long enough, the rift energy permeates your body, sort of like the rift allowing others to identify others who live here."

"You think?"

"No one has ever spent time out here and published anything close to scientific research," I said. "No one has ever moved out here and been seen again. I've heard of Guild members going into those mountains to find someone, and that was it."

"Why didn't they kill you?" Heleen asked.

"The people from the settlement vouched for me," I said.

"Maybe Inaxia should send people to go see who's up there?"

I looked over at the mountains, just as a huge flash of lighting lit up the sky. It was dozens of miles away, but the rumble of thunder went through me as though it were directly above. "There are thousands of rift-fused in those mountains. I'm pretty sure Inaxia wants no part of giving them a reason to band together against a common foe."

After several minutes of quiet, Heleen asked. "How long since you were last here?"

"A good few hundred years," I said. "You?"

"We do runs up to the bridge every few months," she told me. "There's a settlement on this side of it called Gnarled Crop. More a hamlet, really. A few dozen people who moved out of Agency and decided that living here was better than under Tess's rule. We tried to get them back, but they've cultivated a little farm for themselves. They're good people. Never had any trouble; never caused any."

The bridge was a hundred meters wide, but even so, I didn't relish the idea of crossing it at night. I didn't relish being out in the Vastness at night.

"Lead the way," I said.

As daytime moved along into whatever passed for dusk in the rift, the bridge soon became outlined against the horizon ahead of us. We had a few kilometres to go before we reached it. Some said it was the dividing part of the Vastness, from where it was a bit weird to where it got *really* weird. I didn't agree with that, but I had to say that the other side of the bridge was more dangerous. The road was less pronounced, the settlements—as few as there were—less welcoming. Plainhaven was over a day's ride beyond the village and apparently close to Mercy, so we had some ground to cover before we reached it.

There were parts of the rift that were dangerous, that were beautiful, but the Vastness was the one part I'd been to where I just felt uneasy. Like the whole place did not want me there. It was hard to explain to those who hadn't felt that oppressive, closed-in feeling it gave you.

It was odd, but as we rode through the Vastness, I now felt the opposite. As if the whole place around me was comforting, was . . . right. It was a feeling I'd had when I'd stayed in the Tempest after the mountain collapsed and Callie died . . . didn't die. Changed. Whatever the hell happened. Valmore hadn't been able to explain it to me, but being around places in the rift that were strong with energy just felt good.

As we left the road, my thoughts came back to concentrating on what we were doing. It was another hour to ride across the plain and through a small patch of woodland where the itch on the back of my head intensified.

We continued on, down a steep bank, and around to the right, away from the ravine, and by a rocky crop that towered over the settlement. The settlement had been sat in the shade of the rocks, set back to ensure they didn't get squashed by landslides. It had a wooden fence around it, and a stable just outside to the right, with a hut beside it. Vegetable gardens sat to the left of the area, with very little produce left. It looked like they'd all been cultivated some time past.

The settlement itself was a dozen buildings of various sizes, all made of the same burgundy wood as the bridge we'd be crossing the next day. They had the appearance of being strong but also of looking like something out of a horrific fairy tale where people got eaten.

"Oh, no," Heleen said, stopping her horse and swinging down to the soft ground.

I stopped Roar and got down too, watching the movement of the tall grass as Heleen ran toward the settlement. I followed behind her at pace, only knowing I'd caught up to her when I almost bumped into her.

She looked back at me. "It's empty. Where is everyone?"

CHAPTER TWENTY-FIVE

The settlement of Gnarled Crop was completely devoid of life. Whoever had lived there had been gone for a while, a few months at least. They'd taken everything they had and left the buildings inside the settlement as empty shells.

We searched building to building, just in case something horrible had happened, and eventually we found a note in a building with several wooden beds that said: *Plainhaven.*

"They must have left here to move along," I said, putting the note down. "You ever been to Plainhaven?"

Heleen shook her head. "Never. Don't even know anyone who has. Heard whispers about it over the years but never anything more."

"Neb said we could trust the person who runs it," I said. "So, I guess whoever left here felt it was a safe place."

"At least we have somewhere to sleep, and that grass out there is good food for the horses."

I started a fire outside of the building and cooked some of our supplies before I took the first watch and let Heleen get some sleep. It would have been a peaceful night if not for the almost-continuous rumbling of the thunder some distance away. It's normal for the Vastness, but it was amazing how you didn't even hear it in Agency.

There was little point in crossing the bridge in the dark, however dangerous the Vastness.

Heleen switched with me after several hours, and I almost immediately fell asleep. I had dreams about the rift, about the terrible power under the Tempest. I dreamt about my surroundings, about the tiny animals that scurried around, hiding from the predators that hunted at night. It was as though I were watching it all from high above, each individual animal a small light blue glow in the darkness. Being in a place with a concentrated rift energy was going to take some getting used to.

I was already awake when Heleen came in to check on me. Dawn wasn't far off, and after a quick drink of water and finishing off the food from the night before, we set off, heading back to the bridge.

My memories of it did not do it justice.

We were, at a push, a thousand feet above the base of the ravine far below. The wind whistled as it passed over the bridge, which swayed slightly. The bridge itself looked sturdy enough and had existed for, at best guess, thousands of years. No one knew who built it, and it was the quickest way to enter the Vastness proper. There was another way to cross the ravine, but it was a three-day ride south, closer to the mountains. And I wanted to go that way a lot less than I did this.

Heleen rode her horse onto the bridge first, moving at the slowest of trots. The opposite end of the bridge—a kilometre away—looked like a dot that I wished was a lot closer. I followed Heleen onto the bridge, feeling apprehensive at Roar's sure footing.

It wasn't that I was scared of heights. I'd jumped out of a helicopter a few days . . . weeks earlier and had been fine with it. It was the general feeling that the rift did not want you on this bridge and was going to voice its displeasure by trying to blow you off it. Or at least make it seem like it was going to.

Oddly, that feeling didn't happen this time. I felt perfectly fine riding across the bridge, although the occasional clawed hand shooting up over the edge made me want to hurry along. I heard chattering from something, and I knew that there were dozens of creatures that lived under it; I could . . . feel their presence. Whatever lived under the bridge could bloody well stay there.

By the time we reached the opposite end, I was ready to not do that again in a hurry. We rode another few hundred meters before Heleen and I got down from our horses and had a drink, letting each horse have a snack for their bravery.

"I forget how horrible that is," she said once back in the saddle.

"Plainhaven is, supposedly, a day's ride from here," I said, looking back over at the bridge as something large and crablike scuttled over it, disappearing over the side. "We need to make it before nightfall if we can."

The horses put in quite the shift as we rode along the path that, after several kilometres, turned into a grassy trail. More than once, the trail vanished completely, and we were forced to go up and over rocky sections before we could find it again.

Heleen slowed to a stop and got down from the horse, crouching beside some tracks as I kept watch. We were in the middle of a great plain that stretched for miles in all directions, the land almost barren. The only thing that grew was a pale yellow raggedy grass that the horses wouldn't touch, and which gave an unpleasant smell if you rode over it.

"Horses," Heleen said. "A wagon too. Heavy wagon."

I looked down at the tracks. "Four horses, maybe more. So, we're looking for at least four horses and a wagon.

She looked up at me. "Judging from the wheelbase, the wagon is big. You could fit six or seven people in one that large."

"Either way, keep your eyes peeled."

We resumed riding, and by the time dusk had started to follow us, we'd crossed through the dry plains, traveling across scorched earth that looked like a volcano had devastated the area. At the end of the plateau were mountains that stretched into the sky, a tunnel carved through the middle of one. By the time we'd ridden through the huge tunnel and come out the other end, an hour had passed, and the snow was two feet deep in places.

We were sat atop a ridge, looking down over a vast snowy forest open one side, with towering cliffs above us on the other. There was smoke in the distance, across the forest, and something flew across the canopy of the trees that appeared to have the wingspan of a large car.

"I can't imagine any reason for anyone to want to come all this way out here," Heleen said as we began a descent through the snow-covered mountain area to whatever awaited us below. "I don't even understand why someone would want to move to Plainhaven. And yes, I saw whatever that flying thing was, and no, I don't know what it is. I'd rather not meet it, though."

"Agreed," I said, calming Roar down with a stroke of his neck.

It took time, but we eventually left the path, finding ourselves at the foot of the mountain, where the snow was now mostly a smattering over an old stone road that looked similar to the ruins I'd seen back near the Crow's Perch in what felt like a lifetime before. We continued on as night started to fall, hurrying our horses into a steady canter.

It was pitch black by the time the lights of Plainhaven came into view, nestled at the edge of the woods. Something roared from inside the forest, and Heleen and I made the horses gallop as a tree came flying toward us from the treeline, narrowly missing my head by inches.

By the time we reached Plainhaven itself, there were a dozen armed citizens, outside carrying swords and spears, at least three of them having turned into horned revenants. They charged past us without giving a second glance our way, and I turned to watch as they engaged a . . . bear . . . thing. Technically, it looked like a bear. But a bear that was twelve feet tall and had tusks emerging out of its mouth that almost touched the horns atop its head. Also, it had six legs. Or arms. Or whatever the hell they were.

I was about to suggest we help, but one of the soldiers shot fire up into the creature's stomach; there was a roar of pain and a squeal, and it was all followed by a cheer of victory.

"They look to be getting along just fine," Heleen said, as if reading my thoughts.

The pair of us continued on to Plainhaven, which, with its forty-foot-tall white stone walls and bridge over a moat, looked like it could take care of itself too. There was an entire garrison of soldiers outside of the city limits, next to a building made of similar stone to Plainhaven's walls.

We reached the edge of the wooden bridge, and I glanced over the side at the luminescent blue water.

"I need to speak to Timo," I said to the guard at the gate, remembering the name that Neb had told me. "I was told to find her."

"Who are you?" he asked, looking between me and Heleen.

Heleen quickly explained who we were and why we were in the middle of the Vastness. The longer the tale went on, the more it was clear the guard thought we were barmy, but when it was over, he nodded. "I'll take you to Prime Timo," he said.

"You have Primes here?" Heleen asked. "I thought they were only in Inaxia."

"We have four," he said. "Stole the idea from Inaxia. Apparently, they don't like that very much. Ask us how much we care?"

Several more guards, all similarly dressed, but with different weaponry, started to chuckle.

"There's a stable just over there, behind the barracks," the guard said, pointing off to behind the large barracks. "Take your horses there; they'll make sure they're well taken care of."

"Thank you," I told him. Heleen and I did as he suggested, then walked back to the bridge as the bear-thing was dragged over it, much to the delight of everyone around.

"What are you going to do with it?" I asked.

"Eat it," a guard said, in a tone that suggested I'd asked something extraordinarily stupid.

"Waste not, want not," a second guard said.

I gave them a thumbs-up, stepped over a large paw of the recently deceased creature, and spotted the guard we'd spoken to earlier.

"That'll feed everyone for a week," he said, licking his lips. "Lots of clothes and armour, too. You brought us a good find there."

"I'm glad to have been chased by something that's so helpful," I told him.

We walked under a portcullis, and the guard nodded to practically everyone we met; we discovered he was called Sam and was the man in charge of the Night Watch for the city.

"Move out of the fuckin' way," he shouted when the crowd became too dense, and everyone did just that.

What I had always assumed was a fairly small village with people eking out their existence out there was actually about the same size as Agency. The buildings were all old ruins, almost an exact match for those I'd seen when I'd last spoken to Neb. Like everywhere else in the rift, people wore a mixture of clothing from all periods of time. None of the people there appeared to be affected by the level of rift energy, either, at least no one I'd seen so far.

"Where are these from?" I asked, looking at the two- and three-storey buildings as we walked by a woman in a black T-shirt and pair of faded blue jeans talking to a man in a purple toga. "They're amazing."

Sam smiled a knowing grin, and we continued on to a courtyard that had a huge fountain in the shape of birds in the centre. I walked over for a closer look. Clear water cascaded out of the beaks of the various bird species into a large circular pool.

"Drinking water comes up from the earth deep below here and out of there," Sam said. "There are pipes that take it all around the city."

"These birds," I asked him. "They're the Guilds?"

"Falcon, owl, eagle, hawk, vulture, and kite," he said.

"No raven," I said with a frown.

"Not here," Sam told me. "That's someplace else."

I wondered why there was so much symbolism to the guilds in Plainhaven that I'd never seen anywhere else in the rift. And as we continued on through the city, I spotted more and more statues of the various Guild birds, and many buildings had them carved into their exterior walls. But no ravens. It was a strange thing to have so many Guild birds represented but one bird missing. Almost as though those who created the city knew that the Ravens wouldn't last.

"You know," I said, looking around as we continued on toward a large building at the far end of the city, "considering the *Vast Death* is meant to be vast and death-like, I haven't seen much of either."

Sam looked back with a sense of smugness in his smile. "But you didn't want to come here, right?"

I nodded. "Went beyond the bridge once or twice but never this far in."

"Can't say it was high on the list," Heleen said.

"The *death* part is back the way you came," Sam said. "You take a wrong turn, and you become a meal. Mostly, we cultivated the name so people *would* stay away."

"You came up with the name?" I asked.

Sam stopped walking in front of a nondescript front door to a building that looked like every other building we'd walked by. "Keeps people away."

"And Mercy?" I asked him.

His face clouded. "You don't want to go there."

"Don't have much of a choice," I explained.

He clapped me on the shoulder. "Then I'm sorry." Sam knocked on the door, didn't wait for a response, and pushed the door open, revealing a large open room with comfortable-looking sofa and chairs, a wooden table, bookshelves, and a desk at the far end, which faced the door. A set of stone stairs sat at the side of the room, leading up to the floor above.

The room was lit by candlelight, with no purple or blue hues in sight. A woman wearing a black three-piece suit got up from the back of the room and strolled over to Heleen and me, offering her hand, which we shook in turn.

"My ladyship," Sam said, closing the door behind him.

"I do wish he wouldn't call me that," the woman said. She was nearly my height, with olive skin, dark brown eyes, and matching dark brown hair, which was put up in an elaborate bun with what looked like two pencils holding it in place atop her head. If anyone ever asked me to describe what *elegance* looked like, this woman was it.

"I'm Lucas," I said.

"Heleen," she said. "From Agency."

The woman looked between us and nodded. "I am Timo. From Knossos. I'm several thousand years old at this point. Also riftborn. I like cheese, but it's hard to get a good cow's milk in the rift, I also like those

CBD gummies they do on Earth, but try to get someone to bring them back for me without having to make it a whole thing."

"You're from the Minoan civilisation?" I asked. "And you're an Ancient."

"And you're from Carthage, so I hear," Timo said with a wide smile. "Shame what the Romans did to that place. Although I guess the same could be said about a lot of places back then. I miss Carthage. Neb told me there was a trader at the market who did an amazing grilled fish with lemon and spices, but I never got the recipe."

"Neb told me to come find you." I asked.

She nodded sadly. "She told me. Look, there's probably a lot to talk about and probably not long to talk about it, so, why don't we go sit in my study upstairs and we can have a drink?"

"We need to get to Mercy," I said.

"Why?" Timo asked.

"Neb's there," Heleen said.

Timo's expression hardened for an instant. "And you know this how?"

"Callie Mitchell told me that she needed Neb to unlock something," I said. "And then she went a bit weird and started talking about me feeling something in the rift. I think it may have something to with an old mythological hero called Ahiram. I've never heard of him until a few weeks ago, but a bunch of people called the Promise Bearers seem to think he's real and is about to come back and save everyone."

Timo nodded sadly. "He's not exactly a hero. He was, once. Now he's . . . well, he's definitely there. Although not *at* Mercy as such. Like I said, there's things you need to know. We've been preparing for this day and hoping it never happens, but I can now see that we're all about to step into some serious dog shit."

We followed Timo up the stairs, to be presented with a small landing and three rooms, none of which had a door. Of the three rooms, one looked like a hurricane had gone through it, with books all over the floor and bed, a second had a desk and more books and scrolls adorning every surface, and the last was a bathroom.

Timo saw me looking over at the bathroom and tapped a button on the wall outside that was almost undetectable to the naked eye. A door slid out of the wall.

"What is this place?" I asked, as Timo took my hand and led me into the room with the books and scrolls.

"Sit," she said to me, and turned to Heleen. "I need you to go find Sam and tell him to bring water . . . wine. Bring wine. I know you want to hear what I'm about to tell him, but it's a Guild thing. I hope you understand."

Heleen looked over at me and I shrugged.

"Sure," she said, leaving Timo and me alone.

Timo sat opposite me, took my hands in hers, and smiled. "Oh, Lucas. Where do I start?"

"At the beginning?" I suggested.

"You're probably not going to like this bit," she said sadly. "Sorry."

CHAPTER TWENTY-SIX

Neb may have kept things from you," Timo said. "When I say *may*, I mean she did. *Absolutely* kept things from you."

"I am shocked to my very core," I said sarcastically.

"Are you?" Timo asked. "Were you being sarcastic? I don't get sarcasm; it's just one of those things my brain can't understand. Like seeing the colour green."

"You can't see green?" I asked.

"Nope, never have been able to," she told me. "Right, so, back to the topic at hand. Neb wasn't *entirely* truthful about a lot of stuff. Not just her but *all* of the Ancients. You've met other Ancients, yes? Apart from me, obviously."

"A few," I said.

"Excellent," Timo said. "That'll save time. You know what we are?"

"Powerful riftborn?" I asked, although my tone suggested that I wasn't actually sure anymore.

"Oh, no," Timo said. "I mean, we are, but that's not what the Ancients were originally. We were the first riftborn to achieve the state of 'Ancient.' We decided that the rift needed to be tamed, that the world we live in needed to be safe. Especially as our interactions with Earth become more regular and more riftborn and revenants started appearing. So, there were Guilds created to help. Most Ancients worked with three or four others and had a Guild who were meant to be loyal to them. Neb had the Ravens. Ahiram had . . . Well, that's more complicated."

"Ahiram was an Ancient?" I asked.

Timo pointed at me. "Yeah," she said sadly. "He was . . . *magnificent.* I think we all loved him a little bit. He seemed like the best of us, like he was going to make sure that these Guilds worked together to achieve the goals set out for the rift. But then he decided that maybe the Guilds would be better served if they served just one master: him. He tried to overthrow several of the Guilds. Some remained loyal to their original creators . . . others fragmented. The Ravens, however, they refused him outright. Not a single one joined him, and he fucking hated them for it. Every Guild member who aligned themselves with Ahiram was excommunicated."

"Not executed?" I asked.

Timo shook her head. "Some of the Guild members who turned on their *own* Guild were executed. The Ancients had no problems with that. I helped create the Falcon Guild, and we lost nearly ten percent of our members, but there we so many who just joined Ahiram because they believed he was going to make things better. We couldn't just kill all of them. After it all ended, the Guild numbers were regulated; the people accepted went under rigorous tests to ensure they were loyal to none of the Ancients, only their guild and the mission. No more rising up, no more trying to overthrow."

"So, where were the other Guild members and Ahiram taken to?" I asked.

"Mercy," Timo said. "When we handed over control of Inaxia, we gave them the garrison, too. We told them who was inside it and why. They wanted the Guilds to do it, but we couldn't risk it. And as one, the Ancients swore that none of us would ever go there. Not for any reason."

"Why?"

"Primarily because we didn't trust each other. We made a pact never to discuss it with anyone outside of the Ancients. Not even those we loved the most.

"But I needed to keep watch, I needed to make sure that everyone was safe, so I stayed here. The other Ancients didn't argue; I was uninterested in power or influence back then, and even less so now. There were some of the Ancients who weren't thrilled with me staying here, but over time, people just accepted it or chose to forget. The garrison was created explicitly because of what happened with the Guilds. Mercy was aptly named because of what Neb did. Although I'm not sure it was actually much of a mercy in the end."

"So, this Ahiram was an Ancient you imprisoned in Mercy for thousands of years?" I asked. "He betrayed you all and after you defeated him, you all made a pact to keep it quiet, and it's all coming to bite you on the arse?"

"At first, Ahiram wanted to control the rift, the power of the rift, and we thought it might actually be beneficial. We started to operate new tear stones, all across the rift; we found ways to use them to move across the rift itself. But over time, his motivations changed, or maybe he just hid them well; he decided to merge the rift and Earth. To unify them into one place. Everything ruled by him and his people, no more accidental revenants or riftborn, no more random tears. No more chaos. He would make sure *everything* was controlled. His betrayal was something we never saw coming until it was too late, because we agreed with him to begin with."

"Wait, what?" I asked, interrupting. "You found a way to teleport around the rift?"

"Yes," she said. "These old ruins are conductors to tear stones. Instead of the small ones that riftborn move in and out of the tear, they also let people move between the sites of buildings like these. He used to use them to move his people around the rift, attack us from ambush, and teleport to somewhere else to do it all over again. There would be battles, and we'd suddenly have a small group of his people get into a city on the other side of the rift, burn it down, and flee. We could barely keep up. He played hit-and-run tactics with us for months until we managed to get a handle on it all. It's not something we want to go back to."

"How'd it work?"

"You call them ruins, but back then, we called them home. The stone is taken from the quarry inside the Vastness. Vast Death was designed to stop people taking it. To stop people from coming here. Those people who live in the mountains, you've probably heard about them."

"The monsters who kill and eat people," I said.

Timo laughed. "Is that what they do? They're protectors of the stone. Of the quarry. We can't have just have anyone going through there. Not to say that there aren't people out there in the rift that live a little too close to constant flow of rift energy, especially by the Tempest, but I don't think we've turned the rift into the *Cannibal Holocaust* just yet. You seen that film? Don't bother."

The change in conversation was jarring, but I'd also spent a long time with Nadia, so thankfully, I was a little used to it.

"The ruins?" I asked. "Like the ones that are scattered around the rift? They used to be able to teleport people around? Who broke them?"

"Ah, well, we destroyed a few of them in the war and decided not to fix them again once we won. The Ancients kept their use to only us anyway, as we were worried about outside influence. We were power-hungry, petty. Sometimes, I think that Ahiram is our penance. Anyway, we couldn't risk Ahiram breaking out of prison and getting to them to start moving around the rift. We kept a few intact, put cities on them, like this one. Like Nightvale."

"How many people are at the prison near Mercy?" I asked.

"Ah, Mercy," Timo said. "Mercy isn't the garrison; it's the prison itself. Outside of the garrison is a lake. A huge lake. The garrison sits alongside it, but in the middle of the lake is an island. That's called Mercy. It's . . . a *really* big island. I'm unsure how else to describe it. It's bigger than Nightvale. Maybe. Hard to say.

"It holds hundreds of traitors, maybe a thousand. No one has been added to their number since it was sealed. The garrison is staffed by people picked though allies of mine in Inaxia. They think it's a place we sealed off to stop the flow of rift energy from overwhelming the area. That those inside can never be released because they're infected with something. Stops the garrison members from wanting to peek inside. I think so; it's been a while since we made that up.

"Anyway, the prison holds Ahiram and those Guild members who betrayed us and joined him. At least, those who weren't killed in the war or executed after. I guess we should have executed them all, but . . . no one had the stomach for it after so much fighting. The water surrounding it is that icy blue shit. You know, the horrible stuff that kills you if you swim in it, or drink it, or touch it for too long. Rift-energy-tainted water. A boat goes from the garrison to the prison once every few weeks, taking supplies."

"And you just let people rot in a prison for thousands of years?" I asked.

"There's a barrier around it," she said. "Everyone inside of it moves at a slower pace than everyone outside. Food and water last longer; people age slower. Everything takes a long time to get done. Our conversation here would take weeks inside the prison. Or it would feel like weeks to us but normal to them. The prison does weird stuff to people in it. There's rift energy that flows all through it, pumped up from the lake. It's potent stuff. Puts people into a sort of stasis for years at a time. It's why the soldiers are moved out so often. The prisoners wake up, spend a few decades back among the walking and talking before the rift energy puts them back in stasis."

"That's inhumane," I said.

"It is," Timo said. "It's one of those things I wish I'd never allowed to happen. But once it happened, it was too late. You can't go in and remove

---

it without removing the prisoners. And unleashing those men and women on this land would . . . be a magnitude of evil I can barely comprehend."

"So far, all you've said is that he staged a coup and lost," I said. "I understand he betrayed you all, he killed people in war, but what else?"

"He massacred people on here and in Earth," Timo said. "Like I said, he wanted to merge Earth and the rift, and he needed to keep us busy. Ahiram took his army of riftborn to Earth and conquered so much of it. We had to stop him, and we did. Thousands died. Cities turned to rubble. He stood against us and proclaimed himself leader of the rift, and he murdered hundreds to do that. Ancients, Guild members, innocent civilians, no one was immune to his fury at being told no. I watched friends die at his hand. I wanted him executed. I wanted his head on a spike adorning the walls of this city.

"We managed to keep most of what he did on Earth a secret, it was easier to do back then, but he killed and hurt a lot of people. And when we finally defeated him, he refused to back down. If he ever gets out, he's going to go right back to trying to merge the two worlds again."

"You stuck Ahiram and a bunch of highly trained Guild members in a prison for thousands of years?" I asked.

"At least two thousand, five hundred years," Timo said, mentally figuring it out in her head. "Before you were born. Before you became riftborn. Before you became a Raven Guild member."

"It might have been kinder to execute them all," I pointed out.

"Maybe, but there's a reason we couldn't," Timo said. "There were twenty-four Ancients. There were *always* meant to be twenty-four Ancients. We didn't know back then what would happen if we killed one of us."

"It feels like you're not telling me something," I said.

"The Ancients," Timo said. "We were just riftborn to begin with. Like so many others in the rift at the time. We went into the Tempest. We, I can't remember why, decided that we should be *part* of the rift power. That if we were one with the rift, we could make this whole place a haven. Like I said, we were power-hungry. We reached the power of the rift. The core. Under the mountain. All twenty-four of us."

Timo shook her head.

"You okay?" I asked.

"I don't remember what happened," she said. "None of us do, but we walked out of that place linked together. We didn't know what happens when one of us dies. We revelled in how much power it gave us, and we took over the rift, and that's when we decided to create the Guilds, to separate ourselves from one another. That's when Ahiram put his plan into action. We almost ruined the rift, stopping him."

"Neb's the key to unlocking the prison?" I asked. "Maybe, anyway. Callie said Neb was a key."

Timo laughed. "That would be a shit prison if it could be opened by one of us just being there."

"She also said that maybe she was wrong and that I needed to come here. Why would they want me or Neb?"

Timo shrugged. "I wish I knew."

I stood to leave and Timo grabbed my hand. "We're not done," she said, her tone no longer friendly.

There are few things that are certain in the rift, but one of them is when an Ancient tells you you're not done, you either sit your arse down or you get ready to defend yourself. I sat down.

"Ahiram created his own Guild," Timo said. "Back when we created them, he in secret created his own."

"Vipers," I said.

"You know," Timo said, sounding surprised for the first time.

I removed one of the medallions from my pocket and passed it to her. "Took these off two Guild members trying to kill me in Agency. Figured they were named after a snake, but no idea which one."

"When he took people from the Guilds, he used them to create the Vipers," Timo said, staring at the medallion. "He always liked to be different. They were bad, Lucas. No other word for it. They were his elite guard. His assassins. His . . . whatever they needed to be."

"And they've had two and a half thousand years to let that just fester in prison," I said.

"Like I said, to them, it isn't two and a half thousand years. To them it will be hundreds of years, maybe."

"And they have Neb. And Callie Mitchell is helping them."

Timo nodded. "There's more."

"Of course there is," I said. "What horrendous stuff is added to the ever-growing list of horrendous stuff?"

"If Callie is involved, so are the Blessed. Neb told me you had a run-in with them."

"She was one of them, yes. Most are dead or imprisoned," I said. "Actually, I think two of them are still about. One is Prime Roberts in Inaxia, and one is Congressman Spencer Mills. We got him already."

"He dead?"

I shook my head. "Probably not enjoying his time, though. His friend Elliot Webb was told how to make the boxes by Callie. He was taking them through into Earth and using them to create huge tears. More powerful tears. More frequent. What do Ahiram and the Blessed have to do with one another?"

"I don't know," Timo admitted. "But it's more than a coincidence that the architect of the Blessed, Callie, had Elliot working for her to help create these boxes that attract tears. I only met her once, and I got the impression she wasn't someone who did anything without thinking it through. Neb said I should be careful of her. And that was before she died and was apparently resurrected."

"Wait, you and Neb communicate," I said. "How?"

Timo stood and walked over to a drawer, removing a golden mirror, passing it to me. Instead of a shiny surface, there was a one gigantic piece of magenta promise crystal.

"The recipients of promise crystals can talk to one another in their sleep," Timo said.

"This is a bit bigger than the one you wear around your neck," I said, passing her the mirror back. "You've spoken to her recently?" I asked.

"She said she was coming here," Timo said. "Going to Agency first. Told me that you'd be here if anything happened."

"Maybe lead with that next time," I said.

Tomi stared at the mirror for a moment before returning it to the drawer. "Sorry, there was a lot to get through."

"How does it work?"

"You don't need to wear it; when it's this size, you just need to own a piece. This one is about two thousand years old. We both made a promise to the other, and we kept the crystal. The promise can never be fulfilled, so we can use them forever. I just need to have the crystal in the same room as me. I haven't been able to talk to Neb for nine days. So, she's too far away from the crystal to talk to. I try every night. She's not dead. I would feel it. All I know is my friend is out there in the company of people who wish her harm, Lucas. Neb tells me you are a good man. The last Raven. The man who just would not die. Find her."

"That's the plan," I said. "I have to go to Mercy. Neb might be okay now, but I have no way of knowing how long that will last. And I can't bring anyone from Plainhaven with me."

"Says who?" Timo asked.

"Callie Mitchell. She told me to come to Mercy and stop here first but bring no one from this city to the garrison."

"She told you to go alone?" Timo asked.

I shook my head. "Just no one from here."

"How peculiar."

"Having spoken to her, I got the feeling that *peculiar* is her new thing." A thought came to me. "How often do you go to check out the garrison?"

"Every few months," Timo said. "I don't go personally, but I send an attachment of guards there to check everything from afar. None of us step foot on garrison ground, we meet someone from the garrison on the plains outside, everyone has a nice chat, and we go our separate ways."

"What if that someone was lying about everything being okay?"

"If the barrier around the prison had been physically breached, we'd know," Timo said. "The rift power would rush out, wash over everything across the Vastness. So long as that barrier remains, no one gets inside."

I had a thought about something Timo had mentioned. "You said that you don't know what happens when an Ancient dies, but some have died."

Timo looked sad for a moment. "We didn't know what would happen until after we imprisoned Ahiram. Turns out that each of us *is* linked to another. We don't know who is linked to whom, but when one of us dies, all of us feel it, but the person linked to them loses their connection to the rift as an Ancient. They're still riftborn, but they lose their connection to the rift itself."

"Meaning?"

"They wither," Timo said. "They have maybe a few years. A riftborn with power but no connection to the rift can't access their embers. They can't come through a tear without a rift-walker. They grow old and they die."

"How many have died?" I asked.

"A dozen in total," she said. "Twelve of us left, eleven discounting Ahiram. After the first death, no one wanted to go kill Ahiram and risk losing their connection. We are more powerful than a normal riftborn, we heal faster, we are better. And we lose that when we lose our connection.

"Two Ancients in the same city at the same time used to be a cause for a joyous celebration. There were parties and feasts, but those days are long gone. Ancients are studied with suspicion, with outright hatred in some cases. Neb tells me that you don't trust us."

"Everything you've just told me is pretty much why," I said. "You have secrets upon secrets. You might well have good intentions, but the secrecy is what kills you all in the end."

"A fair assessment," Timo said.

"What can I expect at Mercy?" I asked. "I assume the garrison isn't just going to let me waltz into the prison."

"I don't know," Timo said. "We have heard nothing bad from the garrison, so I'm unsure why Callie would want you and Neb there. Surely, that would cause some kind of commotion. Thankfully, with the amount of rift energy in the lake, everyone inside Mercy will be powerless. It's why it was built there."

It felt like this was just one extra thing on a seemingly never-ending list of things. It was beginning to feel like a house of cards that just kept having more piled on it from one person, while another put a big fan beside it.

"Everyone in the prison being basically human is probably not a bad thing," I said after a few seconds of considering it. "Should make it easier to get in and out without having to deal with a group of super-powered, highly trained, exceptionally angry criminals, if a fight occurs." *When*, I mentally added.

There was a knock downstairs, and Timo told me to wait as she went to check. She was gone a few minutes, so I leaned up against the wall behind me, closed my eyes, and tried not to think about what else Neb had lied to me about or kept from me other the years. Almost certainly a lot. When this was all done, I was going to have to sit down and talk to her about her trust issues.

Timo returned with a bottle of wine and two glasses.

"Sam is taking Heleen for a walk around the city," she told me, passing me an empty wine glass.

"Why Plainhaven?" I asked.

"Ah, we just wanted something nondescript," she said. "Calling it the Jewel of the Vastness was probably going to get more people turning up than we wanted. We've been here a long time, making sure that no one tries to come out here and stake a claim for themselves. Or decides to start looking into using the old ruins to unlock travel around the rift again. Or worse."

"Like helping Ahiram get free from prison," I said. "I assume that's Callie's plan, but we still don't know what Callie actually wants. Or what Ahiram will do once he's freed. Maybe he's a changed man after so many years."

"We can hope so." Timo poured me a glass of sweet-smelling white wine. The liquid was cold, and little drops of condensation cascaded over my fingers. When I had half a glass full, she stopped pouring and I took a sip; it tasted nice. Not as sweet as the scent had led me to believe.

Timo poured herself a full-to-the-brim glass and knocked it back in one swig. She poured a second glass, put the near-empty bottle down, and sat back in front of me. "So, there's one more thing."

I drank the rest of the wine. "Okay, let's go."

Timo looked genuinely uncomfortable and poured me a second glass. "I'm pretty sure that Ahiram was behind the murder of the Ravens."

CHAPTER TWENTY-SEVEN

I said nothing and just sat and stared at Timo.

"What?" I asked eventually.

"Ahiram killed the Ravens," she said softly. "Or, at least, I'm pretty sure he had his people kill the Ravens. They were helped by a man by the name of Matthew Pierce."

I nodded as though I understood, although I wasn't entirely sure I did. I knew about Pierce. He was a piece of shit I hoped was dead. The last time I'd seen him, I'd caught him in the throat with a knife as he was escaping the rift. I'd searched for him after but had found no trace, but he was a cockroach and notoriously hard to kill.

"Tell me what you're thinking," Timo said, and lifted the wine bottle. "Do you need more wine?"

I was concerned I might start shouting if I said what I really felt, and it wasn't Timo's fault nor her place to be the one I allowed that anger to be thrown at. "How can he contact people outside of the prison?"

"We're not sure," she admitted. "But after Neb called and said that she saw his name in graffiti, that he might have something to do with the attacks on towns. She said she was coming here, and I figured we'd discuss it further, but then she never arrived and I learned she's at Mercy."

"Callie got her first," I said. "In a roundabout sort of way. Did Neb know who killed them?"

Timo shook her head. "I don't think so. She never mentioned it, and the Ravens were *her* Guild. I don't think anyone considered that Ahiram would be behind it, considering we all thought that Matthew was just working for Callie Mitchell. But Callie didn't do it. So, that leaves Ahiram. Somehow."

"No, Callie would have told me," I said. "She'd have gloated if it was her plan. She also wouldn't have needed to buy a Raven guild medallion. So, there's a chance that inside Mercy is a very powerful Ahiram who has, somehow, been using his power to talk to people outside of the prison. That about sum it up?"

Timo nodded. "If Callie is in contact with Ahiram, he will certainly know who you are and will try to use that information against you. You can't let the anger you're feeling right now dictate your response. If you try to fight him, he might kill you."

"Am I just meant to go to this garrison, get to Mercy, and ask them nicely if they can give me back Neb and her people?"

Timo shook her head again. "They want something. Neb is too vital to kill. I hope."

"That's a lot riding on hope," I pointed out.

"Sometimes, that's all you have," Timo said. "And I think we're done here. I understand if you need time to yourself after the information you've been given. I wouldn't take long, though. While Callie told you to stop here on your way, I doubt it was for a nice holiday."

"How far from here is the garrison?" I asked.

"A half day's ride," Timo said, getting to her feet and stretching. "I'd suggest getting some food and sleep before you leave. You can use my home."

"Why aren't there any ravens in this city?" I asked. "There are ornaments and statues of the other guilds, but no ravens."

Timo crossed the room and opened a shuttered window on the far wall, revealing a large portion of the city.

I got up and joined her, looking out across the white stone of Plainhaven.

"There," she said, pointing off to a waterfall in the distance. "You see it?"

Next to the waterfall were the heads of two large raven statues.

"Every Guild had a city of its own," Timo said. "You didn't know that. Though why would you? No one knew that. For hundreds of years, these cities stood. There are, I think, maybe two left now. Inaxia was meant to be the neutral ground. The ruins by Nightvale were one, one was in the far north, beyond the tempest. There's another to the northeast of here. People from Inaxia or something had started to try and excavate them after the tears became more frequent, but we pushed them on. This place right here was the home of the Ravens. Please, feel free to go look around. I'll make sure the spare room is made up for you and your companion. Not together, or together, I don't really want to judge."

"We're not together," I told her.

Timo patted me on the shoulder with what I suspected was meant to be sympathy and walked away. I looked back out of the window. The darkness had well and truly settled in for the night, and it was simply no longer safe to travel the Vastness. Seeing how I had a few hours to kill and a lot of stuff in my brain to work out, I set off through the streets of Plainhaven toward the waterfall.

The streets were busier than I'd expected them to be, and there were multiple streetlights using the usual rift energy but also several using a warmer white light. People nodded to me and said hello in the street, which felt odd, considering how I'd always been led to believe that this part of the rift was nothing but danger and death. It was all so . . . pleasant.

After a short walk, I reached the waterfall, which also wasn't what I'd expected. The whole area was a giant amphitheatre-like structure, the waterfall on one side and the entrance—where I stood—opposite it. The water from the fall fell into a reservoir, which cascaded down a crisscross of channels into a large pond in the centre of the amphitheatre, several flights of stairs below where I stood. I watched for several minutes, but the water—despite being a constant stream—never overflowed. There were seats arranged in neat pale-stone rows on either side of the entrance, and dozens of people were sat on them, with more walking around the garden area at the bottom, next to where the water flowed.

I took a nearby seat and realised the sound from the falls was nowhere near what I'd expected, considering it was over fifty feet high. It was all so . . . peaceful. I remained seated for a few moments and looked around the area, settling on the two raven statues. Each one was the same height as the waterfall, and each was an anthropomorphised version of a crow. One held a sword and shield, one two daggers, both wore armour similar to the leather armour worn by the Queen of Crows. Neither bird looked like someone you wanted to meet in a dark alleyway.

This city belonged to the Ravens, I thought to myself as people walked by, staring at me or saying hello. I got the feeling that they didn't get many newcomers. I got up from my seat and did a lap of the garden below, enjoying the array of colours until I found myself standing at the base of one statue. *The city of Ravens* was printed on a bronze plaque and fixed to the base. I walked around to the other Raven, and there was an identical plaque.

I walked back up the steps and retook my seat.

Sam from the Night Watch sat beside me, forcing me to budge up the row of seats. "You were a Raven, yes? Sorry, you are a Raven, yes?"

I nodded. "No one ever told me a place like this existed."

"You're the last of the Raven Guild," he said. "That makes you a bit of a celebrity in this city."

"Is that why people keep saying hello to me?" I asked.

"The Guilds, when they were first created, were beacons of hope to a lot of people," he said. "They only really lasted that way for a few hundred years, and everything was very quiet and hush-hush by the time you'd joined. Several cities were gone, destroyed during the war with Ahiram. We burred the mythology and fiction with the truth, and soon, people couldn't remember one from the other."

"You never joined?" I asked.

Sam shook his head. "I'm not a Guild member. I'm . . . I protect the city. I protect the people. But the Guild, they're an ideal that most can never hope to obtain. They're meant to be the best of us."

"Meant to be," I said.

"You haven't decided to restart the Guild, then," Sam said. "Isn't that your job?"

I nodded. "Meant to be. I don't . . . Several of the medallions are still missing. I don't know where they are. Someone, a rich arsehole, purchased one on the black market. And Callie had one too. She found the Guild fascinating. She had tattoos of the birds on her arms. No snake, though. When I last saw her, she said she found the vipers unpleasant. Or words to that effect."

"I don't know who that is," Sam said, getting to his feet. "It was a pleasure to meet you, Lucas. If you need anything in town, come let me know."

I shook Sam's hand and he left me to my watching of the waterfall. I closed my eyes for a moment and opened them to find Timo sat beside me.

"You were asleep," she said, patting me on the hand. "I didn't have the heart to wake you."

I wiped my mouth, blinked, and tried to force myself awake. "How long was I sleeping?"

"An hour or so," she said. "I assume you find this place peaceful."

"Neb should have told me it existed," I said. "This is part of the Raven Guild, for crying out loud. This is the city of the Ravens. Apparently, I'm a celebrity."

"Of a sort," Timo said.

"Why weren't you a Raven Guild member?" I asked. "I asked Sam the same thing."

"I was an Ancient," Timo explained. "We weren't allowed to be Guild members, too. Power corrupts and . . . Well, I'm sure you know the rest. Once Ahiram did his thing, the cities were disbanded from Guild influence."

"You should have killed him," Lucas said.

"Maybe," Timo said. "We were afraid. And after his imprisonment, we had thousands of years of peace, Lucas. Or, at least, we had thousands of years to forget Ahiram existed."

I stood and stretched. "I need actual sleep. And tomorrow, I'm going to ride to that prison and I'm going to find Callie, figure out what is going on, and try to get out of there with Neb in one piece."

"Tomorrow, when you leave, you need to be aware of something," Timo said. "Beyond here, there are more forests, but they won't be an issue. The creatures in them are mostly nocturnal, and so long as you're not inside the forest, you shouldn't have a problem. The difficulty is the open plains beyond. They'll take you all the way up to Mercy. The weather changes in an instant out there; it'll be cold."

"Any chance cannibals might attack us?" I asked, thinking back to what she'd told me about those who were feared for apparently no reason back by the bridge.

"There are small . . . tribes, I guess, of people who hunt on those plains," Timo said. "We don't always have issues with them, but you're both going to be unknown; if you see horses or oxforth riding toward you, don't stop to say hi. Get to that garrison."

"There's always something or someone who wants to kill me," I said. "One day, I'll come to the rift and no one will try to stab me for it."

"We all want a peaceful life, Lucas," Timo said, looking across to the waterfall.

"Thank you for telling me about this place. It feels like somewhere I'd like to return to," I declared.

Timo smiled. "You're welcome here anytime. This is, after all, your home."

I glanced down at her. "The home of the Ravens."

"No, Lucas," she said gently. "*Your* home. You just didn't know about it until now. All the Ravens have a place here, but you hold their future on your shoulders. I can't think of anyone else more deserving of a place to call home. To rest and feel content among those who wish him nothing but good things. The home of the Ravens. The city of the Ravens will be here when you're ready to come back."

CHAPTER TWENTY-EIGHT

I woke to the sounds of birds outside of the window as light streamed in. Heading downstairs, I found Timo and Heleen drinking what smelled like coffee. Timo poured me a large mug, which I drank with a contented sigh. It was good, but it didn't quite taste like coffee. It was considerably sweeter, for one. I followed it up with some pastries that were delicious. It felt almost normal to do such things. Probably a far cry from the rest of the day I had ahead of me.

"Where'd you get the coffee?" I asked.

"We grow it," Timo said. "It's not quite the same as the real thing, but getting it imported from Earth in quantities that allow it to be a regular drink is near impossible."

"You ready?" Heleen asked after I finished my second cup of coffee.

I nodded.

"The horses are ready," Timo said. "When you're done, come back and let me know you are safe. I think the rift needs to change, and maybe Plainhaven needs to be more open about its existence. I would like to discuss how best to do that. Also how best to reestablish the Raven Guild. I think it's important, Lucas."

I agreed, although I had no idea how to actually go about it.

The roads through Plainhaven were quiet, but once again, those few we did pass said hello.

"Everyone seems to be nice here," Heleen said as we reached the outer wall of the city. "And it doesn't feel like one of those times when people are being nice to just betray you and feed you to a monster or something. It feels like people are genuinely decent. Are people like this on Earth? I haven't been there in a long time."

I laughed so hard, she looked at me like I was mad.

Shortly after, we were on the road east again, and not long after that, the city of Plainhaven was a dot on the landscape somewhere behind us. The people of the city had given us thick coats and gloves to wear on the journey, and the horses had new fur-lined coats too. There were big fur boots for Heleen and me, although we'd been given strict instructions not to wear the pale blue clothing until we were off our horses, as they were too big to use the stirrups.

"I've been thinking about something," Heleen said. "How do Callie and whoever is helping her hope to get into the prison? Are the garrison members just going to sit back and watch?"

"That's one of many questions I want answers to," I said. "It makes me wonder what happened to the garrison. And whose side they're on."

"I don't fancy fighting a whole garrison," Heleen said.

"Me neither," I admitted, although somewhere inside of me hoped I would be able to punch someone.

There was more forest all around us for several miles of riding, until it petered out and became open plains. Snow remained on the ground, and a cold wind whipped across the whole area. Timo had told me that it was cold, but there's cold and then there's feel-it-in-your-bones *cold*. This was the latter, and I wished I'd worn several more layers than just the wonderful thick coat.

I removed the large Russian-styled hat from the pack and put it on, relishing the feeling of warmth in my ears again.

"Timo said it would be cold," Heleen said. "This is a bit more than just cold."

As if in reply to her complaint, the wind roared across the plain, bringing another biting blast over us. We rode on in silence after that, although we picked up the pace.

It took a few hours until we saw the tower of the prison in the distance. A large black monument that stretched up into the sky, a translucent shimmering bathing the whole prison. In all honesty, even from the few kilometres of distance, I half-expected to see a fiery eye atop it.

The winds died down a short distance after, although the cold persisted, but it was enough to be able to hear one another again. "That is . . . ominous," Heleen said, pointing to the tower.

"Doesn't scream *come visit*, does it?" I said.

The garrison consisted of an outer stone wall with three ramparts on top of it. The wall was forty feet tall, and there was a metal portcullis that was closed. The combination of the garrison and the tower helped make it look like the least welcoming place ever. It didn't help that it was long enough to stretch around the sides of the lake, making it not only unwelcoming but imposingly so.

"No fires," Heleen said, nodding to the ramparts. "No soldiers patrolling."

I would expect to see both somewhere as cold and remote as this, especially when your entire job was to actually guard the dangerous criminals in the nearby prison. I'd definitely want to keep warm while out doing patrols.

We stopped the horses by the portcullis and I climbed down, looking through the holes in the entrance to the courtyard beyond. There were multiple stone buildings not far from the entrance, but I saw no guards, no soldiers, not even a garrison pet cat.

I turned to smoke and moved through the portcullis, my body forcing itself back to my usual form the moment I'd crossed the threshold. "No powers in here," I said.

"Timo mentioned something about the constant rift energy here making them impossible," Heleen said. "You see a lever to lift this? I don't fancy a climb."

The lever wasn't hard to find, although it took a bit of effort to pull it toward me, releasing the lock and moving the portcullis up into the wall above with all the subtlety and quietness of a herd of elephants on a rampage through a bubble-wrap factory.

"I guess everyone knows we're here now," Heleen said, bringing both horses into the garrison and nodding to the portcullis. "You think we should close it?"

I looked around. "No," I said. "Just in case we need a quick exit."

We tied the horses to a nearby water trough, which had surprisingly warm water inside it, and left them alone as we set about trying to figure out what the hell was going on.

The garrison was bigger than I'd assumed from the outside; it was built alongside the bank of the lake, creating parts of it that were considerably deeper than others. Apart from the dozen stone buildings of various sizes, there were also several dozen green tents. Each tent was made from thick tarpaulin, which I assumed someone had brought over from Earth, and they were filled with beds and covered in rugs. The warmth the place gave off was a welcome respite from the cold outside.

"No one?" I asked Heleen, exiting one of the tents and finding nothing.

She'd just exited the tent beside mine and shook her head. "It's like everyone vanished. No signs of life, no food going rotten, no fires left lit, no nothing. It's been abandoned for weeks at least."

"So, where did they all go?" I asked, looking over at the looming presence of the prison.

"The boat is still here," Heleen said, pointing farther around to the side of the garrison where there was a dock built on the banks of the lake.

The lake's cobalt-blue water chopped unpleasantly against the bank. I could see the bottom of the lake, where there were only rocks. No vegetation or life of any kind.

"It's weird, isn't it?" Heleen asked.

"The lake or the missing soldiers?" I replied.

She pointed to the lake. "The rift energy makes this water deadly to anything and everything, yet there are other bodies of water that come from the same place as this does, and they're completely safe. I assume it's because this goes through an area of high rift energy and it just keeps absorbing it, but . . . the rift is weird."

Couldn't argue with that.

"So, what do we do now?" Heleen asked. "Take the boat over to the prison and check for anyone who might just be there that shouldn't? Because pretty sure if Neb and her people are in there, Ahiram and his people are waiting for us."

"Lucas," someone called out, causing me to be momentarily confused about what I'd just heard.

"Did you hear that?" I asked Heleen.

"Lucas," someone shouted again before Heleen could reply.

I looked around, trying to figure out where the voice had come from, and eventually spotted someone I recognised walking toward me.

The man had dark skin, a bald head, and long black beard braided with colourful beads, and a scar that ran across his face—from left cheek to right ear. He had the appearance of someone who had seen his fair share of battles. He looked hardened. The kind of man who you just *knew* you didn't cross.

"Kuri," I said, walking over to him as he embraced me, slapping me on the shoulder as he moved away. "Neb went looking for you. What the *hell* is going on?"

"I left with Commander Pike to search for those responsible for the attacks on settlements," Kuri began. "We were attacked, separated, I spent weeks moving through the wilderness here, arrived just in time to see the entire garrison march out two nights ago. Been trying to figure out how to get over to the island and inside the prison without getting killed or stuck inside."

I turned back to Heleen. "This is Kuri; he's Neb's bodyguard."

"A pleasure," Kuri said. "Is it just the two of you?"

I nodded. "For now. So, where is Neb?"

Kuri pointed to the prison. "I assume so, anyway. I haven't seen her."

"Have you seen anyone else arrive?" I asked him.

Kuri shook his head.

"How many of you are there?" I asked Kuri.

"Just me," he said. "I've been trying to figure out how to get into the prison without getting killed the second I step foot on their land. If I get caught, does Neb die? Does me getting caught mean they torture me until she gives up what they want? I don't have any good answers. Come, look at this."

Heleen and I followed Kuri through the garrison until we were at the pier. The boat was large enough to sit a dozen people at once, with large white sails that were currently down across the ship.

"It's not a one-man job," he said, sounding frustrated. "If we can get the sail up, the anchor released, and push away from the pier, we can sail that boat across the lake. I've been here before; it takes about thirty minutes with a good wind. The water in this lake doesn't make for speedy manoeuvrability. You sure you don't have anyone else coming? We're going to need help if something goes wrong."

"I wish I could tell you different," I said. It didn't feel like there was any need to explain about Ji-hyun's people. They were at best days away. Whatever was going to happen in that prison would have happened by the time they arrived.

The prison island of Mercy was maybe a kilometre offshore. I could walk it in less than thirty minutes, but that wasn't going to be an option anytime soon, and with the amount of rift energy in the area, it meant I wasn't using my powers. While it had recently felt like a smart decision to put the prisons for awful people in areas where the rift energy makes using powers impossible, it was beginning to become annoying.

I stepped onto the pier and stared out across the blue lake at the darkness of the prison beyond. There was a pier on the opposite side to where I stood, but I saw no signs of life. "Okay, so we get the boat ready, gear up, and go find out what's happening on that prison," I said, turning around, and gasping when the needle went into my chest.

A dozen people left the tents, and Heleen drew her sword, ready to fight, as I crashed to my knees, my world going dark. I watched in impotent horror as someone snuck up behind Heleen and drove their sword into her back. She dropped her own sword and tried to move away, but her attacker slit her throat with their free arm and pushed her away.

"You should be out by now," Kuri said, kicking me onto my back. I couldn't move, couldn't talk, but every impulse inside of me screamed in useless rage. Heleen's killer walked over to me, lowering the hood on their black cloak to reveal Matthew Pierce.

"Sleep now," Kuri said, as Matthew looked down at me and smiled as a gigantic tear lit up the sky directly above the prison and garrison.

Kuri crouched beside me and whispered in my ear. "Welcome to your new life."

CHAPTER TWENTY-NINE

There's no good place to wake up after you've been drugged unconscious by a gang of traitorous arseholes, but to wake and discover you're strapped to a bed, naked, in a cold, dark room with a lot of sharp-looking implements on nearby trays is probably the worst way.

I had a pillow under my head, which was a level of comfort I hadn't expected, considering the rest of my predicament. Still naked, still strapped down. Still next to sharp implements. The pillow actually felt weirder, the longer I considered it.

There was a window over to the side, but it was about twelve inches long by six inches wide and had bars on it. The only thing escaping through there was small enough to not have to worry about being strapped naked to a bed in the first place.

I'd woken up captured by people in the past and never really enjoyed it all that much, but there were things I'd learned. The first was that it was depressing that it had happened so often that I'd learned anything. The second was not to shout and scream but to keep calm and figure out where you are, who has you, and why.

The who was easy, seeing how they were the people who had drugged me. The where was presumably the large prison tower, considering the black stone all around me. The why was . . . harder to figure out.

I tried to turn to smoke but couldn't, so the effect of the rift energy coursing through the landscape was going to remain an issue. I wiggled my hands, trying to free them from the straps, but they were tight, made of leather, and thick enough to have been difficult to break or cut even with suitable implements to do so.

I tied to raise my feet, but they too were strapped down, so I had little else to do but wait. I wasn't going to give anyone the satisfaction by yelling for help.

The door opened after thirty-six seconds—I know because I counted—and a large man stepped into the room, flanked by Matthew Pierce and Kuri, the latter of whom stayed by the door.

"Mr. Lucas Rurik," the man said, pulling up a seat and sitting beside me. He was tall, lean, with pale skin, clean-shaven, and with dark eyes that exuded menace. He wore a charcoal-grey three-piece suit with black boots, the latter of which didn't quite go with the rest of the look. "The drugs that were put inside of you are still there; it'll be a few hours before they're gone. You're going to be dozy and light-headed on and off."

"You do see me naked, strapped to a bed, yes?" I asked. "Because if not, the drugs you gave me have done weird things to my head."

"We cleaned you up," the man continued. "We needed to check for anything that could be used to track you. Obviously, you have allies coming here to help, although I think you'll find that is harder with what we've done to the embers."

"You haven't actually told me who you are," I said.

"Oh, I'm sorry, I thought you knew. I'm Elliot Webb."

"The aide to Congressman Mills?" I said. "I know that you took those boxes through from here to Earth, but you're in charge? I thought you were Ahiram."

Elliot Webb laughed.

"Which part is funny?" I asked, feeling like I was missing something important.

"Congressman Mills is a simpleton," Webb said.

"Yeah, I got that impression. I assume it's always been you." I stared at Elliot Webb and something dawned on me. "You changed your name, you set up your ex-Blessed pawn to be congressman, and you controlled him. There were no photos of you on the congressman's website. No pictures of you with him, no pictures of you at all. It was like you had a very small online footprint, I assume because people would recognise you."

Elliot smiled broadly. "Very good. I worked with the Blessed during their time here, I saw them betrayed, I saw them exiled. I worked with Callie to facilitate everything she needed, including finding rift-walkers for her use. In return, I was given Spencer Mills as someone to use for my aims. I was to remain out of the public eye, though; I couldn't risk someone recognising me and destroying my plans. The only person who knew who was really in control was Callie. I thought my secret had died with her, and then she returned. Although she is not the Callie of old."

"Yeah, I got that impression too."

Elliot patted me on the shoulder. "You have Spencer in your custody, too. He will have to be dealt with. The Blessed were so easily manipulated into what Callie wanted them to do. I was only too happy to help if I got my own aims fulfilled."

"To kidnap me and Neb?" I asked.

Elliot laughed again.

"So, what was your plan that you needed me and Neb for?" I asked. "That you needed to stay out of the public eye for?"

"The public-eye thing is easy," he said. "I wasn't sure who knew what about me on Earth. Couldn't risk being recognised."

"How were you bringing the water back from here to Earth?" I asked. "I always thought you were a rift-walker."

"Callie had acquired a lot of primordial bone and rift-fused water during her experiments in the Tempest," Elliot said. "She knew the next phase of the plan was to weaken the barrier between Earth and the rift. I'd been taking stuff for some time from her to prepare. She was meant to have control over the rift, though, or at least be able to target where the tears opened within the rift. Needed to keep the RCU and rulers of the rift busy while slowly doing what needs to be done."

"You're going to strengthen the link enough that you can open a tear above Mercy," I said, taking a shot at what I thought was going on. "You can get Ahiram out when the power floods out, breaks the shield, and you all go free. That about it?"

Elliot laughed again. "The tears interfere with the shield around this prison. Every time there is one, the shield falters, meaning we can get people in and out."

"So, why haven't you escaped yet?"

"I needed to ensure that Ahiram is being made ready to join us," Elliot said.

"I do not understand."

The man smiled again. "You know, we are similar."

"Oh, this is going to be good," I said. "How are we similar?"

"We were both betrayed by the people we thought we could trust," Elliot said. "We go to great lengths to correct that. We believe in justice. In truth. You came here because Neb needed you. I'd hoped that Neb alone would be enough, but Callie said we needed you, too. She said Neb wouldn't be able to do it. So, we took her to get you."

"Not a single piece of that makes sense," I told him. "Before we continue, can I just say something?"

Elliot motioned for me to continue. I looked over at Matthew, noticing the deep red scar on his neck that I'd given him the last time we'd met. "You didn't need to kill Heleen."

"Those who oppose us will die," Kuri said.

"What's up, Matthew; can't talk?" I asked.

Matthew let out a low growl.

"He worked for you for a long time?" I asked Elliot.

"I'm not sure this is the part where you question me," Elliot said with a wry smile. "But yes, many centuries."

"He helped kill the Ravens," I said. "He helped kill my friends. The last time we met, he almost killed me."

Matthew's gaze bore into me.

"Next time we're alone, I'm going to kill you, Matthew," I told him. "This time, I'll make sure the job is done right."

Elliot clapped his hands and laughed. "You're naked, strapped to a bed, in a prison, and you're making threats."

I looked over at Elliot. "Thank you for the pillow."

"You're welcome," he said. "The straps are for our protection and yours. The pillow is just because I feel like you should be comfortable. You're going to be here a long time. A last piece of comfort is for the best."

"You had the Ravens killed," I said. "Timo said that she thinks it was Ahiram, but it wasn't, was it? Matthew works for you, and it was your order."

"I did," Elliot told me. "Do you know why?"

I shook my head.

"I'll tell you what," Elliot said. "You tell me something I want to know, and I'll answer one of your questions. When we're done, I'm going to take you to Neb—she's alive—and after that, what happens, happens."

"You going to answer the question, then?" I asked him. "Why kill the Ravens?"

"One reason," Elliot said. "I just always hated them. They stood against Ahiram, the only Guild to never support him. I knew that by killing the Ravens, it would make Ahiram happy when he finally woke."

"You murdered my guild to get in with Ahiram," I said. "A man you've never met."

"I have met him, dozens of times," Elliot said. "He speaks to me in dreams. He showed me what *really* happened. How the Ravens betrayed him, how Neb had him imprisoned."

"He's asleep?" I asked.

"Comatose," Elliot said, waving away my comment. "He speaks through dreams. The conversation is slow, lengthy; it takes months to hear all you need. But by being here, you learn the truth."

"The garrison didn't just get up and march out," I said. "They work for you."

Elliot nodded. "It took a long time to get the people I needed in here, but yes, they are my Vipers."

"His power is to speak through dreams?" I asked with a chuckle. "That's what the great and powerful mythological hero can do? I see why he lost."

Elliot's smile diminished, replaced with something dark, as he picked up a scalpel from a nearby tray. "His power is not your concern, but I would advise you to keep a civil tongue in your mouth, lest I remove it."

"Let me," Matthew said, his voice hoarse and unpleasant.

"First of all," I snapped, looking over at Matthew, "fuck you. You ran away screaming because I killed all of your people. You let me out of this and see what happens. And second of all, if you want me here, you're not going to kill me. So, let's just get on with whatever the fuck is going on, so I can put on some goddamned clothes."

Elliot replaced the scalpel. "Kuri will give you clothes; he will unfasten you. You will not do anything but what he says. You will be taken from here to Neb's location. I have waited a long time to see Ahiram wake and lead us all into a united world. The rift and Earth as one, with him at its head. As it *should* be. And if you jeopardise that, I will make you watch as I remove her entrails." He loomed over me. "Understand?"

I nodded.

"Heleen died because she was not needed," Elliot said, standing to his full height. "Ensure you do not fall into that category."

He strolled out of the room with Matthew following but lingering for a second to give me a look of pure hate. I'd earned that look; it warmed my heart.

Kuri removed my clothes from a wicker basket in the corner of the room and placed them on top of it. "I'm going to release you. If you do something stupid, Neb will pay for it."

"You betrayed her," I said. "Money, power, or revenge?"

Kuri laughed and removed a chain from beneath his tunic, showing me the Viper medallion I'd seen before. "I've been one of their number for a long time," he said. "I couldn't wear what I had earned out of fear of reprisals. I did not betray Neb; she betrayed all of us."

"Revenge it is," I said. "I'm not going to do anything stupid."

Kuri unfastened my feet first, before my hands. He stepped back out of kicking range as I sat up on the bed.

"Get dressed," he said. "I will wait outside."

"You needed to know if I had people with me," I said. "That's why you waited for us to get to the boat."

"Also, I didn't want to carry you through the garrison," he said. "I am sorry about Heleen. She was . . . That wasn't meant to happen."

"It's what happens when you work with psychopaths," I said.

Kuri stared at me for several seconds. "You missed your shot. Maybe aim better next time."

I was about to reply, but he left before I could, and I settled for flipping him off before getting dressed. Unsurprisingly, my weapons were all missing. I checked everything to make sure there were no nasty surprises but found nothing out of the ordinary.

When dressed, I knocked on the door, and Kuri opened it. "Shall we?" he asked.

I didn't reply, as I was staring out of the barred window behind him, across the lake to the garrison, which was now a hive of activity. "Who are those people?" I asked.

Kuri smiled. "We've been moving people out of here a few at a time. We had to pause when we heard you were close, but we have resumed plans to leave now."

"Did all of the garrison members really join you?" I asked.

Kuri shook his head. "Not all, but over the centuries, people were placed there who had an allegiance with Ahiram or Elliot. It took a long time to replace hundreds of soldiers, but eventually it happened; we hurried it along by removing the last few dozen who would have stood against us. You hastened it all along, in fact. Thank you for that."

"How?"

"Callie's death and resurrection," Kuri said. "She was the catalyst for hastening our departure. So, I guess we have you to thank for it. She came to Elliot, explained what we needed to do. Told him the way forward, to get Ahiram out of this prison. To finish what he started all those centuries ago. You started that by letting Callie die."

He shoved me in the back, and I walked along the black stone corridor, pale blue lighting illuminating dimly. We stopped in front of a black metal grate, and Kuri pushed the button on the side to bring the lift up.

The constant squealing as the lift made its journey up toward us was not a comforting sound, considering I was about to get on it. The grate moved aside as the lift arrived, and Kuri motioned for me to get onboard.

I stood at the rear of the lift and watched Kuri as he followed me, closed the grate, and selected the *Up* button. Apparently, up or down were the two options available.

We stopped at three floors as we went up the tower, with Kuri re-pressing the button each time until we'd reached out destination.

"Come on," Kuri said, motioning for me to now leave the lift.

The floor looked identical to the one I'd just left, complete with a large, barred window, although this one gave a more pleasant view of the sur-rounding area, not that there was an awful lot to look at.

Near to the end of the corridor were a set of cells, four in total, with a wooden door sat at the far end. Each cell had a bed, furs on the floor, a sink, and toilet, the latter of which I didn't even want to think about. Neb was in the last cell, lying on the bed, staring up at the ceiling. The others were empty. We reached the third cell door, which was opened, and I was pushed inside.

"Lucas," Neb said, looking over at me. "When you get the chance, can you kill Kuri for me?"

I looked back at the man who had been a trusted member of Neb's inner circle. "Sure," I said. "You *really* should have stopped Matthew from killing Heleen."

"Can I assume that you and this Heleen came alone?" Neb asked, sit-ting up, her legs off the side of her bed. She wore the exact same outfit I'd seen her in the last time we'd spoken, although she had bruises around her eyes and mouth, and one finger was badly swollen.

"You have five minutes." Kuri walked away without another word, exit-ing through the wooden door.

"Your people?" I asked her.

"Dead," she said. "Most were executed in front of me. Kuri told me he killed Pike the second they stepped foot on the island, although I haven't seen a body, so I'm disinclined to believe him. Elliot told you why you're here?"

I shook my head. "Not entirely. Something to do with waking up Ahi-ram, although I don't really understand how. It sounds like they took you because they figured you could do it, and then realised you couldn't."

"They need an Ancient to wake him," Neb said. "I figure you're here because they can threaten or hurt you until I do it."

I considered what Callie had told me earlier. "Callie said I was the key."

"Mitchell is alive?" Neb asked.

I nodded. "You didn't know?"

"She was taken into the core at the Tempest, touched by the power of the rift itself. I thought you said she'd been vapourised."

"There's a lot I haven't figured out," I said. "Oh, have you met the Vipers?"

Neb nodded. "Quite a few of them are inside the prison. Ex-Guild members we probably should have killed instead of showing them the mercy they didn't deserve. There are garrison personnel among their number, too."

"There are a few less since they ran into me," I said.

Neb smiled and winced. "That's the Lucas I remember. You know that they used the tear above to break the shield, letting people get in and out?"

I nodded and told her everything about what I'd been through: Tess's death, the resurrection of Callie, everything that Timo had said, and ending with Heleen's murder at the hands of Matthew. I made sure to explain that I was going to kill him for it. Permanently this time.

"Tess is one of the few people who ever managed to get one over on me," Neb said. "I knew she had ties to criminal elements in the rift, I knew she was an arms dealer, but I didn't think for a second she'd be involved with this lot. And by the time I did figure it out, I was being drugged and kidnapped."

"Do you have a plan on how to get out of here?" I asked.

Before Neb could speak, the door opened, and Elliot stepped out into the hallway. "Neb, tell your protégé exactly how you plan to escape from Mercy. *Mercy.* I think I might hate you more for naming this place."

"There's no escape," Neb said. "You need the boat to cross the lake; they have the boat. They've broken the shield, so they can all leave. There's no powers, no way to move freely without using the lift, which makes enough noise to wake the damn dead. This whole tower is floor-to-ceiling cells. The cells are automated from inside that room, just there. No one gets out unless you have access to that room."

"And how long have you had access?" I asked Elliot.

"Oh, two hundred years, give or take," Elliot said, standing in front of my cell, his hands behind his back. "It's been a painstaking process of going through the prison, cell by cell, waking people up, removing anything that allows the stasis and slowness that curse its inhabitants. Started at the bottom and worked my way up. Some took longer than others to wake, and Ahiram the longest. You really made sure that not only was this place surrounded by a shield but his own cell was, too."

"Couldn't be too careful," Neb said with a shrug.

"He escapes and then what?" I asked. "You conquer the rift? Earth? Callie's plan was to control the tears, and it looks like you've used her know-how to do that."

Elliot smiled. "When Ahiram wakes, we're going to finish what he started. First, he's going to kill everyone who ever stopped him all those years ago. After that, we're going to destroy Inaxia and everyone who supports that jumped-up shithole, and then we're going to make sure that those people who have spent their lives, the lives of others, making themselves the powers within the rift and Earth are turned to dust."

"Revenge," I said. "That's it?"

"Oh, that's just the beginning," Elliot said. "We're going to bring the rift and Earth together as one. As it should be."

"Killing untold numbers in the process?" I said.

Elliot shrugged.

"So, why am I here?"

"You're going to come with me," Elliot said. "You're going to wake Ahiram up."

"He's not an Ancient," Neb said. "He can't do it."

Elliot looked over at Neb. "Callie said he can, and honestly, I believe her more than you. If you refuse, Lucas, I will hurt your master."

"I won't refuse," I said. "But I also know you can't kill Neb."

"*Can't* is such a strong word," Elliot said.

"The Ancients are linked," I said. "You kill one, and a random other one loses their connection to the rift. Makes them weaker, considerably so. And then they wither and die. There's a possibility that the one you make weaker is Ahiram. I don't think he'd thank you for that."

Elliot smiled. "I didn't think you knew that. You are a surprise. I have no intention of killing her, but I do think we could take up a long period of torture. Maybe we could go to Plainhaven and see how many we can hurt until you do as you're asked."

I raised my hands in surrender. "Okay, let's go."

CHAPTER THIRTY

The cell was unlocked, and I was marshalled out, taken back to the lift and up to the very top of the tower, where the lift opened into a short corridor with only one door at the end. Elliot gave me a small shove and I started down the corridor, walking through to the door into a room I was not expecting.

It was a lavish room with large four-poster bed carved from dark wood, a window overlooking the lake and mountains in the distance. There were dozens of throw pillows of various shapes, sizes, and colours, and thick, welcoming rugs in shades of green and blue adorned the floor.

In the corner were a small desk and a wooden chair, next to an oil lamp. It looked more like a room designed for a couple's getaway to a ren faire than a prison cell.

On a small bed next to the desk was a comatose man. He wore black robes and a mask with a snake on it.

"Who is that?" I asked.

"A hero," Elliot said.

I turned to look back at Elliot and noticed several bright blue scorch marks all around the inside of the door.

Elliot turned to glance at them too. "They were quite difficult to remove."

"How long have you been in here?"

"Few weeks now," he said. "I used a box to get in, started to wake up the prisoners. Callie brought the box for us to get out."

"You put a lot of trust in her," I said.

"I've worked with her a long time," he said. "We want the same thing."

"Ahiram awake," I said, and looked back at the bed where the prone form I assumed to be Ahiram lay. He was a large, muscular man, with olive skin, long, dark curly hair, and a thick, dark beard. His eyes were closed, and he looked to be at peace.

Beside him sat Callie Mitchell, who looked identical to the time I'd seen her near Agency.

"Is he dead?" I asked, unable to see his chest rise and fall.

"He's in a stasis still," Elliot said. "You will bring him out of it."

I looked back at Elliot. "How?"

"Callie will show you," he said. "I have things to prepare. Do not disappoint me."

When we were alone, Callie said. "I assume you want answers."

"Honestly, I don't care anymore, I have no idea what the fuck is going on." I took a seat at the desk. "I don't know how to wake him up; I don't know why you think I'm a key to anything."

"You touched the rift," she said, looking back at me. "We *both* touched the rift."

"Well, you got vapourised by the rift, so that's a little different," I said.

"I was reborn," she told me. "I remember being under the mountain with you, and then I remember pain, and next I woke up in some ruins to the north of the Tempest. I know what I need to do."

I stared at her for several seconds. "You're not Callie Mitchell. Not the one who died, anyway."

Callie smiled. "You said that back at Agency, and it's not quite true. I am her. Mostly. I have her memories, I have her mind, I have her tenacity, but the rift showed me so much, so quickly. I am Callie; I am just one with her need for . . . validation and desire for her own vengeance removed. I always wanted to free Ahiram, I wanted him to help me set everything right against those who had wronged us both. But I was wrong. This isn't about revenge; this is about what *needs* to happen next. Ahiram *needs* to wake up."

"And lay bloody waste to the rift?" I asked. "That seems like a terrible plan."

Callie shook her head. "That's not why I need him. Do you know what his power is?"

"Dream-talking apparently," I said.

"He takes the powers of those he has physical contact with," Callie said. "The power stays if the person is in close proximity to him. The dream-walking is because someone in here is telepathic, and over the centuries, Ahiram has used that prisoner to power himself."

"And is that the prisoner?" I asked, pointing to the man in the corner of the room.

"Yes," she explained. "Ahiram's people would give their lives to him. It took a long time for the seals on this cell to be broken, to allow this man access to his own power, but I have no doubt that this was a consensual transaction. That man gave his life to ensure that Ahiram could communicate with people. Elliot truly believes he's a hero."

"Why am I here, Callie?" I asked.

"You are the key to what happens next," she said. "Technically, we both are. You see, an Ancient could feasibly unlock his mind, but they're all linked, and Ahiram probably hates them all, considering they stuck him in here. That means they *could* wake him up, but it's also possible his feelings for them could melt both of their brains."

"Wait, I'm going to die doing this?" I asked.

"No, not at all," Callie said quickly. "Let me finish. You touched the rift, but you did not *transcend* as I did. You have no idea what you're becoming now. I can use tear stones to move around the rift with ease; did you know that the ruins were originally designed for people to move freely around the rift? Until they broke them all?"

"They?" I asked.

"The Ancients. Those two dozen men and women touched the rift and took its power, using it to make themselves greater but doing nothing to help this place or its people. They are . . . wrong. They should not be. I am one with the rift; I am an anomaly. You . . . you are stuck. You took some of the power as you tried to help me escape, but it is dormant inside of you. You might have felt an increase in power, or be aware of things in the rift; you sensed me at the body of that mudrider."

"I saw you," I said. "Three of you."

"You saw me move, Lucas," she said. She got up and walked over to me, and sure enough, I saw three of her, all joining together as she reached me. "Did Hiroyuki see that?"

I shook my head.

"No one is meant to be able to see that," she said. "You have been sensing animals, yes? Living things around you."

I nodded slowly. "That and seeing a purple glow around things with a concentration of rift energy. Like you, for example. How are we so different to an Ancient?"

"They took what was not offered," Callie said. "We were given something we did not ask for."

"So, why doesn't the rift want these Ancients dead?" I asked. "Why wake him up?"

"Because it is necessary."

"Can you see the future or something?"

"Your friend Nadia, the chained revenant," Callie started, with no hint of frustration that I was still asking questions. "She sees all of the chains, as she calls them. She tries to navigate them to create the best life for herself and those she loves. I see something similar but for the rift. I see the best way forward for this place and those living in it."

"That means you could want to kill everyone who causes problems," I said. "You could be waking him up so he murders everyone the rift *thinks* is an issue. Assuming the power of the rift has a mind of its own, which I'm iffy on. Why don't you just tell me what you want me to do to save people and I'll go do it?"

"Doesn't work like that," Callie said sadly. "You need to do what you think is right. I just needed you here because . . ."

"I'm the key," I said interrupting. "Sorry for interrupting. So, I need to wake him up?"

Callie shook her head. "I'm going to do that, but it takes time. Days, maybe. Elliot and his people don't know that I can see like your friend Nadia can. They believe I told them that you were the key to waking Ahiram up, but that's not what you're the key to. There is a tear directly above this prison that has destroyed the shield around it, allowing everyone inside who has been here for centuries freedom. They will not use that freedom for good. They wanted Neb because they hate her, and it didn't take much convincing to explain that it was important she was kept alive because I needed you here."

"I do not understand *anything* you've just said. And you haven't actually told me what I'm meant to be the key to."

Callie let out a sigh. "I'm going to go into Ahiram's mind; I'm going to wake him up. It's going to take some time. Elliot and his people are not going to wait around for that to happen. They know you can use the ruins as a way to jump from place to place within the rift."

"And they know this how?" I asked.

"I told them," she said matter-of-factly. "You need to stop them from starting a war, from killing everyone they believe crossed them."

"You brought me here to stop Elliot?" I asked.

"I brought you here to kill Elliot and stop his plan," Callie corrected. "But also, you needed your connection to the rift to become firm, and spending time in the Vastness has done that. That frozen water outside, you felt what it did to you back in Agency, didn't you?"

"It was warm," I said. "I've touched it before and it felt cold and unpleasant, but this was different. Weird. Pleasant."

I didn't like the feeling that everything I'd done over the last few weeks had been because Callie had been pulling the strings to get me where she needed me to be. Preordained shit makes my head hurt. The grin on Callie's face did little to change that feeling.

"Why not just tell me everything I needed to know?" I asked.

"Because you wouldn't have believed me," Callie said. "You still don't, not entirely. Look, I need Ahiram, and you need to stop Elliot and his people. The Vipers. You're here because you are quite literally the only person I know who I can actually trust to do the right thing."

"Why did you leave me with a tear stone?" I asked.

"I needed to leave it somewhere," she said. "And honestly, I know you won't trust me, but you do trust the Queen of Crows. I knew you'd send it there."

"So, despite telling me to send it to the Queen, you knew that I wouldn't on your say so, but would anyway because I trust her, even if I don't trust you." The sentence made my head hurt.

Callie laughed. "My power doesn't work like that. You sent to the Queen because of your own thoughts. You must have been annoyed that I mentioned sending to her before you thought of it. Sorry about that. My ability to see the rift around me is only what is best for the rift, not what is best for individuals in it. Not even myself."

"Are you omnipotent?" I asked. "Immortal? What's the deal?"

"I'm not sure," she said. "I am what the rift needs me to be."

"Superb," I said sarcastically. "Very helpful. How do I get out of this prison?"

Callie shrugged.

"Okay, so, you get me here by telling me and those arseholes out there that that I was the key and that I had to be here to save Neb," I said, feeling a headache coming on. "What am I the key to do?"

"I don't know," she said. "I just know that it's you who does it."

"Does what?"

"It's infuriating, isn't it?"

"Your grin isn't helping," I pointed out. "So, do I actually need to be here right now?"

"I needed to talk to you before I woke up Ahiram," she said. "Please don't try to talk me out of it."

My argument died on my lips.

"Tell them what I am doing, and be honest," Callie continued. "They won't kill Neb because they can't risk it."

"And me?" I asked.

"Oh, they want to kill you," Callie said. "Matthew especially, but I've convinced Elliot you're needed inside the prison, so you'll be a guest here. It was the best I could do."

"This all feels . . . annoying," I said. "Elliot and his people are going to get out of here."

"Yes," Callie said sadly.

"And I have to figure out how to escape, too."

"Yes."

"And you've told them how to unlock moving freely through the ruins of the rift."

"I did."

"You aren't helpful."

"I'm not trying to be. I need Elliot and his people gone from this prison; I can't risk Ahiram waking and they finding him. It would make things . . . awkward. I convinced Elliot that the link between Earth and rift needed to be weaker for the ruins to work properly, but that's not true; he always had the ability to use them, just like you have. I just didn't want him bouncing around the rift, making my life more awkward.

"Elliot is already so keen to make war in the name of a man he's barely ever spoken to, it didn't take much to convince him that I'd stay here and wake him up while he went out and did what he needed to do in Ahiram's name."

I rubbed my temples. "How do I use the ruins to travel?"

"Like Elliot, you already have everything you need to let you do it," Callie said.

"This has been one of the more irritating encounters I've ever had with a person," I said.

"I know," Callie said. "Can I just say that I know you look at me and see a woman who has done horrible things over the years? I'm not her. Not really. I am . . . I have nothing to gain from lying to you. And you know I'm not, don't you."

I stared at her and I did know she wasn't lying. I just didn't know why I knew that. "You left me this vial? The antidote."

"You still have it?" she asked. "Ah, that's good. It's a cure for the baubles that Tess was making based on my designs. She was so proud of them, and she was selling them to anyone who would buy them. Making a *profit* off my creation. I couldn't be having that, so I made a few . . . mentions to a few people in Agency and got her caught red-handed. Selling weapons to a group of outlaws. But then I needed a place to lay low and work on those boxes, and Tess had access to the primordial bone and water I needed, so I had to sort of make nice for a while. Never told her it was me who screwed her over in the first place."

"You've been busy," I said sarcastically.

Callie waved away my tone as if it didn't matter. "I made the vial for myself in case she got ideas above her station, but you should have it."

"What's going to happen to me?"

"You were touched by the rift," she said. "I don't know."

"This has all been as enlightening as mud," I said. "What's stopping me from just killing him and be damned with it all?"

"His death, in this state, could kill another Ancient," she said. "Could be Noah, or Timo, or Neb. That could destabilise a region within the rift or out of it. But more than that, you don't strike me as the *murder a comatose man* kind of person."

I stared at said comatose man. "Damn it."

Callie smiled sadly. "I wish I could give you solace that things will work out. But I can't. Goodbye, Lucas. I am sorry for what happened to you. I'm sorry for manipulating you to get you here. But you really are where you need to be. Tell Elliot I need time alone now; tell him I might need you again. Should mean you won't be locked up. Good luck. I think you'll need it."

Having learned a lot and at the same time very little, I banged on the door. Elliot opened it, and I turned to see that Callie was now lying back in the chair, her eyes closed.

"She said she might need me again," I said. "But it's going to be days, maybe weeks before he'll wake up."

"What?" Elliot shouted.

"This isn't an exact science," I said. "He's been put in stasis for thousands of years, and his brain is moving like treacle. One wrong step and you've got a lobotomised hero to follow." I had no idea if any of that was true, but it felt about as accurate as anything else I could have said.

Kuri stood in the hallway behind Elliot. "We don't have weeks."

"I know," Elliot snapped. "It was always the plan that we would make sure that Ahiram woke to see his enemies vanquished, so he could get on with joining the rift and Earth as one. At last. Get everyone prepared."

Elliot grabbed me and yanked me out of the room, pushing me down the hallway toward the lift.

I was quiet as Kuri, Elliot, and I went back down to where my cell was. I said nothing as I was pushed inside, nodding an hello to Neb as she lay on her bed.

"Don't lock it," Elliot said as Kuri produced a key. "That mad doctor said she might need him."

"We've only got his word for that," Kuri said.

"Fine, lock me in," I said. "I don't care. But if she needs me and can't get to me because I'm in here, it'll probably end badly for Ahiram."

Elliot's anger practically flooded out of him. "Leave. Him. He can die when Ahiram is awake. First, we do what needs to be done."

"I think Matthew will want that privilege," Kuri said.

Elliot laughed. "Matthew really fucking hates you."

"Feel free to let Matthew in here now and we can get it done," I said with a smile.

"I don't think Matthew had a fair fight in mind," Elliot said. "So, while Callie might need you to finish what she's doing, I'm using you as a sort of treat to keep Matthew from doing anything stupid. Do you know that he's unhinged?"

"It's come up," I said.

"Well, if he behaves, he gets you," Elliot said. "If he misbehaves, he never gets to set foot on this island again. I just want to point out that he *really* hates you. I may have said that before, but it's worth repeating."

"Once I'm done with Matthew, I'll make sure to come find you."

Elliot stared at me for several seconds before laughing. "I see why you like him," he said to Neb before turning to me, his eyes hard and unwavering. "You are beneath me, Lucas. Do not mistake your being alive this long for being able to contend with me."

I got up, walked to the bars and stared at Elliot. "I'm going to get out of here. I'm going to find you. I'm going to kill you."

Elliot struck me in the chest faster than I could react. The blow caused me to stagger back, the air leaving my body in a rush.

"I have no powers in here, little riftborn," Elliot said as I struggled to breathe. "All I have done my whole life is learn how to kill people. I am, not to put too fine a point on it, an expert at ending the lives of others. You may think that you are a tough man, a hard man, but you have survived this long purely because you have never crossed my path. Pray you never do again. Enjoy your stay with those prisoners who chose to remain prisoners."

He showed me the rift-energy knuckleduster that had been given to me by Drusilla.

"I think I'll be keeping this," he said with a wide grin.

I watched Elliot and Kuri walk away, the sound of the lift rumbling in the distance, as I continued taking long deep breaths.

CHAPTER THIRTY-ONE

Neb and I were left alone in the cell for a while after that, the whistling of the wind as it whipped across the tower all that broke the silence.

"Are you okay?" Neb asked me after a while.

I'd remained on the floor, leaning up against the stone frame of the bed, looking out of our cell at the hallway beyond. Turning to smoke would end my predicament in less than a second. I moved and winced. The blow to my chest was still sore, but I was grateful that nothing was broken.

"No," I said eventually. "I am far from okay, Neb. I am sat in a prison, with no real hope of escape, while a group of monsters are about to rain down hell on the people of the rift. And probably Earth. Maybe some other places I've never heard of; I assume there are a few of those you've kept from me, too."

Neb sighed. "That's quite petulant to say."

"I feel like being petulant," I snapped back. "I've known you nearly my entire life. And while I always thought that you did your own thing, you lived your own life, and kept your own secrets, I never thought that you would keep things from me if they were important. I am angry at you, Neb. I will remain angry until I don't feel like being angry anymore. And the fact that you had an Ancient imprisoned here for thousands of years is pretty goddamned important. Also, it would have been nice to know about how Plainhaven is the home of the Raven Guild. Or that some of the original Guild members betrayed the others and joined Ahiram and are now called the Vipers."

"I didn't know the last bit."

There was a loud click, and Neb and my cell door sprang open.

Kuri walked into the room and stood before us. He held a spear in one hand . . . my spear. His smile was a lot smugger than I'd have expected from someone who was clearly happy to piss me off.

"This is exquisite," he said, moving the spear around.

"I'll be taking it back from you at some point," I said.

Kuri laughed. "Not anytime soon." He removed the vial Callie had given me from a pale brown leather pouch and showed it to me. "What is this?"

"Drink it and see," I said with a smile.

Kuri stared at me for several seconds before placing the vial back in the leather pouch. "I think not. Let's go."

Neb and I left our cell and walked to the end of the hallway and back onto the lift, before trundling down much farther than my last journey. Eventually, we stopped, and the grate opened, revealing a hallway that looked identical to the one we'd just left, but the smell was anything but. It smelled of stale water and blood. The dozen empty cages to the side of the lift had the appearance of being well used over the centuries, with scratches in the stone of some showing tallies of whatever the prisoner was keeping a tab on.

Kuri shoved me forward, and I stepped out of the lift, placing a hand on the wall to steady myself, and recoiled when I discovered that not only was it freezing cold but wet and slimy, too.

"We're near the bottom of the tower," Kuri said. "This is where most of the prisoners were kept, at least until they all woke up and they moved further up. The nicer floors. Did you know, there's a floor up there that has actual rooms and beds for the guards. Comfortable beds, too, with open, light rooms and fireplaces to keep warm."

"So, you're saying we can't stay there," I said, receiving another shove.

"You betrayed me for people who lived in slime," Neb said.

"You betrayed us *all*," Kuri said. "Riftborn could have been kings of this realm, kings of Earth, too, but you just didn't want to share. Earth and the rift aren't meant to be two places."

We walked down the hallway, stopping by a small window that revealed we were almost at eye level with the ground outside. The garrison was still awash with activity, and people were still being brought over on the boat. A slow process. There was a cobalt-blue mist rolling over the garrison, which wasn't something I'd ever seen before.

Moving away from the window, Kuri opened a large metal door, the hinges squealing in protest, and beckoned us both through. I was pretty sure that between the two of us, we could take Kuri, but he had a spear, and we had the power of positive thinking, and I was pretty sure that wasn't going to cut it in a fight. Besides, even if we did beat him, we had an unknown number of his allies waiting between us and freedom.

Beyond the door was a short hallway leading to a dark staircase.

"Down," Kuri said.

I *really* didn't want to go down there.

"If we'd wanted you dead, you'd be dead," Kuri said.

A valid point. I descended the steps carefully because they too were slippery, but they were also steep and jagged. They'd been carved out of the stone with very little care for anyone having to come up and down them.

I reached the bottom of the steps and looked around the large open room. There were five cages on opposite sides of the room, each one a few feet from those either side of it. Between the cages was a large table with chairs, and at either end of the room were large metal doors similar to the one that Kuri had opened.

The cells were all occupied by people who looked like they'd been kept in cells for a prolonged period of time. They barely gave us any attention as Kuri shoved us toward the far-end door, which opened by the time we'd made it halfway through the floor.

The thing that came through the door was eight feet tall and weighed two of me at least. It had a metal helmet over its huge face that gave it the appearance of a bull. It wore a bronze armoured breastplate, shoulder guards, shin guards, and the remains of a tunic jutting out of the armour around its waist. It was barefoot, although considering the size of the feet, I wasn't entirely sure how you'd find footwear to fit them.

"You made a minotaur?" I said.

"Callie wasn't the first person to start playing around with the genetics of the rift-fused," Neb said. "She won't be the last."

The monster removed its helmet, revealing a large, scarred face, with tusks that protruded out of its mouth a short distance and a long, black horn on either side of its forehead. Its small eyes were full of nothing but hate and evil intent. It had no hair on its head, and its skin was the colour of putrid green. Whatever this thing was, if it had once been human, that humanity had died long before.

"This is Donis," Kuri said.

"Oh, dear boy," Neb said softly. "*This* is what became of you?"

Donis made a dismissive nose and replaced its helmet, which I now saw was designed to almost perfectly mimic his actual head.

"You know him?" I asked.

"He trusted Ahiram," Neb said.

"Until this *dear boy* betrayed him," Kuri finished. "Tried to kill him. Was captured and passed over to Vel."

"Who the hell is Vel?" I asked.

Donis roared at me, and I figured that meant to shut up, so I did. Apparently, the name alone was a sore spot.

We were marched through the open door, and Donis motioned to two open cells beside one another. Apart from one cell having what looked like a mound of fur blankets on the floor, there was no one and nothing else in the identically furnished room from the one before it. Although another metal door at the end made me wonder just how far these cells went.

The cell doors were closed behind us, and I sat on the stone bed and looked around. It was the same as the cell in the upper levels of the tower, except we didn't have a bloody monster walking around up there. Unless you counted Ahiram.

"Enjoy your new home," Kuri said. "I advise you to not piss off Donis. We'll leave a key with Callie to come let you out if she needs you."

Donis huffed in our direction and strolled out of the room, with Kuri beside him.

"Who the hell is that?" I asked Neb. "And who the hell is Vel?"

"Donis was a Greek warrior," she said, testing her new bed before laying down on it. "Horned revenant. He joined Ahiram in his initial war. I think he just wanted revenge on everyone who had turned him into a horned revenant and then killed him for being a horned revenant. At some point, he realised that Ahiram was worse than the people he hated, and turned on him. Tried to slit his throat at night. In punishment, Donis was obviously passed over to Vel. Vel is a riftborn. A lot of his early work is what Callie hoped to perfect with her nightmarish creations you killed."

"Donis is the first of those monsters that needed primordial bone to kill?" I asked.

"I don't know, really," she said. "This is the first I've seen of him in two thousand years. I thought he died. I think maybe that would have been preferable to . . . whatever this is."

"So, how are we meant to get out of this one?" I asked. "I don't fancy spending a few centuries sat in a cell while possibly occasionally becoming frozen in time. Sounds like something I would find unpleasant."

"I say we wait," Neb said.

"For what?" I asked.

"Nightfall," she said. "Shouldn't be long now."

"Neb, what did we just discuss about you keeping secrets?" I asked.

"Ah, you'll like this one," she said, looking over at me with a twinkle in her eye.

It was pretty clear that despite our current circumstances, Neb wasn't too worried, which meant she probably had a plan in place.

"Those prisoners in the other room," I said. "They refused to work with Ahiram."

"Are you wondering why anyone would choose to stay here?" Neb asked. "They could agree with him, leave, and run."

"They'd be running their whole lives," I said. "Staying was the only thing in their power that they could do."

"Would you stay?" Neb asked. "If you were here and offered the chance to join him, I mean."

"I'd have tried to kill him," I said.

"You'd have failed," Neb replied firmly.

I shrugged. "I'd have died on my feet, not in a cell."

"Why not fight upstairs, then, when you had the chance?" Neb asked.

I remained silent for several seconds.

"Because it would leave me still here," Neb said softly. "It would leave me in his clutches."

"Yeah," I almost whispered.

It was Neb's turn to say nothing for several seconds. "You are a good man. Better than you think. Better than I probably deserve to have as a friend."

"Where will Elliot go first?" I asked, changing the subject to something I was actually comfortable talking about.

"The Crow's Perch," she said quickly. "Ahiram hates the Queen of Crows, so Elliot will want to bring her to him for when he wakes up."

"I don't understand," I said. "She's only centuries old. She was put in the Crow's Perch after the attempted coup by the Blessed. Why would he hate her?"

"She was not always called the Queen of Crows," Neb said. "She is older than you by several centuries. She was there when the Guilds were made. She stood beside me when they were named. She stood beside me when we went to war with Ahiram. I was the one who led the Guilds to stop him, but *she* beat him. It hurt her greatly, and it took her a long time to recover. His power to absorb the abilities of those near him almost caused her to become little more than human for years, but she beat him. Sword to sword in front of his army, she crippled him and left him to bleed out on the sand."

I stared at Neb. "Who is she, Neb? I know you two are close, but she was scared for you. She wanted to come with me, I think. Wanted to fight. I've seen her fight; she's good. Very good."

"Not as good as she used to be," Neb said. "The fight with Ahiram hurt her badly. Vel made a gas, a compound with Ahiram's blood in it; I'm not entirely sure how it worked. There was a lot of rift energy. Either way, her winning cost her. She gets tired quicker now. Her body never really healed, even after all this time."

I stayed quiet.

"Her name is Darice," Neb said eventually. "She's my great-granddaughter."

CHAPTER THIRTY-TWO

Your great-granddaughter," I said after sitting bolt upright.

"I had children before I became a riftborn," Neb said. "Three. Two girls and a boy. They went on to live ordinary lives for the time. All had families. I kept an eye on them, just to see how they were doing. Eventually, one of my grandchildren married a man from a Greek tribe and they had a daughter; Darice. Darice was . . . *exceptional.* At twenty-two she was murdered by a guard. She became riftborn. I found her, because this was the time before Inaxia was so organised, and I trained her. She excelled in everything.

"We discussed her becoming a Raven, but she declined. I think mostly because I was related to her and she didn't want anyone thinking there was any nepotism. Instead, I trained her to be whatever we needed. Someone who could strike from the shadows unseen, someone who would do what was needed. I suppose, in a way, she's where the Guild Talons originated.

"After her injury, after everything that happened with Ahiram, she wanted nothing to do with the Guilds, with this life. She left to live on Earth. Spent a thousand years there, wandering, learning, just living among the humans. She returned to the rift and did the same here. Mapping a lot of the places we know about now. She spent time in the Tempest, and in places I'm not even sure anyone has been to. And eventually, she decided to join the Blessed.

"They were meant to be the best of us all. But as Ahiram showed, the best can be corrupted by greed, by the need for *more*. Darice agreed to take the mantle of Queen of Crows. She wears the mask because . . . well, because otherwise, she looks like a paler version of me. Neither of us wanted the other to be used as a way to get at us."

"Didn't people notice that when she first arrived in the rift?" I asked.

"I met her the second she arrived," Neb said. "I explained who I was, who she was. She accepted it. Decided to wear a mask almost from the beginning of her time here. It was a simple black mask to begin with, but eventually, she changed it. Darice has spent almost her whole life in the rift wearing one mask or another. If people discovered who she was to me, she might be in danger. By now, she's racked up her own list of dangerous enemies, who would use me to get to her. The Queen of Crows is someone who scared those in Inaxia who need scaring. Like Prime Roberts."

"What happened to Vel?" I asked.

"No one knows," Neb said. "And I mean that. There are rumours he lives in an isolated cabin atop a mountain somewhere on Earth, occasionally taking people, and making them think it was the abominable snowman. He's a large man, heavyset, so it's possible. Like I said, no one knows."

"Does Ahiram know?" I asked.

"About Vel?" Neb replied. "Maybe."

"And he definitely knows about Darice and you," I said.

Neb nodded.

"Can she stop him again?"

"Whatever shit Vel made up had an effect on her ever since," Neb said. "We've tried everything to heal her, but nothing quite works for longer than a few years. It's not killing her, it's not making her worse, it's just . . . *there*."

"Why didn't he use it again?" I asked.

"I don't know," Neb said. "We tried to find him, but he's elusive. I sometimes wonder if he's trying his best to keep his head down so *I* don't find him."

The look on her face suggested it would be a bad day for Vel.

"Do you actually have a plan?" I asked, without looking over at Neb.

"I'm going to rest for a bit," she said. "And when I wake up, I'm pretty sure you'll have an answer one way or another."

It wasn't like there was much else I could do from inside the cell, and apart from yelling and generally exhausting myself out in a futile attempt to escape, I was just going to have to wait until whatever Neb had planned happened. I really hoped it didn't involve setting fire to the whole prison.

I looked over at Neb, whose eyes were closed. She looked at peace.

It probably involved setting fire to the prison.

CHAPTER THIRTY-THREE

I woke up to discover that nothing was on fire. Considering the low expectations I had for whatever I was going to find when I opened my eyes, I took that as a win.

Neb sat on the end of her bed, leaning against the bars. "You snore," she said without turning around.

"I'll add it to the list," I said.

"What list?" she asked, turning to face me.

I sat up. "The list of things I don't much care about."

Neb smiled. "Still mad at me."

"I'm still alive, so yes," I said. "When I die, I'll still be mad at you, but I'll be dead so won't care as much."

"Some people in the Church say we all go to our own version of heaven," Neb said.

"Some people in the Church sniff glue," I replied, a tad sharper than I'd expected. "I'm not saying there's a correlation; I just think some people have too much time on their hands."

"Doesn't your friend Gabriel run a part of that Church?"

I nodded. "He's never told me I'm going to heaven, Neb. I'm pretty sure he spends most of his time just trying to have faith that there are still good people in the world."

Neb's smile faded. "You don't think there are good people in the world."

"I haven't had enough coffee before I start my theoretical heresy for the day," I said. "I assume there won't be any brought in."

"I don't think we'll be getting croissants, either," Neb said. "Shame, I like the almond ones."

"Okay, I'm awake now; what's the plan?"

Neb's smile slithered back in place. "Who says I have a plan?"

"You always have a plan, Neb. It's one of the more infuriating things about you. I assume you've had a plan since the moment you arrived. You've probably had a dozen and changed them on the fly as you went."

There was a loud crash from somewhere outside of the room, followed by a thud, another crash, and someone's muffled screams. The lefthand door to the cell was pushed open and Commander Marcus Pike entered the room. He wore a hodgepodge of armour—both leather and metal—and his breastplate sat over a white tunic. He carried a bastard sword in one hand and a buckler shield in the other. He was a lanky man with pale skin and had grown a large beard since I'd last seen him, and his hair was now shoulder length. He had several cuts on his face. He was also covered in blood.

The screaming turned to whimpering, which turned to wailing.

"What the hell is that?" I asked.

"Someone lost a hand," Pike said, using a set of keys to open Neb's prison cell door. "My lady."

"Marcus," she said with a smile as she opened the door.

"How did you get in here?" I asked.

"Kuri stabbed me, left me for dead; he thought I'd gone in the water, but I climbed in the boat and hid," he said. "Healed up okay, but I had to climb out of the boat and get around to the rear of the island. Couldn't get back over to the garrison without taking the boat, and that would have alerted everyone, so I just had to wait and figure out how to get inside the prison. Got a lot of help when the shield came down, and I managed to climb up the tower and get in through one of the windows below. I've had a long few days."

"Did you know he was coming?" I asked Neb.

"I did say I hadn't seen the body," Neb told me. "Also, I saw him climbing around the rear of the prison one night just before you got here, so odds were good he was still alive."

Pike opened my door next and I thanked him. The first time we'd met, I'd thought he was a gigantic pain in the arse. Admittedly, the first time we met, I thought he was working for Prime Roberts, which had made Pike a douche by association. Turned out he was actually undercover, and since then we'd become friendly, if not close.

"Raven," he said to me with a slight smile.

"*Lucas* is fine," I told him.

I walked over to the door and saw six prisoners, all with swords, all stood over Donis, who was busy holding one wrist in the opposite hand as blood pumped over the floor. The missing hand was several feet away, next to a nasty-looking hammer, the end of which was the same size as my head.

"Monsters die just as easily as men," Pike said.

"So long as you have a sword," I pointed out.

"He was our jailer," one of the six men snarled.

"My name is Neb," she said, her tone having commanded armies, having told kings and queens exactly what their reality was. Six armed men in a prison had no hope of challenging her. "You may have heard of me. You may not have. But you've all been in prison for some time, and I assure you, the first one who attacks Donis again, dies."

"He deserves to die," one of the men repeated.

"Did he mistreat you?" Neb asked. "Any of you?"

The men all shared a glance, and everyone took a step back. Good to know none of them were idiots.

Neb walked over to Donis and crouched beside him. "You have a choice," she said.

The man still wore his bull helmet, which was splashed with blood. He looked up at her.

"I will treat your wound; you will help us," Neb said softly. "You attack me, and you die here. You refuse to help, and you die here. I will make your death quick. Painless. I cannot, however, make your life mean something. No one can but you."

Donis tried to remove his helmet one-handed but couldn't manage it, and Neb helped him, dropping the helmet on the floor when they were done.

"I cannot leave this place," Donis said softly.

"Cannot or will not?" I asked.

"Whichever one you prefer," Donis said.

"You know how to get out of the prison, don't you?" I asked Neb.

She nodded. "There are tunnels under the lake. Haven't exactly had a chance to use them."

"That information might have come in handy," I said.

"I didn't know until Donis told me," she explained.

"You know where they are, don't you?" Neb asked. "The tunnels."

Donis nodded.

"Our weapons," I said.

"They took your spear," Pike said from behind me. "Saw Kuri with it."

"Why haven't you ever escaped, Donis?" I asked.

"I am simple Donis," he said as the medical supplies were returned from wherever they were kept, and Neb set about wrapping the wound that had already cauterised itself. Apparently, whatever was done to Donis had allowed him to keep his ability to heal within the prison grounds. "Simple, stupid jailer. Man who betrayed our master."

The word *master* was spat with a lot of venom.

"Escape not escape if you run straight into a garrison," Donis said. "Can't open door to tunnels, anyway."

"Why?" Neb asked.

Donis stared at Neb for a second. "Need key. Don't have key."

"That could be a problem," Pike said.

"Pike, find every prisoner," Neb said. "Unlock them, bring them here."

"And if they don't want to come?" Pike asked.

Neb shrugged. "They come with us or die here."

"Die on feet, not on knees," Donis said.

Several of the prisoners who had been willing to kill their jailer only moments earlier nodded in agreement.

"How many of these prisoners actually did something awful?" I asked.

"That's subjective," Neb said. "What is one man's freedom fighter is another man's terrorist."

"Yeah, I've heard that once or twice," I said. "I mean, prisoners who won't work well with others. Who will try to kill us, drug us, betray us the first chance they get, or any combination of the three."

"All left with Elliot," Donis said. "These are the guards who worked in the garrison and refused to follow Elliot. He gave them to Matthew to break. They are loyal to Inaxia. Those who survived still are."

"Need an armoury," I said, not wanting to think about the horde of horrors that would be helping Elliot do whatever it was Elliot was out there doing.

"Next to the medical room," one of the prisoners said. "It's been partially emptied, but there's still some weapons in there."

"Go get them," I said to the prisoners. "Get everything out and bring it here; we'll see what we're working with."

"And what are you going to do?" Neb asked me.

"I'm going to go have a look out of that window nearby and see if everyone leaving this prison has left," I said, took a step, and paused. I looked back at Donis. "Do you know what the blue mist is out there?"

Donis shook his massive head. "They spoke about planning . . . *welcome*. I didn't understand."

"We'll figure it out," Neb said as she finished up helping Donis.

I left them all to it and moved through the prison to the small window I'd seen while being brought down there. There was still the mist clinging to the garrison, but I couldn't see anyone actually there. It wasn't great news that they'd all run off to cause whatever havoc they were planning, but there was little we could do until we were outside.

Someone cleared their throat behind me, and I turned to find Marcus Pike stood there.

"They're going after the Queen," he said, the tension in his voice easy to hear.

I nodded. "That's what Neb said, too."

"You know who she is," Pike said, and I wasn't sure if it was a question or not.

I nodded.

"A lot of innocent people in the Crow's Perch are going to die," Marcus said eventually.

I nodded again. There weren't any words that would make that fact better.

"You ever been here before?" Pike asked, standing beside me to look across the lake.

"No," I said. "Can't say it was on the list of places I even knew existed. Now I kind of wish I'd stayed at home and never left."

Pike laughed again. "You think we can do this?" He was suddenly serious.

I looked out of the window again. "We don't have a choice. We either stop him, stop them, or people we care about die."

"If he's hurt my Queen . . ." Pike's words trailed off, as if he couldn't bring himself to finish that sentence.

I patted Pike on the shoulder. "Let's go get ready."

We went back to the room with the cells, only to find it was now filled with twenty-one more prisoners. Everyone was picking up weapons from a stack on the floor, and several of the prisoners now wore armour, and not the prison-issue clothing of black tunic, leggings, and sandals. The remaining were still finding armour to wear or a weapon to use.

In total there were twenty-nine prisoners, with eight of them being women and the rest men. All of them looked like they needed a haircut and a good meal, although none looked to be malnourished, and all of them were keen to fight.

"Who of you has fighting experience?" I asked. "Or battle experience?"

Nearly everyone put their hands up, a product of humanity in a nutshell. "Right, we'll get kitted out, and we'll figure out how to open a door we don't have the key for."

"I know how to open the door," Neb said. "It's fine."

I shrugged. "Excellent; it's fine, everyone. Neb knows."

I walked by everyone and back into the room where my cell was, feeling a presence behind me a moment later. I turned to see Neb in the doorway.

"Timo said you all made a pact to keep this place and Ahiram secret, but people have died because you did exactly that. She said you didn't kill him because you were all afraid about what his death might do. You thought of yourselves, not the rift. Not the people. It's exactly why I don't trust the Ancients."

Neb nodded.

I removed the Raven medallion from my neck and stared at it. "Elliot killed the Ravens. He arranged it because he thought it would bring him favour with a comatose Ahiram who was talking to him through his dreams."

Neb stared at me.

"Yep, not in a million years did I think of that one," I said. "Matthew helped, and a lot of good people died to help one man get over himself after thousands of years of grudge-holding because the Ravens actually remained loyal to the Ancients."

"You were the only ones who actually posed a threat," Neb said. "The Ravens wouldn't join him, and they were still trusted by the Ancients, while the other Guilds had to rebuild not only their numbers but trust among us. He hates you for it."

"I'm going to get out of here and I'm going to kill Elliot. I'm going to make sure he dies *hard*. I trust there are no objections."

"Absolutely none," Neb said.

CHAPTER THIRTY-FOUR

I t felt like forever to get everyone geared up and ready to go, and while Neb vouched for everyone we'd set free, I didn't know any of them, so I followed from the rear of the pack for the entire journey. Which had the benefit of everyone leaving me alone.

A number of our new recruits were the guards from the garrison who had been kept alive so that Elliot and his allies could torture them. There didn't appear to be a reason for the torture beyond being angry that they refused to join him. Another reason to dislike him.

It was a long climb down a spiral stairwell for several minutes until we reached a large set of double doors, which Donis opened. There were lots of books, most on shelves, and lots of scrolls, most on tables, but there was no time to search everything to see what might be interesting.

"No one came down here?" Neb asked Donis.

The big man shook his head.

Inside the large area, there was an archway in one corridor, beyond which was a study. It contained a large wooden table, three wooden chairs, several bottles of varying coloured liquids sat on a shelf, a large mirror, and the faint smell of perfume. Something flowery. Maybe to dull the smell of anything else that happened down there.

I picked up one of the vials of liquid, a bright sky-blue concoction that turned to a gas when I shook it. I decided that shaking it was a bad idea and put it back.

On the other side of the large space was the inevitable medical area . . . experimentation area. There were arms on the wall that appeared to be made of metal, and a cupboard in the corner revealed legs, hands, and metal spheres that were roughly the size and shape of a human head. It was a deeply disturbing place to be. There were shackles on the walls, and no amount of perfume was going to get the smell of blood out of the bare stone floors. It felt like evil the second I stepped inside.

"Here," Donis said, crossing the floor of the medical room and placing his hand against the stone wall at the far end. "Riftborn has to do it."

Neb and I shared a glance. "Why?" she asked.

"Vel used to think me stupid," Donis said, "after all he did to me. He thought he could share his secrets. Not all. But some. This was his escape but also his last little joke. A door that has no key but I can never open. It needs riftborn blood, but what he did to me bonded me to this place. I can never leave. Vel was angry that he couldn't change this to let only him through; had to be riftborn blood. Not a lot; just a scratch."

Neb cut along the palm of her hand. In Hollywood films, cutting along your palm and then making a fist, produced a veritable torrent of blood. In real life, cutting along your palm is a ludicrously stupid thing to do if it doesn't heal soon after doing it. It was one of those things that always bothered me.

I finished ranting in my head and watched Neb place her hand against the stone, which lit up bright orange and yellow as if it had burst into flames. The stone made a noise that did not sound good whilst stood under hundreds of tonnes of it, and slid across the wall.

Pike, who stood beside me, let out a breath he'd been holding. "I wasn't sure what was going to happen there," he said.

"I'm never sure about anything that happens in the rift," I told him.

"What about light?" one of the prisoners asked from the doorway.

"I'll go get one," Pike said, and left the room, retuning a few moments later with two lanterns that burned a light blue. "Found them in the study," he said, placing one on a nearby table and holding onto the second.

"Everyone out," Neb shouted.

Pike went first, with a nod to Donis. "Thank you," he said.

Donis bowed his head, and we watched Pike disappear into the darkness of the tunnel, the light of the torch still visible as he waited for the prisoners to catch up.

Neb and I stepped to the side as all of the prisoners filed out into the dark tunnel, most of whom looked like they were prepared to fight. Although I wondered how many would think that when faced with actual fighting for the first time in what could have been centuries. Some of them nodded to Donis, but most were just fixated on not being in prison anymore.

Eventually, it was just Neb, Donis, and me. Neb went through, leaving the big man and me alone. Donis turned to me. "I will not be a jailer anymore."

I stared at him for a second before nodding. "Callie and Ahiram are on the top floor; I would be grateful if they didn't leave before we return," I said. "I don't know what she's doing, but from previous form, it's never good."

"They will not leave," he assured me.

"Thank you, Donis," I said from the doorway. I closed the door and ran down the tunnel, catching up to everyone after only a few hundred metres.

Everyone did exactly that, and despite the meagre light, we were all soon jogging down the tunnel. The tunnel got wetter with every step, until it was dangerous to do anything but walk slowly on increasingly slippery stone.

No one spoke as we continued on, the splash of water under our feet the only sound made. There was an occasional noise like something straining against metal or stone, and that hurried us on for a while, the slipperiness be damned. I was not being crushed to death or drowning in the rift-energy water above us.

Eventually, we reached a metal door with a wheel on it, which needed to be loosened to remove the seal. It took Pike and I to force the wheel to move after being stuck solid for who knew how long, but we managed it and pulled open the door, letting everyone out.

"Where are we?" one of the prisoners asked as we all found ourselves in a small stone room.

Neb and I closed the hatch, with an echo-inducing *clang* as it shut fast again.

"There's no door," Pike said, using the lantern to look around.

Neb cut her hand again and placed it on the wall opposite the hatch. The stone wall burned orange and yellow as before and slid to the side with the same level of noise. A stealthy approach was now out of the question.

Once the wall was open, it revealed a stockroom, full of . . . well, stock. There were a few items of food—although none of it looked or smelled fresh—and barrels of water, along with some weapons and pieces of armour. It was the room where stuff got stashed.

At the end of the room was a small door, which I walked over to and pushed open, letting everyone out into the fresh air once more. Although "fresh air" was probably not the right thing to suggest, considering the blue fog that we were met with.

"What the hell is this?" Pike asked as the fog swirled around everyone's feet.

I stepped outside into the garrison, my hand on the hilt of my sword. There was no one there. The boat was sat in the water, bobbing slightly as it awaited Elliot's return to a wakened Ahiram. I intended to spoil that reunion.

After a few minutes of looking around, the fog began to glow before sinking down into the hard soil beneath our feet. "What is this stuff?" I asked.

"I do not know," Neb said.

The fog was all but gone now, the garrison guards stood in the open, all looking around. Some of them were staring at the tear above our heads; some of them held their weapons in a tight grip, ready for trouble.

"Pike," I said. "Go check the ramparts; let's make sure we're not about to have any trouble."

The ground rumbled.

"Bollocks," I said softly.

Pike ran to the door of the nearest tower, practically sprinting through it without stopping, with Neb and me following closely behind. We bounded up the spiral stone staircase two at a time, and I wished I had access to my power. I wished it even more so when we reached the top of the tower and looked out across the landscape to see a large number of angry-looking people running toward us from the cover of the nearby hills.

They all had weapons and armour and gave the appearance of people who were not there to discuss how everyone felt after getting out of the prison.

"Get the gates shut," I shouted down to anyone who might hear me, and ran back down the stairs when I realised we didn't have time to mess about.

I sprinted through the garrison toward where the gates were and found that the lever was destroyed.

Donis's words came back to me, *a welcome*.

"They knew we'd get out," Neb said from behind me.

"No," I said. "This isn't for us. They were expecting people to come here and help us. They left them something to stop them."

"The mist," Neb said.

There was a scream from back where the prisoners were congregating. Neb and I ran back the way we'd come, only to discover that the earth had broken open, and metallic human-shaped monsters were crawling out of shallow graves all around the garrison.

"The people running have stopped," Pike shouted as he reached us. "It's like they're waiting for . . . Fucking hell, what is that?"

The metal creatures continued to tear their way out of the ground as everyone moved away, putting distance between themselves and the new threat. All of the creatures had the Viper Guild mark on their forehead, and it blazed red as they started to move toward us.

Neb ran up to one such metal creature and buried an axe in its smooth, faceless head. The blade dug into the head, but the creature continued to try and pull itself out of the ground. Neb tore the axe away, and blue mist billowed out of the three-inch-deep chunk missing from the metal face of the creature.

"Vel made these," Neb said.

I remembered the metal arms in the laboratory under the prison. "Why does everyone who knew him want to make monsters?" I asked.

"Who put them there?" Pike asked. "The ground doesn't look disturbed."

Now was not the time for answers, and I ran at one of the creatures as it pulled itself free from the ground. My sword caught it in the neck and had a sharp-enough edge to travel a few inches, forcing the head to flop back on itself, exposing the neck, as mist poured out of the body. It kicked out at me, forcing me back, and I noticed the talons on each foot and the same on each hand.

There were a dozen of the mechanical monsters once they were free from the ground, although the garrison guard we'd taken from the prison had started to attack them well before that, and nearly all of the monsters were bleeding the blue fog. It didn't slow them down.

The creatures continued coming, taking blow after blow as if it were nothing. One of them caught one guard across their stomach, opening it up, and kicking the guard in the chest as they fell forward. The crunch of metal meeting bone was enough for everyone to move back, dragging the seriously injured man with them.

One of the monsters attempted to launch itself at me, but I ducked the blow, driving the sword up into their chest, where their heart would have been and tearing through the side of the torso.

"The metal is soft," I said. "It's easy to injure, but it doesn't seem to matter what you do to them."

Those not injured ran back into the fray, hacking at limbs with a variety of bladed weapons. The arms and legs of the mechanical things fell off, but the creatures themselves kept coming. Only when having lost a few limbs and its head did the creatures fall unmoving to the ground.

Unfortunately, by the time you'd caused enough damage to one of them, they had managed to cause a lot of injuries of their own, and our side were losing people rapidly. As the seventh creature fell unmoving to the ground, we were forced farther and farther back toward the main gate of the garrison, with six of our own group too injured to continue. And with the lack of power caused by the rift energy in the area, we weren't going to be healing back to full health anytime soon.

Neb and I fought in unison, moving through three of the metal creatures, hacking at legs and arms as we continued through them. Three more dead mechanical creatures, but both Neb and I were bleeding from a host of small but occasionally deep wounds.

By the time we reached the main gate for the garrison, there were seven of our group dead and another eight with injuries that left them close to useless.

Before the last of the creatures were killed, I heard a roar of anger behind us and turned to see Kuri and fifty soldiers, all fully armed and armoured, and all charging toward us.

"That's mine," I said as I walked toward the shut gate.

Kuri raised his fist to stop once they reached the garrison grounds, spinning my spear in one hand.

Kuri shrugged. "Mine now."

"The trap is linked to your Viper Medallion," Neb said from beside me.

"The second you stepped on the land and triggered the mechanical monsters," he said, showing his Viper guild medallion, "we had to stop and come make sure they finished the job. Guess we didn't leave enough of them."

"There's only fifty of you," I said. "And you're stuck out there, while we're in here. Unless you can walk through solid stone and metal, I think we'll be fine."

Kuri laughed. "These are all highly trained garrison soldiers. Not old men and women who have barely held a sword for hundreds of years. This is your last chance. Surrender. Have an honourable death."

"What do you know of honour?" Neb shouted, her face red with anger. "You little scab of a man. You come here yourself and best me in combat if you dare. You cowardly piece of shit."

"So be it," Kuri said. "I will enjoy ending you all. You should know those creatures need to be dealt with better than you did. See you soon."

The sound of metal scraping against metal got my attention as the twelve mechanical beasts began to repair themselves.

"Oh, fuck off," Pike said.

I picked up the limb closest to me and threw it into the lake. It touched the near-frozen water and hissed unpleasantly, like someone letting the air out of a tire, before vanishing from view in a bubble of water.

"Get them in the lake," I shouted, and everyone who could picked up a piece and threw it into the lake. Some of the pieces had to be hacked off the main body again, but we managed to get them all back in the lake, with only two of us taking an injury, and none of them were major.

The group outside the garrison began banging their shields. We were stuck between a lake that would kill us and a bunch of crazed psychopaths who would kill us.

I picked up a ruined shield from the ground and tossed it aside, settling for just using the longsword instead. "How many of you have fought in a shield wall?" I asked.

Those who had, which turned out to be nearly all of them, formed a dozen-man shield wall, where at least half of that number were walking wounded. Still, I didn't see a better way for them to possibly survive.

"How many people were in the garrison here?" I asked Neb.

"Two fifty, three hundred," Neb said.

"He knows how to use the ruins to move around the rift, but where would he go?"

"Plainhaven is the closest place with ruins," Neb said. "He'd go there, force his way in."

"Oh shit," I said. "I sent a tear stone back to the Crow's Perch for safekeeping."

Concern crossed over Neb's face. "We have to get to Plainhaven. Now."

"How many could he take with him?" I asked, keeping an eye on the approaching fifty soldiers.

"A dozen, maybe," Neb said.

"So, where are the rest of the soldiers?" Pike asked.

The soldiers outside of the garrison stopped banging their shields. Kuri made a hand gesture with each hand, and hooks were thrown up and over the side of the garrison walls.

I looked from Kuri to the walls as more soldiers scrambled over them, dropping down into the garrison with murderous intent.

"Do we keep the shield wall?" one of the guards asked.

"Do what you can to survive," I told them.

"We can't win this," Pike said as Kuri started to laugh again.

I stared at Pike. He wasn't scared, he wasn't trying to suggest we run, he was just making a case for the fact that we couldn't beat three hundred trained soldiers with what we had. "Take as many of the bastards with you as you can when you go," I shouted.

CHAPTER THIRTY-FIVE

The soldiers came over the walls, dropped down into the garrison, and moved toward our group in one unified block of murderous intent. Someone opened the garrison gate, although I didn't see who or how, just the slow, lumbering ascent of the portcullis. Kuri and his squad remained on the opposite side of the entrance, waiting for the entrance to be fully open.

We were trapped. There was no getting out of this fight, and there was certainly no winning. We were outnumbered twenty to one, we were essentially human, and all of us were injured to some degree or another.

Unfortunately for those who decided to attack us, we were all too stubborn to actually just lie down and let them kill us.

We stayed in something resembling a formation, keeping those forming a shield wall—including Neb, who had taken command—to the right. Pike, and anyone else who could stand, did so with me facing the left. It was, frankly, a ludicrous last stand.

I glanced over at Kuri, who was pointing and laughing. He had the pouch that Callie had left for me with the antidote in it. I was going to get that back. "The great Neb," he called out. "How long I waited for this moment."

The two sides continued their unstoppable march toward us. No running, no chanting, just a slow, steady walk toward our inevitable deaths. I always knew I'd die in battle; it was the life I'd led. I would have preferred to have gone out taking those who had put me in that battle to begin with, but few get to choose where and when they go.

"On my command, slaughter them," Kuri said to the soldiers behind him as the portcullis finished rising, and we'd all backed up as far as

possible before getting into the water. "Goodbye, Neb. You're an unpleasant bitch. Kill them all."

It was my experience in the world that bad people often like to gloat.
I don't mean monologue à la James Bond villains, but bad people like to
make sure you understand who is killing you; they want to see that fear,
see the knowledge in your eyes that they beat you. The worse the person, the more pontificating they do. And Kuri struck me as a particularly
unpleasant little arsehole. I honestly didn't know how Neb never noticed.

The fifty behind Kuri charged toward us, screaming bloody murder.
Our small group had to quickly move to face the new threat, and although
the shield wall was all but useless with so few people against so many, I
was genuinely impressed that they maintained it as they moved.

They intercepted the first group of soldiers with an almighty crash,
while the remaining prisoners, Pike, and I tried to make sure they didn't
have to deal with anyone trying to get to one of the sides of the shield-wall
group.

The wall lasted about twenty seconds before it all descended into anar-
chy, with the dozen of us who were capable of serious fighting against the
fifty of the soldiers who were clearly trained killers. It didn't take long
before it was just Neb, Pike, and I against the horde, and while we put
down more than our fair share, it wasn't long after that all three of us
started flagging.

"Back," Kuri commanded, and the group left us on our knees in the
now-chewed-up ground. We were panting and bleeding and generally
looked a right mess, but we were alive.

"I wish to end her myself," Kuri said.

This was a spectacularly bad idea. I wouldn't have tried to pick a fight
with Neb unless she was already dead, and even then, I'd do it from a
distance, just in case. If there was one thing that Kuri should have learned
during his time with her, it was that if there was life in her, there was the
ability to kill in her.

Kuri strolled through the cheering crowd of imbeciles like he'd just
run up the steps like Rocky. He was slapped on the back by several of
his soldiers, and he twirled the spear . . . *my spear* . . . like a damn baton.
Whatever horror was about to befall him was deserved.

He stood over Neb and looked down at her, a smug grin on his face.
He used the tip of the blade on the end of my spear to lift her head to
look up at him. "For so long, I have worked for you, I did what you asked.
I became a bodyguard, a confidant, a man you relied on to do what you

needed done. All this time, you never knew that I was working against you. The mighty Neb got caught out. I want you to know that . . ." His chest exploded before he could say anything else.

Kuri topped forward onto the dirt beside Neb as everyone looked around to try and figure out what in the world had just happened. A second later, two soldiers' heads were turned into plumes of red mist as they vanished. A third died the same way before the people in the garrison's main entrance figured out something bad was happening and turned to see what was going on. Their boss was dead; several of their friends were dead. No one seemed to know why.

"*Zeke*," I said, picking up the spear as I got to my feet.

Two more dead soldiers collapsed to the ground as a dirt cloud erupted across the plain behind the garrison.

Hiroyuki dropped from the ramparts above the entrance, his katana slicing through the neck of one soldier before he turned and drove it into the chest of another, sending the entire group into a disorderly retreat.

"Kill everything that moves," I said, feeling revitalised as more and more horses could be seen riding toward us.

"Cavalry," Neb said, getting to her feet too.

Despite being vastly outnumbered, no one on either side of us appeared to want to take the first steps to fight us, considering several of their comrades were now missing their heads.

I brought the fight to them, charging into the group closest to me, using my spear to great effect as I cut through one, two, three soldiers, before the rest of them realised that they outnumbered me a hundred to one and decided to fight back.

By then, it was too late.

Zeke rode into the garrison, leapt off his horse, two six-shooters drawn and firing at anything that moved. He unloaded on everything around him, dropped the guns, and started using a Winchester rifle to headshot everything in the vicinity, while I kept the mass of soldiers at bay with my spear.

Eventually, the rest of the group caught up. Dozens of them; most I vaguely recognised from the RCU. Ji-hyun had sent her people to help. The numbers went from a hundred to one to about even.

Drusilla charged into a group of retreating soldiers, a claw on each hand, slashing through anything that moved as Neb used a sword and shield to make anyone running wish they hadn't bothered. The pair worked in tandem as I moved through the ranks of the now-petrified soldiers. No command structure, no one to tell them what to do, and we weren't just sitting down and dying. This was not their plan.

Some turned, found a backbone, and started to fight back, but by then, our cavalry were all inside the garrison, and the combined might of those of us fighting back was enough to make sure that the tide was turned.

There were casualties on our side, but they numbered less than a tenth of the overall force, whereas everyone who had come to kill us was either dead, about to be dead, or wishing they were dead.

I cut the pouch from Kuri's belt and affixed it to my own, and turned as Drusilla dragged someone who was alive but bleeding badly from several wounds over their body. She stopped beside me and dropped the badly injured soldier at my feet.

"Kill me," he said softly.

"Where has Elliott gone?" I asked. "Don't bother to deny knowing; I'm not in the mood. You die here. It's just how painlessly that depends on you."

"Ruins to the north," the soldier said, his voice hoarse. He was dying.

Good; hope it hurt.

"How many went with him?" I asked.

"Two dozen," he said. "Matthew and the elite Guild who were brought here."

"Elite Guild?" I asked.

"Vipers," the man corrected. "He went with his Vipers."

The man started to cough up blood. "Please end it."

I turned and walked away, leaving him to die in pain. He didn't deserve a clean death, and I was in no mood to grant him one.

"Had to climb up from the far north side of the garrison," Hiroyuki said. "Sorry I wasn't quicker."

I slapped him on the shoulder. "Thank you, but we're not done yet."

"We need to get after Elliot," Neb said. "He's gone after the Queen of Crows."

"He's gone to some ruins to the north of here," I said.

"He's planning on using the ruins to move around the rift," Zeke said, the rifle slung over his shoulder. "One of the soldiers told me. You all go; I'll stay here, clean up."

"Do they work?" Drusilla asked.

"We agreed to not use them again," Neb said. "If you know how to connect with them, you could, but you unlock one, you unlock all of them. I fear this could be the start of something we can't stop."

"Elliot already started that," I said. "We need to stop him before he makes it worse. What's more important, Neb? Stopping Elliot and saving the Queen's life, or keeping your secrets secret? We need to get to Plainhaven."

"Any chance he has more people waiting to help him when we get wherever he is?" I asked.

"Yes," Neb said. "Tess had a lot of people on her side in Agency when she was outed. I don't know where they all went, but my guess is we're going to start seeing people moving toward the Crow's Perch. When Elliot and his Vipers get their powers back, we're going to have a lot of bodies in their wake."

"Best get going, then," I said.

She rode out first, with half a dozen guards and Neb beside her, Hiroyuki and Pike behind them, and me between Zeke and Drusilla.

"You doing okay?" Drusilla asked me, reaching over and squeezing my hand.

I nodded. "It's been a long few days," I said. "Too many good people died here. How long has it been on Earth?"

"Six days when we left," she said.

I let myself have a smile, just thinking about it. "Did Dani bring you?" I asked.

"She's resting in Plainhaven," Drusilla said. "It was a lot to take just us all through. We had to ride all the way from Agency to Plainhaven, too. Timo wanted to bring people, but we told her to get ready for anyone coming her way. I hope they've had enough time to prepare. It's been eight days since you arrived here, from our point of view."

"Several less for me," I said, looking over at Zeke, who looked to be in his element. "Guns?"

Zeke could make his weapons rift-tempered just by holding them, although that didn't mean the bullets would take the charge.

"Not rift-tempered unless I want them to be," he said. "I don't go anywhere without them. Timo said the land around the prison didn't allow for abilities, anyway. And a good time was had by anyone not shot in the face."

"I'm grateful for your timely intervention," I said. "There was a guard who came with me from Agency; her name was Heleen. They murdered her when we arrived. Elliot will pay for her death. Matthew Pierce too."

"Wait, he's alive?" Zeke asked. "For fuck's sake, that man just won't die."

"He will next time," I said. "I'm going to make sure I watch him die."

We rode on for a few hours until we reached Plainhaven, and my heart did a little leap at seeing it again.

"You're smiling," Drusilla said.

"This might sound weird," I told her, "but Plainhaven was a city of Ravens. There are statues there and everything. It feels like home of a kind."

"A City of Ravens?" Zeke asked. "Seriously?"

"Hundreds of years before I was born," I said. "It was kept quiet after . . . well, after there was a war."

I took the time to explain everything I'd learned about Neb and her part in Ahiram's imprisonment. Neither Zeke nor Drusilla said anything until I was finished, and then Zeke let out a long whistle.

Drusilla's expression softened. "I'm sorry, Lucas."

"Me too," I said.

"You can tell them if you like," Neb said, looking back at me. "It's going to come out now."

I nodded a thanks and saw the tug of a smile on her lips. "The Queen of Crows is Neb's great-granddaughter."

Apparently, I'd spoken a little louder than was necessary, because everyone turned back to look at me. "Seriously?" Hiroyuki asked.

"Yes," Neb said, without looking back at the rest of us. "Darice is my great-granddaughter."

"The Queens name is Darice?" Zeke asked. "I always expected something more . . . you know, regal. Like Esmerelda. Or Boudica."

Neb looked back with an expression of puzzlement. "No" was all she said before turning back around.

It was nighttime when we reached the gates to the city. We left our horses at the stable, while we raced through after the guard who I certainly hoped knew the way. The guards were still outside, and nothing appeared to be out of the ordinary.

"We need to talk to Timo," I said to one of the guards. "There's a Guild of people called the Vipers. It's complicated, but in case any of them decide to head this way, you need to get ready."

We got down from our horses and the guards began to mobilise their defence.

As we were running through the fairly empty streets of the city, I spotted Dani running toward us. "Hey," I said as she joined.

"I was told you were coming back," she said. "Why are we running?"

"City ruins are a rift teleporting system," I said.

Dani glanced my way for a second. "The rift is fucking weird."

Couldn't really disagree with that one. "We need to find Timo," I said.

"She's up there," Dani said, pointing up toward the highest part of the city.

We started up the steps with Dani leading the way and took a left at the top. I glanced back down over the city and wondered if I'd ever get to come back there. I shook the thought loose and continued on until we came to a cave set into the side of an area that had a sign with RESTRICTED ACCESS written on in it in red lettering.

We walked through the cave, and I realised that we were behind the waterfall, the sound of the water echoing around the cave, until we exited and found ourselves atop the waterfall itself. There were ruins everywhere. Most were poking out of the ground, but many had been excavated, and thick rope had been placed in a cordon around them, like medieval police tape at a crime scene.

The ruins looked like the white-and-grey stone throughout the city, but in the middle of them was a tiled circle on the floor. It was twenty feet in diameter and had ten-foot stone columns jutting out of the dark soil that hadn't been swept away. The tiles were black and grey, depicting several ravens in flight. At the top of the circle of tiles was a charcoal-grey stone lectern with a place where something could be fitted.

"Your medallion," Neb said to me. "That's what's used to activate it. It's part of the reason why you have them in the first place."

I removed my medallion and looked at it. "Callie said I already had everything I needed to be able to do this. So, only a Raven medallion will activate this one?"

Neb shook her head. "Any medallion can activate any of these sites."

"Hence the Viper medallions," I said. "Callie said Elliot always had what he needed to use them, just like I do. She didn't want to tell him until she'd gotten what she needed."

"Ahiram," Neb said.

I nodded.

"Teleportation in the rift," Hiroyuki said. "I was really hoping we were done finding weird shit here."

"You and me both," I said. "So, is this instantaneous?"

Neb nodded.

"Does it need power?" Drusilla asked, getting a good look at the lectern.

"It uses the power of the rift to work," Neb said. "It's going to open a tear in the sky above us. It's going to flood this whole place with rift energy."

"That can't possibly be a good idea," Zeke said.

"It's one of the reasons we stopped using them," Neb said. "You're unleashing a lot of rift energy over a wide area."

"And any animals unlucky enough to wander into it," Drusilla said, leaving the rest unfinished.

"Your guards need to be ready," I said to the guard who had led us through the city.

"They are," he told us. "But I'm going to join them just in case. I wish you all good luck."

"How does this work?" Dani asked.

"I just explained," Neb said. "The medallion goes in—"

"No, I mean with *us*," Dani said. "How does it work with us? Is this like *Star Trek*, where we're one place, then another? Or is it more our molecules are torn apart and put back together, where we feel every single second of it? The second one sounds bad."

"It's not painful," Neb said. "It's . . . disorienting. It feels weird, as if your whole body has pins and needles."

"Not painful, just unpleasant," Zeke said with a sigh.

"Yes," Neb said. "We need to leave."

"How do we select the destination?" I asked. "It's a piece of stone with a hole in it."

Neb gestured for me to hand over the medallion, which I gladly did. "We're going to be heading into a bad place," she said, inserting the medallion into the hole in the lectern. Two metal clasps grabbed the medallion, holding it in place, as ten blue lights illuminated on top of the lectern, all around the medallion.

"Ten destinations," Neb said. "Each one is a different set of ruins. A different city."

"It's a map of the rift," Hiroyuki said.

"Yes," Neb replied, turning the clasped medallion, making different lights flick on and off with every turn, until she settled on the one she needed.

"Get us to the tear stone I sent to the Queen," I said.

"Are we all ready?" Neb asked.

"No," Zeke said.

Everyone ignored Zeke, and Neb placed her hand on the medallion and pushed. And nothing happened.

"That was anticlimactic," I said.

"There's no stone to access," Neb said. "It's not there. We'll have to go to the ruins near the Crow's Perch."

"Let's do it, then," I said, feeling anxiety grow inside of me.

Neb performed the same action as before, and the world went white.

CHAPTER THIRTY-SIX

On the plus side, no one threw up. It worked, too, so I guess there was that.

We ended up in the ruins where I'd met Neb and the Queen what felt like months earlier. Everyone lay on the ground; the weather had changed from cold but dry to a fine drizzle.

No one moved for several seconds; pain raced through my body. It was a little like pins and needles, in the sense that it was as if someone was stabbing me all over my body with tiny needles. It hurt like hell, and while it only lasted a few seconds, those few seconds sucked.

"I don't ever want to do that again," Zeke said.

Hiroyuki sat up. "I taste perfume in my mouth."

"Sometimes, your tastebuds go weird," Neb said.

"This is an astonishingly bad way to travel," Drusilla said, using some nearby rocks to pull herself to her feet.

I followed suit and pulled myself up onto a horizontally lying piece of stone to wait for the dizziness to go away.

"You get used to it," Neb said.

"Nope," Dani replied. She was the last person to get back to their feet. "Just absolutely fucking not."

I looked up at the tens-of-miles-long tear that had been ripped open in the sky above us. "I'd like to agree with Drusilla; this is a terrible way to travel."

Everyone else looked up.

"It looks like we opened a nebula above our heads," Hiroyuki said.

Neb got to the lectern, removed the medallion, and threw it over to me, and I caught it with one hand, replacing it around my neck. "This was already excavated," I said.

Neb looked down at the tiles on which the lectern sat. The tiles were sky blue and showed no creatures at all.

"The ones with the birds were changed from a plain colour," Neb explained. "Elliot's people uncovered this since we were last here. They were preparing for this."

"What did the Queen of Crows do?" I asked. "She didn't notice that someone had been excavating them, or put guards here?"

"Questions to ask when we see her," Neb said.

I looked over at Zeke. "Can you move around to the south, head toward the front of the city? We'll cut straight there, but if you see anyone at that gate and want to thin their numbers . . ."

"On it," Zeke said, and ran off toward the tall grass to the south of the Crow's Perch.

"We need to move," Hiroyuki said.

No one disagreed, and we were soon on our way across the landscape of the rift toward the Crow's Perch. The Queen had said it was a few hours of riding, and with no way of getting there quicker, we were going to have to do it by foot.

We found fresh horse tracks outside of the ruins. I didn't know how many there were, because I stopped counting when I reached twenty individual animals. There were too many prints that crossed over one another. *More than twenty* was enough.

The Queen had been right about the terrain, too; it wasn't made for hard riding. One horse putting its hoof in one of the myriad of holes that littered the area, and you've got a thrown rider and horse that will never walk again.

It took a few hours before we saw the black smoke in the distance, and we picked up the pace, spotting the city of the Crow's Perch not long after. We were at the top of a steep hill, with nothing but open land from the bottom of it to the city, where fires had been set all around the exterior of the city, and I spotted riders outside of it. While they'd started fires on part of the wall, preventing anyone from climbing over to escape, they were congregating around other parts, presumably waiting to attack anyone who tried to get out of the city. Or waiting to help Elliot escape. Neither were great options.

Pike, who had been unusually quiet since we'd left the garrison, moved at a flat-out sprint after he saw the flames. Neb was close by, and everyone else was running after the pair of them. I knew I could just turn to smoke and billow down there, but once I got there well ahead of everyone else,

I was going to be outnumbered and quite possibly going to make things worse while everyone else caught up.

As we reached the bottom of the hill and began sprinting toward the city, several of the horsemen spotted us. Two of them turned their horses toward us and set off in a gallop to intercept. I was in no mood to be intercepted.

I turned to smoke and billowed across the ground, outpacing everyone behind me, until I was close enough to re-form, leaving my finger as smoke in the box on the staff. I threw the staff at the closest rider, catching them in the chest and pitching them off the back of the horse. I turned back to smoke, snapped to the staff instantly, re-formed, grabbed the staff and did the exact same thing with the second rider. Both were dead in seconds, but there were still a dozen more outside of the city, all of whom looked more prepared for our arrival.

Pike swung up onto one of the horses, and Neb—who was the closest to me—jumped up on the other one.

"Clear these out," Neb shouted over to everyone else. "Meet us inside."

They were off before anyone could stop them.

"How are we meant to clear them out?" Dani asked.

"I better go after them," I said, watching Neb and Pike ride toward the front entrance.

The horsemen outside of the city had clearly made their decision about which of the two groups they needed to deal with and went for us.

Hiroyuki drew his katana, the air around him become freezing cold, his breath visible. "We'll be fine," he said.

"Go stop them doing something stupid," Drusilla told me with a wink.

"Yeah, leave the large, armoured people on horses to those of us on foot," Dani said, sounding less than convinced. "Sounds like a brilliant idea all around. Really glad I came."

Four horsemen were charging toward us now, the horses kicking up soft earth as they showed no attempt to slow down despite having seen what happened to their friends.

"Gonna need a horse," I said.

"Pick one," Drusilla said.

"I got this," Hiroyuki told us, creating a sharp cone of ice and throwing it at the four horsemen. The cone got within ten feet, forcing the soldiers to move aside, and detonated, peppering the men with shards of ice.

Two of them jumped off their horses, turning into their horned revenant forms before landing with a crunching thud and running toward us.

One of the four took a shard through the neck and was pitched off the side of the horse and dragged along for twenty feet before the horse decided there was something more interesting to do. The last horseman stopped and got down slowly, his eyes on the rest of us as the two horned revenants engaged with Hiroyuki and Dani.

"Go put that idiot out of his misery," Drusilla said, her eyes locked on the soldier walking toward them. They held a flail in one hand, the large, spiked ball moving freely by their knee.

I left Drusilla to it and ran after the errant horse as its rider tried to untangle themselves from their predicament and was having a difficult time of it.

The horse eventually slowed to a stop, although it hadn't helped the rider much, as his head had bounced off the ground the entire distance. I took hold of the reins, risking a look back at my friends as they fought against those who would side with Ahiram.

"Revenant or riftborn?" I asked the bloody and battered passenger.

"Riftborn," he said. "I can talk to animals."

"Why not tell the horse to stop?" I asked.

"He thinks I'm a prick," the man snapped. "Being able to talk to them doesn't mean they like you."

The horse made a neighing noise that sounded a lot more like a chuckle than it probably would have if I hadn't just heard what the soldier said.

"What's Elliot's plan?" I asked.

"I had to fight for him; I had *no* choice," the soldier pleaded. They pulled off their black helmet, revealing long blond hair and the face of a man was probably considered more beautiful than handsome. At least it would have been before it was covered in blood from a broken nose.

I placed the tip of the spear against the throat of the soldier. "Choose again."

"Get the Queen, burn the city," the soldier said.

"After that," I said.

"Run to the Tempest," he said. "When the time is right, Elliot is going back to the prison for Ahiram. Until then, we wait. That's all any of us know. We were told to come to the ruins, await his arrival, and that was it. He's not exactly one for being chatty."

I removed his trapped foot from the stirrup and let him fall roughly to the ground. "Find somewhere else to be," I said, patting the horse before pulling myself up. "If I see you again, I'll kill you."

"You can't beat Elliot," the man said, still lying on the ground.

"Start running," I said, and brought the horse around to face the city.

"You're a dead man," the soldier shouted. "Do you hear me? Dead. He's going to kill the fucking lot of you."

The horse bucked, kicking him in the head, and the soldier stopped talking and decided to make a weird wheezing noise instead, as the front of his face was caved in from the force. "Good horse," I said, patting him on the neck.

A moment later, and after risking a glance over to my friends, who I saw were now three to one against the surviving horned revenant, the horse and I were riding toward the Crow's Perch.

Even with the distance between myself and the city, the sounds of battle inside were overwhelming, with screams of pain mixed with roars of those currently engaged in combat. I hadn't been to the city for a while, but I knew the way to the Queen's palace, and I also knew that there were a lot of alleyways and places shrouded in shadow where an assassin or two could easily be hiding. I didn't want to have to spend the time moving slowly; I didn't have time.

I turned the horse north, toward the nearest tear stone, one I'd used before. If I was going to go into the city, I needed more than just myself and a horse, and my friends were engaged with the horse riders.

It didn't take long to reach the stone. I climbed down from the horse, stepped onto the stone, and opened a tear to my embers.

I had to wait a few seconds for Casimir and Maria as they moved toward me from the other side. Casimir was in the shape of a large grizzly bear, and Maria sat on Casimir's head in the shape of a small wood mouse.

"I need help," I told them. "If you both come out, and you get hurt, you know it might end badly for you."

"We are eidolons," Maria said. "You have never taken both of us out before."

I nodded. "I know; can you do it?"

Maria hopped down off Casimir's head, turning into a Siberian tiger as she did.

"We are with you," Casimir said.

I looked between them both. I'd learned a lot about the eidolons and my connection to the embers over the last few years; I had learned about how to get in and out of them without needing a tear, although I wasn't in the Tempest, so it didn't count. I also learned that most riftborn didn't use their eidolons in the way I did; they kept them inside their embers at all times, afraid of what might happen to them if let out.

This was the first time I'd asked them both to leave with me. Something I'd always assumed was impossible. Sometimes, it felt like as long as we lived, we didn't really know much about the world we lived in.

"We are weapons to be used," Maria said, stepping out of the tear beside me.

"We are with you," Casimir said, leaving the tear, which snapped shut behind them.

I looked between them and smiled, the horse beside me remaining remarkably calm. "Let's go to war, then."

CHAPTER THIRTY-SEVEN

Dead guards littered the ground at the smoke-filled entrance of the Crow's Perch; all had blade wounds to their heads and necks. The gate had been obliterated, with pieces of it all over the ground around me. I got down off the horse and walked toward where the gate would have been, and quickly dodged a knife throw from somewhere beyond the smoke.

The horse wisely ran to the side of the gate as I dodged a second knife throw. I turned to smoke, moved through the gate, re-formed next to the knife thrower, and drove my spear into her heart. Her Viper medallion tumbled out from beneath her layers of clothing.

Casimir and Maria were behind me, following me into the city proper. They took up positions in front of me, able to sniff out trouble before it reached us. We walked at a quick pace through the city, with Casimir and Maria attacking anyone who posed a threat.

The last time I'd been there, it had been a bustling town full of life, and now there were clouds of smoke wafting through the streets, revealing the dead as they dissipated. The sounds of battle raged farther into the city; the citizens wouldn't go down without a fight.

Barricades had been erected at some streets, giving me the impression that the city had been preparing for war well before it had reached them.

There were dead littering some streets, a mixture of black-armour-clad Vipers and the citizens of Crow's Perch. Occasional gunshots rang out from farther into the city. "There are a lot more of these then I thought there would be," Casimir said as they sniffed at the body of another dead Viper, this one missing its head.

"This plan has been in motion for a long time," I said, turning down an alleyway to avoid one of the residents of the Crow's Perch who was flinging balls of fire at a group of soldiers, who were trying to hunker down behind another barricade. "The residents of the city appear to be a lot hardier than the Vipers had anticipated."

"The Queen of Crows must have spent time preparing them all after the last time the city was attacked," Maria said.

At the end of the shadow-covered alleyway was a large, open square with a fountain in the shape of a large fish in the middle and stalls all around the outside. Not including where we'd entered, there were four exits from the square, two in front and one either side. Directly in front of us, between the two exits, was a large bell tower.

I went out first and told Maria and Casimir to hold back as I stepped out into the open. Maria ignored me, turned into a mouse, and ran up my back, hiding in one of the pockets of my armour, while Casimir did as they were told. Which made a change.

The last time I'd been there, the square had been noisy with large numbers of people shopping or just milling around. Now it was deserted for the exception of Matthew, who stood beside the fountain; five dead Crow's Perch guards lay at his feet.

Matthew held a buckler shield in one hand and a broadsword in the other; he swiped the sword up and down, removing some of the blood it had obtained.

"I hoped we'd meet again," he said, stepping over the body of a decapitated guard.

I smiled. "Me too. You were the one leading all of the attacks on villages, yes? The unnecessary levels of violence screamed you."

"The boxes brought the fiends out," Matthew said. "And for the first few, that was all I was meant to do. Then we needed an escalation. Something to draw Neb in. She sent her people instead, so we needed them to go missing, but we needed something *more*. I hoped that when Neb went missing and a village turned up destroyed, you'd get brought into it. Wanted to finish off what we started. No bears falling out of the sky this time."

He removed a bauble from his belt and threw it at me. I let the smoke move over me, my power immediately removed. I took the vial from my pocket and drank it. If Callie had been lying, it had been a weird thing to lie about, considering the effort she'd gone to in getting me to her. My power flooded through me, and I stepped through the smoke with a smile on my face.

He reached out, his power to amplify my own ability slamming into me, turning my body to smoke and pulling it apart as he grinned that stupid smug grin. I stopped walking, and my body re-formed; the pain at being forced to turn to smoke, forced to dissipate, left me.

The smug grin vanished in an instant. "Wait, how?" He asked.

"It turns out that things have changed since we last met," I said, not moving. "I can make sure your power doesn't affect me. I've been working on myself for the last few years; it's amazing what you can discover even after you think you know it all."

The smug grin returned. "So, you can't fight, can't do anything but stand there and look stupid?"

I nodded. "Pretty much."

Matthew laughed. "Oh, I'm going to enjoy this."

There was a roar behind me as Casimir stepped out of the shadows on their hind legs, towering over me by several feet.

Matthew's eyes went wide.

"Remember me?" Casimir asked, as if you ever forget an encounter with a grizzly bear where the bear tries to tear your face off.

Matthew raised the sword at Casimir. "I will kill your eidolon this time," he stammered. There was a lack of confidence in his words.

"No," I said, taking a step to the side so the fountain was between Matthew and me. Matthew tracked me, occasionally moving back toward Casimir.

At some point, I wasn't entirely sure when, Maria had jumped out of my pocket and run around the outside of the courtyard, keeping under the market stalls and to the shadows until they were behind Matthew.

The Siberian tiger that stepped out between two stalls growled. "We haven't met," Maria said, their words dripping with potent venom as they padded softly toward Matthew.

"I will take one of you with me," Matthew shouted.

"No," I said, and threw the spear at him. It caught him in the chest, throwing him back into the claws of Maria, who drove Matthew to the ground, sinking her teeth into his shoulder.

Matthew pleaded with me to let him go. He deserved worse than the death the eidolons would give him. But I had better things to do. I drove my spear into his brain, killing him instantly.

The fighting was fiercer the farther into the city I ran, although I avoided most of it by turning to smoke and moving around where I needed to, until I arrived at a second courtyard. It was similar to the first but without the fountain and market stalls. On the opposite side to the only entrance was the palace. It was a three-storey building, much like many others in the city, although it was considerably longer than any other near it.

The dead who lay on the ground were of the Queen's personal body-guard. The doors to the palace were closed, judging by the amount of hammering on them Elliot was doing.

"Make sure nothing gets to me," I told Casimir and Maria before walking through the courtyard.

"Damn you," Elliot screamed.

"This doesn't appear to be going your way," I called out.

Elliot turned back to face me. "You all got out," he said. "Kuri said I should have killed you all at the prison. I couldn't risk it harming Ahiram, though."

"Kuri was smarter than you are," I said.

Elliot carried a large war hammer in one hand but held no shield or secondary weapon, I could see. As if in response to that, he drew a dagger from behind his back.

"That belongs to me," I said, recognising the weapon. I continued to walk toward him, my hand gripping the shaft of the spear. I stopped by a dead guard and removed the small buckler shield.

"It does," Elliot said, moving his hand to show the primordial-bone knuckleduster. "This too. It's good. I like it. So, Matthew is dead, yes?"

"Very dead," I said. "Matthew. Everyone you left at the garrison. Any-one outside. Most of the Vipers you arrived with. All dead. This didn't go how you planned, I think."

Elliot laughed, sheathing the dagger, and picking up a buckler of his own from the ground. "I'm beginning to think that Callie played me and you. She said we needed to kill the Queen, that we needed to attack the cities of the rift. I have Vipers all across the cities right now, killing and maiming with impunity. She said you would be kept in the prison, that you were needed to wake Ahiram. But I think she was lying."

"She wanted you out of the prison," I told him. "I think she's planning on using Ahiram for her own aims. I think she probably wanted us all busy."

Elliot smiled and shrugged. "Well, as I'm here, I may as well finish what I came to do. The Queen is going to die by my hand."

I mimicked his shrug. "I think we should find out. You killed my friends, you killed people I cared about, you murdered my guild."

"I'd like to say it wasn't personal, but it was," Elliot said. "They refused Ahiram's hand of friendship. Hand of leadership. I knew that if I arranged their deaths, it would make him happy."

"He told you this?" I asked. "Over those months and months you spoke to him while he slept?"

"I did," Elliot said proudly. "He *hates* you. Hates the Queen, too. With both the Ravens and the Queen gone, I will have done for him for no one else ever could."

"I'm going to kill you for it," I said. "You should know that."

Elliot put himself into a fighting stance, the hammer's head low, the shield up. "You really want to do this?"

"Gods, yes," I said, and charged forward.

Elliot removed a bauble from his belt and smashed it on the ground, covering the area in blue smoke and removing my power once again. I had no vial to drink. I had no way of quickly recovering my ability. It was going to have to be done the hard way.

CHAPTER THIRTY-EIGHT

My spear met his shield, and I blocked his hammer blow with the buckler, although the vibration from the strength of the blow went up my arm, forcing me to move back and put some distance between us. I had no powers. I couldn't even feel them, and it was something that sat in the back of my mind, like an anxious thought that wouldn't go away. I had to push the thought out. I had no choice in the matter. Either I pushed that shadow of doubt aside or I would die. There was no room to have my thoughts on anything but the fight.

Each attack by Elliot or myself was deflected, parried, or avoided by the other. Attack was met with defence and counterattack again and again. Each time he brought his hammer down onto my shield, the jolt of pain that ran up my arm became increasingly difficult to ignore. It was becoming obvious that I needed to end this fight before I was too hurt to defend myself properly.

Elliot darted toward me, bringing his hammer down, but instead of stepping back, or using the shield, I stepped to his inside. His eyes opened in surprise as I took a glancing blow on my shoulder and drove my spear toward his chest. He moved back, quickly using his shield to block the blow, but the tip of the spear hit it at an angle, deflecting down and cutting across the side of his thigh.

He kicked out, trying to put distance between us, but I raised my knee and twisted my body, taking the blow on my own thigh, as we both separated.

Blood fell in slow, steady drops onto the ground by Elliot's foot, while I rubbed the soreness on my shoulder, thankful that I had armour to mitigate a blow which could well have broken bones.

We hadn't been fighting long, but it felt like an age, and if Elliot was anywhere near as sore and in as much pain as I was, I hoped it wasn't going to continue for much longer.

Elliot threw another bauble at my feet, the smoke obscuring my vision for a moment, and he used the second to charge toward me. I avoided the wild swing and stabbed at his face with my spear, which he moved to deflect with the side of his shield, but I moved the spear at the last second, bringing it down toward his chest. He moved his body slightly, and the spear tip cut along the armour by his shoulder. He brought the shield down on the head of the spear, trapping it against his body, and brought the hammer up toward my ribs.

I twisted as much as possible but couldn't get the spear away in time to stop the blow, so I released my grip on it and moved to intercept with the shield. The hammer smashed on it at an angle, causing my arm to move back and exposing my side for Elliot to use the knuckleduster on his hand to punch me in the ribs.

The air left my body in one long rush, and I half-stepped, half-fell back, narrowly avoiding the hammer as it sailed by for a second attempt. I gritted my teeth and snapped back toward Elliot, smashing the butt of my shield into his elbow, which made an horrific noise as the bone broke. He brought his knee up into my ribs. If they weren't broken from the knuckles, they were now.

I staggered back, my side feeling as though it were on fire, and watched the spear clatter to the ground, while Elliot put distance between us, his arm held against his body, the hammer on the floor at his feet.

It hurt to breathe, and I desperately wanted to move as far from Elliot and the smoke stopping my power as I could get. Instead, I used the shield to help me get back to my feet, making a loud groaning sound as my ribs yelled at me for daring such a thing.

I rolled the spear shaft over my foot and flicked it up, catching it in my hand, which once again made my ribs protest. I *really* didn't feel like fighting anymore, and from the look in Elliot's face, he didn't seem all that enthused either.

There was another crunch as Elliot straightened his broken arm, and he screamed in pain while more awful sounds left his body. I dropped to my knees, retrieved a dagger from one of the bodies on the ground, and threw it at Elliot. It hit him in the back of the hand, which wasn't where I was aiming, but at that point, so long as it hit something, I was going to count it as a win.

Elliot's hammer dropped to the ground with a clatter as he pulled the dragger out and discarded it. "You are an irritant," he snapped.

"I get that a lot," I said between clenched teeth.

I got to my feet as Elliot walked toward me. He pushed aside my feeble attempt to stab him with the spear and punched me in the ribs again. The spear clattered to the ground as I dropped to my knees, and he kicked me in the ribs, forcing me to roll back. Another kick to my stomach made me try to roll away, but a kick to the back of my head made the world go dark for a moment.

Elliot stood over me as my vision darkened.

I flipped Elliot off and felt pretty good about it until he stamped on my ribs again.

"Most heroes die well before anyone will have ever heard of them," Elliot said. "And when I kill everyone who's heard of you, I'll never have to think about you again." He lifted his foot to stamp down again, and an arrow slammed into the side of his knee.

I blinked. I wasn't sure if the arrow was actually real, although the screams that left Elliot's mouth were definitely real. He backpedalled, letting me lie on the cool stone ground and get a good view as a second arrow hit Elliot in the stomach. He doubled over as a third hit his shoulder, and a forth sailed by where his head had been.

The Queen of Crows, holding a handheld repeater crossbow, casually walked out of her palace. She removed the drum where the arrows were kept, and reloaded it with another that hung from her belt. She fired twice more, each of the arrows slamming into Elliot's shield with a satisfying thud.

"Bitch," Elliot screamed.

"That's *Queen* Bitch to you, motherfucker," the Queen shouted back, firing two more arrows, hitting Elliot in the knee with one of them.

I thought of a witty quip about adventuring that I was sure no one had ever said before, but decided now was neither the time nor the place. Besides, I wasn't actually sure I could talk without causing myself more agony, so I just lay still and enjoyed the show.

The Queen stood in the square, next to the dead members of her guard, and reloaded the crossbow. She appeared to be in no hurry, but Elliot was going nowhere, and it gave me the time to pull myself up against a nearby wall and try to get my breath back.

"You okay, Lucas?" the Queen shouted over without turning to look my way.

"Peachy," I called back, feeling nothing of the sort. I hoped that Casimir and Maria were okay. I hoped that the rest of the group were winning against the Vipers on horses outside of the city.

Elliot, who was now fully behind a stone wall at the edge of the square, remained quiet, which might have been the smartest thing he'd ever done. He threw something over the wall that landed at the Queen's feet.

The Queen barrelled into me, taking us both over a nearby wall as the object exploded, showering the area in shrapnel and red smoke.

When the smoke dissipated, I glanced over the wall to find that Elliot was no longer behind it.

The Queen helped me to my feet as Casimir and Maria ran into the square. They stopped beside me. "You both okay?" I asked, picking up my dagger from the ground where Elliot had dropped it.

"Yes," Maria said.

"Elliot?" Casimir asked.

"Gone," the Queen said, looking behind the wall where Elliot had been.

"That's okay," I told her, retrieving my spear. "I know where he is."

Before anyone else could say something, part of the exterior wall of the city exploded.

I moved toward the newly created hole in the wall, climbing through it as Elliot climbed up onto a horse and began to gallop away. There were two more horses, both with soldiers atop them. I threw a dagger at one of the men, who tried to move aside, but the blade buried itself in his forearm. I turned to smoke, wrapping around the other man as he tried to get the horse to gallop.

I re-formed behind the soldier, cut his throat with another dagger, and pushed him to the ground before giving chase on his horse after Elliot, who had gotten a considerable head start on me.

The horse was fast and steady on its feet, and I was soon catching up to Elliot, who appeared to be slowing down as he reached the apex of the hill, where we'd all entered from the ruins. He jumped off his horse and ran into the ruins.

As I reached Elliot's abandoned horse, I jumped down from my own, turned into my smoke form, and moved as quickly as I could across the ruins, re-forming as I barrelled into Elliot.

The pair of us fell over a set of stone pillars, slamming into the hard ground as Elliot's medallion glowed.

A second later, the world went white.

CHAPTER THIRTY-NINE

Elliot headbutted me before I could figure out where I was, kicking me away and over the side a hill. Blood streamed down the front of my face as I bounced down the tree-covered hill, hitting what felt like all of them on the way down.

I hit the bottom hard, the breath leaving me in one rush, and lay there for a moment as blood kept streaming down my face. I was pretty sure I had a few more broken ribs, considering how much my chest felt like it was on fire. I stayed there for as long as I could while my body protested the fact that it existed.

I didn't have time to waste, though, and eventually forced myself back to my feet, using a nearby tree to make sure I didn't immediately fall over again.

Everything was a kaleidoscope of shades of blue and purple; the rift energy there was immense. I turned back to smoke and moved as quickly as possible back up the hill, and by the time I got to the top of the hill and re-formed, any pain inside of me was gone. My nose and ribs felt fine.

I turned back to smoke and moved down the hill toward the garrison in the distance. Elliot had used his time to put some distance between us, and I moved as quickly as possible, hoping to gain ground and stop him before ... actually, I didn't know. Presumably, he was going to go back and help Ahiram get out of the prison, but if he was still unconscious and Callie was still working on him, that might not end in Elliot's favour.

I reached the edge of the garrison and re-formed, walking by the littered dead who had attacked us not long before.

Elliot stood by the pier, twirling a blade in his hand. He walked down the pier, by the boat, which continued to bob gently in the lake.

"I *knew* you weren't going to let it go," Elliot said. "You expect me to come with you and the group I'm sure you've brought with you?" When I was ten feet in front of him, he raised his arms out in front, wrists next to one another. "Going to arrest me?

I barrelled into him, taking him off his feet and slamming him into the tree behind. I avoided a swipe of the blade, but he managed to kick me in the chest, sending me sprawling.

I rolled to my feet, drew a knife of my own, and readied myself.

He came at me, swiping up, dropping the blade from one hand to the other and forcing me back. I waited until he moved forward again, and I sprang toward him, moving him back when he managed to dodge my cut across his face. We moved around the top of the hill, avoiding each other's knives as best we could, but after only a short time, we were both bleeding on our hands and arms. You don't get to walk away from a knife fight unscathed.

I managed to deflect a blow and smashed my elbow into his sternum before catching him under the chin with an uppercut that rocked him back. I was quickly on him, trying to stab him with my own knife, but he brought his knee up to block the blow and caught me in the throat with a jab. I coughed, giving him enough time to disarm me and try to stab me with his own dagger, but I moved around him, locking out his arm, and tried to force him to open his hand. When all else failed, I bit his hand, and he let out a yell, but it worked, and the dagger fell away.

Elliot ran toward the garrison entrance, but I came after in a flash, and tackled him just as he reached it, both of us rolling through the garrison entrance.

Heat radiated through my body, and I had to kick myself away as the ground around him burst into flame. I rolled back to my feet, both daggers several feet from either of us.

His upper body glowed white-hot, the tactical armour around his torso melting away in places, revealing the Viper Guild medallion around his neck. He tore the remains of the armour free and tossed it aside.

Elliot spat on the floor. "That hurt," his voice rough where I'd caught him with the uppercut.

He removed something from one of the pockets on his still-intact trousers and threw it onto the ground beside me. I didn't look down.

"Go on; you know you want to," Elliot said.

I took two steps back to keep him in view and saw the Raven Guild medallion nestled in some grass beside my foot.

"A lot of us took them as rewards," he said. "We didn't get them all, but we got enough. We still have them, still look at them every time we walk by our little museum of people who weren't as good as we are."

I walked slowly toward Elliot, stepping over the Raven medallion, ignoring it.

"You want to fight?" he asked, putting his fists up. He kept the smirk on his face as he bounced from foot to foot. When I was only a few feet away, he drew another knife from a sheath against his leg.

I didn't stop walking.

He lunged for me, and I stepped aside, knowing full well what pain was about to lace through my body and trying to ignore it, but the dagger bit into my side, just under my ribs. I bit down a scream of pain and stepped into Elliot's almost-embrace.

"It's best like this," he whispered, twisting the knife. "Let's go for the killing stab next."

"I just wanted to get in close," I said through gritted teeth.

"I'll tell them you died fighting," he said, pulling out the knife and causing a lance of white pain to go through my body.

I placed my hands on his face. "I'll tell them you died screaming, you little fucker." I turned to smoke.

I didn't like touching living flesh when I turned to smoke, because it tore apart whatever my hands were on. Elliot's face came apart like peeling an orange, big, long strands of flesh and muscle coming away as I moved back across the hill, still in smoke form. The man screamed as blood poured like a fountain out of the gore-filled hole where his face used to be. I'd taken his nose, lips, eyelids, ears, and everything connected to them.

He dropped to his knees, trying to hold his face with his hands as I re-formed beside my dagger. I was bleeding profusely, but I grabbed the dagger, walked over to Elliot, and buried it in the top of his skull, right up to the hilt, with a satisfying crunch. He'd deserved worse.

I looked around, found Hiroyuki galloping his horse toward me, over a dozen riders behind him. I dropped to my knees, bloody, beat, and exhausted.

"Can you walk?" he asked as more than two dozen sets of eyes looked down on me from horseback.

"Yes," I said, giving him my hand and allowing myself to be helped up to my feet. My body began to heal itself, although the pain was still substantial. "We need to check the prison."

Hiroyuki nodded and didn't argue as he ordered the soldiers to stand guard before he helped me into the garrison. We were walking by the lake bank when I had an idea. "Wait," I said, disengaging myself from using him as a walking stick, dropping to my knees by the water.

"What are you doing?" Hiroyuki asked, using the same tone to say that someone was an idiot.

I scooped the cobalt-blue liquid up in my hands.

"What the fuck, Lucas?" Hiroyuki shouted and took a step toward me.

"Wait," I said. "Please."

Hiroyuki didn't look happy about it, but he waited.

The water felt warm in my hands, that warmth spreading up my arms. Much like how I'd felt in Agency when touching the water, I felt . . . better. I poured the remaining water over my head and looked up at a horrified Hiroyuki.

His gaze softened. "How are your cuts healing?"

I looked back down at the water. I had no idea what was happening to me. This water should hurt, should be killing me, but instead, it was healing me, making me feel better.

"We need to get into that prison," I said, and got to my feet. I didn't have time to heal myself fully, and I wasn't entirely sure what would happen if I submerged myself in a liquid that I'd seen dissolve someone not that long before.

"Boat looks okay," Hiroyuki said.

We boarded the boat and took the slow journey over the lake, with Hiroyuki at the helm and me wondering what the hell I was going to do when I got onto the island, when I got to see Ahiram again. Callie was right; I wasn't the type of person who murdered comatose people. Defenceless people. But Ahiram was a conqueror. A monster. A killer. His plan of unifying the Earth and rift would bring ruin to both.

The boat pulled up to the pier, and we disembarked, weapons in hand, ready for whatever was going to happen the moment we were inside.

It took the pair of us to push open the unlocked door, as someone had piled up old chairs and a piece of rug behind it. In the gloom of the prison entrance stood Donis, holding a makeshift club in one hand.

"You came back," he said, sounding like he was exceptionally surprised about that.

"Anyone been in here?" I asked him. "Oh, Donis, Hiroyuki, and vice versa. You can trust one another."

The two men nodded a greeting.

"No one has been since you left," Donis said. "No one has been to see Callie and Ahiram. I swear."

We walked through the prison and took the lift up to the top floor, and I still wasn't sure what I was going to do *when* I got into that room again. Donis stayed at the lift while Hiroyuki and I went to the room.

"You ready?" Hiroyuki said, his hand on the door handle.

"Let's get this done," I said.

He pushed open the door, and we both stepped inside to find Callie sat cross-legged on the bed, with no Ahiram lying motionless in the bed. An IV line left his arm, looped up over the bed post, and ended in a blood pouch on a tray beside it.

"What the hell?" I asked.

"Nice to see you, too," Callie said.

"You are a monster," Hiroyuki said. "You should be dead."

Callie smiled at him. "Was a monster, not a monster. Was dead, not dead."

"What are you doing to Ahiram?" I asked.

Callie swung her legs off the bed and stood before stretching. She walked around the bed and unplugged the IV line from the pouch, putting the now-sealed pouch in a bag on the floor, which I could easily see was filled with more pouches.

"You didn't answer my question," I said.

"I thought you were just exclaiming surprise," Callie said. "I'm taking his blood. It's why I needed everyone gone; couldn't have too many weird questions from Elliot and his people."

"You set him up," I said. "He figured that bit out by the end."

"He wasn't as dumb as I thought then," Callie said. "Elliot is dead I assume."

I nodded.

"And his Vipers?"

"Scattered," I said. "More than a few are dead."

"Good," Callie said.

"Was all of this just to get some time alone with Ahiram?" I asked. "I thought you wanted him up and about."

"Oh, gods, no," Callie said. "Maybe once, but he doesn't really care about the rift; he just wants to rule it. Opening a permanent tear between rift and Earth was just a means to an end for him. A way to get more power."

"So, you're going to bleed him dry?" Hiroyuki asked.

"No," Callie said. "I'm taking some blood because he's an Ancient and it's going to come in handy for what I need to do. I thought about taking him to the rift and doing it there, but I think this is cleaner."

"Do what?" I asked.

Callie, now stood by Ahiram's head, removed a dagger and slit his throat in one smooth motion. She drove the dagger into his heart and left it there as Hiroyuki and I stood in mute shock.

"He can't get out," Callie said.

"One of the other Ancients is going to die now," I said.

"Not *now* now," Callie said. "They'll lose their connection, they'll wither, and eventually die, but it takes time. Besides, I don't care."

Hiroyuki took a step toward Callie, his hand on the hilt of his katana.

"See you soon," Callie said.

She vanished.

"What the hell just happened?" Hiroyuki asked.

"I've been asking myself that a lot recently." I checked to make sure that Ahiram was as dead as he looked, and when satisfied, I said, "I guess this one is no longer a problem."

No one wanted to stay in the prison a moment longer.

We used the boat to cross back over the lake and walked out of the garrison. We rode back up to the ruins where Timo had gone, only to find Timo and her people with no bodies of any Vipers. Or anyone else, for that matter.

All of us rode back to Plainhaven, where I told Hiroyuki I'd see him soon. He was keen to get back to Noah and check that Ahiram's death hadn't affected him.

I told Timo that I'd return to Plainhaven when I could. It was something I wanted to do soon; I felt like the place was somewhere I needed to know more about.

Timo took me through the city to her home, where the tear stone sat on a table. "The Queen sent it here with your friends. Not figured out where to put it, but it'll come in handy, I'm sure. Ahiram really dead?"

I nodded.

"Good," she said. "I don't know which one of us is going to lose our connection, but I don't think it's me. Not Neb, either."

"She okay?" I asked.

"She's gone back to Nightvale," Timo said. "I think she's got a lot of things to think through. You should go see her."

"I will," I said. "But there's something I need to do first." I thanked her, opened a tear into my embers, and stepped through.

Maria and Casimir were both happy to see me, although both were worried as the embers set about fully healing me. I had to stay the night in a building; listening to the sounds of the embers at night was less than pleasant, especially when you were healing.

When I was done the next morning, I stepped out of the building I'd been in to find Maria and Casimir waiting in the street. Casimir had turned into a red panda, while Maria had gone back to the bird forms they loved so much, in this case a raven.

"What will you do now?" Casimir asked, as they perched on a wooden fence outside of the door I needed to use to get back to Earth.

"What I should have done a long time ago," I said.

"We will always be here to help," Maria said.

I thanked them both, opened the door, and stepped out into my New York apartment bedroom. The building was opposite Prospect Park, but I hadn't been back there for several months. I showered and was happy to change into clothing that felt more comfortable than bloodstained armour.

I removed the bag from the closet and opened it, taking out the half dozen Raven medallions inside and placing the one I'd taken from Elliot with them. I picked them all up, put them in a small holdall, and carried them through into the front room, where Nadia was seated, eating a large plate of nachos while watching a film on the TV. A laptop sat open on the table in front of her.

"You look happy," I said. "How many times have you seen this one now?"

"It's Aragorn," Nadia said. "He's unlocked an awakening in me."

I laughed.

"So, it's been two months," she said.

I closed my eyes and took a deep breath. "What have I missed?"

"Dani went back to find you, and Timo said you'd gone," Nadia said. "So, no one panicked. I heard you tore Elliot's face in half."

"Something like that," I replied, placing the holdall on the chair next to me. "Anything else?"

"The tears have stopped going bonkers, although they're still more regular than they were. I guess you were just unlucky that they stopped while you were in the embers."

"Any word on which Ancient drew the short straw?"

Nadia shook her head. "Whoever it is, they're keeping it quiet. How's the variety of injuries?"

I patted my side. "Good. How are you?"

"I'm okay. Drusilla waited here for the first month you weren't back," she said. "We didn't know if it would be here, or Gabriel's, or even back on the island. Timo said that Hiroyuki said you got another Raven medallion; I figured you'd want to put it with the others."

"That it?" I asked.

Nadia turned the laptop to show me, and I bent forward to read the screen. "That's a list of Viper Guild members," she said, scrolling through it with one hand while the other held the nachos. "Names, locations, powers. It's not every single member, but the congressman knew a lot more than he was meant to. It says *Talon* times three. No names."

"Holy shit," I said. "It's a good start."

"So, we're going after them?" Nadia asked.

"We're going to find their base of operations," I said. "And then we're going to take back all of the medallions that they took from the Ravens. And I'm going to re-create the Guild."

Nadia smiled. "Sounds like a plan. I'll help however I can."

I stood, removed a medallion, and placed it in front of Nadia. She stared at it, looked up at me, stared at it again, placed the nachos on the coffee table, and went back to staring at me.

"You okay?" I asked.

"Are you serious?" she asked me.

"Nadia," I said. "I would be honoured if you could help me remake the Raven Guild, with you as a member."

Nadia picked up the medallion and stared at it before wiping her eyes as she began to cry. She looked up at me, tears rolling down her cheeks. "Of course," she said, placing the medallion chain over her neck. "Let's go get these bastards."

"I'm glad you're with me," I told her.

"But first, I need to finish watching this film," she said, picking up her nachos again.

I sat beside her, and she offered me some food.

ACKNOWLEDGEMENTS

So, the first four Riftborn books are done. They've been a pleasure to write, and I hope you enjoyed Lucas' journey so far.

There are, as always, numerous people who have helped me get this book written, edited, and published.

My wife, Vanessa, and my daughters, Keira, Faith, and Harley. Their support can't really be measured. They're part of the reason I write; they're part of the reason I ever decided to try and get published in the first place. Thank you for everything you do.

To my parents, who have always been supportive of my writing and read every book I publish, thank you for being there all these years, and I am sorry (not really) for the amount of space the wall of my covers now takes up.

To my family, my friends, all of those people who have supported me, who have contacted me to tell me they've loved my work, who listen to me going on about ideas and complaining about how my brain won't shut up for five minutes to let me work on one thing, you're all awesome.

My agent, Paul Lucas, is a hell of a good guy and one I'm privileged to be able to call my agent and friend. Thank you for all you do.

To everyone at Podium. I've been working with Nicole, Victoria, Leah, Cole, and Kyle for a few books now. It's been a genuine pleasure to work with them all and I look forward to what the future brings.

My editor, Julie Crisp. An incredible editor who helps make my work better and who manages to translate the sometimes word salad that is an early draft of my book. Thank you for being awesome to work with.

To Pius Bak, the artist who did the incredible covers to all three Rift-born books. Thank you for your amazing work.

Last, but by no means least, to everyone else who picks up my books, whether this is the first one or those who have followed my work for years, thank you.

ABOUT THE AUTHOR

Steve McHugh is the bestselling author of the Hellequin Chronicles. His novel *Scorched Shadows* was nominated for a David Gemmell Award for Fantasy in 2018. Born in Mexborough, South Yorkshire, McHugh currently lives with his wife and three daughters in Southampton.

 **Podium**

DISCOVER
STORIES UNBOUND

PodiumAudio.com